LOVE AND LAUGHTER

"But as it happens Susan's father isn't to blame for my lack of attention," he continued. "I was thinking about you."

Taken by surprise Laura couldn't help commenting, "No wonder your mood seemed so black."

Davey's laughter was full of good humor and soon Laura joined in. The sound brought Davey up short.

"Do you know that's the first time I've heard you laugh? You really should try it more often," he recommended listening to the soft, tinkling strains of musical mirth drifting through the air.

Laura stopped laughing as their eyes met and held. She tried to see beyond the velvety brown irises of the man looking back at her from a mere arm's length away. The horses drew closer together and Laura's knee brushed Davey's thigh. Though jolted by the contact she didn't move away. She couldn't have moved if her life depended on it.

Davey found himself staring into twin pools of liquid gold. Mesmerized by their depth and clarity, his head dipped lower until their lips were just inches apart.

"What were you thinking about me?" Laura whispered. Her warm, sweet breath stroked his face like a gentle caress.

"I was trying to figure out why I insisted on taking you back to River Ridge. Now I know."

And then his mouth came down to cover hers in a kiss that left Laura reeling in mindless ecstasy . . .

KATHY WILLIS

SOUTHERN SURRENDER

ZEBRA BOOKS
KENSINGTON PUBLISHING CORP.

ZEBRA BOOKS are published by

Kensington Publishing Corp.
475 Park Avenue South
New York, NY 10016

First Printing: April, 1994

Printed in the United States of America

This one is for my son-in-law, Dan Jamison, as promised.

Prologue

Florida, 1845

The ancient buckboard bounced along the rutted road pulled by two swaying nags plodding ahead with a slow but steady gait. Like the animals, the driver appeared old and bent. His face was hidden by the slouch hat he wore; the reins were held loosely in his gloved hands, leaving it up to the horses to find their own way on this moonless night. It wasn't difficult for both sides of the trail were lined with towering pine trees and dense underbrush.

When the plaintive call of a night bird sounded softly from somewhere close by the wagon drew to a halt. The animals bowed their heads waiting patiently for the familiar clucking noise that would signal them to resume their laborious pace. Their master slumped forward seeming to have fallen asleep. He made no move to rouse himself even when a large, shadowy figure emerged cautiously from the woods, taking time to study the road ahead and behind the dilapidated conveyance. Only after the ghostly apparition had satisfied himself that no one else was about did he motion for the trembling forms crouched among the bushes to come forward. Quickly he shifted the bales of hay in the wagon bed making room for the two to climb aboard. Just as quickly he covered them with a blanket and loose hay and then vanished among the forest of trees as if he had never been.

Without raising his head, the driver clicked his tongue against the roof of his mouth and the animals trudged onward. Soon they were swallowed up by the darkness as they disappeared into the silent night.

Chapter 1

Clad only in her shift and petticoats, Laura stared out the window above the neatly manicured lawn where lanterns glowed invitingly, illuminating the paths that wound through the garden of tropical flowers. The scent of honeysuckle and jasmine hung heavy in the air and the sound of water playing in the ornate fountain could be heard from the patio below accompanying the odd assortment of notes carried on the breeze as the orchestra tuned up in the ballroom. She looked past the formal gardens and neatly cropped grass, but without the benefit of a moon she could not see the acres of cotton, sugarcane, and citrus trees beyond.

Just as she leaned daringly over the sill to peer down at the flagstones below, the door swung open and Delilah entered the room carefully carrying a freshly pressed gown of emerald green taffeta cradled across her arms.

"Lord have mercy, Miss Laura! Come 'way from dat window 'fore somebody seez yore naked body!"

the young negress chided, draping her burden upon the bed so that she could wag her finger in a gesture that had become familiar to Laura since her arrival at River Ridge plantation.

"I'm hardly 'naked,' Delilah. Besides there's no one out there to see me," Laura replied laughingly.

Her good humor was greeted by a frown from the pretty dark-skinned woman who immediately ceased her wagging to place her hands on generously rounded hips. "You jus' never knows what's out dere in de woods." Delilah softened her warning by adding, "Anyways de important peoples is downstairs waitin' to meet yo'!"

Laura's unusual amber-colored eyes twinkled with amusement. "I thought those important people below had come here to celebrate Florida's newly acquired statehood!"

Delilah reached for the gown not bothering to hide her exasperation. "Well, dat's part of it," she admitted. "Mistah Dunstan's worked mighty hard to make dis territory a state, but dat's not all dis party's 'bout. De mistah he figgers it's high time yo' met some of his friends and neighbors. I heard him say as much to Miz Hester just t'other day. He said 'High time dat gal puts her grievin' to rest.' Din he said 'Way to do dat is have her meet up with some of dem young bucks 'round here.' Dat's what he say and Delilah don't lie!"

Enveloped in the yards of material floating over her head, Laura managed to stifle a laugh as she pictured the distinguished, well-spoken Fowler Dunstan making such a speech. But by the time the

10

gown was smoothed into place, her mood was reflective. She wondered if her uncle was concerned because she had shown no outward signs of mourning over her father's untimely death. During the past few weeks he had urged her not to keep her feelings bottled up inside. But how could she possibly tell her kind, sensitive uncle that she had scarcely known the wealthy Boston banker who had sired her and that, if anything, his passing had been a relief?

She had no recollection of her mother who had died of some mysterious malady when Laura was still in the nursery. Once she had overheard a whispered conversation among the servants about a broken heart but it meant little to her at the time. What she *could* remember was the series of expensive boarding schools in New England and then Europe where she had spent her childhood making friends only to have to say goodbye as she was shuttled from one elite institution to the next, finally completing her education at Miss Haversham's Academy for Young Ladies in London.

Only on a few occasions was she allowed to visit her father in Boston and those times proved to be a strain for them both. Her father had been a handsome man with dark brown hair that gleamed red in the sun and topaz eyes which Laura grudgingly acknowledged as so like her own. He was successful in business and, as she'd come to realize years earlier, successful with the ladies as well. During one of her rare visits, her father had entered the breakfast room with a woman on his arm. Though Laura could not recall the woman's name, she remembered her as being young and beautiful, and she had worn a look of satisfaction on her face after spending a night in Franklin Dunstan's bed.

As Laura grew older she worried about her future knowing she could not remain in school forever, yet equally certain she would be no more than an unwelcome visitor in the house of the man who was obligated to care for her but preferred to do so from a distance. She often thought it fortunate that Franklin had no use for religion or surely he would have shipped her off to a convent to spend her life in prayer and supplication. Under the circumstances, Laura felt little remorse when, one month before she completed her schooling, she received word that her father had died of a heart attack. Upon returning to Boston she gained a fuller account of his death, again through servant gossip, but the fact that he had been in bed at the time with a young woman no older than Laura came as little surprise and was of no concern to the young heiress who suddenly found herself in possession of a town house in the city, a mansion in the countryside, and a sizable fortune to sustain her. Some might call it a poor substitute for years of loneliness and a lost childhood, but Laura, who could not miss what she had never had, found it just compensation.

She thought Fowler Dunstan would probably understand her lack of emotion where his brother was concerned if she could find the courage to unburden herself to the Southern planter who had come seeking her out, offering comfort in what he assumed to be her hour of need. But Laura was reluctant to criticize her father, a man whom others seemed to view as warm and generous. She didn't want to risk her own standing with the uncle she had never heard of until a little over three weeks ago when he had appeared on her doorstep.

Older than Franklin and not quite as tall, the man who'd introduced himself had reddish-brown hair winged with gray along the temples. His skin had a weathered look as if he spent a great deal of time in the sun. Laura might have viewed Fowler's unexpected arrival with suspicion had it not been for one thing. There could be no mistaking the Dunstan eyes—deep amber irises flecked with gold—a color she had rarely seen except when she looked in her mirror.

Laura's shock at suddenly finding she was not without kin as she had been led to believe, demanded an explanation which Fowler was quick to give though his answer was somewhat vague. Smiling sadly her uncle confessed that he and his brother had been estranged for many years due to what he termed a minor difference of opinion. He'd learned of her father's death through a Boston newspaper which had eventually reached him at his home in Florida. Brushing a tear from the corner of his eye, he expressed his regret over not having attempted to mend their relationship before it was too late. Though Laura was curious as to what had caused the breach, the man's sorrowful countenance left her reluctant to pursue the matter, but she never doubted for a moment that the fault must lie with

13

her father. Her uncle had nothing but kind words for Franklin—so many kind words that Laura was tempted to argue his opinion but held her tongue knowing it was unseemly to speak ill of the dead.

To her astonishment Fowler had urged her to return with him to his plantation where she could meet the rest of the family—her aunt Hester, her cousin Angel, and his stepson, Bradley Kincaid. His entreaty could not have come at a more opportune time for Laura had readily grown tired of Boston society, tired of the foppish young suitors vying for her affections, their interest, she suspected, enhanced by her newly acquired wealth; and their dour-faced mothers who considered it scandalous for a snip of a girl "scarcely out of the schoolroom" to control her own fortune. Where were those rugged American men the silly girls at Miss Haversham's whispered about so incessantly? Certainly not in Boston from what she had seen!

And so restless and longing for adventure, Laura eagerly agreed to accompany her uncle on his return journey south. Though she was curious about this newly discovered family of hers, she viewed the trip to Florida as merely the first step along the road to even more daring explorations. She had no responsibilities to tie her to one particular place and she had always enjoyed traveling back and forth between Boston and England. Now with the means to go wherever she chose and do whatever she wished to do, Laura decided to see the world. She would meet the rich and famous people she had only heard about. The beautiful and exotic places which were no more than names in books would become familiar haunts. She might eventually plant her roots on some foreign soil but not until she had experienced all life had to offer.

"Where is yo' at, Miz Laura?" Delilah asked, finishing braiding a green silk ribbon through Laura's thick tumble of auburn curls.

Smiling up into the mirrored concern on the puzzled maid's face, Laura replied, "I'm sitting right here, Delilah, waiting patiently for you to declare me ready to join the others downstairs."

"Yore body's here. No doubt 'bout dat!" Delilah conceded taking a step backward to admire the beautiful, sweet-tempered visitor who treated her like a friend rather than a slave to be ordered about. "But yore mind be somewheres else. Yo's woolgatherin' 'stead of paying attention to what I been saying 'bout the people yo' gonna meet tonight."

"I'm sorry, Delilah. For a moment there I was caught up in memories." And plans for the future, Laura thought as she stood and smoothed the front of her dress. "Now that I've apologized, I promise not to 'woolgather' again. If you'd care to continue I will pay the utmost attention."

"Yo's already late," declared the maid shaking the finger of one hand as she patted Laura's skirts with the other, ushering her toward the door. "Just 'member—don't go lettin' dat Benton boy take yo' on no walk in de garden 'cause he ain't to be trusted even in de lamplight; and watch where Tom Seaver puts his hands if'n yo' have to dance with him 'cause he's fresh as a just laid egg; and don't yo' go lettin'

15

nothin' Miss Angel sez rile yo', yo' hear? 'Cause yo' is gonna be de bell of de ball and dat little prissy ain't gonna like it one bit!"

Delilah's admonitions followed Laura down the thickly carpeted hallway to the head of the wide circular staircase. Laura smiled as she began a graceful descent. She would do nothing to embarrass her uncle in front of his friends and neighbors, she vowed. But should the opportunity arise to put her snooty little cousin's nose out of joint, she knew she would be hard-pressed to let the chance pass her by!

Davey Logan thanked the groom who had taken the reins of his big black stallion, leaving the man with his mouth agape for never had a visitor to River Ridge so much as acknowledged the negro's existence. As the slave made his way toward the stable pausing occasionally to cast a bewildered glance back over his shoulder, Davey stood where he had dismounted, gazing up at the imposing structure before him.

Lamps glowed from every window of the stately two-storied mansion, illuminating the wide round columns fronting the entrance. Long minutes passed during which he considered, then discarded, the numerous reasons why he should not take those final steps to the door. He didn't belong here, he didn't want to be here, and he certainly wouldn't be welcome among the planters assembled inside. Every instinct told him to call for his horse and head back to Fort Brooke. Only the knowledge that he might learn something important, something he could use, forced him to stay his retreat.

The sounds of music and laughter drifted through the open windows setting his teeth on edge. What right did they have to be happy when so much misery surrounded them? Or were those within blind to the suffering they generated through their ignorance and greed?

Davey patted his coat pocket to make sure the invitation was still there, an invitation addressed to "Lance Logan and Family." His lips curled in a wry grin for he doubted the sender had intended to include the half-breed son of the famous army scout who had recently been elected to the newly formed state legislative council. As luck would have it his father had been in Tallahassee on the day the invitation arrived, the same day Davey returned home after several weeks' absence. At first Rebecca had tossed the buff-colored vellum aside, her green eyes igniting with anger as she proclaimed Fowler Dunstan to be a damnable blackguard spawned by the devil himself. Davey could understand his stepmother's sentiments for she'd fought as hard as anyone against men like Dunstan. The entire Logan clan had argued in favor of Florida's entry into the union as a Free State, but much to their sorrow the money and power of those who dealt in slave labor had eventually decided the issue.

Glad to be back for a brief respite and too tired to think about anything except a hot bath and a soft bed, Davey let the matter of the unexpected invitation drop. But later that evening after she'd had time to think it over, Rebecca had approached him with that peculiar light in her eyes that meant she was about to suggest something he didn't want to hear. Davey had wished his father was there for Lance Logan was the only man able to curb Rebecca's reckless nature. Though she would soon celebrate her fortieth birthday, Rebecca had lost none of the adventurous spirit that had brought her to the primitive wilderness of the Florida territory twenty-one years ago.

Davey had been smoking a cheroot, listening to the sounds of the crickets and night birds when she came out onto the porch to join him. It was her sigh of resignation as she seated herself in the rocker as much as the expression in her eyes that alerted him to the danger ahead. Rebecca never sighed unless she was plotting something. Certain he would not want to hear what was on her mind, he'd allowed the silence to grow heavy.

Finally she'd said, "It might not hurt to have someone attend the party. After all, how often is one invited into the enemy camp?"

Davey shook his head now just as he had that night two weeks ago when he had sworn he would not give in to his stepmother's harebrained schemes again. Yet here he was at River Ridge Plantation— precisely where he did not want to be!

He stepped back as a shiny black carriage swung around the circular drive coming to a halt in front of the smooth stone walkway. The door of the conveyance opened and before the driver could scramble from his perch to lend assistance, an elderly bewhiskered gentleman alighted, then turned to extend his hand to a young woman with flaxen hair and sparkling eyes that perfectly matched the blue of her gown. She began to follow but was brought to an abrupt halt when the wide skirts of her dress stuck in the narrow opening. The older man muttered an oath as he tried to wrench her free.

"Please, Papa!" Davey recognized amusement in the gently scolding voice. "It will spoil the evening if you pull my arm from its socket before I have a chance to dance the first waltz."

"Don't know why you women have to wear so many dang fangled petticoats! Just a waste of good cotton!" came the disgruntled response.

"And, pray tell, what would happen if we women gave up our outlandish fashions?" The girl proceeded to answer her own question without giving her father a chance to reply. "I'll tell you what would happen! The demand for cotton would drop in half. Fifty percent of the crops would wind up rotting on the vines. In no time at all we'd be paupers not knowing from whence our next meal would come." Placing one hand over her breast she continued dramatically, "With all due respect, Papa, you should be kissing the feet of each and every lady whose frivolity ensures against our becoming beggared!"

From where he stood hidden in the shadows of a tall shrub, Davey fought the urge to applaud her performance, though it was obvious the girl's father was not the least bit impressed.

19

"Dammit, Susan! How many times do I have to tell you cotton doesn't grow on vines? And as for respect, young lady, you haven't the least notion of what the word—"

The remainder of his discourse was cut short as the dress unexpectedly came free and *Susan* popped like a cork from a bottle right into the arms of her slightly built father landing them both in a heap of lace and ruffles at Davey's feet. The sound of deep rumbling laughter caught the pair off guard. Both looked up toward the one who found their situation so amusing.

The girl sprang to her feet despite the cumbersome skirts which had caused the calamity in the first place. Her father was not so spry, and Davey found himself reaching out his hand which the other readily accepted.

"Dammit, Susan! Look what you've done now!" her elder spluttered, brushing at his once-immaculate suit, now wrinkled but only slightly begrimed, for the walkway had been swept clean of dirt and debris in preparation for the grand ball.

"If you could postpone the lecture, Papa, I believe you owe this gentleman a debt of gratitude for getting you back on your feet," Susan suggested, giving Davey a conspiratorial wink which brought an unbidden smile to his lips.

She was an impish miss. There was no denying it. Probably spoiled beyond reason from what he had seen and heard so far, yet for Davey something in her manner struck a familiar chord. Though there was no physical resemblance between the two, the girl reminded him of Beth, his free-spirited cousin who had lead them all on a merry chase until a half-breed like himself had won her heart and pulled the reins in on her daredeviltry.

Susan eyed Davey curiously. He was an exceptionally tall man and she couldn't help noticing how his wide shoulders strained the material of his black broadcloth coat. She wondered who he could be and why he had secluded himself in the bushes instead of joining the merrymakers inside. The questions lent an air of mystery to the darkly handsome stranger.

"Dammit, Susan! I don't need you telling me who I owe and who I don't. You're not my accountant!" her father flared belligerently. With that he turned to Davey. "The name's Henry Ashe and this is my daughter Susan. I appreciate your help, young man, but not your laughter. There's nothing funny about being saddled with a flibbertigibbit female who can enter a carriage without a hitch, but must shoot out like a rocket on the Fourth of July as soon as we arrive at our destination."

A trace of humor in Henry's voice belied his gruff tone. Even the third "Dammit, Susan" lacked the rancor of a full-fledged oath, and Davey felt himself warming to the crusty old patrician.

Davey extended his hand once more. "I apologize, sir, for making light of your predicament. I'm Davey Logan from Fort Brooke and I'm pleased to meet you both." Nodding to Susan he was surprised to find his words were true, his smile genuine. The last thing he expected was to meet a planter he liked.

Of course he didn't know much about the man. Ashe was probably as self-serving as the rest of his ilk. Still it never hurt to keep an open mind especially since his lovely daughter was not only a delight to the eyes, but full of spunk to boot.

Henry peered up into the face of the stranger. Though the light was muted he could see the outline of high cheekbones and black brows that slashed above dark, deep-set eyes. "David Logan," he repeated. "Wouldn't happen to be related to Lance Logan, now would you?"

"My name is just Davey, sir. Not David, and Lance Logan is my father."

Henry chuckled heartily. "Well, *Just Davey,* you've ridden a long way to attend a party. Things must be a mite dull at the fort."

A long way indeed, Davey thought. Fort Brooke was located on the central west coast of Florida near the growing settlement of Tampa, a name the Indians had given the little town and which the settlers and soldiers saw no reason to change, while Fowler Dunstan had built his plantation on a rise overlooking the Saint Johns River some two hundred miles to the northeast. The sparsely populated land in between was fraught with danger. Though the remaining Seminole warriors who had fought so valiantly for the right to live in the territory had retreated to the great swamp that made up most of the southern part of the state, there were plenty of wild animals—bears, panthers, bobcats—waiting to attack any man foolish enough to venture into the forests, and one had to be constantly on the watch for snakes and alligators which resided in and near the many rivers and freshwater lakes dotting the countryside. But Davey felt safe in the woods. It was the towns that seemed to rise up overnight and the people who inhabited them that made him wary.

"There's no lack of excitement or entertainment at Fort Brooke, sir," Davey assured him, smiling as he recalled the lively times to be had at Flora Mae's whorehouse on a Saturday night. "I'm visiting a friend in the area and since my father is unable to be here, I've come in his stead."

"The more the merrier," the planter chortled clapping Davey on the shoulder. "Your father's a fine man. Oh, we have some differences of opinion as to how this state should be run," he qualified, "but the important thing is that we are a state now. That's something we've all fought to achieve and we all have a right to celebrate the victory together."

"Sounds like a fine idea," Davey replied, amicably offering his arm to Susan who had not said a word since he had introduced himself.

While his smile hid his inner thoughts he couldn't help wondering how much "celebrating" would be done in the mean, dirt-floored hovels behind the big house he was about to enter. He knew better than to raise the question for it would defeat his purpose to alienate his new acquaintances at this stage of the game. Let them think they had won, Davey decided as Susan took his arm, looking up at him with an unreadable expression in eyes as blue as the sky on a cloudless day. Accom-

23

panying Henry Ashe and his daughter toward the laughter and light, Davey knew only time would tell if the victory the planters celebrated was premature.

Chapter 2

Laura rounded the curve in the staircase, then stopped to admire the floating sea of color created by the gowns of the ladies dancing with their partners beneath the glittering lamps in the ballroom. She was not surprised to observe her cousin Angel, *a misnomer if there ever was one,* she thought uncharitably, dancing with Fowler's stepson, Bradley Kincaid. The flirtatious redhead appeared to be giving Brad her undivided attention but Laura suspected she was furtively cutting her eyes at every eligible bachelor in the room. It hadn't taken long to discover that her cousin was always on the lookout for a new conquest, someone to satisfy her endless need for adulation.

The last strains of music died away just as the front door opened and a gray-bearded, slightly disheveled-looking gentleman entered followed by a handsome couple walking arm in arm. The term "ideally suited" immediately came to mind as Laura stood poised with one hand resting lightly on the bannister. The girl's creamy skin and golden-blond hair made a perfect foil for her companion's dark, rugged good looks. His head was bent toward her, his lips drawn up in a smile. Laura wondered what it would be like to have someone smile at her in that special way.

Unable to take her eyes off the man standing in the foyer, Laura was gripped by a peculiar fluttering feeling in her stomach. It was probably because she hadn't eaten since noontime. Surely her indisposition could have nothing to do with that unusually tall personage whose large frame filled the doorway, blocking out the night, and whose hair was so black it gleamed blue as a raven's wing in the lamplight. Laura noticed how the muscles of his broad shoulders flexed, stretching the material of the black coat he wore as if he was unused to the restrictions of formal attire. When without warning her look was returned by a pair of soft brown eyes that locked with her own and refused to let go, new symptoms of distress were added to the queasiness which she had at first attributed to hunger. Her heart quickened its beat sending pulsating sensations coursing down her limbs and setting her fingers and toes to tingling. The hand that rested upon the wooden railing tightened its grasp while the other moved involuntarily to her throat. Her chest rose and fell in time with the pounding of blood racing to her head, leaving a crimson blush on her smooth white cheeks. In one breathless moment the words "rugged" and "virile" had taken on new meaning, and the schoolgirl whisperings about American frontiersmen she had scoffed at seemed not so far-fetched.

Davey, whose senses were honed to a razor sharpness, having spent all of his life in a land where danger lurked in unexpected places, felt Laura's eyes upon him before he raised his head. As he returned her stare, he saw her hand move to touch the milk-white skin of her long, slender neck. He was aware of the way her small breasts rose and fell, straining against the fabric of her gown's low-cut bodice. But it was her eyes that held his attention for they were neither brown nor gold but a fascinating combination of both, reminding him of river rocks glistening in the sunlight.

The spell was broken when a man Davey assumed to be their host approached to greet the Ashes with enthusiasm, pumping Henry's hand, then brushing a light kiss across Susan's cheek.

"And this is our friend, Davey Logan, from Fort Brooke."

Davey quirked a dark brow in Susan's direction for she had managed to make the introduction sound as if they were old acquaintances. In answer to his unspoken question she smiled and gave his arm a familiar squeeze. Davey raised his muscled shoulders in a shrug, deciding to pursue the matter later should he be so lucky as to find himself alone with the charming Miss Ashe. Turning then toward the planter he'd come two hundred miles to meet, Davey found himself looking into a pair of eyes identical to those of the young woman he'd seen on the staircase. He glanced up quickly but she was no longer there. Davey had heard rumors that Dunstan's only child was a vain little creature with a reputation for throwing herself at anything wearing pants. Somehow he found it difficult to apply that description to the stunning vision in green, yet there could be no mistaking the likeness of her remarkable amber eyes and those of the man to whom he had just been introduced.

He suppressed the urge to wipe his palm against his pant leg after dutifully shaking the hand Fowler Dunstan extended though the man was nothing like Davey had imagined. If not the devil himself with horns protruding from his head, he'd at least expected the infamous slaveholder to be a daunting figure. Instead Dunstan was only slightly taller than Henry Ashe with reddish hair just beginning to gray around the edges and a ready smile that appeared genuine as he welcomed Davey in the friendly, gracious manner for which people of the South were known.

Davey knew what would come next.

"Any relation to Lance Logan?"

He had grown used to the question for his father was a legend among those who had chosen to make Florida their home. Lance had come to the territory nearly thirty years ago and had fallen in love with the natural beauty of the wild, rugged land. He'd worked hard to befriend the native Calusa Indians. He'd worked harder still to protect them from the white settlers determined to drive them out.

Davey barely had time to reply, repeating the explanation he had given Henry Ashe for his presence at River Ridge, before Susan whisked him off toward the huge formal ballroom from which the lively strains of music flowed once more. A row of elderly matrons were seated in chairs placed along one wall for their comfort. Davey and Susan excused themselves as they passed in front of the chattering women. Susan spoke to several by name but made no move to introduce her companion. Davey could see curiosity in their expressions and he wondered if it was because he was a stranger among them or because they recognized the distinctive features of his mother's people in his face with its high cheekbones and dark features. It didn't matter to him one way or the other for he had long ago learned to ignore prejudice when it was directed at him.

When they reached an empty alcove partially screened by a huge potted palm, Susan stopped, glanced briefly at the dancers, then ducked into the small recess. Since she still had a firm grip on Davey's arm he was forced to follow. He grinned down at the pretty blonde. If she wanted to be alone with him in some secluded corner, he wasn't about to argue. Stealing a kiss from her soft pink lips was certainly preferable to standing around watching others dip and whirl.

As if she had read his thoughts Susan quickly disspelled the notion that she was given to light-hearted dalliances with men she scarcely knew. "Don't even consider it!" Her snapping blue eyes held a warning. "I have the bite of a rattler and I strike just as fast!"

Davey threw back his head and laughed. He couldn't help himself. The blue-eyed little spitfire sounded just like Beth when she got her dander up. Looking pointedly at the arm still holding his, he grinned and said, "Apparently I owe you an apology but frankly I don't understand the rules to this game we are playing."

Susan had the grace to blush, at the same time releasing the grip she had on his sleeve and clasping her hands together. "You owe me no apology, Davey. I know how it must look and I'm the one who is sorry. But I had to find a place where I could talk to you alone. As to the rest, if it is a game I play, it's a deadly one for a single rule broken could cost a man his life—or a woman hers." The grave expression on her pretty face put an end to Davey's teasing.

He placed his hands on her shoulders and felt her tremble but the response was not that of a woman desiring a man's touch. It was a quivering that stemmed from fear and he wanted to know the reason. "We're alone now, Susan," he reminded, his voice low and soothing. "Tell me what you are afraid of." Perhaps it was because she reminded him of Beth. More likely it was the sense of purpose he glimpsed beneath her superficial capriciousness that made him add, "Whatever is troubling you, I'd like to help."

"I was hoping you would say that. We desperately need men like you."

As often happened when he was alone on the

trail, Davey smelled danger ahead. Warily he asked, "Who is 'we'?"

Susan chose not to answer directly, saying instead, "I've heard a lot of talk about your father. He's not a popular man among the plantation owners because of his stand on the issue of slavery."

"It's no secret that Pa is opposed to one man owning another."

"And what about you, Davey?"

There was more than idle curiosity in the question for the depth of emotion in her voice was reflected ten-fold in eyes that burned bright with the fervent spirit of one dedicated to a cause. Davey thought his answer over carefully. He had no idea where the conversation was leading, but the tense expectancy in Susan's stance and the inner excitement she held barely in check led him to believe she had something important on her mind.

"You say you've heard about my father. But did you know that my mother was a Calusa Indian princess, my grandfather a chieftain of the tribe?"

Susan cocked her head and pursed her mouth as she studied the lines of his cheeks leading down to a strong square jaw. "So that's why you look so . . . foreign. But I thought your mother was from England."

"How alike you white people are to decide we natives look 'foreign.' "

"Oh, Davey. I . . . I didn't mean . . . I mean . . ." Stammering in embarrassment, Susan colored to the tips of her dainty ears.

Davey grinned, revealing straight white teeth.

"My stepmother is from England though she's as much an American as any of us now. The point I was trying to make is that the Calusa fought against becoming enslaved for hundreds of years, first by the Spanish, then by the whites, which should answer your question as to my own feelings. Now could we get back to what's bothering you and how I can be of help?"

Susan's eyes darted nervously toward the dancers passing by so closely she could almost reach out and touch them. "There are people—some right here tonight—who feel the same way you and your father feel, and they're doing something about it. There's a movement afoot to help the negroes who want to escape their bondage. I was hoping you might want to be a part of it."

Davey's dark eyes widened in surprise. "Abolitionists? Here?" Before she could answer a shadow blotted out what little light touched the alcove.

"Quick!" she whispered, urgently rising up on her toes and leaning into him. "Kiss me!"

Bradley Kincaid had to speak Laura's name three times before she became aware of him standing at the bottom of the stairs. With an effort she forced her attention away from the handsome stranger talking to her uncle and managed to give Brad a tentative smile as she closed the distance between them. Pointedly ignoring her cousin, Angel, who had attached herself to her half brother's arm like a tight bandage, Laura held out her hand allowing

Brad to assist her down the last few risers which he did quite handily despite the beruffled leech clinging to his personage.

"Laura, you look lovely," said Bradley, leading her toward the crowded room.

Laura glanced at Angel knowing her cousin would not take kindly to hearing a compliment directed at another. Sure enough, the glare she got in return could have curdled milk.

Before Laura could properly thank Brad for his approval, her cousin remarked with barely disguised enmity, "How gallant of you, Brad, to overlook Laura's faux pas. Apparently she doesn't know that pastels are more appropriate for a summer ball. I'm sure she had no intention of making a spectacle of herself."

It galled Laura to hear Angel speak as if she wasn't there but she paid little heed to her spiteful words. She had already seen a number of women dressed in brightly colored gowns. One of her uncle's more imaginative guests had even fashioned an ensemble which combined a skirt of red and white stripes with a blue bodice from which white stars glittered.

While Laura chose to ignore her cousin's petty jealousy, Brad was not so forgiving. Releasing his hold on Laura momentarily, he pried the other girl's fingers from around his arm. His narrow face was pinched in an expression of annoyance. Finely drawn lips tightened below his neatly trimmed mustache.

"I will not tolerate your rudeness to Laura any

longer. If you cannot behave like a lady I suggest you remove yourself from this gathering." His words were sharp and brittle as he thrust Angel away from him.

It was an embarrassing scene for Laura to witness. If someone had spoken to her in such a manner she would have burst into tears and fled to her room. Instead Angel gave her a look of such malevolence, Laura felt herself flinch as if she'd been struck. Then her cousin turned on her heel and disappeared among the crowd.

"I'm sorry, my dear," Brad apologized contritely. "I'm afraid our Angel is in reality full of the devil. I've offered on more than one occasion to thrash her soundly but Fowler won't hear of it, though a belt properly applied to her backside would do her a world of good. Come, let's dance."

For the second time in the space of a few minutes Laura recoiled. Where she came from a man didn't hit a woman even one as spoiled and undisciplined as her cousin. Yet something in Brad's manner led her to believe he might look forward to the prospect of punishing Angel for her misdeeds. Surely she was mistaken, for Bradley Kincaid was a gentleman. Though he refused to give in to his half sister's childish tantrums she could not imagine him hurting Angel or anyone else for that matter.

Shaking off her unease, Laura watched the odd gleam fade from his pale, sea-green eyes. He took her in his arms and as they began to glide gracefully across the floor, she noticed more than one young lady casting an envious glance in her direction. Her

34

partner was a good-looking man, a little taller than most with sandy hair and sharp features that seemed in keeping with his somber temperament. She had never heard him laugh and on the rare occasions when she had seen him smile it was no more than a slight upward tilt to the corners of his lips.

As she studied him more closely, the edges of those very lips she had been thinking about twitched, then lifted. "Do you like what you see, lovely Laura?" he asked in a silky, seductive voice that prickled the hairs at the nape of her neck.

Shyly she answered, "I do now. You should smile more often."

His mouth again hardened into a thin, firm line. "It's difficult to find much humor in life when someone is trying to stab you in the back."

Laura missed a step and stumbled, but Brad's strong arms quickly righted her as she glanced around anxiously. His voice held a trace of impatience. "I don't mean literally. No one would be that foolish. I'm talking about a few self-righteous individuals who are determined to wreck the cotton industry and put an end to the livelihoods of the planters."

"That's terrible, Brad. But how could a small number of people do such a thing and what exactly is it they are doing?" Even before he answered Laura found herself resenting this unknown enemy. She might not understand much about plantations but she knew the whole world depended on cotton!

"Never mind," he answered offhandedly. "I'll take care of whoever is responsible."

Responsible for what? Laura wondered as the music drew to a close and they stopped in front of a dimly lit alcove. She was about to ask when she heard the rustle of petticoats, followed by Bradley Kincaid's quick intake of breath. She turned around just in time to see the woman in blue locked in a warm embrace with her escort. The two figures were melded into one, the man's big hand positioned on the woman's satin-covered hips, pressing her against him while their lips entwined. At the sound of Brad's hiss the couple sprang apart but not before Laura had a good look at what they were about. She had seen her cousin entice men with her coquettish behavior. Now to discover another young *lady* displaying affection for a man in front of God and anyone else who happened by caused her to wonder if all Southern-bred females behaved in such an indecorous fashion.

"Susan! What the hell is going on here?" Brad growled, his face more pinched than usual.

Stupid question, Laura thought. It certainly didn't take a genius to know exactly what was going on!

"Why, Bradley. How nice to see you," Susan effused in a pronounced drawl as she stepped into the light while her companion remained in the shadows. If she felt any embarrassment at having been caught kissing the fellow, she kept it well hidden beneath a smiling facade.

Brad scowled. "I asked what you were doing," he

replied in a steely voice that demanded an answer.

Susan batted innocent blue eyes in his direction. "Why we were conducting an experiment. Yes, that's it . . . an experiment!"

Her reply was met with a deepening frown from her interrogator. "What kind of experiment?"

"A secret experiment," Susan whispered placing one finger over lips still swollen from the force of the kiss she had shared with the man who chose that moment to come forward. "One that could revolutionize the cotton industry," she added dramatically.

Davey's face gave no clue as to what he was thinking. An end to slavery would certainly *change* the cotton industry, but "revolutionize"? That was stretching it a mite far. Susan had said "we" when she spoke of those who shared the belief that slavery was wrong. Surely the daughter of a planter could not be involved in the abolitionist movement; yet she was willing to risk her reputation rather than reveal the real reason they were together in the dimly lit alcove. He would give a lot to be rid of the two intruders so that they could resume their conversation which for the time being left more questions than answers.

"Now Bradley. If you'll stop acting like a thundercloud ready to burst I'd like you to meet a friend of mind. This is Davey Logan from Fort Brooke. Davey, this is Mr. Dunstan's stepson, Bradley Kincaid."

Davey purposely put as much muscle as he dared into the handshake. His mouth quirked with satisfaction when he saw the other man grimace beneath the pressure.

His gaze shifted to Laura, his black brows arching in surprise as he recognized the woman he believed to be Fowler Dunstan's daughter. For one reputed to play fast and loose her shocked expression seemed out of character. Two rosy circles of color dotted her smooth cheeks, contrasting sharply with the natural whiteness of her complexion, a sure indication that she was embarrassed at having caught him kissing Susan. Davey's appraising eyes lingered on her full, slightly parted lips. When her small pink tongue darted out nervously to lick the bottom of the perfect bow he felt his knees go weak. It was all he could do not to imitate her gesture, his own mouth gone suddenly dry. Wanton or not, she was a beauty with her topaz eyes and auburn curls.

"And you must be Laura Dunstan. Bradley seems to have left his manners out in the cotton fields. I'm Susan Ashe from Pine View Plantation."

Confused, Davey looked from one woman to the other. Why would Susan have to introduce herself to Dunstan's daughter when she obviously knew his stepson well?

With an effort Brad Kincaid brought his anger under control. "Forgive me, ladies. Indeed Susan, this is Fowler's niece, Laura Dunstan." Turning to Laura he said, "Susan and her father are our closest neighbors and two of our dearest friends."

Despite his words, Brad's tone indicated that he wasn't feeling very friendly toward Susan at the moment.

Susan laughed, not the least put off by his brusque manner. "I'm so glad to meet you Laura. You're absolutely gorgeous and that gown makes you look as regal as a queen. I'll bet Angel is fit to be tied."

Susan gave Laura no time to respond to her candid remarks.

"This is Davey Logan from Fort Brooke," she went on, "Davey, Laura is visiting from Boston."

Davey nodded his head in Laura's direction. The news that she wasn't Fowler Dunstan's wayward daughter brought a feeling of relief. He wasn't sure why it should make a difference, but it did. And Susan was right. Laura Dunstan did look like royalty in her expensive green ballgown. A regular monarch exuding about as much warmth as a north wind in February. Ice princess would more aptly describe this stiff-necked Yankee, he decided, studying her tall, unbending form with a critical eye.

Brad took Susan firmly by the arm, then addressing both Davey and Laura he said, "Please excuse us for a moment. Susan and I need to have a word in private, but I assure you we will return shortly."

Blue eyes sparkling, Susan allowed Brad to propel her through the crowd and out into the hall.

Laura noticed the way Davey's gaze followed the pretty blond until she was out of sight. Susan Ashe was not only pleasing to look at but vivacious as well. What man would not want to be around someone so delightful and bubbly? What a dullard she must seem in comparison for she had not been able to get a word in edgewise.

Davey knitted his brow as he watched the two vanish around the corner. He didn't like the high-handed manner in which Brad Kincaid had forced Susan to accompany him. Hell, he didn't like Kincaid period! But Susan seemed well able to hold her own with her arrogant neighbor and he knew it would accomplish nothing if he made a scene and got himself thrown out on his ear. He'd wait five minutes before he went looking for them. Not one minute more!

Chapter 3

Laura shifted her weight nervously from one foot to the other as she sought for something clever to say but nothing would come. *Don't just stand here like a ninny,* she chided, feeling more self-conscious with each passing second.

"So, Mr. Logan, you are from Fort Burke?" she said when she could stand the silence no longer. Not particularly adroit as conversation goes but it was a start, or so she thought until she realized Davey hadn't heard a word she'd said. He was still staring at the door through which Susan and Bradley had disappeared. His inattention pricked her vanity though she was loath to admit it. Making up her mind to match his rudeness stroke for stroke Laura gingerly plucked at his sleeve.

Davey felt a tickling sensation on his arm and without bothering to look down, he brushed his hand along the fabric of his coat much as he would have done to rid himself of a pesky fly.

Truly angered now, Laura tried pinching that

same arm as hard as she could but there was nothing beneath his jacket except rock-solid muscle—not an ounce of loose flesh to get a grip on. Her impulsive action did finally gain his notice, but by this time she was so intrigued with the feel of the iron-hard sinew beneath her fingers that she failed to see Davey's puzzled gaze trained on her bent head. She couldn't know that trails of red flames highlighted by the illumination from the lamps danced among her auburn curls setting her hair aglow.

Davey observed Laura curiously as she continued poking and prodding. After several more jabs Laura felt the muscle flex expanding to fill the sleeve like an inflating balloon. Slowly she lifted her head to find deep-set brown eyes focused on her forefinger poised an inch or so from its target.

"Blast!" Her favorite expletive came out in a barely audible groan. She had achieved her objective in gaining the man's undivided attention. Too bad that in so doing she'd also made an utter fool of herself.

Davey's lips twitched. Laura thought she detected amusement in his eyes as well but she could not be sure. Suddenly that odd queasiness in the pit of her stomach was back in full force. Why didn't he say something? Demand an explanation for her unseemly conduct? Oh, Lord! What a wretched idea!

Hastily considering her alternatives, Laura decided to ignore her indiscretion and hope that he was gentleman enough to do the same. "So, Mr. Logan, you are from Fort Burke?" Reverting back to her previous query she waited to see if he would simply answer her question or insist on pursuing an incident best forgotten.

He kept her in suspense a long moment before he replied, "No ma'am, Miss Dunstan. I'm from Fort Brooke."

Laura felt the heat rising to her cheeks.

"Blast!"

"I beg your pardon?"

"For what?" She didn't like the way this conversation was getting away from her.

Davey cocked a thick, dark brow wondering if the amber-eyed beauty might have had one too many cups of punch. She seemed a trifle moonstruck and he still hadn't figured out what she found so fascinating about his arm.

He nodded toward the French doors leading to the garden. "Maybe a breath of fresh air would clear your head."

Laura looked at the open doorway, then brought her gaze back to Davey. Drawing herself up until her gently sloping shoulders were on a horizontal plane she replied haughtily, *"Mister* Logan. I am not like *them! I* am from Boston!"

After imparting that bit of information which he already knew, she turned and flounced away, leaving Davey to wonder what he could have said to get her so riled.

Brad Kincaid lead Susan down the hall and into his stepfather's study keeping a firm grip on her arm until they were behind the closed door. He released her then but kept himself between her and the ready means of escape.

"Really, Bradley. I've never known you to act quite so boorish." Her smile had been replaced by a look of annoyance which Brad met with a glare, his slender nose lifting, reminding her of a fox on the trail of a rabbit.

"I demand to know what possessed you to behave like a slut out there—and don't give me any cock-and-bull nonsense about an *experiment!"*

Susan wasn't intimidated by his show of temper. She knew he couldn't afford to make a scene with the house full of guests. It would not be in keeping with the image of a gentleman he sought to portray, which meant she could afford to bait him.

"My, my! We are in a snit tonight, aren't we? What's the matter, Bradley? Did Fowler's beautiful niece spurn your advances?" Her false show of concern was transparent, just as she meant it to be.

"Rest assured, Susan, you are solely responsible for my foul mood. Have you any idea who you were trifling with beneath this very roof?"

"Trifling? Why, Bradley, what a quaint way to describe an innocent kiss between friends," she replied with a coolness that served to further incense her accuser. "But of course I know who he is. Didn't I introduce you? Besides I would hardly 'trifle' with a stranger," she added smuggly.

Brad seized her upper arm in a painful grip, sneering, "That man happens to be Lance Logan's half-breed bastard. When did the two of you become 'friends'?"

Deciding she had pushed him as far as she dared, Susan lied without conscience. "Davey often has business in the area. Not that you've any right to ask but we've met on several occasions. Besides, if the Logans are so offensive why were they invited to the party?" Her question held no little amount of contempt as she wrenched her arm free.

"As a courtesy, Fowler sent invitations to all of our newly elected government officials and their families, but he never expected that rabble-rouser Logan or his by-blow to show up here tonight."

Susan bared her teeth making plain her dislike for the man facing her. "Life is full of surprises, isn't it Bradley?"

Instead of replying to her sarcasm in kind, Brad's manner turned conciliatory. Susan wondered what he was up to. She didn't have long to wait before she found out.

"And just what is this business that brings Logan across the state so often?"

"His business with *me* is strictly personal. Anything else you will have to ask him yourself."

Brad moved aside as she reached around him to open the door, but he covered her hand with his own before she could fully turn the heavy brass knob. "Remember this, Susan. People who play with fire tend to get burned. We've had more than our share of runaways at River Ridge recently. I'm convinced the darkies are getting outside help. When I discover who is responsible I intend to see that the person or persons pay a high price for breaking the law."

Susan looked him straight in the eye without blinking, even when he removed his hand allowing her to open the heavy oak door. "You can't hang a ghost," came her grave reply. "You'll never catch *the Specter.*"

Before he could answer she was gone, leaving him to worry and wonder where she could have heard that dreaded name—the sobriquet the negroes had given the black-caped figure seen more than once riding through the darkness. And always the morning after the apparition was spotted a planter would wake to find that his labor force had diminished overnight.

Just as Davey started down the hall in search of Susan, a door opened and she breezed out in a whirl of blue skirts. She smiled when she saw him but the smile failed to reach her troubled eyes. At his sides Davey's fists curled for he felt sure Kincaid was responsible for whatever was bothering the young woman, and it wouldn't take much in the way of an excuse for him to punch the arrogant son of a bitch in his aristocratic nose.

Seeing his tight-lipped expression, Susan muttered through gritted teeth, "He deserves to be brought low but this isn't the time or the place."

"Did he hurt you?"

"No," she assured, sensing instinctively that were she to say otherwise it would be impossible to stop the large, angry man from challenging Fowler's stepson. "But I don't doubt he would have if he thought he could get away with it," she added bitterly. "Brad Kincaid enjoys inflecting pain on those who can't fight back."

Susan felt Davey's body tense; saw his strong jaw clench. "I wish he'd try something with me. I'd like nothing better than to beat the hell out of him!"

This time Susan's smile was real. "I hope you get that chance one of these days, and if you do I would like to be around to see it."

Davey forced himself to relax, even managing to return her smile. "But not tonight?"

By now they had reached the crowded ballroom and as her gaze swept over the distinguished group of ladies and gentlemen circling the polished wood floor Susan giggled. "Definitely not tonight!"

Only half pretending a look of disappointment, Davey sighed resignedly. "Then since fighting is out of the question I guess we might as well dance."

Without giving her a chance to object, he swept her into his arms, leading the way as they joined the other couples swaying to the music. He moved with unexpected skill and grace for someone who had been raised in a primitive wilderness.

Unable to hide her surprise Susan asked in her typically candid way, "Who in the world taught you to dance so beautifully?"

Davey's dark eyes sparkled with mischief. "Why, Miss Ashe, dancing is a tradition among us natives, though we usually do it around a camp fire with a lot more whooping and hollering."

Susan's infectuous laughter trilled through the air, drawing attention to the handsome twosome as they glided around the room. Davey grinned down at the woman in his arms unaware that they had become the focal point for more than one pair of eyes.

"Actually it was all my stepmother's doing. Rebecca convinced me that Beth's entire future rested in my hands."

"Beth?"

"She's sort of a cousin by marriage. As Rebecca explained it, Beth couldn't possibly learn to dance without a partner. Naturally I told her that what she suggested was beneath the dignity of a Calusa warrior, but . . ." Davey grinned. "I guess you'd just have to know Rebecca to understand."

"I'd like to meet her. She sounds like a brilliant strategist."

"She puts the army's best generals to shame," Davey bragged. "The only reason I didn't rebel more vigorously is because Beth hated the dance lessons even more than I did. It was always a challenge to find her when the time came. Once I'd tracked her down, hog-tied the little hellion, then dragged her into the parlor, I couldn't very well walk away."

Davey told the humorous tale without missing a step, his rugged features softening to reveal the obvious love he felt for two more members of his remarkable, if unorthodox, family. Earlier Susan had recognized the pride in his voice when he spoke of his father. Now she knew he also held his stepmother in high regard. And what about the "sort of" cousin, Beth, who he deemed "a little hellion"?

"I'd like to continue the discussion we were having before Kincaid interrupted."

Davey's reminder gave her no further time to ponder. "We can't talk here. Brad will be watching us like a hawk. Where are you staying?" she asked him.

The music ended. Members of the small orchestra laid their instruments aside and headed for the refreshment table. Still Davey remained with his arms about Susan, his face close to hers, a certain wariness evident in his eyes.

Susan waited unmoving beneath Davey's careful scrutiny. She could not blame him for being cautious. He'd made clear his feelings where the issue of slavery was concerned. Proof that the daughter of a well-to-do planter shared his views would require more than mere words, especially since she dared not chance arguing her case while standing in the middle of Fowler Dunstan's ballroom. So she continued to wait, holding her breath, hoping he would see something in her face that would convince him to trust her.

"I'm staying with a friend, Wade Callahan. He has a little farm a few miles southwest of here on the road to Fort King."

His words meant she had passed the test and Susan expelled her breath, her relief enormous. "I take a ride every morning before breakfast. There's a little church set back in the woods. It can't be far from your friend's homestead."

Davey nodded. "I know the place. I'll meet you there at dawn."

When she nodded her agreement his admiration for her increased another notch. She was lovely to look at, courageous when it came to standing up against the likes of Brad Kincaid, and she was dedicated, though to what cause he was not quite certain. He doubted if many of the women present tonight would stir from their beds until noon. But Susan rode out early every morning and tomorrow would be no exception.

Sky-blue eyes peeked at him from beneath a fringe of honey-blond lashes. "I'm afraid since Brad discovered us kissing you're stuck with me for the evening. It will look most peculiar if we go our separate ways now."

Taking her small hand in his much larger one and patting it reassuringly, Davey dipped his head in a mock bow. "Miss Ashe, it would be my pleasure to play your devoted swain for the rest of the night."

Susan laughed gaily enjoying his teasing banter. Davey glanced over her shoulder noticing Brad Kincaid standing not far away, giving him a look that promised trouble ahead. That came as no surprise. What did startle him was the glare he was getting from Laura Dunstan who stood at Kincaid's side. Davey didn't know what he had said or done to offend the ice princess from Boston but she sure acted like a hound with a burr in its tail. And from the way she was scowling at him you'd think he had put it there.

* * *

Laura watched Susan Ashe and Davey Logan dancing together with that perfect rhythm and timing usually demonstrated by couples who had been partners for a long time. Yet Brad, a close neighbor and friend of the Ashe's said he had never met the man who circled the room with a fluid grace which put the other men's efforts to shame. There was a mystery here which aroused Laura's curiosity and begged to be solved.

When the music ended and Davey continued to hold Susan in his arms, Laura gave an unladylike snort. The man was a rake and a bounder for hadn't he invited Laura herself to accompany him outside just minutes ago? And when she'd rebuffed him he immediately returned to the pretty blonde who obviously enjoyed his touch and his kisses, judging from her smiling face and delighted laughter.

What, Laura wondered, would have happened if she had been bold enough to walk with him through the lamplit gardens? Would he have held her in those hard-muscled arms the way he held Susan Ashe? Would he have tried to steal a kiss from *her* in the dark? Remembering his wide, well-formed mouth, watching his lips move as he bent his head to whisper something close to Susan's ear, Laura felt her knees go weak, her cheeks grow hot, and everything in between begin to tingle.

"I must speak to Henry about putting his daughter on a tighter leash," sneered Brad coming up beside her. "Susan has always been a bit outrageous. Probably because her mother died when she was very young and Henry tends to let her have her own way, but I've never known her to behave with such total disregard for propriety. Someone should take a firm hand to her.''

Laura frowned at her uncle's stepson. There it was again. The suggestion that women should be kept in line with physical force. Still frowning she turned back just in time to catch Davey Logan's eyes on her, dark unreadable eyes that masked his thoughts. But there was contact just the same. Laura felt as though an electrical charge had flashed between them giving her a jolt. Perhaps that's how it is with rakes, she mused. Maybe some men are born with a certain indefinable charisma which women find irresistible. Most women, Laura amended. She, of course, was immune to any such attraction. Hadn't she already made it clear that she was not interested in what he had to offer?

He certainly hadn't been very persistent when she had rejected him, but then why should he be concerned when he had Susan Ashe and who knows how many other young women falling at his feet? Not that she cared if they wanted to make fools of themselves over the man. Come to think of it he really wasn't *that* handsome. His hair was a little too long to be considered fashionable and those penetrating brown eyes set in his darkly tanned face below thick black brows embodied the description of the pirate villain in a book she once read.

He was definitely unlike any other man attending the party, though Laura could not put her finger on what it was that made him unique. It was true that none of those present were as tall or as broad in the shoulders as he, but it was more than just his stature, more than his coloring or the texture of his skin. It had something to do with how he held himself aloof looking down from his loftly height at those around him. Yes, Davey Logan was different. And Laura had a feeling he liked it that way.

"Fort Brooke must be a good distance from here," she mused aloud.

Brad gave her a surly reply. "Fort Brooke is on the western coast of Florida and that's where Logan ought to stay. But what made you think the fort was not close by?"

Laura was perplexed by Brad's open hostility toward the man he had just met.

"Mr. Logan doesn't seem to know anyone but Susan Ashe," she answered hesitantly. "And he seems . . . I don't know . . . different, that's all."

Brad's thin lips curved upward. For a moment Laura actually thought he was going to laugh but he caught himself in time and snarled instead. "Oh, Logan's different all right. He's a *breed,* my dear. Part man, part beast."

At first Laura thought Brad was teasing her but such a thing was not in keeping with his serious nature.

"It's true the high and mighty Lance Logan is the man's father but his mother was a full-blooded Calusa Indian. Needless to say there was no marriage to formalize the union which makes Susan's latest conquest a damnable half-breed bastard."

Laura was too shocked to reprimand Brad for his vulgarity. Though she knew little to nothing about Indians, had in fact never seen one, the Dunstans referred to them all as savages which led Laura to form her own mental picture of what one must look like. She had been relieved when Fowler assured her that those remaining in Florida stayed hidden in a huge swamp far to the south.

"You mean Mr. Logan is a . . . a . . . *savage?"* she gasped.

Seeing the fear and horror on her face, Brad Kincaid smirked in satisfaction. "I can think of no better way to describe him, my dear!"

Laura awoke sometime in the early morning hours, her heart racing, her nightgown drenched with perspiration. She got up, hurrying to the open window where she pulled the curtains aside, letting in the feeble light from a waning moon. All around her the land was blanketed with an eerie quiet that seemed to magnify rather than diminish the memory of her nightmare. Clearly she recalled her fear. She was running through the woods chased by a huge hairy animal. For a while she was able to elude the creature, then suddenly the trees and bushes took on human forms reaching out with giant leafy branches to snatch at her skirt and yank on her hair until she was trapped in a tangled net of vegetation which would allow her to go no farther.

Her pursuer stopped right behind her. She could hear his ragged breathing, feel his heated breath on her neck, sending shivers of fright up and down her spine. She didn't want to look back, but she had no choice for such is the way with dreams. One glimpse brought her to her knees shaking uncontrollably, screaming like a banshee. It was the sound of her screams that finally released her from the nightmare's grip. Even now she could hear them echoing in her mind as she tried to erase the image that had caused her panic.

He had the body of a grizzly with huge fur-covered arms and handlike paws from which sharp rounded talons extended. The girth of his chest was as large as a mighty oak but his head was that of a man with long raven-dark hair. Familiar deep-set eyes gleamed red in the light and when he opened his mouth in a grotesque grin, there were two yellow fangs dripping blood.

"Blast, Brad Kincaid!" Laura fumed aloud. It was all his fault for spouting that nonsense about Davey Logan. *Half man. Half beast.* Ridiculous! He might be a rake and a womanizer but he certainly appeared to be *all* man.

Yawning, Laura decided it was time to forget the silly dream and return to bed, but as she started to turn away she heard the jingle of harness barely audible in the distance. By now her eyes had adjusted sufficiently so that she could see the outline of a slow-moving mule-drawn wagon just topping the rise to disappear over the other side.

She yawned again, then closed the curtains and felt her way back to bed. Raising the covers up to her chin she wondered drowsily where the buckboard could be going in the middle of the night. Either someone was out awfully late or up disgustingly early she decided just before she drifted off to sleep.

Chapter 4

It was a pretty little church built of whitewashed timbers nestled among a stand of oak and pine. The parishioners were poor farmers who thanked God for what he had given them and tried to give back something in return. The meeting house was a tribute to their efforts with its neatly cropped yard and well-tended cemetery.

Davey walked among the plots, glancing at the markers. He stopped when he came to one particular stone partially covered by a climbing rose bush. Dew dripped from the petals of the delicate pink blossoms to fall like tears upon the grassy mound. He didn't have to move the thorny branches to see the inscription for he knew what it said.

NELL CALLAHAN
1820–1844

Less than a year ago he had watched Wade chisel the letters and numbers into the granite slab with loving hands, then carefully uproot his wife's favorite flower, the one that grew right outside the front door of their tiny farmhouse, transplanting it to this spot beside her.

Hearing a rider approach Davey turned as Susan dismounted, then crossed the wet grass to join him. She looked at the gravestone, then at the tall, solemn-faced man holding his hat respectfully in his hand.

"Someone you knew?"

Davey nodded. "Nell Callahan. Wade's wife. She was only twenty-four when she died."

"How tragic. Was it the fever?" she asked softly. Yellow fever, an all too common form of death in Florida, had no respect for age, striking young and old alike. So far its cure was as much a mystery as its cause.

"No. Nell drowned in the river attempting to save someone else." His voice held bitterness as well as regret.

"I'm sorry." It seemed inadequate but Susan didn't know what else to say.

Davey shrugged his broad shoulders. It was not an insensitive gesture, more an effort to shake off the anguish he felt whenever he thought about Nell's senseless death. Taking Susan by the hand he led her to a bench that had been erected between two sturdy oaks. "It's too late to help her now," was all he said. Once they were seated he came straight to the point. "Last night you spoke of a movement underway to assist escaping slaves in finding their way to freedom. You hinted that you might be one

58

of those involved in the illegal operation. I hope I misunderstood because I'd sure hate to see that pretty neck of yours at the end of a rope."

Susan eyed him sharply. "And *I* hope I didn't make a mistake in assuming you would be in sympathy with those held in bondage."

Davey watched the bright gold rim of the sun edge its way up over the treetops turning the gray sky to blue, but his thoughts were not on the landscape. "I think I've made it clear that I don't hold with the idea of one man owning another, but what happens between the planters and their 'property' isn't any of my business and it shouldn't be yours either. Aiding and abetting runaway slaves is a serious crime, not a game little girls should play."

Thinking she might be placing her life in danger for the sake of a few thrills to relieve the boredom of a humdrum existence made Davey angry. But Susan was angry, too. Angry and disappointed.

"Obviously I misjudged you. Having heard so much about your father, I thought you would care about the people we are trying to help."

So much for any doubts. Her words confirmed her involvement with the abolitionists. She was clearly one of them and knowing it was true scared the hell out of Davey. He quickly racked his brain for a way to make her understand the seriousness of the situation. "Maybe if I knew more about what was going on . . ."

He left the sentence unfinished, allowing Susan to think she could sway him to her side. It worked. Taking his words as encouragement she related in vivid detail the abuse many negroes received at the hands of their masters—the beatings, the rapes, husbands, wives, and children often separated from one another by sale or trade.

"It isn't right, Davey. They're human beings but they're being treated worse than animals. Why most planters treat their horses and cattle *better* than they do their slaves."

The fervent spirit of the crusader was back and Davey wondered for the first time if Susan's determination to rescue the unfortunates might be more than just a passing fancy. It was vital that he find out for sure.

"You talk about caring. Why do you care what happens to them? Your father is among those you are working against."

"No! Papa would never harm one of our people! He treats them like children."

When Davey cast her a doubtful look she refused to back down in her father's defense. "It's true. Those that work at Pine View have never shown any discontent. Papa may not go so far as to set them free but he doesn't abuse them. And someday when the plantation is mine I will see that they have their freedom."

"Then how will you afford your fancy ball gowns and expensive riding outfits?" He hadn't failed to notice the well-tailored blue habit she was wearing or the matching hat perched jauntily on her head. "If you and your friends succeed in turning loose those who work to keep your closets full you might be forced to dress like us common folks."

Running her eyes down the length of him from his soft deer-hide shirt to the knee-high moccasins laced over form-fitting pants, Susan replied, "I would probably look rather fetching in buckskins."

Remembering the way Beth looked in tanned leather, Davey chucked. "You just might at that!"

"I don't care about fancy clothes." There was no amusement in Susan's voice when she returned to the subject foremost in her mind. "But I'll tell you what I do care about. There was someone very dear to me. She was my maid but more importantly Rhea was my friend. She fell in love with a young man named Benjamin who belonged to Fowler Dunstan. When I told Papa he offered to buy Benjamin so the two could be married, but Fowler refused, saying money couldn't pick cotton. That's when Rhea and Benjamin decided to run away together. I knew about their plans. I suppose I even encouraged them. It seemed like something out of a romantic novel." She paused, choking back a sob.

"But this story didn't have a happy ending. Benjamin was caught trying to escape. He was dragged back to the quarters and whipped to death. The other slaves were forced to watch in case they had any ideas about trying the same thing. The next morning we found Rhea hanging from a rafter in the barn where she had taken her own life."

Davey was not unmoved by her story but he managed to hold his emotions in check. "Did Dunstan order the beating?"

Susan shook her head. "I'm sure he was aware of

what was happening but, no, it was Brad Kincaid who wielded the whip."

It took a lot of lashes to kill a man. Davey's gut twisted with anger as his mind conjured up a picture of what must have taken place that night. "So you decided to set all of the slaves free to avenge the deaths of Rhea and Benjamin."

Again Susan moved her head from side to side. "It wasn't like that at all. I wanted to do something to protest the atrocity but I felt so helpless. However, I did talk about the incident with several close friends. Not long afterward I received a note asking me to become part of a network being formed to aid the negroes who were being mistreated."

"Who sent the note?"

"I don't know. The organization operates in secret. No one knows all of its members. We work like a chain. If there is a weak link or if someone gets caught the chain may be temporarily broken but never completely destroyed."

"It still sounds dangerous to me," commented her listener, "but I'd like to hear more."

Unable to guess by his dark inscrutable eyes what he was thinking, Susan continued hopefully. "There's a hollow tree down by the river. When an escape is planned a message is left there. I gather food and clothing and place it in the boathouse. The next morning it's gone along with a few more slaves from one of the neighboring plantations, usually River Ridge."

"So you don't even know who your contact is?"
"No."

Davey rubbed his chin with a calloused palm. "Sounds like you're at the bottom of the chain. It would be interesting to know who's at the top."

Before she could think better of it Susan replied, "The Specter." She clamped a hand over her mouth, but not before she had Davey's full attention.

"The *who?*" His voice rang out loudly through the quiet morning air startling a blue jay in the tree overhead.

The bird took flight screeching his objection at having been disturbed. Susan wished she could call back her carelessly spoken words but she knew it was too late. "I don't know who he is but the negroes call him *Specter* because he dresses in black and no one has ever seen his face. He arranges transportation for the fugitives. Once they reach the Florida-Georgia border there are 'safe houses' along the route north where they can rest and get a good meal before they continue their journey."

"And you have no idea who this man might be?" Davey studied her features carefully looking for some indication that she knew more than she was telling, but her ingenuous face assured him she was holding nothing back.

"Like I've said I have no idea who he is though I'd certainly like to meet him some day. To the slaves he's just one step short of God and I must admit he's become a hero to me as well."

The reverence in her tone when she spoke of the one called *Specter* deepened the furrow between

Davey's brows. "He's only a man, Susan. If he's caught he'll be hanged like any other thief."

"He won't be caught."

Her illogical certainty caused Davey to feel both uncomfortable and impatient. No man was invincible and to think otherwise was only deluding one's self. But he doubted he could convince Susan of the fact, so he decided to let the matter drop for now.

"Suppose I was to agree to help you and your friends?" He held up his hand when he saw her expression brighten. "I didn't say I would. We're just supposing. But if I did, what role would I play in your little drama?"

He didn't seem to be taking her seriously but Susan was not put off. "I'm sure *Specter* could use your help in getting the people to Georgia. You're an outsider able to come and go at will."

Davey grimaced. She had things all figured out. "You seem to forget that my home is two hundred miles away."

"How long will you be visiting your friend?"

"A few weeks at most."

Susan put her hand on his arm and smiled beguilingly up into his handsome face. "All I ask is that you think about my proposition. Even if it's only for a short time I know you could prove invaluable to the cause."

Before he could argue she went on. "Tomorrow night Papa is giving a small party. Nothing fancy. A few of our neighbors are coming to dine and play cards. I wish you would come?"

"Will the Dunstans be there?"

Susan hesitated, wondering if he would be more likely to accept her invitation if she said "no." But it wasn't her nature to be less than honest. "Yes," she replied holding her breath as she waited for his answer.

Davey didn't look forward to spending another evening with Dunstan and his insolent stepson. Then he thought about the haughty, amber-eyed Laura. Funny how he hadn't been able to get her out of his mind. He kept seeing the shock on her face when she'd caught him kissing Susan in the dark; the way she had looked at him with disdain after his dance with Susan had ended as if she herself would shrink from the touch of a half-breed. It would be a challenge to find out just how far he could go with the prim and proper Miss Dunstan, and if there was one thing Davey thrived on it was a challenge.

"How can I refuse such a gracious invitation?" he agreed as he helped Susan mount.

The smile she gave him was triumphant. "Dinner is at eight." Kicking her horse in the flanks she called back over her shoulder, "And bring your friend, Mr. Callahan."

Davey shook his head laughing silently. It would be a cold day in hell when Wade Callahan sat down at a slaveholder's table!

As their horses cantered up the long sweeping drive, Davey cut his eyes over at his friend. "You don't have to do this you know."

65

Wade's mouth curved in a smile giving his round, freckled face that cherubic look that often fooled people into thinking he was tractable. "Now that's where you're wrong, Davey. After the way you've raved about your blue-eyed protagonist who prefers poverty to wealth and thinks the word 'revolutionize' is synonymous with 'abolition,' I'll never know another moment's peace until I meet this remarkable young lady for myself."

Davey wondered what Wade was really up to. He had shown no interest in women since Nell's death and knowing his friend's hatred for the plantation owners, Davey had been understandably surprised when Wade agreed to accompany him tonight.

Wade whistled through his teeth as they handed their reins to a groom and walked toward the entrance of the two-storied brick mansion where a negro dressed in red and black livery waited to attend them. Wade gave up his battered, wide-brimmed headpiece but declined to part with the black leather gloves he always wore. While Davey was dressed much as he'd been at Fowler Dunstan's party, his companion had chosen to don a fawn-colored vest over a plaid cotton shirt which was clean but faded as were his heavy brown twill pants. Wade had clothes more suitable for the occasion and if it was his intention to embarrass Henry Ashe and his daughter, Davey would have a few things to say to him on the ride back to the farmhouse.

* * *

Laura sat on the sofa in the comfortably furnished drawing room sipping a glass of sherry and chatting with Susan. Despite her first impression of the young woman, Laura found the Southern belle to be a delightful hostess who had twice been to London and shared her interest in the many art galleries and museums scattered throughout the famous city.

The men stood clustered around the huge empty fireplace, some smoking cigars, all with whiskey glasses in their hands. Angel and several of her friends whose names Laura could not remember hovered nearby giggling occasionally in an effort to gain the men's attention. Instead they were rewarded with stern looks from their mothers who had elected to congregate on the far side of the room where they could gossip about those who had not been invited.

Laura wondered if Hester Dunstan had anything to contribute to the conversation. She glanced over to where the ladies had gathered and shook her head sadly. Her small, silver-haired aunt sat on the fringe of the group, her head bent over the neatly folded hands clasped in her lap. She looked like a child in the high-backed chair which dwarfed her tiny person. Laura found her aunt's meekness annoying at times though she doubted the woman could help herself.

Hester rarely spoke, perhaps because when she dared to voice opinions her views were met with contempt by her son and daughter. Angel was openly vicious in the way she treated her mother.

Though not as cruel, Bradley's patronizing air rubbed Laura the wrong way. She had never heard Fowler speak harshly to his wife but neither had she heard him upbraid the other two for their lack of respect. It was a strange household but then what did she know? Never having been part of a family before she had little with which to compare the Dunstans' relationships toward each other, yet common sense told her there must be a more amenable way of living together.

So lost was she in her musings it was several moments before Laura realized how quiet the room had suddenly become. Above the rim of her crystal wine glass she saw the men staring at the door, disapproval clearly etched their scowling faces. From the women's corner she heard more than one gasp. Angel's nervous titter brought Susan Ashe quickly to her feet.

"Davey, I'm so glad you could come," she greeted, hurrying to where he stood bedazzled by the bright lights from the chandeliers. Then extending her hand to Wade she said graciously, "And you must be Davey's friend, Mr. Callahan. Welcome to Pine View Plantation."

She seemed not the least disconcerted by Wade's informal attire or by the smooth leather gloves he wore, and when her father moved to shake the hands of the two newcomers everyone relaxed visibly as Susan and Henry made the introductions.

Laura watched them move about the room. Davey Logan was as handsome as she remembered. Now that she knew he was a savage she could iden-

tify the specific features which made him unique—
deep-set eyes above high cheekbones, a facial structure that narrowed only slightly before reaching his
strong masculine chin. His dark skin was burnished
by more than just the sun and the shadow of a beard
marked the lower part of his face. She seemed to
recall having heard that savages had no body hair.
If so, she guessed white blood was responsible for
his having to shave each day. Remembering the
terrible nightmare she'd had after the party at River
Ridge, Laura could not help but smile. Savage
Davey Logan might be but he was also the most
magnificent specimen of maleness she had ever seen.

From the moment Davey entered the brightly
illuminated room he had known exactly where
Laura was. He saw her immediately, sitting on the
sofa holding a glass of amber liquid so like the color
of her unusual topaz eyes. Even from a distance he
could feel her presence, smell the scent of jasmine he
remembered from their brief encounter two nights
ago. He planned to remain cool and aloof, pattern-
ing his manner to parallel her own haughty disregard, but already his palms were sweating and he
found it hard to swallow. Running a finger around
the stiffly starched collar of his shirt he tried to
concentrate on matching names with faces as Susan
introduced him to her neighbors, but soon those
around him blurred into a droning sea of voices.
Only one person among the throng stood out as an
entity unto herself. Laura Dunstan.

The rich turquoise splendor of her gown set
against flawless alabaster shoulders and arms made

69

her appear not quite real. She reminded him of a porcelain doll belonging to Beth's sister, Mandy. No human being could be as perfectly put together as Laura and it was that very perfection which made her seem cold and untouchable, like the doll now kept high on a shelf out of the reach of grubby little hands. Davey tried to envision the proud beauty with her hair loose, blowing in the wind or a smudge of dirt on her face. Not the ice princess, he decided with a wry grin.

She raised her eyes to meet his and he was transfixed by the shimmering golden lights that flared to life in her irises. Try as he might Davey could not break the contact. He fought the urge to unbutton his collar which seemed to grow tighter with each breath he took. Dammit! She had no right to make him feel this way. No one had ever strangled him with a look!

Laura watched Davey's expression change from amusement to confusion to anger. And he was staring straight at *her* while the transition took place! What could she have done to provoke him? She hadn't even spoken to the man since he'd entered the room and she hoped she would be able to get through the evening without having to do so. Her hopes were dashed moments later when dinner was announced and Laura found her place card next to that of the very one she wished to avoid.

"Blast!" she muttered grudgingly, taking her seat.

There was little consolation in hearing a disgruntled sigh to her right. Obviously Davey Logan was equally displeased about the arrangement.

70

Chapter 5

Most of the space in the large, high-ceilinged dining room was taken up by a beautifully appointed table with seating for twenty-four people. Centerpieces made up of flickering candles in silver holders surrounded by greenery added a touch of color to the snowy linen cloth. The young people had been grouped together for the meal with Susan at one end of the long table. Closest to their hostess, Laura and Wade sat facing each other. Angel was seated across from Davey who was positioned between Wade and Bradley Kincaid.

As soon as everyone was settled Brad began to speak loudly, picking up where he had left off in a conversation he was having with his friend, Hal Barker. "I'm telling you something has to be done! Yesterday morning we discovered two more of our field hands gone. Vanished during the night without a trace!"

"Almost seems as if someone has it in for you and your stepfather," remarked Hal as a steaming bowl

71

of soup was placed in front of him. "Most of the thievery has occurred at River Ridge."

Brad didn't appreciate being reminded that his stepfather's plantation had been hardest hit. Pale green eyes narrowed to tiny slits. "That's no reason for the rest of you to be complacent. All of the planters run the risk of losing property until those responsible are caught and hanged."

"Just what do you expect us to do?" Hal asked impatiently.

Brad straightened. His answer was accompanied by an attitude of smug satisfaction. "I'll tell you what *I've* done. I took a little trip to Fort King yesterday and hired a dozen extra men, and the guns strapped to their hips were the only references I needed. From now on there will be guards posted around the quarters day and night. In addition to their wages I've offered a hefty bonus if they catch any negroes trying to escape or anyone found trespassing on Dunstan property."

The silence that followed Brad's pronouncement was broken by the sound of silver hitting china and all eyes focused on a crimson-faced Susan Ashe who was mopping the bodice of her dress with a napkin. Davey and Wade exchanged worried looks. It was the first time Davey had seen Susan flustered. Even when they were discovered kissing in the dark she had managed to make light of the situation. Apparently she viewed Kincaid's new hirelings as a real threat to the freedom movement with which she was involved.

Surprisingly it was Angel who came to the rescue.

"Now see what you've done, Bradley, with all your frightening talk about thieves and gunmen. Why just thinking about such things makes me positively lightheaded."

Davey heard what sounded like a snort and turned his head to find Laura Dunstan frowning at the simpering redhead across the table. *What the hell was wrong with the woman now?* Angel had been right in objecting to talk of violence at the dinner table. Besides she'd managed to divert attention away from Susan and for that she had earned his gratitude. But it did make him a little uncomfortable the way she kept staring at him and fluttering her eyelids. Brad gave his stepsister a quelling look but he made no further mention of the labor problems plaguing River Ridge plantation.

Susan seemed determined to put Wade at ease by keeping up a constant flow of chatter about vegetable farming and the best way to get the crop to market. Fine for Wade but that left Davey feeling obliged to try and carry on a conversation with Dunstan's stiff-necked niece.

He cleared his throat searching for something they might have in common. His mind came up blank. Finally in desperation he asked, "Do you ride, Miss Dunstan?"

Laura started at the sound of his deep baritone voice close to her ear. *Miss Dunstan.* The vivacious blonde seated next to her was *Susan* while *she* was *Miss* Dunstan. Not that Laura wanted to be addressed familiarly by a savage. No, it wasn't that. *What was it then?* If she were honest with herself she'd have to admit her irritation stemmed from Davey Logan's easy acceptance of her previous rejection. Since her father's death she had grown used to having men fawn over her, even going to great lengths just to be near her, yet this uncivilized lout seemed impervious to her charms. Even now she had the feeling he was only talking to her because the lady on his right was engaged in a discussion with Hal Barker and Brad Kincaid.

Laura's amber eyes flared with indignation sparking to life the perverse little devil that occasionally took control of her tongue. "Why yes, Mr. Logan. Of course I ride," she replied airily. "I rode on a ship from London to Boston, a train from Boston to Savannah, and a steamer from Savannah to River Ridge. Or did you think I could sprout wings and fly from one place to the next?"

"No ma'am. I never thought that," Davey assured her with a shake of his head. *Hell! She didn't need wings. All she had to do was grab a broom!* He almost felt sorry for Fowler Dunstan having to play host to the sharp-tongued vixen whose rapid, clipped way of speaking rubbed a man raw.

How simple it would have been to tell him that her education had included lessons in horsemanship and that she was a superb equestrian. But then Laura would have missed the fun of watching the rogue flush and run a finger nervously around his collar!

Once dinner was over Davey thought his misery would end. Such was not the case. Card tables had been set up in the drawing room while they ate and now couples paired off joining in groups of four to play whist. He found himself standing beside an empty table with Susan, Wade, and Laura but when he started to pull out a chair, Susan suggested they walk in the garden instead. Certain a vegetable farmer would know nothing about the genteel entertainment, she sought to spare Wade embarrassment. Since every place at the other tables was now occupied, Davey was again stuck with the ice princess from Boston. He considered telling them he was ill and taking his leave. It would not have been entirely a lie. Everytime Laura Dunstan opened her mouth his stomach tied in knots. But he didn't want Susan or her father to think something he'd eaten at their table was responsible for his distress.

Arm in arm Susan and Wade passed through the open French doors and out onto the terrace leaving Davey and Laura to follow. Laura wanted to scream. How could Susan do this to her just when she thought they might become friends? And why was she leaving her savage to fend for himself while she went strolling off in the dark with that ill-bred farmer? Why, Wade Callahan hadn't even bothered to remove his gloves during dinner.

Blast! All these questions were giving her a headache—or could it be the musky masculine scent of the tall man standing next to her? She dared to glance up, then wished she hadn't for Davey Logan was scowling ferociously. Thick black brows were drawn together, forming one dark line above angry brown eyes that looked ready to do battle. His jaws were tightly clenched and his firm chin jutted out at a stubborn angle. She wondered if he would go after them; demand that Susan come back. *Oh, Lord!* That would leave *her* with the farmer. Never had there been such a classic case of having to choose the lesser of two evils!

"Mr. Logan, since we seem unable to avoid each other's company do you suppose we could declare a truce for the remainder of the evening?"

"I wasn't aware we were at war, Miss Dunstan," he said indifferently, still watching the path where Susan and Wade had disappeared.

The man was so concerned about his lady love he couldn't even look at her when she asked a simple question, Laura thought peevishly. "Oh come now," she countered. "Ever since I refused to leave the room with you the other night you've gone out of your way to annoy me."

Davey's mouth twitched. His ears must be playing tricks on him. Even a woman as self-centered as Laura Dunstan couldn't have mistaken his lack of interest in her for wounded pride, could she? She certainly seemed to believe what she was saying and now the minx was actually looking down her nose at him. Quite a feat, for despite the fact she was tall for a female she was still considerably shorter than his six foot three inches. Much to Laura's dismay Davey threw back his head and roared with laughter. The deep rumbling sound that erupted from his chest went on and on drowning out the voices of the nearby card players.

Struggling to suppress his mirth, Davey chortled, "Miss Dunstan, no one has to 'go out of his way' to annoy you. You're as sour as a persimmon that's picked before it's ripe and as testy as a hound dog with a thorn in his paw."

Laura felt the hot flow of blood rising to her cheeks. Her temper began to ignite starting at the core of her being and rapidly fanning out in all directions. How dare he insult her in such a manner. The uncouth provincial was making it sound as though she were to blame for the discord between them. Too furious to trust herself to speak she stormed out the door wanting only to get away from the hateful laughter that still rang in her ears.

Davey watched her flounce across the patio and realized he had gone too far in letting her know he was unimpressed by her uppity ways. He had seen hurt as well as anger in her face and knew he had inflicted the pain. Ashamed of himself, he quickly followed in her wake. He might not like her but his rudeness was inexcusable. She deserved an apology and come hell or high water she was going to get it!

Laura's eyes misted with tears, making it difficult to see where she was going but she refused to stop. She would not give her tormentor the satisfaction of witnessing her humiliation even though his opinion of her mattered not a bit. He was nothing but a half-breed bastard just as Bradley had said. She didn't see the steps leading down to the garden until her foot found only empty space and she pitched forward into a pair of strong arms that clamped about her slender form like an iron vise.

"Whoa there, lady. You forgot to sprout those wings."

Shaken by her close call, Laura grasped the lapels of Davey's coat as shudders rippled through her like waves upon the ocean.

"Easy, Laura. You're all right now," he soothed, rubbing his hand along her spine in an effort to calm her fear.

At the use of her given name, Laura raised her head. It sounded different coming from his lips. Almost like a caress. Davey felt his heart contract when he saw the moisture shimmering in her lustrous topaz eyes.

"Thank you," she whispered shakily.

Davey leaned back to study her face more clearly in the dim light. "Don't thank me. It was my fault you fell. I don't usually behave like such an ass." Which was true, leaving him to wonder what it was about this woman that brought out the worst in him.

Laura gave him a tremulous smile and, in spite of the tears that clung to her lashes like dewdrops, Davey knew it was the most beautiful smile he'd ever seen.

Grinning back he said, "If that offer of a truce is still on I'd like to reconsider."

Before Laura could answer, Susan and Wade appeared out of nowhere.

"Miss Dunstan, if this man is bothering you I'd be glad to call him out."

Wade's suggestion was laced with a goodly bit of humor. Davey released her reluctantly as she hastened to explain what might be misconstrued as an embrace.

"I'm afraid I took a tumble down the stairs, Mr. Callahan. Davey . . . I mean Mr. Logan, happened to be there to catch me."

Remembering Davey's description of his first meeting with the auburn-haired beauty, Wade mumbled just loud enough for his friend to hear. "Been at the punchbowl again, eh?"

From the drawing room they heard a chair being scraped against the hardwood floor, then Brad Kincaid's voice shouting angrily, "Dammit, Angel! A horse wearing blinders could play a better hand than that! I'd rather be partnered with a tree stump!"

"Little Angel must have trumped the devil's ace," commented Wade with a negligent shrug.

Davey chuckled while the two women stared at the ragtag farmer in disbelief.

"You know how to play whist?" Susan's question held a considerable amount of disbelief.

Wade winked over her shoulder toward his friend. "Shall we give the ladies a lesson or two on the fine points of the game?"

Without waiting for an answer he took Susan by the arm and guided her toward the light and laughter. Davey hesitated. He wasn't sure he could handle any more challenges tonight. He'd wanted to see how near he could get to Laura Dunstan before she ran like a rabbit back to her hole. But remembering the feel of her soft supple body wrapped in his arms, the sweet smell of jasmine that wafted up from silky auburn curls tucked beneath his chin, he knew she had allowed him to come much closer than it was safe to be. He didn't like the strange emotions she stirred in him.

She stood in the lamplight waiting for him to make a move, her lovely face mirroring his own confusion over what to do next. After the way he had treated her earlier he hadn't the heart to turn and walk away, though every instinct told him to do just that. No, he would play the gentleman tonight, but after this he would make sure he put plenty of distance between himself and Laura Dunstan. Better she remain high up on the shelf, for to have her within his reach could spell disaster for them both!

"While you were alone with her in the garden did Susan say anything more about the abolitionists?"

"She didn't have a chance. I spent the whole time apologizing for dressing like a country bumpkin. I should have worn my formal duds, but I was so damned determined to show them I wouldn't bend to their rules, I wound up looking like an ass and embarrassing myself in front of a very nice young lady."

The road was dark with only a glimmer of moonlight sifting through the trees overhead. Davey could not see the expression on his friend's face but Wade's voice was filled with chagrin.

"So you liked Susan, did you?"

Wade took his time answering, drawing deeply on his cheroot. They ambled along at a leisurely pace neither man in any particular hurry to get back to the lonely farmhouse even though it was well after midnight.

Exhaling a puff of smoke he said, "She wasn't at all what I expected. I guess I wanted to see contempt in her eyes for this lowly gaffer who dared enter the hallowed halls of Pine View dressed like a rag picker. Then she would have fit neatly into the mold of a rich planter's daughter. But Susan didn't seem to notice what I was wearing. I guess she did though. Why else would she stay at my side the entire evening?"

"Maybe she was mesmerized by your charm and wit."

"I don't think so," Wade countered, ignoring the teasing note in Davey's rejoinder. "I believe she was trying to protect me from the condescension of her guests."

They rode on in silence each lost in his own thoughts. Davey was glad the evening had gone smoothly but they had been foolish in taking such a risk. To socialize with the slaveholders was to tempt Fate and he could already see problems ahead. He'd hoped his friend would eventually find a woman to care for now that his sweet Nell was dead, but Wade's fascination with Susan Ashe could only lead to trouble. And that kind of trouble was the last thing they needed right now!

Staring up at the pale blue canopy Susan found sleep to be elusive. Every time she closed her eyes she saw a round, freckled face with a devil-may-care smile beaming at her from behind her lids. *Drat the man!* After the solid trouncing she and Laura had taken playing whist, the least he could do was let her rest in peace. Imagine being outfinessed by a vegetable farmer and a half-breed Indian!

Susan smiled and stretched beneath the flowered counterpane like a contented kitten. She tried to decide what it was about Wade Callahan that she found so intriguing. He was only of average height and build; not nearly as impressive in stature as Davey Logan. His light brown hair and boyish features held none of the dark mystery one saw in his tall, handsome friend from Fort Brooke. If she passed Wade on the street she probably wouldn't give him a second glance, yet there was no denying she was attracted to him. Perhaps it was the way he snubbed his nose at convention. He was a rebel, someone with whom Susan could relate for she was much more likely to swim against the tide than go with the flow.

While his looks might hold no mystery, the man himself was certainly an enigma. He had the vocabulary of a scholar and played the sophisticated card game with remarkable skill. He spoke of foreign places with the firsthand knowledge of a frequent traveler. So why, she pondered, was someone of his ilk growing beans and corn on a tiny farm in rural Florida?

Wade Callahan was hiding something. Susan was willing to bet her life on it and as she rolled over, thumping her pillow with a balled fist, she decided it would behoove her to learn more about the man.

Hopefully she could begin her investigation first thing in the morning. How fortuitous of her to have mentioned the direction in which she would be riding!

Chapter 6

Laura paused outside the door to the breakfast parlor hesitating to interrupt the argument coming from within. She recognized Fowler Dunstan's voice though she had never heard it raised in anger before. Since Angel and Hester seldom made an appearance before noon she assumed her uncle must be talking to Bradley Kincaid. Seconds later her suspicions were confirmed.

"Those lazy darkies need a firm hand or they'll be running River Ridge instead of us!" came his thunderous response to something Fowler had said.

"*Us?* You listen here, boy! *I* run this plantation and *I* give the orders around here!"

Laura could almost hear the china vibrating, such was her uncle's fury. His next words, though spoken in a more moderate tone, were commanding nonetheless. "Put that thing away or I just might be tempted to use it on *you!*

Curious, she peeked around the door frame. The two men stood facing each other a few feet apart.

Her uncle's face was flushed with rage. Though Brad's back was to her she could see the coiled leather whip in his hands, smooth and black like the body of a snake. She watched unable to take her eyes from the wicked-looking scourge as he stroked it, much as one would a favorite pet. Surely Fowler could not have been serious about using the lash on his stepson! The idea made her stomach churn.

No longer hungry, she slowly backed away, then hurried through a side door and headed for the stables. It was still an hour before she was to meet Susan Ashe but she felt an urgent need to be out in the fresh air and sunshine. She would leave word for her new friend to join her down by the river where it was peaceful and quiet. No loud voices raised in anger; no idle threats to spoil her appetite!

She rounded the corner of the barn nearly at a run only to come up against what felt like a solid brick wall. She would have been knocked off her feet if two wiry arms hadn't reached out to steady her.

"Well now, what have we here?"

Laura looked up into the face of a nightmare. Shoulder-length hair darkened by an accumulation of sweat and dirt framed the hideous features of the man she had plowed into. A jagged scar puckered his left eye, ribboning its way down a swarthy cheek to end at the corner of a smirking mouth. She choked back a scream as cold ebony eyes peered from above a crooked nose that had been broken more than once.

Struggling to free herself from his hold she

gasped out breathlessly, "Who are you and what are you doing here?"

The nightmare laughed without humor. "I might ask you the same thing, little darlin'," came his raspy drawl.

Gathering her courage, she replied, "I'm Laura Dunstan and my uncle owns this plantation. He doesn't like trespassers on his property." The tremor in her voice took much of the impetus out of her admonition.

Tightening his grip the stranger pulled her closer to his rank body. "Man's got to protect what's his, all right. That's why me and my boys were hired. The name's Bart Harmon and if there's anything I can do for you, little darlin', it would be my pleasure—and maybe yours, too," he added with a self-satisfied leer.

So this was one of the dozen gunmen Bradley had recruited at Fort King. She shuddered to think what the other eleven must look like, but knowing the odious creature was in her uncle's employ served to put the starch back into her quivering limbs.

She faced him without flinching, confident that she was now in control of the situation. "There are several things you *will* do to pleasure me, Mr. Harmon, that is, if you desire to continue working at River Ridge plantation. First you will remove your filthy hands from my person. Next you will call me Miss Dunstan, not *little darlin'*. Last and most immediately you will step aside and let me pass!"

Before Bart could sort out her rapid-fire instructions, Laura hauled off and kicked him hard in the shin with the sharp pointed toe of her boot. He yowled in pain, releasing her so quickly she staggered backward, but her furious gaze never left his ugly visage.

"Damnation!" hollered the surprised ruffian, lifting his injured limb and hopping on one foot. "You nearly broke my leg!"

Laura darted out of reach to the safety of the stable where Old Jake had a horse saddled and waiting before she taunted boldly, "Too bad, Mr. Harmon. I was aiming higher!"

Laura guided her mare along a well-worn path which skirted the plantation's cotton fields. An army of workers was already moving quietly up and down the rows beneath a golden ball of sun that promised to broil the land in a few short hours. Even so early in the day she could feel rivulets of perspiration trickling down the valley between her breasts. The shaded pinewoods ahead looked cool and inviting as she nudged the horse to a faster trot. Once hidden within the forest of trees she unfastened the top two buttons of her blouse and pulled the fabric away from her heated skin.

Reaching the bank of the river she dismounted and strolled to the water's edge. A variety of small trees and bushes competed for space, their foliage intertwining, their limbs adorned with gray festoons of Spanish moss. Schools of tiny minnows swam among the slimy roots growing out into the water while a turtle sunned atop a fallen log.

The wide Saint Johns was unlike most rivers of the United States in that its two hundred eighty-five mile course flowed from south to north, paralleling the Florida coastline, then veering east at Jacksonville to empty its waters into the Atlantic Ocean. The Seminole called it *Welaka,* a word meaning "River of Lakes," but which also carried with it the idea of tides moving upstream. To the early Spanish explorers it was the *Rio de corrientes* or "River of Currents," so named because of the spectacular way the currents at its mouth met the surf.

The cotton and orange growers living along its tree-lined banks as well as the inland produce farmers depended on the river to get their crops to market. Each plantation had its own dock. In addition, many sported boathouses built out over the water to protect their private crafts from the elements. The less prosperous farmers had to bring their goods by wagon to the public dock at the end of Store Lane where the general store and post office were located.

Unable to resist the temptation offered by the river's gentle flow, Laura plopped down on the grass, then tugged off her boots and hose. Lifting her skirt to mid-calf she dangled her feet in the water, startling the fish who swam away only to return seconds later and cautiously nibble at her toes. The sound of a warning blast woke the sleeping turtle who rolled off the log and disappeared beneath the surface just as a steamboat rounded the bend heading upstream. A man in the pilot house waved to her as the craft chugged by leaving behind a cloud of black smoke.

"So here you are," Susan greeted, sliding from her horse. "Looks like you've got the right idea. Whew, it's hot!"

Soon she too was trailing her bare feet in the water and chatting nonstop about the success of the card party at Pine View the night before. Her frequent references to Wade Callahan did not go unnoticed, which as far as Laura was concerned confirmed the old adage that there was no accounting for taste. The darkly handsome savage seemed a more likely candidate for Susan's attention yet she hadn't mention Davey Logan during her discourse.

"I had a lovely time," Laura agreed when Susan paused for breath. To her astonishment she realized it was true, though she could not say why. She'd been embarrassed, humiliated, then made to look like a novice at a game she normally played with skill. It didn't make sense but then nothing seemed as it should be in this uncivilized land where men wore guns and carried whips. Not at all like London or Boston. There people were predictable. Boring, she acknowledged, but predictable.

Susan kicked a spray of droplets into the air. "Did you notice how Wade . . . Mr. Callahan apologized every time he won a hand? Don't you think that was gentlemanly of him?"

"It would have been more gentlemanly had he let us win a time or two," Laura retorted. "Besides his partner deserves a fair share of the credit in bringing about our defeat."

Blast! Now she was championing the rogue who had done nothing but put her down since the moment they met.

"They do make a formidable team, don't they?" giggled Susan glancing over her shoulder toward the pinewoods.

"Formidable indeed. I must say you seem quite smitten with Mr. Callahan."

The color in Susan's rosy cheeks deepened. "I don't know him very well, of course, but I find him most fascinating. He's so . . . so . . . different."

Now there's an understatement if there ever was one, thought Laura disparagingly. "He's different all right. Not many people can shuffle cards with their gloves on."

Laura frowned as Susan pivoted to look behind her once again. Following her gaze, she asked, "Are you expecting someone?"

"No, of course not." Innocent blue eyes gave credence to the lie.

"Do you think his hands are deformed?"

"They felt perfectly normal to me." Her face now crimson, Susan stammered, "I mean . . . Wade . . . that is, Mr. Callahan . . . well, the garden path was dim and he didn't want me to stumble in the dark."

"So he took off his gloves and held your hand?"

"Not exactly. I mean he didn't take off his gloves but I could tell he had all ten fingers."

Biting her lip to keep from laughing, Laura remarked, "That's fascinating all right!"

The jingle of harness from close by brought both

women whirling around in unison, though their reactions when they saw Wade and Davey emerge from the woods were nothing alike. Susan's face beamed with pleasure while her companion's expression showed suspicion and dismay mingled with apprehension.

"Blast you, Susan Ashe! You planned this, didn't you?" Laura hissed.

Ignoring her accuser, Susan smiled sweetly and lifted a dainty hand to wave a welcome. "Good morning," she sang out merrily. "What an unexpected surprise."

Laura groaned and gave her friend a well-deserved pinch. The truce she had declared with the overbearing Mr. Logan was a temporary thing meant only for one night. Afterward it was her intention to avoid the man whom she could not seem to stop thinking about. Now, thanks to Susan, for it was obvious this little assignation had been prearranged, the very one who had haunted her dreams and muddled her thoughts was sitting not ten feet away upon his huge black horse staring down at her with those eyes that gave nothing away. His mouth was fixed in a firm line, the hard planes of his face showing not a trace of humor. Apparently the grinning farmer hadn't seen fit to inform him of his planned tryst with Susan for he seemed none to pleased to find them here.

Davey sought to reconcile the girlish figure sitting in the grass with her skirt hiked up and her legs dangling over the edge of the bank, with the aloof, citified woman he secretly thought of as the "ice princess." Instead of the sophisticated upswept hairdo that fitted her image of cool refinement, her mane of thick auburn curls hung loose beneath a floppy straw hat. Her smooth cheeks were already tinted pink by the sun. Or was it annoyance that brought out her heightened color? Annoyance. No doubt about it, he decided as he watched her amber eyes flare and her teeth clamp together tightly.

Damn the woman! She looked as if she thought he'd planned to find her here instead of happening upon her accidentally. Did she really think he'd go out of his way to subject himself to more of her acid-tongued ridicule? She must be blinded by her own conceit but he'd set the record straight real quick!

"I'm afraid we've caught the ladies at an awkward moment, Wade. Besides we've got things to do and we'd best get at it."

Though he spoke to the man at his side, his deep brown eyes raked Laura up and down. She could feel his disapproval and when his gaze rested on the vee of pale skin exposed by her open blouse, her face flushed scarlet while trembling fingers fumbled to fasten buttons whose holes were suddenly too small.

Susan scrambled to her feet. "Why, Davey, surely you're not in that big a rush. You haven't even said good morning," she pouted.

Obediently Davey touched the brim of his hat. "Morning, Susan. Miss Dunstan."

Laura cast a scathing look in his direction not bothering to acknowledge his salutation. There it was again. *Susan* and *Miss Dunstan*—the setting apart as if he knew she didn't belong here and was going to make certain she knew it, too.

"Come on, Wade. The boat's probably at the dock by now with those tools you ordered."

"Those tools aren't going anywhere, Davey," Wade replied making it clear he was in no hurry to leave.

"You and your shortcuts! We should have stuck to the main road," grumbled Davey.

Susan clucked her tongue. "My goodness we're in a foul mood this morning. By all means don't let us keep you from your business."

Seeing the disappointment on Wade's face, she brightened. "As a matter of fact I told Papa I'd pick up a few things we need from Mr. Cawthorn at the general store so if it's no trouble we'll just ride along with you."

"No trouble at all," Wade grinned as the shapely blonde turned her back while she put on her stockings.

Laura fumed inwardly. She should simply refuse to go with them but that would mean Susan couldn't go either, not alone and unchaperoned.

"Are you coming, Laura?"

Laura scowled up into pleading blue eyes, then sighed and reached for her boots. She and Susan needed to have a long talk about farmer's and planter's daughters, but it would have to wait until another time.

The path along the river was wide enough to ride two abreast. Susan wasted no time in positioning her mount beside Wade Callahan's roan, leaving Laura and Davey to trail behind. The couple in the lead talked animatedly, laughing often at what one or the other had to say while their counterparts followed in stony silence. Soon they crossed a narrow wooden bridge over the irrigation ditch that served as a property line between River Ridge and Pine View. When they reached the dock and boathouse belonging to Henry Ashe they drew to a halt.

"Listen. What is that?" Laura asked in bewilderment, cocking her head to catch the chorus of voices harmonizing in the distance.

"Papa's field hands. They always sing the old spirituals while they work."

"It's lovely. I don't believe I've ever heard my uncle's slaves singing."

Davey and Susan exchanged knowing looks. "Maybe they don't have anything worth singing about," came Davey's cryptic reply.

Laura had no idea what he meant and since she'd decided not to speak to him she let the remark pass as they continued on their way. Holding her tongue was one thing but it was not so easy to bridle her thoughts which kept straying to the dark, brooding man at her side. She wondered what kind of life he'd had growing up with mixed blood in this newly settled land. Finally her curiosity combined with the sustained silence got the better of her resolve to stay quiet.

"Do you have any brothers or sisters, Mr. Logan?"

It seemed an innocuous enough question but the

look she received made her feel she was prying into something that was none of her affair.

Just when she thought he wouldn't answer, he replied shortly, "Yes, ma'am."

Laura waited. As seconds ticked by and he said nothing more, impatience gave way to irritation. "Well?"

"Well, what?"

"Which is it? Do you have brothers or sisters or both?"

"I have four brothers."

"Younger or older?"

"Younger."

"Do they look like you?"

"I never noticed."

Obviously savages were incapable of carrying on a polite conversation so Laura gave up and once again lapsed into silence.

"They're my half brothers. I have a stepmother. My real mother died when I was just a kid."

His deep voice was so unexpected it gave Laura a start but she quickly digested the information he had volunteered. His father had remarried after his mother died. No that wasn't accurate if Brad was to be believed for he had said the senior Logan never married the Indian woman he lived with.

Before she could sort it all out, Davey asked, "What about you? No, don't answer that!" He rubbed his chin thoughtfully. "I'll bet you are an only child."

Laura's eyes widened in surprise. "How did you guess?"

His sardonic expression was answer enough. He knew nothing about her, yet for some reason he had stereotyped her as a spoiled, self-centered brat! It wasn't a very flattering description. What's more it was totally untrue. Not that his opinion mattered in the least! She should have stayed with her original plan and kept her mouth shut!

Sticking her slender nose in the air, she jabbed him with one final query. "Tell me this, Mr. Logan. Are your brothers as rude and insufferable as you?"

"Not yet, but they're working on it."

Seeing the steamer tied to the dock just ahead, Davey again touched one hand to his hat in a vague salute and spurred his horse into a gallop, leaving Laura to choke on his dust.

Blast the ill-mannered rustic! If there were four more at home like him, his stepmother certainly had her sympathy!

Chapter 7

After Susan completed her purchases and Wade collected his tools, Davey told them he would not be returning to the farm right away. Saying he'd heard about some horses he wanted to look at in a neighboring settlement he hastily took his leave of the trio without looking back.

Susan had been right. He *was* in a foul mood. Course he hadn't been in a foul mood when he got up this morning. Hell no! He'd been in a great mood until he discovered he'd been duped by a man he thought was his friend. Their meeting with Susan Ashe and Laura Dunstan had been no accident. And it didn't take a genius to know Wade was setting himself up for a big fall even if Susan was a sweet gal. Henry Ashe seemed like a fair man and to Davey's knowledge there had been no discord among the people at Pine View but Ashe was still a wealthy man as well as a slaveholder, and he was not likely to support a match between his only child and a dirt-poor farmer.

Davey urged the stallion to a faster pace but he couldn't outrun his disquieting thoughts. If Wade wanted to make a fool of himself that was his business but Davey had no intention of helping him do it! And he damned sure didn't intend to put up with Fowler Dunstan's ill-tempered niece so that Wade and Susan could continue their *chance* meetings!

He resented the woman's questions about his family. She'd sounded as if she really cared but he knew she didn't. Why should the affluent Bostonian concern herself with a half-breed from a place she'd never heard of? *Fort Burke* she'd called the army post named after his father's good friend, George Brooke. Of course it was possible Dunstan put her up to asking questions just to find out what he was doing here. If so the old man was going to be disappointed. His terse answers had given nothing away, had in fact discouraged her interrogation. He'd only slipped up once volunteering information she hadn't even asked for.

It was funny how that had happened. There they were just riding along in silence when suddenly he'd found himself wanting to talk about his family. Not just his little brothers but about his cousin, Beth, and her husband, Robin, who was a half-breed like himself, and Beth's brother, Edward, who lived with his wife, Maggie, and their kids near Fort King. And then there was Mandy, Beth and Edward's irrepressible half sister who had hair as black as night and eyes that sparkled like sapphires.

Thinking about his family went a long way toward restoring Davey's good humor but imagining himself trying to explain all the "halves" and "steps" in the complicated Logan/Townsend clan to someone who couldn't even get the name of the fort right made him laugh out loud.

Anyway, he reminded himself, his family was of no concern to her and neither was his reason for being here. She'd caught him off guard with her unexpected questions but next time he would be ready for her. Yes, sir. It'd be a cold day in hell before the amber-eyed beauty wheedled any more information out of him!

Laura paused at the far end of the formal garden watching the negroes move up and down the rows of vegetables grown for the family's use, their backs bent as they plucked weeds or hoed the sandy soil. Again she was struck by the silence as they worked beneath the relentless midday sun. She was not the only one observing their progress. Dotted around the perimeter of the cultivated acreage stood the overseers and drivers along with the dark-clad, gun-toting hirelings whose job it was to put an end to the disappearance of Dunstan slaves.

Spotting the tall, rangy figure of Bart Harmon in the distance, Laura averted her gaze to the ridge where trees of ripening oranges grew in columns spaced so that from whatever angle one looked they formed perfectly straight lines. It was then she re-membered the wagon she'd seen crossing the rise several nights ago. She wondered if the mysterious buckboard could have anything to do with the two slaves discovered missing the following morning.

Laura didn't know much about the workings of a large plantation like River Ridge and up until now she'd had no particular desire to learn more, but from listening to her uncle and his friends she did understand that slaves were vital to the cotton industry and in exchange for their labors the men, women, and children who toiled in the fields and the manor houses were provided by their owners with food, shelter, and clothing.

At first it seemed like an equitable arrangement. After all she employed servants to perform much the same tasks as the slaves, and though she paid a fair wage, those who served her had to depend on the money they earned to support themselves. But the sight of the armed guards ringing the area quickly changed her view by demonstrating the fundamental difference between the two groups. Servants had a choice as to whom they would serve while slaves did not.

Never having contemplated the issue before and finding it too miserably hot to do so now, Laura decided to explore a wooded track she had noticed jutting off the main path that lead to the river. She couldn't venture far on foot, but she was not ready to return to the house nor did she want to attract the attention of the men by remaining where she was.

The trail was strewn with pine needles dropped from the tall trees overhead though their sparce foliage provided little protection from the fierce rays of the sun. Pulling a dainty handkerchief from the pocket of her dress, she wiped at the trickles of perspiration ribboning down her flushed cheeks. Soon she could wring the salty moisture from the small scrap of material as she continued to make her way under the damp blanket of humid heat.

Perhaps Angel was right when she'd said only a fool or a Yankee would take a walk in Florida during the middle of the day, but her spiteful cousin was the main reason Laura had chosen to do just that. At least it was a way to escape the little witch for a few hours. Laura was tired of listening to Angel brag about her many conquests among those of the opposite sex while taking pains to point out how men preferred petite females with well-proportioned curves and peachy complexions to tall, skinny women whose pale skin made them appear anemic. She hadn't quite gone so far as to name Laura among the emaciated and sickly creatures deserving one's pity, but the implication was there in her superior attitude and falsely sympathetic smile.

As much as she would have liked to put the hateful words down to petty jealousy, Laura couldn't help but remember the years when her father had forced her to live abroad clearly demonstrating his lack of affection for his only child. And while it was true that after Franklin's death she'd had a gaggle of young suitors, she always wondered in the back of her mind if they were courting her or her inheritance. Then there was the savage! At least, she admitted, Davey Logan was honest about his feelings. He didn't like her and he didn't bother to pretend otherwise. She was still smarting over his abrupt leave-taking at the dock this morning—and without even giving her a chance to tell him she'd decided to extend their truce! Not that it mattered. After all he was nothing but an ill-mannered halfbreed. Still, he had added to her insecurity just when her confidence needed a boost!

"Blast the man!" Laura kicked a pine cone right into a clearing near the door of a small cabin she hadn't known was there. Like the slave quarters the structure was built of tabby, a stone made of crushed oyster shells, sand, and water. It looked stark and alone here in the middle of the woods far from the main house with its surrounding outbuildings. It also looked deserted. Curious, Laura crossed to the door and rapped lightly not really expecting anyone to answer her knock. She jumped back with a start when the panel flew inward and she came face to face with a furious Bradley Kincaid.

"Who the hell . . . ?" By his astonished expression Laura knew he was as surprised as she.

"Laura! What are you doing here?" He stepped quickly into the sunlight, pulling the door securely closed behind him.

She thought she heard a moaning sound coming from within the dark interior of the windowless structure but she couldn't be certain.

"I . . . I was . . . taking a walk," she stammered wanting to ask Brad the same question but hesitating in view of his foul mood.

"Alone?" His pale green eyes shifted nervously

from side to side as if he thought someone else might be concealed in the heavy underbrush.

Afraid she had wandered onto forbidden ground, Laura answered cautiously. "Why, yes, but I had no intention of trespassing. I didn't realize anyone lived so far from the house."

Brad took her firmly by the arm, steering her back toward the path. "No one does. This place is only used to store surplus tools and equipment."

Laura's brow knitted in a frown. The cottage seemed too remote to serve as a convenient storage shed but she had no reason to doubt Brad's explanation. Still she was troubled by what she had thought was a noise coming from within.

Looking back over her shoulder she gave voice to her concern. "I could have sworn I heard something when you opened the door."

Brad appeared briefly disconcerted, but recovered quickly. With the expertise of a practiced liar he replied, "Nothing to worry about, my dear. One of the men out hunting small game met with a slight accident. Luckily there were first aid supplies in the cabin. I'd just finished fixing him up when you arrived."

"Shouldn't you stay and make certain the injured man is all right? He sounded as if he were in considerable pain."

"I can assure you he's fine. I'm much more concerned over finding you out here alone. These woods can be quite dangerous. Aside from the snakes and wild animals that inhabit the area, you could easily have lost your way."

Though Laura prided herself on her sense of direction, especially where there was a path to follow, and she'd come a goodly distance without seeing an animal of any kind, wild or tame, it meant a great deal to know Brad cared what became of her, cared enough to see her home safely. And he was rather nice looking when he wasn't frowning, she concluded, as they moved arm in arm down the trail. By the time the house was in sight, her companion had visibly relaxed.

"Now that you've been with us for a while, tell me what you think of our plantation."

If Laura hadn't accidentally overheard the argument between her uncle and his stepson that morning, she would have thought nothing of the way Brad used the words *us* and *our,* but now she couldn't help wondering what Fowler Dunstan would say if he were here. Would he again remind the young man that River Ridge was his and his alone?

"It's very different from London or Boston. Life moves at a much slower pace. I like that," she answered with guarded enthusiasm.

"Florida weather is too hot to inspire haste."

Laura looked up at Brad in wonderment. It was the closest he'd come to saying something funny but his solemn expression told her he hadn't meant it as a joke. Like her uncle's slaves he had a somber disposition. Laura was curious as to whether melancholia might be contagious and if so who was infecting whom?

They continued on for some minutes without

speaking, then Brad stopped and turned, placing his hands lightly on her shoulders. His look was so intense, Laura felt self-conscious and a little alarmed but his words, when they came, left her more bewildered than frightened. "Have you ever considered staying here with us, my dear? I know it would please Fowler and my mother if you came to think of River Ridge as your home, too. And since we are your only remaining family . . ."

"I appreciate your kindness, Brad, but you know I have my heart set on seeing the world. Besides I doubt Angel would jump for joy at the prospect of having me for a permanent guest." Laura laughed lightly hoping to provoke a smile. Instead his pale eyes darkened with renewed anger.

"Angel is a spoiled child who's bound to come to a bad end if something isn't done about her soon."

His harsh words held an unspoken threat as his fingers tightened painfully, digging into Laura's soft flesh. A picture flashed through her mind of the man stroking his lethal-looking black whip. She wanted to pull from his grasp and flee from the charged atmosphere, but she held her ground reasoning calmly, "I agree Angel has some growing up to do and perhaps she is spoiled, but considering how Uncle Fowler and Aunt Hester have indulged her that's no more than to be expected. I'm sure she will change once she marries and has a family of her own."

"Who in his right mind would marry her now?" Brad shot back, his narrow features twisting into a grotesque mask of contorted lines. "She's already given herself to half the men in the State!"

Not knowing how to reply Laura looked around glad to find that no one else was within hearing. Embarrassment brought twin red spots to her cheeks.

Brad drew a deep breath, struggling to regain control after his outburst. "I'm sorry," he apologized. "One of your innocence should be shielded from the ugly truth. But it makes me so furious when my friends laugh and ridicule Angel behind her back."

In an unexpectedly tender gesture Laura would have thought impossible following so closely upon his display of temper, Brad put one hand beneath her chin, turning her head until their eyes met. "We've gone far afield from where we began. I can assure you Angel will have no say in what you decide to do but for what's it's worth, I would like you to stay."

He almost smiled then. Not quite but there was that slight tilt to his thin lips and his voice held a note of pleading sincerity. For a few brief moments, Laura considered his suggestion. To be with people who wanted her after a lifetime of loneliness and rejection sounded like a dream come true. Yet she knew nothing was as simple nor as perfect as one would like it to be. She could not escape that niggling little voice that told her something was not quite right here at River Ridge.

There was the inexplicable undercurrent of gloom among the workers. And then there was the family itself. She often found it difficult to be patient with Hester Dunstan's timidity, her cousin Angel was openly antagonistic, and the only emotion she had seen Brad Kincaid display, with the exception of a brief softening when he'd asked her to stay, was anger. Fowler seemed to be the only normal one of the bunch but she was not entirely at ease with her kindly uncle either for there was still the question of why he had remained a secret until after her father's death.

"You're very kind, Brad, but in addition to my wanting to see new places I have responsibilities in Boston—two houses, the people that work for me, my father's business investments—"

He held up a hand to silence her. "We can sell the houses and handle the investments from right here."

We? Just then she knew how her uncle must have felt earlier that morning when he'd had to remind his stepson that River Ridge belonged to him. Laura considered herself an intelligent, well-educated woman capable of managing her own affairs and she resented any threat to her hard-won independence. Though she had yet to decide how best to dispose of her holdings in New England, of one thing she was certain. She alone would make the decisions and she would do it in her own good time.

"Let's wait and see," she replied hoping to postpone any further confrontation.

They parted company and Laura walked across the wide lawn toward the stone terrace without looking back. If she had, she would have seen the impotent rage again distorting the man's handsome face.

"I did what you told me to do," Brad sulked, slouching down in the well-padded leather chair across the desk from where his stepfather sat drumming his fingers on the rich mahogany. "It's not my fault she didn't fall at my feet in gratitude when I suggested she stay."

Fowler Dunstan glared angrily at the one who had failed him. "Isn't it?" he countered, his ruddy complexion deepening to a crimson hue. "I should have known you were incapable of courting a lady properly. You have about as much charm as a water moccasin!"

"Now wait just a damn minute!" Brad roared straightening as his own temper flared. "I do all right with the ladies."

The older man leaned forward steepling his fingers together. "Ladies? Ha! I know how you get women to spread their legs for you," he derided scornfully. "Don't think I'm unaware of what goes on out there in the woods, boy!"

Fowler's gleaming amber eyes challenged Brad to deny what he knew to be true.

"That's another thing." Brad's whining voice grated on Fowler's nerves. "She almost caught me with Delilah. Can't you keep her from roaming around where she doesn't belong?"

The muscles in Fowler's face tensed. "You listen to me, boy! Until we get this thing settled I want you to stay away from that cabin and from those darkies you like to pump on! I'll not have my plans going awry because you can't keep that rod in your pants. Do you understand me?"

After a lengthy silence Brad nodded his head, his eyes filled with undisguised enmity for the man he was forced to obey in order to continue enjoying the benefits derived from being second in command. Someday soon all that would change, he reminded himself, finding comfort in the thought that eventually River Ridge would belong to him.

Fowler was not quite finished putting Brad in his place. "If it weren't for you, I could be rid of that blue-blooded niece of mine right now and have the inheritance that belongs to me!" His voice hardened ruthlessly. "But I can't afford any more questions. The neighbors are already suspicious about the discontent among the slaves here at River Ridge."

He paused, his eyes boring into those of his stepson. "My only recourse is to keep Laura alive until the talk dies down. By marrying you she will have to remain at River Ridge and control of her fortune will be in my hands."

Brad frowned up at the picture on the wall above his stepfather's head. The landscape concealed a safe containing the infamous document he had been forced to sign, a document turning over Laura's estate to Fowler once she and Brad were wed. He had protested loud and strong before agreeing to his stepfather's terms. Not until Fowler threatened to throw him out and cut him off without a cent had Brad put his name on the official paper.

But once the ceremony was over, who was to say Fowler wouldn't be the one to meet with an unfortunate accident? Brad could not hide the smug satisfaction he felt as he plotted the planter's demise. Soon it would all be his; the money, the plantation, and Laura Dunstan. He would show her who was master and he would teach her about the pleasures of the flesh. He was an expert in the art of arousing a woman's desire by applying just the right amount of pain prior to copulation.

Not often was Fowler Dunstan taken by surprise especially when it came to anticipating his stepson's reactions to any given situation but this was one of those rare occasions. He would have understood anger, resentment, possibly rebellion after the tongue-lashing he had administered. What he did not expect was the decadent smile which curved Brad's lips as his eyes focused on something only his depraved mind could see.

Chapter 8

Laura and Susan sat on the shaded terrace sipping the delicious juice squeezed from the golden fruit of the orange trees that grew along the ridge. Two days had passed since Laura's unexpected meeting with Brad Kincaid and still she had found no answers to the questions that bothered her.

It didn't take long for Laura to notice her friend was not paying the least attention to anything she was saying. "What's wrong, Susan? You don't seem quite the thing today."

"I'm worried about Papa. I wish he had stayed home." Henry Ashe had accompanied his daughter to the Dunstan plantation and was now closeted with Fowler in the library.

"Why? Is he unwell?"

Susan glanced nervously toward the house. "No. He's mad as a wet hornet. I just hope he doesn't lose his temper completely and go for Fowler's throat."

Laura could not imagine Susan's mild-mannered father committing an act of violence but one look at her companion's face told her the concern was real.

"Has my uncle done something to upset your father? I thought they were friends."

"They used to be, but lately . . . well . . . there comes a time when a man can no longer condone injustice. Not that Papa ever did," Susan was quick to emphasize, "but after what happened last night . . ."

When Susan didn't go on Laura prodded impatiently. "What *did* happen last night?"

"Papa found one of the Dunstan slaves near the irrigation ditch. He'd been badly beaten and left for dead."

Laura gasped. "Was the man trying to run away?"

"He swears he wasn't."

"Then why was he assaulted? Who would do such a dreadful thing?"

Susan was too distraught to guard her tongue. "That scar-faced animal Brad Kincaid hired was responsible for nearly killing the man but you can bet Brad gave the orders."

"That's a lie!"

Both women turned to find Angel Dunstan standing directly behind them, hands on her well-rounded hips, face livid after overhearing the accusation against her stepbrother.

"It's the truth and you know it!" shouted Susan, coming to her feet and taking a step toward the diminutive redhead.

Angel put her hands up as if to ward off an attack

as Laura hurriedly rose and stepped between the two combatants.

"Stop it!" she demanded, feeling like she'd been caught in the middle of a windstorm.

Thinking herself safe with Laura blocking Susan's way, Angel smirked, "If the man was beaten I'm sure it was no more than he deserved."

At that Laura had to physically hold Susan back.

"Why you little whore!" Susan spat in a fit of rage. "No one deserves to be beaten like that. In this case the victim was a man whose only crime was being too old to work as fast as the others!"

Laura watched the tears spring to Susan's crystal blue eyes.

"Jealousy doesn't become you, Susan. Just because the only man you can get is an ill-bred sod-buster who probably wears those awful gloves to hide the dirt under his fingernails is no reason to disparage my popularity," Angel retorted patting her fat, perfectly curled ringlets.

Laura tightened her grasp on Susan's arm as she lunged once more. "Blast you, Angel! If you're not out of sight by the time I count to three I'm letting her go! One! Two!"

Laura breathed a sigh of relief as her malicious cousin disappeared around the corner. She felt Susan's body tremble. The tears her friend had managed to hold in check spilled over to roll down her cheeks. Susan whispered brokenly, "Angel's wrong, Laura. He's not dirty. He's good and kind and . . . wonderful."

Laura didn't have to ask who the *he* was. She

already knew and her heart ached for Susan. She wondered how many times her friend had sneaked off to meet Wade Callahan and how far the affair had gone. It was all too obvious Susan was falling in love with the man and the realization brought with it a terrible sense of dread.

"Let's go, daughter," came Henry Ashe's gravelly voice as he stepped through the back door. "We're no longer welcome here," he added gruffly, slapping his hat on his head.

"Oh, dear! I was afraid of this," Susan pulled from Laura's embrace, wiping at her eyes as she started to go to her father, then rushed back to hug Laura goodbye.

Laura wondered when or if she would ever see Susan again. She had wanted answers but not the ones she was getting. She didn't want to believe Brad Kincaid was the heartless creature Susan described. It was easy to imagine Bart Harmon as the villain but surely she was mistaken about Brad.

Taking her seat beneath a waxy-leafed magnolia tree Laura tried to sort out what she knew as fact and what was only supposition. A man had been seriously injured and, if he were to be believed, Bart Harmon was the culprit, but apparently there was no actual evidence linking Brad to the atrocity, only supposition on Susan's part. The simplest way to discover the truth was to ask Brad what really happened. Unfortunately he was on his way to Jacksonville to take care of some plantation business so she would have to wait until his return.

Meanwhile perhaps she could do something

about Susan and Wade. But what could she do that wouldn't look like interference? Should she go to Susan? Try to make her see that there was no future for her with a penniless farmer? No, she thought dismissing that idea. A Dunstan probably wouldn't be welcome at Pine View right now. Besides, if Susan was as infatuated with Wade Callahan as she appeared, Laura doubted the girl would listen. That left Wade himself. He seemed like a reasonable man. She would talk to him, plead with him if necessary, but somehow make him understand that to continue whatever relationship had begun between he and Susan would only bring heartache to them both. If he refused to listen, at least she would know she had tried.

Early the next morning Laura ordered her horse saddled and headed south along a rutted road canopied by huge live oaks, their branches draped with streamers of Spanish moss waving gently in the breeze. The sun was high in the sky before she met anyone else traveling the narrow trail, but eventually she was forced to move aside to let an old man with a wagon load of vegetables pass. From the driver of the conveyance she learned her destination was just around the next bend.

Wade Callahan's place was about what she'd expected. The farm was little more than a clapboard shack surrounded by a field of corn. Other vegetables grew in a small garden plot near the dilapidated wooden structure. A barn tilting crazily to one side stood in the rear. Half a dozen piglets chased each other about the yard squealing and scattering the chickens who flapped their wings in annoyance. Laura would have laughed at the idea of Susan Ashe living in such squalor had the situation not been so serious.

She tied her horse to a sagging picket fence, then lifted the latch on the gate. As she crossed the porch and raised her hand to knock she had a fleeting feeling of déjà vu but unlike the door to the cabin in the woods, today she received no answer to her persistent rapping. Moving to a window with flowered curtains drawn back and tied, she peeked inside. Clothes were scattered about and dirty dishes littered a wooden table with no cloth. The curtains seemed inconsistent with the rest of the unkempt interior. A woman's touch? But then who and where was the woman?

Disappointed at finding no one home, Laura decided to check the barn before beginning the long trek back to River Ridge. Shooing chickens out of her path while holding the skirt of her riding habit above her ankles, she tiptoed toward the open double doors trying to avoid the offal that was everywhere attracting flies and smelling to high heaven. She almost made it when without warning an enormous black beast came flying out of nowhere, sending her sprawling backward into the refuse. She landed with a splat right in the middle of a mud puddle beside the watering trough. Before she could open her mouth to scream the hairy monster was in her face licking her skin with a rough, moist tongue.

Hearing a hoot of laughter, she pushed against the mound of fur. "Get it off of me!" she cried, finding out the hard way that she should have kept her lips sealed, for the long, lapping tongue skimmed across her teeth moving from one cheek to the other.

"Heel, Brutus!" At the sharp command the animal's head came up. Slowly he backed away and, panting and drooling, settled on his haunches at the feet of the man who had issued the order.

To give him his due, Davey tried hard to suppress his laughter. "Bad dog!" he scolded, scowling at Brutus who acknowledged the rebuke by happily wagging his tail.

Laura wiped her mouth, then scrubbed at her teeth with the sleeve of her jacket. "You call that thing a dog? Miniature horse is more like it! He's . . . he's . . ."

Brutus's tail thumped against the hard-packed dirt.

"Make him stop smiling!"

Davey bent to scrutinize the dog's massive square head. Button eyes in a face comprised of flabby skin falling in rolls all the way down to a thick neck looked back at him. The animal's wide mouth below a leathery pug nose did seem to be smiling, though it was hard to tell with his tongue lolling from side to side.

After careful study Davey said, "Nope. He's not smiling."

"How do you know?"

"You can't see his teeth."

"What?"

"When Brutus smiles his teeth show. Here, let me help you up."

Laura stared at the outstretched hand connected to a bare arm bulging with muscles. Her amber eyes widened as she followed its length to where the limb joined one immensely wide shoulder atop a brawny chest—a *naked* brawny chest. Until now she had been too preoccupied with the devil dog to notice that Davey wore nothing but a pair of fringed buckskin breeches, calf-high moccasins, and a beaded headband. He looked every bit the savage she had pictured from the tales she'd heard about the heathen redskins.

His stance was totally masculine, legs spread apart, magnificent chest extended, bronze flesh glistening with sweat. Mesmerized by the awesome sight of potent male virility, Laura found herself unable to move. Only when Davey shrugged his broad shoulders and started to turn away did she come out of her stupor.

"Wait!" Her brusque command gained her a look of cool assessment from beneath thick raised brows.

Davey took his time considering the advisability of repeating his offer of assistance after the stubborn woman had refused his help to begin with. *What the hell was she doing here in the first place?* he wondered, his observant eyes taking in the finely tailored brown skirt and jacket she wore. A jaunty little hat made of matching material and a white blouse with ruffles of lace hiding the buttons completed an outfit more appropriate for the English countryside than the Florida backwoods.

"Last chance, princess. Take it or leave it," he sighed, thrusting out his hand once more.

Laura could tell by his tone that he didn't particularly care which she did. Before he could change his mind she grasped the hand he extended and pulled. Mud sucked at her bottom making a squishing noise as she was hauled none too gently to her feet.

Once upright she craned her neck to survey the damage. "Blast!"

Davey cocked his head to one side. "Do your folks know what a foul mouth their gently bred daughter has?"

Laura was in no mood for criticism. "My parents are dead, Mr. Logan. My only remaining relatives are my uncle and his family."

"That's a shame."

Laura had a feeling there was some double meaning behind his commiseration but good manners required her to thank him. "I appreciate your solicitude, Mr. Logan, but what I need right now is something dry to wear."

"Your wish is my command," he replied, disappearing into the barn, then returning seconds later holding his buckskin shirt stretched between the thumb and forefinger of each hand.

Laura drew away from the offensive piece of tanned deerhide. "I can't possibly wear *that!*" she assured with a lift of her aristocratic nose.

"Suit yourself, princess."

"Stop calling me princess!" she demanded with a stamp of her booted foot.

Hooded eyes raked her up and down. "What would you prefer? Your highness? Your grace? Your muddiness?"

"My name is Laura and I'll thank you to remember it!"

"Laura."

It wasn't the first time he had used her given name but this time was different. Whispered softly like a gentle caress, the word lingered in the air. She could almost reach out and touch it. Her heart quickened its beat as blood flowed fast through her veins and her palms began to sweat. Shaken by a reaction she couldn't understand, Laura snapped more sharply than she intended, "You must have something more appropriate that I can wear for I certainly can't ride all the way home like this!" She wiped at the still wet mud coating her backside which only made the situation worse. Now her hands were as dirty as her skirt.

Davey wondered what she'd do if he volunteered to take over the messy job she'd started. It might be kind of fun to rub his hands up and down her slender rump even if it was covered with grime. She'd probably run screaming all the way back to River Ridge, he decided, dismissing the idea with a shrug.

"Come on in the house. Maybe we can find something fit for a queen."

Suddenly wary, Laura shook her head. It was one thing to stand out in the open with the man but to go in the house? Alone with a half-breed Indian? Not bloody likely! She'd rather suffer the discomfort of a wet behind than risk what might happen once they were inside. "I've changed my mind, Mr. Logan. I think I'd best be on my way."

Having been snubbed by people like Laura all his life, Davey was quick to understand what she was thinking and he felt his temper begin to rise. When she started to move away, he reached out and clamped his hand around her arm.

"Let me go," Laura hissed, unable to break the hold.

"What's the matter, princess? Afraid I might contaminate you with my touch?"

More angry than afraid, Laura snarled, "I said let me go you . . . savage!"

Savage! Why the ignorant little she-devil! He'd show her "savage"! Davey propelled Laura toward the house. She kicked at his legs and pommeled him with her free hand, shouting curses every step of the way, but her struggles were useless against his vise-like grip.

Thoughts too awful to dwell on flashed through Laura's panic-stricken mind. What was it the Indians did to their victims? Torture? Rape? Murder? From the fiendish look on Davey Logan's face she imagined all three making her certain that death, when it came, would be a welcome release.

Davey burst through the back door jerking Laura with him. When he continued on into the bedroom she knew her worst fears were about to become reality. Still holding her firmly by the arm, Davey circled the wide double bed that took up most of the space, then came to a halt before a battered old trunk. Wrenching the lid open Davey flung her away from him. "Take what you need and get out!"

Before she could gather her wits, he stalked from the room. Laura gazed down at the neatly folded dresses which filled the trunk. With a trembling hand she touched the gown on top. A delicate scent of roses drifted through the air as she lifted and gently smoothed the wrinkles from the green-and-white checked gingham. Remembering the thoughtless words she had hurled at Davey, she was suddenly assailed with guilt. He hadn't hurt her even though she had treated him abominably by calling him names and behaving like the snobbish creature he thought her to be. Maybe he was right. She'd certainly done everything she could to reinforce his low opinion of her. Scarcely aware of what she was doing Laura undressed, and after locating suitable undergarments she donned the soft cotton gown. It was several inches too short but her boots would cover her ankles. Who could the clothes belong to? The same woman who had hung curtains at the windows? It seemed likely.

She picked up her soiled skirt and made her way through the untidy little house. To her relief Davey was nowhere in sight. She crossed the yard, then dunked the mud-soiled garment in the watering trough swishing it around. After wringing it out the best she could, she draped it over a fence rail to dry.

Laura wasn't sure what to do next. She wished Davey had just sent her on her way instead of being nice to her even when he was so very angry. Now she guessed she would have to apologize for calling him a savage—which, after all, he was. Of course it wasn't his fault that his mother was an Indian. On the other hand, facts were facts. Indians were savages. Uncle Fowler said so and he had been in Florida long enough to know.

It certainly was quiet. Maybe he had ridden away while she was getting dressed. In that case she could leave him a note saying she was sorry for being rude. *Please,* she prayed. *Let him not be here.* Cautiously she stepped into the barn, afraid the huge dog might jump out of the shadowy darkness at any moment. As her eyes adjusted to the dim light she could make out a row of stalls. The first two were occupied by a pair of mules standing with their eyes closed. The next was empty. Just when she thought her prayer had been answered she heard a whinny and spotted the big black stallion near the rear of the building, his head held high, eyes flashing nervously, ears flattened back.

Davey Logan stepped from the stall holding a currying brush in his hand. His barely leashed anger was like a tangible thing stretching across the space that separated them, causing her throat to constrict when she tried to swallow.

"Goodbye, Miss Dunstan." Clearly he was not going to make this easy for her.

"My skirt is wet. I washed it in the trough." Laura hated the tremor in her voice but she was not used to being faced with such utter contempt.

Studying the tips of her boots below the too-short gown, she mumbled, "I'm sorry for what I said."

Her apology was met with silence. Just as she was beginning to think she would have to repeat the words she found so difficult to say, he asked defiantly, "Why?"

The single syllable brought her head up. Their eyes met in a clash of wills. "Because it was rude of me. I shouldn't have lost my temper."

Davey's strong jaw tightened. "Let me see if I have this straight. You're sorry you called me a savage because it was rude and you lost your temper. It's not the sort of thing a lady says even if it's exactly what she believes."

"Yes. NO!" she corrected. "It's not like that at all!"

In a voice as cold as ice Davey said, "You have insulted my lineage, Miss Dunstan. Don't insult my intelligence as well. Why did you come here today?"

Why did you come here today? The question echoed in her mind. So much had happened since her arrival, she couldn't at first remember the purpose behind her visit to the run-down farm. Wade Callahan! She hadn't given him or her friend, Susan, a single thought since she'd been bowled over by the hairy brute of a dog.

"I came to see Mr. Callahan."

"Wade isn't here. I don't expect him back until this afternoon."

Laura wondered if Wade and Susan were together. It was a troubling thought. "I wanted to speak to him about Susan." What she had to say was really none of Davey Logan's business but perhaps she could enlist his help, convince him to speak to his friend, saving her from having to broach a subject which would probably prove embarrassing to both her and the farmer. The scowl on Davey's darkly handsome face wasn't encouraging and Laura knew she had no right to expect any favors from the man, but surely he would have to agree that no good could come from the forbidden liaison.

Davey's hand tightened on the brush he was holding. He put aside his own concern for the star-crossed lovers. *So that's what this is all about. Miss Hoity-Toity had seen what was happening between Wade and Susan and decided to meddle. She'd come here to put Wade down, remind him of his lowly station, and demand that he discontinue his association with the rich planter's daughter. Well, she wouldn't get any help from him!*

"I'm sure Wade would enjoy talking about Susan to anyone willing to listen, Miss Dunstan," Davey assured, managing a rakish grin. "He's completely taken with her. I suppose we all know that and who can blame him? Susan is beautiful, charming, and then, of course, there's all that money." He gave Laura a conspiratory wink. "Yep! Old Wade's just been waiting for a gal like Susan to come along. Since his poor wife died this place has gone to wrack and ruin, but I bet Susan will have it in tip top shape again before you know it."

Laura's mouth worked up and down but no words came out. So Wade Callahan intended to wed her dear friend and install her here in a filthy hovel to take up the drudgery that probably killed his first wife. At least now she knew where the trunk full of clothes came from and the curtains at the windows. Naturally, the idea of a marriage between Susan and Wade was preposterous. Henry Ashe would never allow it and once Susan got her head out of the clouds long enough to realize what she would be giving up she would come to her senses. Then Davey Logan would not be so smug. He seemed to think the matter was all but settled. Well he would have another think coming!

She was about to tell him as much when the dog's barking and a distant shout cut her off. Davey rushed to the door where he met Brutus and a barefoot, towheaded lad both panting for breath.

"What's the matter, Johnny?" he asked, recognizing the son of Wade's closest neighbor.

"It's Pa! He cut his leg with an ax. He cut it real bad." The boy's round eyes looked too large for his pale, frightened face. "Please, Dr. Logan. You gotta come quick!"

"Go to the house and get my bag." Davey gave the order without hesitation. "It's beside the fireplace," he yelled after Johnny who was already halfway across the yard.

Ignoring Laura, he led the big black from his stall. Setting the horse in motion with a swat to his rump, Davey began to run. As soon as the animal cleared the double doors, he leaped into the air, landing on the stallion's wide bare back. By this time Johnny stood near the house clutching a leather satchel to his meager chest. With one arm Davey snatched the child up in front of him. Then horse and riders galloped away with Brutus barking at their heels.

Laura's knees threatened to buckle as she watched them disappear in a cloud of dust. The thunder of hooves continued to pound in her ears, drumming a steady rhythm that soon evolved into a chant, the words repeating themselves over and over inside her head. *Dr. Logan. Dr. Logan. Dr. Logan.*

It was really too much, she thought, collapsing onto an overturned bucket to wait. Soon she would wake up in her comfortable bed and laugh about this silly dream she was having. After all, what other explanation could there be?

Chapter 9

Wade Callahan and Susan Ashe were indeed together, but instead of meeting in a secluded hideaway as Laura imagined, they were seated in the comfortable parlor at Pine View. Wade had come to try and talk some sense into Susan. He liked her. He liked her a lot and he didn't want to see her get hurt. Through Davey he knew of her involvement with the abolitionists and her reasons for wanting to help the repressed and he applauded her sentiments, but he was sure she did not fully understand the danger she would face should she be caught. Aiding and abetting slaves was against the law. In Susan's case, should her activities become known, she would be looked upon as a traitor as well as a thief.

"Would you care for some coffee, Wade?" Susan could not have been more pleased by the man's unexpected visit.

"No, thank you. I had thought we could talk outside." Wade shifted self-consciously.

Susan, dressed in a pale blue daygown with her

honey blond hair hanging in ringlets down her back, looked so right among the perfectly matched furniture and flowered wallpaper while he felt cloddish and out of place in his work clothes and scuffed boots.

"What would your father say if he were to walk in and find me here?"

Susan laughed lightheartedly. "Knowing Papa, I imagine he would offer you whiskey instead of coffee."

Wade looked down at his clean but faded outfit. "Just because he allowed me to stay the other night when I interrupted the party doesn't mean he would welcome me on a regular basis."

"You didn't interrupt the party. I asked Davey to bring you, and you're wrong about Papa. He doesn't judge a person by the clothes he wears or how much money he has. It's character that's important. Papa believes things like honesty and decency are what count when taking a man's measure."

"Does he think it's honest and decent to own slaves?" Wade already knew the answer for there were over a hundred slaves at Pine View. He also knew he was treading on dangerous ground, but he was doing so to make a point and hopefully to convince Susan to discontinue her activities with the underground.

Susan stood up and went to the window. "Come and tell me what you see."

Standing so close to the lovely young woman, Wade found it hard to concentrate on anything but her nearness. Forcing himself to look at the scene outside he noticed that the tabby cottages in which the slaves lived had been built closer to the main house than on most plantations but at first he saw nothing else that set them apart. Then he realized nearly every one of the two-room structures had a large individual garden plot in the back where a variety of vegetable plants grew healthy and well-tended.

Smiling Susan answered his unspoken question. "The people are encouraged to grow their own crops. What they don't need for their own families Papa helps them sell."

"But when do they find time to work their own gardens?"

"Papa runs Pine View by the task system. Instead of forcing the people to toil from dawn until dusk, each man and woman is assigned daily tasks. When their work for the plantation is done they are free to work for themselves. In addition, they are given two days off each year, one in the spring to plant, and one in the fall to harvest."

Wade started to speak but Susan held up her hand. "There's more that you might find interesting. See? Each dwelling has a fireplace for cooking and heating." She leaned close, touching his arm as she pointed out the brick chimneys. "And all of the cabins have wooden floors which add warmth in the winter."

No wonder the slaves at Pine view were content with their lot. Though it didn't change Wade's opinion that slavery was wrong, he had to admit he was impressed with the living conditions here. It was certainly a more tolerable arrangement than any he'd seen yet.

When they returned to their chairs Susan rested her chin in the palm of her hand gazing pensively at the man seated across from her. "I've answered your question in the only way I can. Papa believes that without slavery the agricultural South would shrivel up and die like plants without water, but the people out there are his children and he treats them fairly."

Wade cleared his throat. "And what would he say if he knew his daughter was doing everything she could to cut off the water supply?"

"So Davey told you." It was a statement not requiring an answer, but Wade nodded his head in confirmation.

"We all do what we have to do," was all she said, but it was enough to reinforce Wade's fear for her safety. Susan had no intention of backing away from the cause she believed in even if it meant siding against her own father.

Henry chose that moment to walk briskly through the door as if he had materialized from Wade's thoughts. Wade jumped guiltily to his feet prepared for a well-deserved lecture on propriety. Not only was he here uninvited, but he and the man's daughter were alone without a chaperon. Not something a father would take lightly.

"Good to see you again, my boy," Henry effused, clapping Wade on the shoulder, then bending to plant a kiss on Susan's cheek.

Wade was too stunned to return the greeting. Instead of the reprimand he'd expected, the old planter seemed not at all put out at finding him here.

"Papa, where have you been? It's too hot for you to be out in the middle of the day."

Henry laughed jovially. "I was attending to some very important business and I think you will be pleased with what I have accomplished."

"If you will excuse me, I'd best be going."

Wade started to leave, figuring Henry would want to discuss his news with Susan in private, but he was brought up short when Henry said, "You needn't go, son. What I have to say will be common knowledge before long. Sit down, my boy."

"All right, Papa. What have you been up to?" Susan asked once Wade had resumed his seat.

Henry strutted about the room picking up a knickknack, then setting it down again. "I've been making the rounds this morning talking to our friends and neighbors. They are as disturbed as I am by the way Fowler has allowed Brad Kincaid to abuse the workers at River Ridge especially now that he's hired Bart Harmon and the rest of those no-account drifters. And we intend to put a stop to it."

Wade heard Susan's sharp intake of breath. "Papa, you and the others are no match for those ruffians."

Henry chortled confidently. "We don't need to use force to make Fowler see reason."

"Then what do you plan to do?"

"Since talking to him has done no good, we intend to band together and ostracize the Dunstans from every social gathering that takes place in these parts. They won't even be welcome in church—not that they attend often enough to care about that. But as for the rest . . . to be totally cut off from society will be a sentence worse than death for a man like Fowler."

"Oh, Papa! What you are proposing sounds extremely dangerous. You know the importance Fowler places on social status."

Wade frowned as he listened to the two. It seemed incredible that a group of men could bend another to their will simply by withholding a few party invitations. But then the priorities of the gentry were different from those of the common folk who rarely had time for anything but work.

"That's what we're counting on," reminded Henry. "Fowler enjoys his power and influence in the community. He will give in to our demands rather than be shunned by his peers."

"King of the haut monde," Wade muttered without thinking. Realizing his slip, he looked up to find Susan staring at him, her blue eyes narrowed in thought.

Soon Henry excused himself saying he had some letters to write in the library. "Do come again, my boy. You're welcome anytime."

Once Henry was out of earshot, Susan rose and went to stand behind Wade's chair. She didn't say a word but her silence spoke volumes.

"I'd better be going. Davey will be worried."

Even to Wade the excuse sounded feeble. When he started to move, a small hand clamped down firmly on his shoulder.

"Surely, Mr. Callahan, you don't intend to leave before we finish that very interesting discussion we were having before Papa arrived. You know . . . the one about honesty and decency?"

Wade felt beads of sweat pop out around his collar and across his wide forehead. "I thought we finished that particular conversation."

Susan rounded on him then, placing her hands on the arms of the chair, and leaned forward until their noses nearly met. Blue eyes sparked with indignation. "I'm not certain I understood what you were trying to say. Why don't we go over it again? This time *in French!*"

"I'd like to explain." But he knew he couldn't. Not yet.

Doubting she would find any explanation satisfactory, Susan hissed, "From the beginning I felt you were hiding something. Now I know I was right. Can you explain why a man with the vocabulary of a scholar, a man who talks knowledgeably about foreign places, plays whist, and speaks French is trying to pass himself off as a poor farmer?"

Wade bristled. "I never said I was poor and there's nothing wrong with being a farmer. It's an honest living."

"Yes, farming is an honest living, only you don't seem to know much about it! Every time I've brought up the subject of crops you have been evasive. I don't think you have the vaguest idea what should be planted when, which leads me to believe you are a 'poor farmer' in more ways than one!"

Wade could not blame Susan for her anger. Though not intentional, he had played her for a fool. He had betrayed the friendship she had freely offered, deceiving her, then compounding his transgression by trying to use honesty as an argument against her involvement with the abolitionists.

"Why, Wade? Why did you lie to me?"

If she had shouted at him, if she had ranted and raved, maybe thrown something in his direction, Wade would have found the situation much easier to handle than her softly whispered question filled with pain.

He cupped her face between his gloved palms. "I never lied to you, Susan. I just didn't tell you the whole truth and I can't tell you now." When she tried to pull away he held her firmly. "Soon, sweetheart. Soon I will explain everything. I promise. But for now, please trust me just a little longer."

Susan could think of a million reasons why she shouldn't Admittedly he was holding something back. He refused to trust her with his secret and now her very life might hang in the balance for he was aware of her part in helping the slaves escape. How could she possibly trust him? Yet as his eyes pleaded, her heart cried out to give him a chance.

Wade was aware of the struggle going on within her, knew the precise second when emotion won out over sound judgment. Her features relaxed and when her lips softened invitingly he could not resist the temptation to touch them with his own. Caught up in a breathless moment of desire, Susan reveled in the feel of his mouth as he deepened the kiss. When at last they drew apart both knew, regardless of what lay ahead, it was too late to turn back.

"What did she say when she found out you were a doctor?"

"She didn't have a chance to say anything. I was in a hurry. When I got back she was gone."

Seated at the scarred table in the little farmhouse, Davey stared broodingly into the empty mug he held.

"I wish I could tell Susan the truth. She knows just enough to jump to the wrong conclusions," Wade worried aloud.

"Maybe she'll jump to the right ones which could be even worse," Davey pointed out glumly. He played with his cup a few minutes letting the silence settle in around them. "Laura Dunstan came here to suggest that you stop seeing Susan."

Expecting something like that, Wade looked up. "What did you say to her *suggestion?*"

"I told her you planned to marry Susan for her money."

"You WHAT?" Davey's bland expression left Wade wondering if he'd heard correctly.

"Well, she made me so damned mad with her meddlesome ways, I couldn't help myself."

"But what if she tells Susan?" Wade was clearly upset. Pacing around the room he said, "She already thinks I'm some kind of fraud. It was all I could do to convince her to trust me, and now this! How could you tell such a ridiculous lie?"

Davey had the grace to look sheepish. "Like I said, she made me angry. You didn't see her, Wade. Prissing through the yard on her tippy toes holding up her skirt, afraid she might get a little dirt on the hem."

Wade stopped on the other side of the table, placing his gloved hands on the wood for balance. "Hells, bells, Davey! The yard is full of shit! What did you expect her to do?"

Davey answered with a shrug, then followed it up by saying, "Laura's right you know."

When Wade bared his teeth in a ferocious scowl, he hurried to amend his observation. "I don't mean you aren't good enough for Susan. I just think you are forgetting her father is a slaveholder."

"I'm not forgetting anything," Wade countered belligerently. "But I'm not interested in her father! Besides you know yourself Susan hates the idea of slavery."

"Which reminds me. Did you get her to agree to stop looking for messages in that tree?"

This time it was Wade who looked abashed. "No. She made it clear that nothing will prevent her aiding the *cause.*"

Davey was thoughtful. "In that case we'll have to work from the top down."

"What do you mean?"

"We'll find out who's leaving the notes and replace the last link of the chain without Susan's knowledge."

"That's going to take some time. The reason the mission has been successful thus far is because each operative knows no one but the person he is to contact."

"Then we'd better get started right away before Susan Ashe finds herself in over her head."

Davey could have kicked himself for his carelessly spoken words when he saw the color drain from the other man's face.

"I'm sorry, Wade. That was stupid of me," he apologized knowing he had reminded his friend of Nell's tragic death.

"You didn't mean anything by it, Davey. I know that. You'd think after a year I'd be reconciled to it by now, but it still hurts like hell."

Davey could read the anguish in Wade's face.

"I didn't want to love again. Not after Nell. But now there's Susan and I can't help the way I feel." His smile was rueful. "Davey, if anything happens to her I just don't think I could go on."

Davey's heart went out to Wade Callahan who had suffered not only physical pain but the far greater torment that comes from losing the one you hold most dear. Determined to do all he could to protect his friend from further hurt, Davey replied with more confidence than he felt, "One way or another we'll see that no harm comes to Susan."

* * *

"Susan! I'm so glad to see you. I wasn't sure Delilah would be able to pass along my message."

It had been a week since Laura had seen her friend. In fact it had been a week since she'd seen anyone outside the family. The shunning Henry Ashe instigated had left the Dunstans with no one but each other for company and Laura was feeling the effects of isolation as much as the rest.

Susan tied her horse next to Laura's and seated herself on the mossy bank. "I'm so sorry about all this. You shouldn't have to pay the price for Fowler's stubborness. How are the others taking it?"

Laura groaned. "Uncle Fowler spends most of the time locked in his study. Angel complains endlessly and Aunt Hester wanders about like a ghost wringing her hands and looking lost."

"What about Brad?"

"I don't see much of him. I guess he's with that awful Bart Harmon and his men," replied Laura, her expression mirroring her distaste. "How long do you suppose this will go on?"

"Until your uncle dismisses Harmon and his followers and puts a stop to Brad's mistreatment of the Dunstan slaves."

"Surely you are wrong about Brad, Susan. I can't believe he would be deliberately abusive. I feel sorry for him. He's not a happy man."

Susan knew it was no use arguing. "Oh, Laura, you are just too nice. You always look for the good in people and refuse to see the bad."

Laura studied the ripples in the water. "You're

wrong there. Sometimes I see the bad which is why I asked you to meet me here. I've been wrestling with my conscience for days now wondering what to do and I have decided I must tell you the truth."

"The truth about what?"

Hoping she was doing the right thing, Laura plunged ahead. "It's about Mr. Callahan."

"Wade?"

"Yes. I went to see him a week ago."

"What in the world for?"

"It doesn't matter. He wasn't there but Davey Logan was. There's no way to make this easy so I might as well come right out with it. Davey told me Wade Callahan intends to marry you for your money."

Once the words were spoken Laura felt better. Susan would be hurt, possibly angry, but it was nothing compared to what she would feel if the cad was allowed to continue with his deception.

Susan's reaction was not what Laura expected. After a brief period of puzzled silence, the pert blonde threw back her head and laughed until tears were rolling down her cheeks.

"Would you mind telling me what you find so funny?"

Susan tried to control her mirth. "Wade doesn't need my money," she finally choked out.

"How do you know?"

"Because he speaks French." With that she broke up again in peals of laughter leaving Laura to wonder if the shocking truth had sent her over the edge.

140

"What does speaking French have to do with anything?"

Sniffing loudly Susan brushed her cheeks with her fingertips. "Don't you understand? Wade isn't a farmer. He's a scholar! And I don't think he's poor."

Laura greeted her explanation with a dubious look. "Then what is he doing growing corn on a broken-down farm?"

"I'm not sure but he is going to tell me soon."

Laura threw her hands up in a gesture of frustration. "While Wade was *not* telling you about himself did he happen to mention that Davey Logan is a doctor?"

"Doctor?"

"That's right." Laura proceeded to tell Susan everything that had transpired during her disasterous visit to the Callahan farm.

"A doctor, eh? Somehow that doesn't surprise me."

"Well it certainly surprised me!" Laura confessed. "What do you suppose they are up to?"

"I have no idea, but Wade promised to explain everything soon and I promised to trust him until then."

"It doesn't seem like a fair bargain to me."

Refusing to be swayed by her friend's logic, Susan replied dreamily. "Fair or not it's still a bargain. And we sealed it with a kiss."

"Oh, blast!"

Chapter 10

Long after Susan left, Laura was still sitting beside
the fast-flowing river trying to sort out her troubled
thoughts. The savage a doctor? Wade Callahan,
a . . . She didn't know what *he* was but he was
certainly not what he seemed to be. And what about
Brad Kincaid? He had asked her again a few days
ago if she would stay at River Ridge. He seemed
anxious to gain a commitment from her and had
been unable to hide his impatience when she tried to
explain her desire to visit all of the strange, exotic
places she had never seen. A short time later her
uncle had approached her adding his arguments in
favor of her staying. But if this week was any indication of what life would be like from here on out she
might as well be on her way for life along the Saint
Johns River had become intolerably boring.

She tried to recall the handsome faces of the men
in Boston who had danced attendance on her after
her father's death, accompanying her to the theater
or escorting her to parties and balls, but without

conscious thought the image of Davey Logan crowded in, relegating the mental picture of her former swains to some shadowy corner of her mind. She willed the unwelcome impression to go away but it was no use. How could ordinary men compete with such virility and masculine potency even in one's reverie?

A rustling noise in the bushes directly behind her caught Laura's attention. The sudden appearance of Bart Harmon had her wishing she'd left with Susan rather than lingering by the river so far from the main house.

"What are you doing here?" she demanded rising to her feet.

Shifty eyes, one drawn down by the hideous scar, raked her from head to toe, then back again, pausing on her slightly heaving bosom. "I was looking for a runaway but I've found me a little darlin' instead. I'd say this is my lucky day."

Laura held her ground as Bart took a step closer. There was no way to retreat without jumping into the river. "I told you not to call me that. Now go away. There is no one here but me and I prefer to be alone." She managed to say the words with scarcely a tremor to give away her fright, but inside her heart was pounding for she knew there was nothing she could do if the man chose to disregard her command.

"Now is that any way to talk? You should be grateful I came along when I did. No telling what might happen to a young filly all by herself in these woods. Why somebody who didn't know any better might think you were waiting here on purpose, setting a man up like your cousin, Angel, does when she has a hankering to get laid."

Bart reached out and ran his hand along one sleeve of Laura's dress. "Is that how it is, little darlin'? You got an itch that needs scratching?"

Before Laura could protest, he grabbed her roughly by the arms and pulled her toward him. She could feel the heat of his fetid breath as he bent his head. Turning her face away she let out a piercing scream. At the same time she brought her leg up to connect with Bart's groin, and the next thing she knew she was flying through the air with nothing but water to break her fall.

Davey told himself he had chosen to take the path along the river because it was the shortest route to the post office. It had nothing to do with Laura Dunstan. It would suit him just fine if he never saw her again. Damned woman with her uppity notions and her funny way of speaking. Served her right to be caught up in the cold-shoulder treatment directed against Fowler Dunstan and his family. If she didn't like it she could pack up and go back to Boston. No one was forcing her to stay. He was surprised she hadn't hightailed it out of here by now.

Maybe she had. He hadn't seen her for a week. Davey wondered why the idea bothered him. Because he had given her credit for more gumption? Possibly. Still, the fact was she didn't belong in

Florida and it would be better for everyone if she left. Then he could stop thinking about her and get on with his business.

Suddenly a scream rent the air followed by a loud splash. Davey nudged the big stallion with his heels and the animal sprinted ahead. Rounding a curve in the trail they came upon the spot where he and Wade had met Laura and Susan a little over a week ago. But this time the only person in sight was Bart Harmon. Brad Kincaid's henchman was bent double clutching his stomach as he retched. Davey knew the scream he'd heard hadn't come from the lowlife scum spilling his guts in the grass, but there seemed to be no one else around.

"Help!"

He caught only a glimpse of Laura before the current dragged her under. In one fluid motion he was on the ground, then in the water, swimming with powerful strokes that quickly brought him to the place where she had disappeared. He dove beneath the surface searching the murky depths for some sign of her. When his lungs threatened to burst he came to the top, then dove again. He'd almost given up hope when he saw her caught in a tangle of weeds, her auburn hair streaming out in all directions like an undulating curtain framing her chalk-white face.

Circling her slender body with one arm he lashed out with the other to free her from the clinging vegetation. Once loose he kicked with all of his might, propelling them upward toward the halo of sunlight shining overhead. Carried by the tide

Davey brought her ashore near the Pine View landing.

Placing Laura gently on the ground, he knelt beside her and began rubbing her arms, then lifted her sodden skirts to massage her long, shapely legs. She felt cold and clammy to his touch. He could see the tiny blue veins beneath the skin of her nearly transparent eyelids, the thick black lashes that fanned out across her pale cheeks, the colorless lips that could smile or pout depending on her mood but now did neither. He brushed the hair from her face, then slapped her hard in a frantic attempt to stimulate some reaction.

"Wake up, dammit! You're not going to die like Nell! I won't let you! You're too stubborn to give up! Fight, damn you! Fight!"

Davey didn't realize he was shaking her like a rag doll just as he wasn't aware of the tears that blurred his vision. The only thing he recognized was a deep, all-encompassing anger that drove him to reach beyond this life into the next and snatch Laura's soul from the one who would take her from him.

From somewhere far away Laura heard the harsh male voice calling her back. She wasn't sure she wanted to obey. Why couldn't he leave her alone? Maybe she would return just long enough to give him a piece of her mind. Yes, whoever was shaking her and shouting like a savage deserved a stern reprimand. *Savage?* Could it be? Laura's eyelids flickered, then opened, but all she could see was a brilliant ball of fire in the sky beyond the dark silhouette of a man jouncing her around until her teeth rattled. Still she knew who he was.

"Who's Nell?" The raspy voice she heard didn't sound at all like hers.

Immediately the vibrating stopped and she found herself caught up in a tight embrace. Her face was pressed against a soggy buckskin shirt making it impossible to breathe. Laura put up her hands and pushed as hard as she could. When a tiny space opened between her and the barrier that threatened to suffocate her she sucked in oxygen, filling her lungs with warm, moist air.

Gasping and wheezing she looked up at the man who held her. "What are you trying to do, kill me?"

Davey's rich, rumbling laughter rang forth as he held her possessively, unwilling to let her go now that he had her back.

Shortly thereafter, he took her to Pine View which was closer than her uncle's plantation. After issuing orders on how she should be cared for he left abruptly, saying he would stop by River Ridge and inform the Dunstans as to what had happened. His manner had been coldly professional, leading Laura to wonder if she could have imagined his tender solicitude. She'd even thought there were traces of tears on his cheeks when she first opened her eyes but it must have been drops of water falling from his wet hair. Men didn't cry, especially strong, rugged men like Davey Logan.

Tucked beneath the covers of Susan's blue-ruffled canopy bed she wondered again about the woman called Nell. Davey had shouted at her saying she couldn't die like Nell. There had been anguish in his voice. He must have loved Nell very much. What would it be like to know such love? How did one go on when the love died?

Tomorrow she would have to return to her uncle and to the dreary house that had become cloaked in a veil of misery. It was cheerful here with Susan and her father. It would be nice if she could stay for a while but she couldn't very well desert her family when the rest of the community had turned their backs on Fowler and his kin.

Surely once her uncle learned about Bart Harmon's abominable behavior which had almost cost her her life, he would insist that Harmon and his unsavory friends leave River Ridge. Then maybe life would get back to normal.

Laura stifled a yawn. She had heard Davey instruct Susan to add a small amount of laudanum to her tea. She felt the drug begin to take effect. Her limbs seemed weighted and she was having difficulty keeping her eyes open. She fell asleep wondering how Davey would explain the accident to her uncle.

Davey was beyond livid as he approached the Dunstan mansion. What he felt was a fury so intense he could taste its bitter acid on his tongue. He hadn't needed Laura to tell him what had happened there on the riverbank. A rabid animal like Bart Harmon ought to be destroyed.

Dismounting before the big stallion came to a full stop, he took the steps two at a time, using the heavy brass knocker to announce his arrival. Metal clanged against metal until the door opened.

"Logan! What are you doing here?" Brad Kincaid was not pleased to see him.

Davey fought the urge to ram the smaller man's teeth down his throat. He wanted to hit something . . . or someone, and he figured Kincaid would do nicely as a target.

Using every bit of restraint he could muster Davey answered. "I came here to tell you Laura has had an accident."

"An accident? Where? How? Is she all right?"

"She's all right, no thanks to you!" Briefly Davey related what had occurred a few hours earlier.

"Thank God, she escaped serious harm." Brad's relief was genuine but it had nothing to do with concern for Laura. She had to stay alive long enough to marry him or his plans for acquiring her fortune *and* River Ridge would be unnecessarily complicated. "I'll speak to Harmon and see that he stays away from Laura from now on."

"Speak to him? Scum like that should be sent packing! You can't keep him here after what he's done!"

Brad's narrow features grew pinched. "I don't need a half-breed bastard like you telling me what I can and cannot do, Logan. I said I'd take care of Harmon and I will . . . in my own way. Now if that's all you came for I'd better get over to Henry's and bring Laura home."

Davey clenched his fists at his side. "Laura is

sleeping. She shouldn't be moved until tomorrow after she's had a chance to rest."

"*Miss Dunstan* is my responsibility, Logan, not yours," Kincaid countered arrogantly. "And not that it's any of your business but Laura is going to be *my* wife!" Unaffected exacerbation gave credence to the lie.

Brad's pronouncement was met with stunned silence. Laura and Kincaid? Surely there had to be some mistake. Davey felt as if he'd been socked in the gut. How could Laura consider marrying a ruthless jackal like Kincaid?

Brad read more than doubt in Davey's eyes and he didn't like what he saw. Had something been going on between Laura and the half-breed that he didn't know about? If so, he would put a stop to it right now.

"Laura is still in mourning over her father's death. As soon as her grieving period is over we plan to announce our engagement."

He sounded confident and Davey could think of no reason for him to lie.

"Stay away from her, Logan. She doesn't want anything to do with the likes of you."

Before Davey could open his mouth, the door closed in his face. Making his way back down the walk he tried to sustain his anger but instead found himself weighed down under a cloud of depression. Kincaid's words hurt more than he cared to admit, mostly because he knew they were true. Laura didn't want anything to do with him. Everytime they were together they ended up in an argument

. . . except this last time when she had been too weak to fight. He winced, remembering how fragile she had looked when he pulled her from the water. They had nothing in common. She came from a different world with different values where money and social standing were more important than love and respect for one's fellow man. Maybe she and Kincaid deserved each other, he thought contemptuously. At any rate he had his own life to live and it sure didn't include a frigid prima donna who'd been born with a silver spoon in her mouth. He'd had to work hard to earn his degree at the School of Medicine in Charleston. It hadn't been easy for someone of his background but he had succeeded and now he was determined to use his skills where they were needed most. Instead of settling in a big city and building a lucrative practice, he had chosen to travel the wilderness trails of Florida, treating the settlers who had no other access to medical attention. Payment for services rendered was usually a home-cooked meal and a heartfelt thank-you. Not something a woman like Laura Dunstan would understand, but it was all the compensation he needed.

Lost in thought Davey didn't see Angel standing in his path until he nearly plowed into her. He reached out, taking her by the arms to keep her from falling. When he would have let her go she moved closer, leaning against him as if she needed his support.

"Why, Mr. Logan, surely you weren't going to walk right by me without saying hello?"

Angel's soft sugary-sweet drawl hinted at affectation. Davey decided he preferred her cousin's rapid-fire, clipped way of speaking. At least Laura didn't make a man feel like a bee being lured to a honey pot.

"Sorry, Miss Dunstan. I didn't see you," he apologized touching the brim of his hat.

Angel pouted prettily. "I'll forgive you if you call me Angel."

"Yes, ma'am." Davey looked around nervously. "I really should be going now."

The pout was replaced by a coy smile which made Davey even more nervous.

"I was hoping you would stay awhile. We haven't had much company lately and a body tends to get ever so lonesome," cajoled the petite redhead, continuing to use him as a prop for her tiny frame.

The way she said "body" led Davey to believe she was referring to more than just a loneliness of spirit.

"Miss Dunstan, I really must go. I have some important business to attend to," he lied, forcing her to stand on her own two feet.

Continuing to block his escape, Angel laced her fingers through the fringe of his buckskin shirt. "You were going to call me Angel, remember?"

Davey remembered no such thing. It had been a long day and he wasn't in the mood for games. He tried to step around her but she moved with him.

"I was hoping you had come to visit me today but I can see I was wrong. Too bad, Davey. I'll bet we could have a real good time together, just you and me."

When he gave her no encouragement her demeanor turned pettish.

"I suppose you came to see Laura." There was a grating whine to her voice when she spoke of Laura.

Impatiently Davey brushed her hands away. "No, ma'am. I came to tell your folks that your cousin met with an accident earlier today."

Anxious to rid himself of the clinging female Davey gave her only a brief explanation saying Laura had fallen in the river and he had pulled her out and taken her to the Ashe's plantation. He saw no reason to mention Bart Harmon.

When he was finished Angel purred, "My, my! Clever Laura. I wish I had thought of that."

"Thought of what?"

The flame-haired temptress laughed meaningfully. "Why, I wish I had thought of jumping in the river to get your attention."

Davey wanted to throttle the heartless little baggage who displayed an appalling lack of concern for her cousin. Instead he caught her by the shoulders and gave her a good shake. "Laura almost lost her life today! Doesn't that mean anything to you?"

Ignoring his question Angel smiled provocatively. "I like men who treat me rough."

Disgusted Davey thrust her away and quickly moved to where his horse stood waiting. He didn't know how to deal with someone like Angel. Touching her made him feel dirty. He mounted and nudged the stallion into a gallop. Racing down the drive he didn't look back but he could hear her high-pitched laughter long after he reached the main road. It was chilling, like the sound of one not quite sane.

Brad didn't go immediately to Pine View. First he stopped by the stables to talk to Bart Harmon. He was enraged to think the scurrilous gunman might have jeopardized his well-laid plans because he couldn't keep his hands off Laura. He found Bart standing idly at the far end of the building gazing out across the fields of cotton and sugarcane puffing on a long, brown cheroot. Without warning Brad uncoiled his whip, then let it fly, cutting the cigar in half while it was still in Bart's mouth.

"What the . . . ?" Bart's protest died in the air as he whirled to face his irate employer.

"Damn you, Harmon!" Brad snarled. "I ought to flail the hide off your back."

Bart knew good and well what had the man so riled, but he'd seen what Brad could do with that deadly piece of leather and he wasn't about to admit his guilt.

"What's the matter with you, Kincaid? I ain't done nothing wrong."

Brad played the whip along the ground, making it slither like a snake, as Bart watched fascinated by the writhing movement.

"You call molesting Fowler's niece nothing?"

Bart thought quickly. There was no point in denying what Kincaid already knew. He was hoping Laura Dunstan and the interferring half-breed had drowned but obviously such was not the case. Now he would have to twist the story to make that haughty bitch seem at fault.

"Listen, Kincaid, all I was doing was searching for the runaway. When I got to the river, Miss Dunstan was there. She come on to me like you wouldn't believe, telling me how lonely she was and begging me to do something about it. All I did was kiss her. Next thing I knew Logan came crashing out of the bushes on that big stallion of his. Laura . . . I mean Miss Dunstan must have been frightened by the horse. She stepped backward right off the bank. The breed, he hauled off and punched me, then jumped in the water after her."

Brad eyed the man sharply. "And you didn't think the incident was important enough to tell anyone about?"

"I saw Logan pull her ashore downstream. Once I knew she was safe I continued searching for the missing slave. I just got back a few minutes ago."

Brad felt almost certain Harmon was not telling the truth. Laura didn't strike him as the type to throw herself at a man, especially a scar-faced gun-for-hire like Harmon. Yet there was just enough doubt to make him stop short of calling the man a liar. If his suspicions were correct there was something going on between her and that bastard Indian. Maybe Laura was as promiscuous as Angel, and her standoffish attitude was just an act to make a man all hot and hard with wanting before she gave in. He looked forward to finding out if that might be the case. Meanwhile he had better make sure Harmon

155

understood that Laura was off limits as far as he was concerned.

He took his time coiling the whip in loops that dangled loosely from his hand. "If what you say is true then your only crime was kissing my intended." He paused to let his words sink in and was rewarded by an astonished look on the disfigured face of his hireling. "That's right," he assured. "Miss Dunstan and I are engaged and although she may not be as virtuous as she pretends, she's all mine. Is that clear, Harmon?" Each time he repeated the lie, it became more and more of a reality in his own mind.

Bart resented the hell out of taking orders. He didn't like Brad Kincaid, who had the wealth and power to buy a man's soul, but Bart needed the money Kincaid offered. "You've made your point," he growled, "but if I were you I'd keep a tighter rein on that little filly."

Brad managed to hold his anger in check as he ordered a gig for the trip to the neighboring plantation, but Bart Harmon was the second man today to offer advice on how to deal with Laura Dunstan and it didn't sit well. It was about time he and the future Mrs. Kincaid had a serious talk.

Chapter 11

Laura awakened with a headache, a terrible taste in her mouth, and a few choice words for the doctor who had prescribed the laudanum. The dim light which bathed the room in a shadowy glow indicated that evening was fast approaching. As she got up shakily and splashed water on her face to clear her drugged senses a maid entered announcing that Brad Kincaid was waiting for her downstairs. Upon questioning, the dark-skinned girl informed her that Henry and Susan were down at the quarters but were expected back shortly.

With the maid's help Laura donned the dress she had taken off to dry. She wasn't looking forward to telling Brad about Bart Harmon's treachery but then maybe he already knew. There was also the matter of Brad's treatment of the slaves which she hadn't had an opportunity to discuss with him since his return from Jacksonville. All in all she would much prefer a good night's sleep to any sort of confrontation but she couldn't very well leave him waiting downstairs alone. Seeing no alternative, she smoothed the wrinkles from her skirt, then left the room.

Brad was standing in the foyer but hurried to assist her as she descended the stairs. "Laura, my dear. Are you all right?" He took in her disheveled appearance, frowning at the now dry but crumpled gown.

"I'm fine, Brad. Just a little tired."

Taking her arm he moved toward the door. "Of course you are. What a dreadful ordeal it must have been but we won't talk about it now. We have to get you home where you can be properly cared for."

"But, Brad," she argued digging in her heels, "I've been very well cared for by Susan and her father. I can't leave without thanking them for all that they have done."

"That can wait, and I'm sure the household staff can be relied on to tell them I've taken you back where you belong. Now let's be going."

Laura found the urgency in his tone disconcerting. After what she had been through she was in no mood to be rushed.

Seeing stubborn refusal in the jut of her chin, Brad sought to appease her.

"Laura, you know Henry Ashe wants nothing to do with those of us from River Ridge. I'm astonished he even took you in. But you can't expect his hospitality to continue now that you are well enough to leave. Do be reasonable and save us all embarrassment."

Not for a minute did Laura believe Susan's father

would insist that she go but he might resent finding Brad here. Under the circumstances at least part of what he said made sense, but she insisted on taking the time to jot a note to Susan before they left.

She scribbled a hasty message thanking her friend and asking that she meet her tomorrow. This time she set their rendezvous spot at the Ashe's boathouse. The last thing she wanted was to cross paths with Bart Harmon again.

When she and Brad reached the main road the moon was rising overhead. They traveled in silence for a while. Finally Brad broached the subject she had hoped to put off until tomorrow.

"The half-breed told me Bart Harmon attacked you but Harmon says it was the other way around."

At first Laura thought he was joking but she knew humor was not his style. Still she said, "You can't be serious?"

As if to reinforce what she had just been thinking, he reminded, "I'm always serious, Laura."

She turned to look at him but could only make out his stern profile. "I'm hardly capable of attacking a man though if I'd had a gun handy I might have considered shooting the odious blackguard."

Brad drew the horses to a halt. "He didn't mean *that* kind of attack. He said you—how can I put this delicately? He said you encouraged his advances, then when Logan showed up you accidentally fell into the river."

"And you believed him?" she shouted in outrage, causing the horses to fidgit nervously.

Keeping a tight hold on the reins, Brad reproved

159

her. "Calm yourself, my dear. Of course I don't believe him. I know you would never deliberately entice a man like Harmon."

Actually Brad wasn't sure whether she would or not and he didn't particularly care, but he knew better than to suggest she might have been at fault.

"Well, thank you for that vote of confidence," Laura said bitingly.

Brad sighed, annoyed by her sarcasm. "I know you are not to blame for what happened, but the world is full of filth like Harmon and you are a very beautiful young woman with no one to protect you from his kind."

He was pleased with his impromptu little speech. There could be no arguing his logic and he had found a way to open the door to the more serious matter of who should take care of Laura—and her money. Just the right amount of sympathy and concern coming at a time when she was vulnerable would hopefully help Laura soften toward him. He could feel her anger draining away and was quick to press his advantage taking her hands and squeezing them lightly.

"Surely you must know how much I have come to care for you, lovely Laura. I had hoped to give you more time but after what has happened today I believe it is vital to your safety and well-being that I declare myself. I want the right to protect you against anyone who might seek to do you harm. Perhaps I didn't make myself clear when I urged you to stay at River Ridge. What I am trying to say

160

is that I would be honored if you would consent to become my wife."

Whatever Laura had expected it certainly wasn't a proposal of marriage. She liked Brad despite his somber disposition, and deep down she couldn't believe him capable of the cruelties for which some accused him. He had been kind and understanding where she was concerned but there was something missing. Brad didn't make her nerves tingle or her heart skip a beat. She pushed aside the fleeting image of Davey Logan. He had nothing to do with her current dilema. The truth was she didn't love Brad Kincaid. And when it came to marriage she would settle for nothing less.

Her head was reeling. This on top of everything else she had been through today was almost more than she could handle yet she felt the need to choose her words carefully. "I'm flattered, Brad. I feel fortunate to have you for a friend. Hopefully nothing will ever change that. But I'm afraid I cannot marry you. It wouldn't be fair to either of us."

The subtle light concealed the angry flush that suffused the man's face. "I don't understand, Laura."

"It's very difficult to explain," she answered giving him a wane smile. "You see growing up without a mother, having little contact with my father, I've never known love. I'm not certain I would recognize it should I be fortunate enough to find it, but I have to keep searching. Until I discover that elusive emotion I've only read about, I can never be complete. I like you, Brad, but I don't love you and I don't think you love me. At least it's not the kind of love I'm looking for."

Brad's hands tightened on the leather straps. He wished he had brought his whip. A sound thrashing would exorcise her stubbornness and put an end to this childish talk of love soon enough. "You are very young, my dear, and your head is full of fanciful dreams. Knights in shining armor don't exist outside the pages of romantic novels. This is real life. I must insist that you be practical."

Laura was miffed by his patronizing attitude. "You may be right, Brad. Perhaps there is no such thing as true love. But as you say, I am young. I have plenty of time to find out for myself."

She had successfully managed to use his own argument against him, and although Brad knew he had lost the battle, he was still determined to win the war. He slapped the reins across the horses' backs to set them in motion. "I realize what a rough day it has been for you having to contend with Bart Harmon, then being left to the mercies of that savage. We will speak of this again after you have had an opportunity to rest." *And come to your senses,* he wanted to add.

Laura knew she would not change her mind but it would do no good to argue the point now, so she sat back and allowed her brooding thoughts to take over. At no time had Brad said he loved her which was odd for a man proposing marriage. And he hadn't said he would get rid of Harmon which left her questioning the depth of his concern for her welfare. But what confounded her the most was the way she had inwardly rebelled when he used the term "savage" to describe Davey Logan. Somehow it no longer seemed a fitting characterization for the man who had risked his life to save her own.

Fowler Dunstan was waiting the next morning when she entered the breakfast room.

"Laura, I can't tell you how sorry I am about what happened yesterday. I do hope you are completely recovered."

Though she had slept poorly and was still feeling the aftereffects of her ordeal, Laura saw no reason to add to her uncle's distress for he looked a bit haggard as if he too had struggled through a restless night.

"I'm fine now, Uncle Fowler. Thank you for your concern."

Taking a piece of toast from the sideboard, she poured herself a cup of tea.

Fowler reached for the silver coffeepot. "I cannot imagine what possessed Bart Harmon to behave so crudely but I can assure you it will not happen again."

Laura felt her spirits lighten. "Has Mr. Harmon gone then?"

"Gone?" Fowler frowned uncertainly.

"Why, yes. I assumed you meant the man had been fired."

The lines in Fowler's wide forehead deepened. "I wish it were that simple, Laura. Unfortunately we need all the men we can get right now. At the rate the slaves are disappearing we won't have enough hands to pick the cotton come fall. We have to put a stop to this insurrection. But I assure you Harmon will not bother you again."

His excuses did little to cheer Laura and his assurance could not alleviate her fear of the degenerate gunman. "I understand your position, Uncle, but under the circumstances I believe it would be best if I continue my travels." She was hurt to think he would put his crop ahead of her safety.

Shaken by the prospect of her leaving, Dunstan let the cup fall from his fingers. A servant hovering nearby hurried to mop up the ugly brown stain spreading across the white cloth but Fowler impatiently motioned him away.

Amber eyes pleaded as he said, "Surely there must be another way to resolve this matter. I can't stand the thought of your being alone in the world when you belong here with us."

Laura sipped her tea, making no reply. In truth she didn't really want to leave—as happened too often lately, Davey Logan's darkly handsome visage intruded on her thoughts—but neither did she want to subject herself to another frightening encounter with Bart Harmon.

Fowler appeared to be pondering his next words and finally said apologetically. "I hope you will forgive an old man's interference, but I am aware of another possible solution which I beg you to consider." He hesitated a moment then amended, "I should say *reconsider*. Brad has told me he asked you to marry him and you turned him down. You must know that as his wife you would be treated with the respect you deserve."

Laura took time to nibble a bite of toast before she replied. "I had thought as your niece I would be safe from the advances of a man like Harmon. I can't see how as Brad's wife I would be any less vulnerable. Besides that's not a very good reason to marry a man when I have the option of leaving."

The elderly man's expression turned sadly retrospective. "I was hoping you would come to think of River Ridge as your home, Laura. Your aunt and I won't live forever. Angel will marry one of her young suitors someday, then all of this will belong to Brad. When I came to Florida this land was nothing but virgin wilderness. I cleared the ground, built this house, and planted the fields. River Ridge is my life. I'm proud of what I have accomplished and though Brad has been like a son to me, he's not a Dunstan. It would mean a great deal to know that my brother's only child, my own flesh and blood, would be here to carry on after I'm gone."

Laura was not unmoved by her uncle's colloquy and she regretted having to disappoint him but she would not be pushed into marriage for all the wrong reasons. "I'm sorry, Uncle, but I don't love Brad."

Fowler managed to hide his frustration behind a mask of tender concern. "Perhaps given time you will change your mind. At least say you will stay a little longer."

"I don't know." Laura didn't want to encourage false hope but even as she spoke it occurred to her that she had not properly thanked Davey for saving her life. And then there was Susan Ashe. A strong bond of friendship had developed between the two women in the short time she had been at River Ridge and she dreaded the thought of not seeing Susan again. There was also the mystery surrounding Wade Callahan's background. It would be difficult to leave with so many loose ends dangling in front of her.

Giving her uncle a winsome smile she yielded to his persuasion. "I doubt I will change my mind about Brad but I would like to remain a while longer. After all, with the two of you to protect me, how could I possibly come to harm?"

"Kill Laura! But you said I was suppose to marry her!" Brad was dumfounded. He had no particular qualms when it came to eliminating someone who stood in his way, but Laura Dunstan was the key to his getting the plantation. Everything hinged around them becoming man and wife. He would turn her money over to Fowler. Then he would arrange a tragic accident to befall his unsuspecting stepfather and it would all be his, including the beautiful Laura.

"Because of your incompetence, I find myself forced to alter our original plan." Fowler glared at Brad in disgust. "Laura has made it clear she has no intention of accepting your proposal which leaves only one alternative. We must get rid of her despite the rumors which are bound to arise as a result of her untimely death. Even if there are some who suspect foul play they have no one in authority to turn to with their suspicions. I had hoped to secure what rightfully belongs to me without violence but now I see no other way. It's too bad for I don't hold Laura responsible for my father's sins. It isn't her fault her grandfather played my stupid mother false leading her to believe he would wed her. His family was rich and she was nothing but a servant in their big house. She allowed him to take his pleasure with her, then when he discovered she was pregnant he threw her out into the streets to fend for herself and her unborn child."

Fowler's face twisted as he recalled the poverty and humiliation he had suffered made worse by his drunken hag of a mother whose bitter resentment never let him forget who his father was; how she had cursed her former lover when he married the daughter of a well-to-do Boston banker.

Brad had heard the story before. He hadn't felt any sympathy for Fowler then and he didn't now. He knew his stepfather to be a ruthless, vindictive man who deserved no pity for the blows Fate had dealt him.

"You did all right for yourself," Brad sneered. "Marrying my mother for her money when I was too young to protest. Using what should have been mine to buy this land and the slaves to work it. Making me dependent on you for what little I have."

Fowler's eyes flashed a challenge. "No one is

forcing you to stay at River Ridge. You're free to leave at any time."

Brad leaned across the desk menacingly. "Not a chance, old man. One way or another this will all be mine someday."

Fowler laughed in the face of his stepson's defiance. "But it won't be by marrying Franklin Dunstan's daughter, which brings us back to the problem of how to dispose of her."

Determined to make this latest turn of events work in his favor, Brad asked curiously, "Once she's dead, how do you plan to lay claim to her money? Legally your name's not even Dunstan."

Confidently Fowler smirked. "Laura is going to leave a will naming me her sole beneficiary. Since she has no family to contest its validity it won't matter who actually signs the document, now will it?"

"What you're talking about is murder," reminded Brad. "There may not be any law and order in the state right now but there soon will be. And the price for my silence is high."

Fowler leaned forward. "How high?"

Brad gave his stepfather a sly look knowing he now had the upper hand. "I want your agreement in writing that River Ridge will be mine when you die," he answered cold-bloodedly.

Fowler gazed out the window making the younger man wait, but both knew Brad would get what he wanted.

After Brad had taken his leave Fowler sat back in his chair contemplating the bargain they had struck.

The price for revenge wasn't really so high. What difference did it make to him what happened to the plantation after he was gone? Besides, he was planning to live for a long, long time.

Chapter 12

"Papa and I were worried when we returned to find you gone."

Laura recognized hurt as well as concern in her friend's voice. "I'm sorry, Susan. I know it was rude to leave without thanking you both for allowing me to stay until I was recovered, but I didn't want to risk a confrontation between Brad and your father."

"You owe us no thanks. We're just glad you're all right, and I appreciate your keeping Brad away from Papa. He's not feeling very charitable toward your uncle or his stepson. It was certainly a stroke of luck Davey happened along when he did."

Susan gave Laura a teasing smile. "Of course, I can't imagine what he was doing on the river path to begin with unless he was hoping to run into you."

Laura blushed. "Don't be silly. Davey can't stand the sight of me. He thinks I'm a spoiled coquette with more money than sense. He was probably taking a shortcut to your house. No doubt he wanted to regale you with stories of the heroic deeds of Wade Callahan so you would marry the poor man and rescue him from poverty."

"Laura Dunstan! That's a terrible thing to say. I've told you Wade is not after my money and no one has to convince me to marry him. All he has to do is ask."

Oh, Lord!" Laura cried truly distressed. "You're in love with him, aren't you?"

Susan gazed down into the water lapping at the pilings on which the boathouse stood. "I sure am," she answered dreamily. "When I'm with Wade I feel all weak-kneed and trembly, and I forget there is anybody else in the world. When he kissed me the sky exploded like fireworks on the Fourth of July. I've never felt like this before. It's wonderful but frightening at the same time."

Biting her lip, Laura gazed across the water. She watched a snowy-white egret drying its wings atop a towering cypress tree bearded with Spanish moss. "The night I first met you at my uncle's party, I could have sworn it was Davey you loved. The two of you looked so beautiful together; so perfectly matched."

Susan's laughter rippled like the river's surface stirred by a gentle breeze. "And when you saw us kissing in the alcove you naturally assumed we were lovers."

"Well, what was I supposed to think?" There was a note of defiance in Laura's question as well as some other emotion she'd prefer not to put a name to. She knew now that Susan didn't play fast and loose with her affections, yet she had seen the pair locked in a heated embrace.

"Anyone who witnessed our passionate exchange was suppose to think exactly what you did," replied Susan giving her friend an apologetic smile, "only the charade was for Brad's benefit, not yours."

A tumble of confused thoughts assailed Laura.

Correctly interpreting her friend's bewildered expression, Susan hurried to explain. "Davey and I were discussing a private matter of vital importance; one I am, unfortunately, not at liberty to share. When I saw Brad headed our way, I decided it would be easier to explain our presence in the dark nook by pretending we were canoodling."

Arching a perfectly formed brow, Laura remarked caustically, "I would hardly call it pretending."

"Oh, Laura! Davey and I had only met that very night," she exclaimed earnestly. "There has never been anything between us except friendship. It's Wade Callahan I love. I'll admit he isn't as handsome as Davey and there are things in his past that he prefers to keep to himself, but he needs me and I need him. Nothing else matters."

Laura experienced a stab of envy along with an inexplicable feeling of relief. "If you saw the hovel he lives in you might change your mind. You can't just turn your back on all of this," she reasoned indicating the acres of fertile fields.

There was more than a hint of regret in Susan's reply. "Your worry is a bit premature. Wade hasn't mentioned marriage . . . yet. But if he does I will say yes without a moment's pause. Don't you see? Material things mean nothing in comparison to the happiness two people share when they love each other."

Laura remembered her conversation with Brad when she told him she would settle for nothing less than love. Apparently Susan had found the very thing Laura was searching for. How could she fault her friend for following where her heart bid her to go? Impulsively she leaned over and gave the smaller girl a hug.

"What a pair we are," she chuckled. "You want a man who won't propose and I get a proposal from a man I don't want."

Surprised Susan asked, "What proposal?"

Thoughtfully, Laura told her all that had transpired after she and Brad left Pine View the previous evening. "It was very strange. He didn't say he loved me. He didn't even try to kiss me. Now that I think back, it was more like suggesting a business merger."

"Thank God you said no. Laura, I wish you would believe me. Brad Kincaid is a vicious man who enjoys hurting people. In some ways I think he's worse than Bart Harmon. At least that scar-faced gunman can be controlled to some extent by those who pay his salary. I hope your uncle told Harmon off good before he let him go."

"I know how you feel about Brad, but I've seen no evidence of the abuse you speak of. It wouldn't be fair for me to judge him by what someone else thinks. And I'm afraid Harmon won't be leaving for a while." When she repeated what her uncle had said about needing the extra men, Susan responded just as Laura expected she would. "Are you telling me that vile creature will be staying after what he tried to do to you?"

Laura nodded unhappily.

"This isolation must have sent Fowler over the edge. Laura, why don't you move to Pine View with us where you will be safe from both Brad and Bart Harmon?"

"You know I can't do that. I'd feel like a deserter. Uncle Fowler promised to keep Harmon away from me and he would be terribly hurt if I demonstrated my faith in him by taking refuge with you and your father. He has so much on his mind right now I simply can't add to his burdens. Two nights ago he lost another slave. He said if something isn't done there might not be enough hands left to pick the cotton crop this fall."

But Susan was no longer listening. Her eyes were focused on the hollow tree some distance away—the tree where she had found no messages for over two weeks.

Wade and Davey were seated at the table discussing the accident and Laura's engagement to Brad Kincaid when a sharp rap sounded on the door.

"Wade Callahan! You open up right now!"

At the sound of Susan's voice Wade paled. Something terrible must have happened to bring her all the way out to the farm.

But it was Davey who rushed to open the panel. "Is Laura all right?" he asked feeling his stomach tighten in dread.

Brushing passed him without so much as a glance, Susan replied, "She was fine when I left her." Like a locomotive with a full head of steam she advanced on Wade, her eyes flashing azure fire. Windblown blond curls framed a face damp with perspiration and rosey-red from the heat of her ire.

Hammering her small fists against his chest she proceeded to berate him, her voice rising steadily. "You snake in the grass! You wolf in sheep's clothing! You . . . you . . . BRUTUS!"

Before Davey could stop him the huge black dog bounded through the door and lunged right at the unknown visitor who had shouted his name, throwing her unceremoniously into his master's outspread arms.

"Down boy!" At Davey's command, a slavering Brutus flopped down at Susan's feet, his tail beating a staccato rhythm against the wooden floorboards.

Taking advantage of the opportunity presented him, Wade tightened his hold on the small body wrapped in his embrace. Susan tried to pull away but she was no match for his superior strength. It was Davey who put an end to the skirmish by suggesting she settle down and tell them what had her so riled.

Rounding on him Susan shrieked. "Another of the Dunstan slaves escaped the night before last!"

"And that upsets you?" asked Wade, knowing full well that was not the reason for her tirade.

Susan whirled back to face the man now holding her at arm's length. "Of course not, you dunderhead! And I'm not upset! I'm furious! There was no message left in the tree. The one who got away did it without my help!"

Davey and Wade exchanged satisfied looks.

"Someone else must have supplied the needed food and clothing," Davey commented with a smile, adding fuel to Susan's already fired-up temper by stating the obvious.

"I'm not stupid! I know someone else furnished the supplies. What I don't know is why!"

"And you think I had something to do with it?" It was Wade who asked the question and though he seemed aggrieved that she would suspect him of duplicity, Susan was not fooled by his pretended innocence.

"You and Davey are the only ones who know about my part in the movement and you've made no secret of your disapproval. I don't know how you did it but you've somehow managed to undermine my efforts to aid in a cause I hold most dear."

Frowning Davey reminded, "We're not the only ones who know about you, Susan. You're forgetting the person leaving the notes in the tree. Or do you think one of us is your mysterious contact?"

The idea made Susan laugh aloud. "You two? Not likely!"

Neither man was flattered by the scorn in her tone.

"What does that mean?" asked an offended Wade.

"It means both of you have made your feelings perfectly clear. You may be opposed to slavery but you prefer to let others take the risks when it comes to saving the oppressed."

"Now hold on. We're no cowards."

Before Wade could say more, Davey interjected, "There are many ways to fight injustice, Susan."

"Yes," she replied heatedly, "And we each must do as our conscience dictates which is precisely my point. I've found a way to aid the cause. Now suddenly my help isn't needed."

She began pacing the cluttered room, stepping over Brutus, moving around a pair of boots which had been left in the middle of the floor where Wade had taken them off. "The *Specter* has relied on me and I've never let him down. It doesn't make sense for him to change a system that has worked so well."

She stopped on the other side of the table to give Wade a studied look. He was hardly an impressive figure in his faded clothes and his stockinged feet. *And those gloves,* she sighed. *Doesn't he ever give his hands a chance to breathe?* Though she cared deeply about Wade Callahan she couldn't see him influencing the leader of the abolitionists. With an apologetic laugh she said as much. "I guess I was wrong. I doubt the *Specter* would change his method of operation just because you asked him to."

Having already been made to feel a coward in her eyes, Wade did not take her apology with good grace. "You talk as if this *Specter* is some sort of God!" he said irascibly.

"I suppose to the negroes he comes pretty close. They rock their children to sleep at night singing ballads about the one who comes to free them from their bondage."

Wade threw up his hands in frustration. "He's a mortal man made of flesh and blood just like the rest of us."

Eying him suspiciously, Susan remarked, "If it weren't so farfetched I would think you know who he is."

"Susan"—she had almost forgotten Davey was in the room until he said her name—"we've talked about this before. Regardless of what the negroes believe, you know the one called *Specter* is no more Divine than I am. I'll say it again. What he's doing is illegal. If he's caught he will be hanged as a thief and his supporters will hang right along with him."

He spoke with a calm that made his dire prediction all the more chilling, but Susan stubbornly argued against his logic.

"And because there is a degree of risk involved you think I should turn my back on those who need me?"

Wade came to where she stood, placing his arm about her waist. "A little while ago you described the cause as being *most dear* to you. Well, you have become *most dear* to me and I will do anything within my power to protect you from danger."

His words wrapped around her like a cloak, enveloping her with warmth and tender caring. He had all but admitted he was responsible for removing her as a link in the chain formed by the freedom fighters but Susan could not remain angry in light of his confessed feelings for her. She still didn't know how he had done it but she now knew why and that was enough. Their eyes locked and held, then Wade brushed a soft kiss across her slightly parted lips.

Only when Davey cleared his throat did they remember his presence, but even then they remained with their arms entwined. The looks of their faces said more than words ever could. Davey knew it would be pointless to remind them of the obstacles that lay ahead so he wisely remained silent. Perhaps their love would be strong enough to survive the truth that was bound to come out soon.

For the first time since her arrival, Susan took time to survey her surroundings. "Laura was right," she moaned, shaking her head. "This place is a mess."

The mention of Laura gave Davey a start. She had been so much on his mind. Now hearing her name spoken aloud was almost like having her walk into the room. He could feel her presence, smell the clean, light scent that followed her, see those jewel-like eyes holding him captive beneath their steady gaze. Suddenly he knew he had to make certain for himself that she was all right after her close call yesterday. He needed to see her for strictly professional reasons, of course. After all, he was a doctor. It couldn't be anything else. No doubt she would scoff at his concern. She probably didn't even believe he was a real doctor. A tribal medicine man but not a bona fide, licensed-to-practice doctor.

He'd be better off forgetting her. He should go

rabbit hunting with Brutus instead. At least he'd have something to show for his efforts. Damn! Why did she have to engage herself to that slimy son-of-a-bitch Kincaid? She ought to get her tail back to Boston where she belonged. Find some mealy-mouthed milksop to marry. A man who would put up with her sharp tongue and haughty ways.

Searching her out was just asking for trouble and Davey knew better than to go looking for what seemed to come his way uninvited. Yes, sirree. The best thing to do would be to go find a couple of nice plump rabbits he and Wade could share for supper.

Having made up his mind, he said to Susan who was already busy picking up discarded articles of clothing and folding them in neat piles, "If you don't think your father would mind, I'd like to ride over to Pine View and make sure Laura is all right. As a doctor I feel responsible," he added to make sure Susan didn't get the wrong idea.

Bustling about like a spinning top, Susan called over her shoulder, "Brad came and got Laura last night, but I saw her this morning and she assured me she was fine."

So, Davey thought more disappointed than he would admit even to himself, *she couldn't wait to be back with her lover. Good. It would save a long ride in the hot sun.*

By now Susan had found an old broom and was making the dust fly. Brutus whined, covering his face with his huge paws while Wade tried to wrench the broom from her hands. He was rewarded with a playful swat to his backside.

"You're going to be as dirty as a chimney sweep if you keep that up," Wade warned with a chuckle, wiping a smudge from Susan's cheek.

"A little dirt never hurt anybody," she replied saucily, "but you don't have to live in it night and day."

Davey found their cheerful banter depressing and turned to leave. He'd go for a ride, he decided. Trail dust couldn't be any worse than the dust being raised inside the farmhouse. Susan's voice stopped him in his tracks.

"Laura said she was fine but she looked a bit peaked to me. Maybe she's just upset because that no good rat, Bart Harmon, is still around. When I left her she was down at our boathouse just sitting there on the dock watching the river flow by."

Without a backward glance Davey stepped out into the sunlight, closing the door behind him, not seeing Susan's smug smile or hearing Wade's sagacious snicker.

Laura knew she should return to River Ridge. Her uncle would be wondering where she had gone. He probably wouldn't understand or approve of her continued friendship with Susan but never having had a close companion her own age, Laura was determined to do everything she could to preserve the affinity between the neighboring planter's daughter and herself. She liked Susan's father, too, but she questioned whether he might be just a bit dotty in thinking there was a morale problem among the Dunstan slaves. True they were a silent group, except for Delilah who never stopped talking, but perhaps the others were simply taciturn by nature.

The sun shone down from above, sprinkling the river with diamonds, but dark clouds hovered in the distance promising an afternoon thundershower. At least the rain would bring temporary relief from the heat. Watching the cattails swaying with the current, Laura felt her eyelids grow heavy. After a poor night's sleep the hypnotic effect of the moving water was making her drowsy.

Strange the way Susan had rushed off. One minute they had been talking about the latest problem to plague River Ridge; the next minute she had mounted her horse and dashed away saying there was an urgent matter she had to take care of. Laura had decided to wait, but an hour had passed and she was beginning to worry. Suppose an accident had befallen her friend? She would stay a few more minutes but if Susan did not return soon she would have to search out Henry and let him know his daughter was missing.

A cooling breeze blew across the water. Laura yawned, then closed her eyes, enjoying the whisper of wind that teased the loose strands of hair around her face. The lapping waves lulled her, soothing away her troubled thoughts and before long she curled up on the shaded bench and dozed off to sleep.

*　*　*

As he made his way along the path leading to the boathouse, Davey kept a watchful eye on the ominous black clouds blotting out the afternoon sun. He heard a rumble of thunder just as a stiff gust of wind nearly sent his hat flying. He told himself he should turn back. Laura would not be at the boathouse with a storm approaching. Still he kept going.

By the time he reached Pine View it had grown as dark as night. The fields were deserted, the negroes having taken shelter in the quarters. A streak of lightning lit the sky followed closely by a loud clap of thunder indicating the storm was directly overhead. It was in that brief moment of illumination he saw her stretched out on the bench beside the boathouse apparently asleep. As if on signal the clouds opened up, dumping their heavy burdens in great gray sheets blanketing the dockside with blinding torrents of rain.

Chapter 13

They ran through the forest hand in hand, laughing at the small woodland animals who scurried to get out of their way. He paused to pluck a fragrant blossom growing wild beside the path. When they reached a tiny stream they fell breathless upon the thick carpet of grass and he twined the flower into her hair. His fingers traced the outline of her cheek, then continued down the curve of her neck filling her with excitement and anticipation. Velvet brown eyes smoldered with passion as his lips found hers. His hands were gentle but then of course they would be for he was a doctor trained to comfort those in need. And her need was most urgent. Within her abided a hunger only he could feed, a thirst only he could quench. He was her sustenance, provider of those basic essentials necessary to preserve life.

His hand slipped beneath her breast, cupping the soft flesh. She arched her back, pressing against his palm until she felt her nipple grow taut, but it wasn't enough to satisfy her body's fevered demands. There had to be something more he could do to put out the fire he had ignited with his touch. If only she knew what it was.

The heat continued to build spreading in all directions. Writhing in agony, tormented by the flames threatening to consume her, she implored his help, certain he would know how to extinguish the blaze. He murmured love words in her ear, his voice husky with emotion. Slowly his hand moved, gliding lightly across her ribs, skimming over her flat stomach, coming to rest just above that forbidden place at the juncture of her thighs. Then the world exploded around her.

Wrested from the dream, Laura found herself plunged into the midst of a nightmare more terrifying by far. No sooner did she open her eyes to the howling wind than she was pelted with stinging drops of rain pouring down from the sky overhead. At first she thought she must still be asleep, but there was nothing imaginary about the barrage of cold water soaking her person. She sat up and shook her head. What was she doing out in the storm-swept night alone and away from all that was familiar? When the next jagged bolt of lightning forked across the firmament, she saw the turbulent river topped with foam-crested waves and her memory came rushing back. She recalled lying down on the bench beside the boathouse to wait for Susan, remembered closing her eyes against the brilliance of the sun, and finding herself transported to a fantasy land of erotic dreams. The summons back to the present had come abruptly and with an excessive amount of noise.

Laura knew she should seek shelter but numb with fear and trembling from the chilly deluge, her stiff limbs refused to obey her brain's commands. A scream tore from her throat as a deafening thunderclap boomed overhead, vibrating the wooden planks under her feet. At the same moment she was whisked up into two powerful arms and clasped against a rock-solid chest.

The man holding her fumbled with the knob as he fought the wind, then ducked beneath the low beam above the entry. The door slammed shut behind them. It was even darker inside the boathouse. Laura could barely identify the shape of the sleek sailing craft belonging to Henry Ashe. Though securely tied, the boat rocked from side to side bumping the narrow walkway running along the wall. Gusty currents of air blew under the large double doors facing the river, but at least the roof shielded them from the driving rain.

"Dammit, Laura! Don't you have enough sense to get in out of the rain? First I find you in the river; now I come across you sitting like a statue in the middle of a gale!"

He let her go but continued to berate her. "Tomorrow I expect to hear you've drowned in your bathtub or fallen into the well!"

Recognizing his voice, Laura sagged with relief. His arms were all that kept her from landing in a heap at his feet. "How did you find me?" she asked, trying to control the tremors that left her knees threatening to buckle. Her teeth chattered together making it difficult to understand what she was saying above a resounding crash of thunder.

"Why do you think I was looking for you?" He spoke close to her ear in order to be heard over the din. His warm breath and husky voice reminded her of the man in her dream. She wanted to close her eyes and return to the grassy bank beside the stream where the sun was shining and the world was at peace, far away from this place being ripped to shreds by nature's fury.

Davey shook her, not roughly but with enough force to keep her alert. He was waiting for an answer. She had none to give. There was no way she could explain to him what existed only in her fantasies.

Laura experienced a moment of panic when he steadied her next to the wall, then disappeared into the shadows. A hand touched her giving her a start but it was only Davey feeling his way back to her side. Soon she was wrapped in a coarse woolen blanket and together they huddled on the narrow ledge, sharing the cover's warmth, listening to the roar of the wind and rain battering their lightless refuge. She rested her head on his broad shoulder and for a time neither felt inclined to talk.

Heat from the blanket added to the cozy comfort of Davey's nearness again stirred Laura's memory of the strange dream. If not for the absence of light the man who had come to her rescue for the second time in as many days might have questioned the crimson blush which stained her cheeks. Instead he allowed his own imagination to take wing on a rare flight of fancy.

When he'd seen her, Laura had resembled a bedraggled Sleeping Beauty just rising with the wind whipping her auburn curls, the lightning revealing amber eyes still glazed from her slumber. But in this fairy tale it was the ferocity of the storm that had awakened her, not a lover's tender kiss. He had been angered by her foolish disregard for danger though he had found it impossible to sustain his vexation. Her helplessness brought his protective instincts to the fore and once he had her in his arms he was loath to let her go. She felt so fragile and smelled so good like a delicate flower whose fragrance is enhanced by a summer shower.

It seemed fitting that she should be here beside him with her head resting on his shoulder. She was right in guessing he had come looking for her. She had needed him; once more he had been there for her as if Fate had played a part in bringing them together. But Davey was a practical man with little faith in preordination and it didn't take him long to realize the absurdity of what he was thinking. Laura Dunstan was promised to another. Brad Kincaid should be the one watching over her, seeing that she stayed out of trouble. It should be Kincaid sitting here in the dark, soaked to the skin. But despite his arguments, Davey's arm tightened about Laura's waist, snuggling her closer.

The boathouse was growing increasingly lighter. He could still hear the rumble of thunder but now it came from farther away, and though rain drummed steadily down upon the roof it was no longer accompanied by the howling wind.

"I believe the storm is over."

Laura wondered at hearing his softly spoken words. She had fallen asleep and dreamed of one who could create a tempest within her more disturbing than anything nature could unleash. She had opened her eyes to find herself in the arms of a man who bore a striking resemblance to the one she had envisioned. Yet she and Davey Logan despised each other. He was her uncle's enemy and therefore hers as well. Was the storm really over or was it just about to begin?

When they emerged, Laura, expecting it to be the middle of the night, was surprised to see late afternoon sunshine filtering through the clouds casting a feeble light on the rain-washed landscape. Davey insisted on accompanying her back to River Ridge which proved fortuitous since her horse was nowhere in sight. Unlike the well-disciplined stallion who came at a run in answer to his master's shrill whistle, the gentle mare had apparently bolted, frightened by the thunder.

In the light of day the comraderie they had shared during the storm disappeared, leaving Laura feeling shy and self-conscious. Davey mounted, then reached down to lift her up in front of him. Unnerved by his close proximity which had comforted her only moments ago, she tried to lean forward putting space between her body and his. But as soon as Davey set the horse in motion, she fell back into arms that locked about her without hesitation.

Striving to ease her tension through conversation, Laura remarked petulantly, "I can't imagine where Susan could be. I was waiting for her when I fell asleep."

"She had an important matter to discuss with Wade so I came instead."

Laura pivoted her head to see his face, and his lips accidentally brushed her cheek. She jumped as if she had been burned, nearly unseating herself. "Then you did come seeking me."

Davey could hardly deny what he had already admitted but he wanted to make sure she didn't mistake his intentions. "You nearly drowned yesterday. I'm a doctor, Laura. I needed to satisfy myself that you were all right."

Disappointment showed in her topaz eyes causing Davey to wish he had said something a little less professional. "I'm not your patient, Mr. Logan. There is no reason for you to concern yourself with me."

She was acting uppity again, showing the side of her personality Davey didn't like. Knowing what she said was true, he snapped back defensively, "And if I hadn't come along just as the storm broke what would you have done? Sat there until a gust of wind blew you away?"

"I was half asleep when you arrived. Given a chance to collect my wits I would have managed quite well, thank you very much!"

"Oh yeah? What if lightning had struck before your wits were collected?"

"I'm not going to answer any more of your 'what

ifs'!" she shouted defiantly. "What I do is none of your business!"

They rode in stony silence until they reached the drive leading to the plantation house. When Davey started to pull the rein left, Laura put her hand on top of his. "I can walk the rest of the way. One of the guards is liable to shoot you, thinking you are the one who has been helping Uncle Fowler's slaves escape."

Davey brought the animal to a halt. "I'm curious, Laura. Why do you suppose your uncle's slaves are so discontented? It seems to be a problem unique to River Ridge plantation."

Annoyed by a question for which she had no answer, Laura snapped, "I have never given it any thought."

"Well think about it now. What if there is a good reason for someone to aid the slaves in their flight?"

"Blast you, Davey Logan! There you go again with those 'what ifs'! The slaves belong to my uncle. No matter his purpose, the one responsible for their disappearance is a thief!"

Infuriated by her stubborn refusal to admit there was a difference between what she termed thievery and an act of human kindness, Davey lashed out angrily. "Would you still condemn him if you knew those he chose to help had been brutally beaten or raped and defiled?"

"Stop it!" she cried out in anguish. "My uncle wouldn't allow such a thing! You are lying to turn me against him but it won't work! Now let me go or I swear I will scream for the guards!"

Davey released her, not because he was concerned with her threat but because if he didn't he was likely to throttle her. As much as he abhorred violence he felt a barely restrainable urge to shake some sense into this woman who could not see beyond Fowler Dunstan's deceptive facade.

Laura leaped to the ground, then glared up at the man who wreaked havoc on her emotions. "Leave me alone, Davey. I don't want or need you as my protector. Just leave me alone!"

Spinning around she began to run, her long auburn hair streaming behind her. Soon she was swallowed up by the gray mist left in the aftermath of the storm.

Once safely distanced from Davey's ugly innuendos, Laura slowed her pace. He had no right to say such dreadful things. He was trying to stir up trouble between her and her family. Apparently it wasn't enough that friends and neighbors had turned their backs on the Dunstans. Now it seemed there was a scheme afoot to plant seeds of distrust among the family members themselves.

She finally had everything she'd always longed for—the financial means to do as she pleased and a family to supply the love her father had been unwilling to give. Stopping to gaze up at the imposing manor house she vowed to protect her hard-won freedom and the generous uncle who had unselfishly welcomed her into his home. She'd be damned if one interfering half-breed was going to spoil things for her.

She made it to her room without being seen but Delilah was waiting for her just inside the door.

"Lord have mercy, Miss Laura! What has yo' done dis time? Yo' looks like a drown kitten! Did yo' fall in dat ole river agin?"

The maid's round eyes threatened to pop from their sockets as she took in her mistress's disheveled appearance. Red-brown hair usually piled neatly atop Laura's head hung in damp ringlets down her back and wet petticoats gone limp left several inches of wrinkled skirt dragging the floor.

Not waiting for an answer, Delilah ducked into the dressing room, returning with an armload of towels. She helped Laura out of her clothes, then set about drying her hair.

Laura watched the coffee-colored woman in the mirror. Though not much older than Laura, herself, Delilah clucked over her charge like a mother hen with only one chick. She could scold, comfort, laugh, or cry depending on the circumstances, and she was always there when Laura needed her. They had spent long hours talking together. Whenever Laura wanted a sympathetic ear she turned to Delilah, pouring out her heart to her willing listener.

She had told her about Franklin, her coldly aloof father who put his own pleasures ahead of his only child. With more insight than Laura would have imagined possible, Delilah had asked why Franklin left his fortune to a daughter he cared nothing about, suggesting he may have loved her but not known how to express his feelings. True or not, it was a comforting thought, one which Laura had never considered.

Laura had been angry and hurt when she described her Boston suitors, admitting her suspicion that they were only after her money, but Delilah made her see humor in the none-too-subtle approaches they used to try and win her over.

Yes, they had spent a great deal of time laughing and chatting together but only now did Laura realize every conversation had revolved around her— her life, her problems, her hopes for the future. How selfish she had been, she acknowledged with no little regret. Never once had she asked about Delilah's family. She didn't even know if she had one. She'd never inquired as to what the other woman did beyond these four walls, whether she had a beau, or how she felt on any given day.

"Well?" The object of her thoughts paused with the brush in her hand. "Is yo' gwonna tell me how yo' gots so wet or is yo' gwonna leave me guessin'?"

Laughingly Laura replied, "I didn't fall in the river. This time I fell asleep waiting for Susan at the Pine View landing. I was awakened by the storm and got drenched before I could take shelter in the boathouse."

"Wasn't yo' scared to go in dat dark place all alone?"

"It was preferable to remaining outdoors. Besides I wasn't alone. Just as I woke up Mr. Logan came by. We waited out the storm together."

Delilah didn't miss the rosey blush that tinged Laura's cheeks at the mention of Davey's name.

"Dat Dr. Logan, he's one fine-lookin' man. Reckon I wouldn't mind bein' in the dark iff'n he was with me."

Laura puckered her brow. "How did you know Davey—I mean, Mr. Logan—is a doctor?"

"Why everybody round here knows dat."

"I didn't until a few days ago."

Delilah resumed her brushing. "Mebbe dat's 'cause he only doctors poor folk."

There was a certain smugness in the maid's tone. She sounded as if she thought the affluent were missing out on something special.

"I understand he lives on the other side of the state. Surely his practice doesn't extend this far." Laura chided herself for encouraging gossip, but she couldn't resist the urge to learn more about a man of medicine who shunned the rich while offering his services to those less fortunate.

"Don't know nuthin' 'bout no practice. I jest know he goes where he's needed."

That seemed to be explanation enough for Delilah but Laura was left more puzzled than when their discourse began. Of one thing she was certain. It was time to change the subject. Just because she couldn't get Davey Logan off her mind was no reason to bring his name into every conversation. She decided the best way to forget him was by concentrating on someone else for a change. She would start with Delilah and make amends for having thought only of herself since her arrival at River Ridge.

"Delilah? You've never mentioned your family,"

she remarked casually, not wanting to appear nosy or prying. "Do your parents work here at the plantation?"

"Oh, no ma'am. Don't rightly know where dey's at. Mistah Dunstan, he bought me when I was jest a little babe."

Laura knew slaves were the property of their owners but the idea of children being separated from their parents had never occurred to her. It was one thing to ignore a child as Franklin had done but quite another to have one's own flesh and blood sold for profit.

"But how did you manage growing up with no one to care for you?"

"I was given to Sulee. She took care of me and taught me everthin' I needed to know 'bout servin' de mastah and Miz Hester."

Sulee was the Dunstan's cook, a huge dour-faced old woman with skin as black as ebony. Laura had only seen her once or twice for Sulee generally stayed in the kitchen which was separated from the main house by a covered walkway.

"Was Sulee good to you?"

Delilah looked blank. "She taught me what I needed to know," she repeated.

"Did she treat you with kindness?" Laura hoped to hear that the woman responsible for Delilah had been a worthy substitute for the girl's own mother.

"I reckon she did," Delilah replied hesitantly. "Iff'n I was good she only whupped me once a week. Sulee sez all chillen needs a good whuppin' least once a week. Yes'm. Ever' Sataday regler as clockwork I'd pull down my drawers and bend 'cross Sulee's knees to get my whuppin'."

Laura felt her stomach revolt. Imagining the corpulent cook with her huge fleshy arms metting out punishment to a defenseless child who had been orphaned because of someone else's greed made her want to lash out against a society who would sanction such brutality. *Blast! She was beginning to sound like Davey Logan.* Perhaps this selflessness wasn't a good idea after all. Delving into the lives of others could be most unsettling.

Chapter 14

"They tried to kill you, Papa! If you don't put an end to this exclusion they're bound to try again and next time Wade and Davey may not be around to run them off!"

"I'm afraid I'll just have to take that chance, Susan, for I don't intend to back down."

Though still pale and shaken, having narrowly escaped being ambushed by a gang of gunmen, Henry was adamant in his determination to continue what up until now had been a war of wills with his nearest neighbor. Only one person in the room had any doubt as to who was responsible for the attack, and even Laura had to admit the finger of guilt seemed to point toward her uncle. It was unlikely anyone else would have reason to want to harm the gentle-mannered old gentleman.

After her disturbing conversation with Delilah last evening, Laura had come to Pine View out of curiosity to find out whether it was common practice to separate slave children from their parents or

198

if the young maid's unfortunate circumstance was unique. When Susan told her many of the slaveholders sold or bartered children with no compunction, she was saddened in one sense, relieved in another. There was some small comfort in discovering her uncle was not the only one seeking to make a profit by heartlessly tearing families apart. Yet in no way could she condone his callous behavior.

Before she'd had time to think further on the matter, Davey and Wade had entered assisting Susan's father who looked on the verge of collapse. Laura sat listening in silent dread as they described hearing shots, then seeing Henry racing through the cane field just ahead of half a dozen armed riders.

"The cowards quickly veered off in the opposite direction when we returned their fire," Wade informed the two women. "We didn't get a good look at them but I'll bet my life it was Bart Harmon and his gang."

"It isn't your life which is at stake!" wailed Susan who knew their suspicions meant nothing without proof.

Wade moved to Susan's side and put his arm around her waist. "Look, honey. If it will ease your mind I'll stick close for a few days. I can bed down in the barn."

If Henry was surprised by Wade's possessive manner toward his daughter he certainly didn't show it. On the contrary, when Susan hesitated he lost no time in accepting the offer for her. "We'd be pleased to have your company, young man, but you'll not be sleeping in the barn. We've plenty of room here in the house. That way if we need you, you'll be close at hand. You're welcome to stay, too, Davey," he added with all the enthusiasm of someone issuing invitations to an impromptu party.

Laura could hardly believe her ears. Didn't Susan's father realize he was paving the way to his daughter's ruination by extending his hospitality to a man like Wade Callahan? Nodding his assent Wade shifted his gaze to Susan who smiled gratefully. Neither saw Henry's own satisfied grin, but Laura did and she wondered just what the old planter was up to.

Meanwhile Davey thanked Henry for including him but said he'd best remain at the farm. "I've been tending one of Wade's neighbors who nearly cut his leg off with an ax," he explained. "And if any other folks have a need that's where they will expect to find me."

"How is Johnny's father?" The question came from Laura unbidden, astonishing her as much as it did Davey.

Giving her a speculative look, he replied, "He's on the mend. Now it's just a matter of keeping the dressing clean so infection doesn't set in."

How civilized their conversation sounded, yet both Laura and Davey were remembering their bitter parting less than twenty-four hours ago when he had accused her uncle of committing vile deeds and she in turn had shrieked at him demanding he stay out of her life. For a timeless moment they stared at one another, each aware of the other's thoughts, both feeling a need to bridge the gap that stretched between them.

"Do you play chess, young man?" Henry's query as he clapped Wade on the shoulder broke the spell they had fallen under.

Laura blinked her eyes, then swallowed, finding her throat suddenly dry. "I really must be going." Her voice quivered ever so slightly as she stood up and gave Henry a quick peck on his bewhiskered cheek. "I'm glad you weren't hurt, Mr. Ashe," she whispered sincerely. "Please be careful."

If anyone found it odd to hear the niece of the man suspected of trying to harm Susan's father expressing concern for Henry's welfare, he kept his opinion to himself.

By the time Laura reached the open portal Davey was by her side. He touched her arm bringing her to a stop, then turned to bid goodbye to the other three. "Since we're going the same way I'll see Laura home," he said, not asking her consent before he ushered her through the doorway.

Laura felt a thrill of excitement at the prospect of having Davey accompany her. She had told him she didn't need his protection but the possibility, however slight, of running into Bart Harmon made her glad to have him with her. From his tall, muscular body emanated an aura of power which would cause other men to think twice before issuing a challenge. but it wasn't his physical prowess that made Laura's stomach do those odd little flip-flops nor was it his darkly handsome features. In all honesty she could think of nothing which would account for her unusual reaction to the half-breed doctor whom she didn't even like. Neither could she deny the charge of energy that shot through her when his hand clamped around her arm as he steered her out of the room.

Without speaking, Davey assisted her onto her horse, then mounted his ebony stallion. How well-suited they seemed, the raven-haired rider and the sleek black animal beneath him. Laura wondered what Davey would do now that he had her alone. Surely he must have had a reason for offering to escort her back to River Ridge but he seemed in no hurry to let her in on it. Before long his brooding silence began to grate on her nerves.

Despite the brilliant orange ball of sun shining down from overhead she felt a chill ripple through her which had nothing to do with the weather. She didn't know what she had expected but it was definitely not this prolonged quiet. Glancing over at her uncommunicative companion whose rigid profile could have been carved from stone, she decided he was waiting for her to make the first move.

Obligingly she ventured, "I haven't thanked you properly for pulling me from the river or for coming to my rescue again yesterday. I'd like to do so now and while I am at it I want to apologize for behaving like a shrew last evening."

Heavily hooded eyes looked in her direction, but Davey's face remained granite-hard revealing nothing of his inner thoughts. When seconds ticked by and he made no response Laura squirmed in the saddle. *So much for that. She should have known he wouldn't act the gentleman and simply accept her expressions of regret. She had been a fool to hope he might.*

Davey was stirred from his own restless musings by what sounded like clipped words of apology. Certain he had heard wrong, he cast a glance at Laura determined to pay more attention should she speak again. He saw her fidget nervously which seemed odd for a woman who normally came across as being in complete control, a trait he found difficult to master when he was in her company. She was like a bothersome itch. To scratch would only cause further irritation; to keep his hands off was virtually impossible.

"Damn!" He hadn't realized he'd spoken aloud until Laura's head swiveled around and he was confronted by questioning amber eyes.

"I said I was sorry. What now?"

So he hadn't misunderstood. No wonder she appeared ill at ease. Davey doubted apologies came easily or often from the lips of the haughty New Englander, and here he'd been so busy trying to figure out why he had volunteered to see her home he didn't even know what she was sorry for. Well, he wasn't about to admit he had missed such a monumental event. He would just have to bluff and hope she didn't catch on.

Taking a stab in the dark he replied, "You needn't apologize. I'm sure you didn't fall in the river on purpose and being new to the area you couldn't know how fast a storm can move in."

Laura stared at him blankly for a moment before

topaz eyes flared. "Blast it, Davey Logan! You didn't hear a word I said. I was apologizing for losing my temper!" she shouted.

So much for bluffing, thought Davey with chagrin. Reining in beneath the shady branches of a wide-spreading oak tree he turned in the saddle to face the irate woman at his side. "You're right, Laura. I'm afraid my mind was on something else."

Remembering how just hours ago Davey and Wade had interrupted the attack on Henry Ashe, Laura thought she understood his preoccupation. How selfish she was to expect his attention to be focused on her after what had taken place.

Thick chestnut lashes fanned her cheeks as she looked down at the pommel of her saddle. "You must be terribly worried about Susan's father." All trace of resentment was gone from her voice.

Davey wasn't about to try and bluff this time by allowing Laura to believe his abstraction resulted from concern for someone else. "It's true I'm worried about Henry. His stubborness could get him in a lot of trouble, not unlike certain other people I won't name."

He softened the well-directed barb with a smile which set loose those devilishly unpredictable butterflies who had taken up residence in Laura's stomach of late. Blast the man for his ability to chastize in such an irresistibly charming fashion, she grumbled to herself.

"But as it happens Susan's father isn't to blame for my lack of attention," he continued. "I was thinking about you."

Taken by surprise Laura couldn't help commenting, "No wonder your mood seemed so black."

Davey's laughter was full of good humor and soon Laura joined in. The sound brought Davey up short.

"Do you know that's the first time I've heard you laugh? You really should try it more often," he recommended listening to the soft, tinkling strains of musical mirth drifting through the air.

Laura stopped laughing as their eyes met and held. She tried to see beyond the velvety brown irises of the man looking back at her from a mere arm's length away. The horses drew closer together and Laura's knee brushed Davey's thigh. Though jolted by the contact she didn't move away. She couldn't have moved if her life depended on it.

Davey found himself staring into twin pools of liquid gold. Mesmerized by their depth and clarity, his head dipped lower until their lips were just inches apart.

"What were you thinking about me?" Laura whispered. Her warm, sweet breath stroked his face like a gentle caress.

"I was trying to figure out why I insisted on taking you back to River Ridge. Now I know."

His mouth came down to cover hers in a kiss that left Laura reeling in mindless ectasy. She swayed dizzily but was soon righted by two strong arms. Caught up in the magic of the moment her lips parted on a sigh and Davey was quick to take advantage, thrusting his tongue into the narrow opening afforded him. Currents of charged energy rippled through her as she grasped his broad shoulders, clinging to him as a drowning victim would to a lifeline. Swept up in a tidal wave of passion she felt herself rise to the top of the foaming crest only to discover a dark and deadly maelstrom of swirling surf waiting below. Struggling to stay afloat she pushed with all her might against the relentless force that threatened to extract the last breath from her body.

Davey didn't want to believe Laura was fighting him, not after the way she had willingly surrendered to his embrace. But the fists beating against his chest made clear her change of heart. Reluctantly he ceased his tender assault on her mouth without relinquishing his firm hold on her. The look of pure terror in her eyes infuriated him for he assumed her fear stemmed from finding herself in the arms of an Indian. A savage she had called him. Davey was also angered by his own body's response. Damn her for teasing him into losing control. Didn't she realize a man could only be pushed so far before he reached a point where there was no turning back?

He ought to take her right here, right now. Show her how a savage treated a woman. It would be no more than she deserved. Without intending to do so he tightened the grip on her arms.

Laura flinched as she felt his fingers bite into her tender flesh. "Let go! You're hurting me!" she cried, fighting to still her racing heart. *God! What had she done? And why was he looking at her like that?* True she should never have let him kiss her though she wasn't sure what she could have done to prevent it.

But now his dark eyes were blazing, burning into her with a fury that threatened to singe her very soul. It was her place to be angry, not his, she railed as her own temper began to rise.

But she hadn't been angry. She had been frightened out of her wits by the feelings his touch evoked. He had unearthed something inside of her she never knew was there. A gnawing empty void begging to be filled. She hadn't wanted him to stop. It was that annoying little voice within her head which finally brought her to her senses warning that she was in danger of losing all she had managed to gain. Important things like wealth, security, and independence. They were important! What's more, they were all she had.

Davey watched her expression change from one of fright to vexation, then bewilderment. What was she thinking? At least she no longer acted as if she thought he was going to eat her alive. Not a bad idea when it came right down to it but he didn't want to see that look of fear in her eyes again. With nothing to stoke the fires of wrath, Davey felt his rage melting away. Releasing his hold he straightened in the saddle.

"I guess it's my turn to apologize. I don't usually behave like a . . ." Dammit! He had nearly used her favorite misnomer. Then again maybe she wasn't so far from the mark. ". . . an ass," he amended giving her a contrite grin.

Laura's troubled spirits quieted as his smoldering eyes softened to their usual velvety brown hue. She returned his grin with a weak smile. "We always seem to bring out the worst in each other, don't we Davey?"

Yet we keep coming back for more, Davey wanted to say but he held his tongue, for to make such an admission would force him to analyze the peculiar allure which continually drew him to her like a magnet.

Gruffly he barked, "It's time to get you home."

He hadn't meant to sound so churlish but his mind was in an upheaval. Common sense told him he had to stay away from Laura Dunstan. Manly desire argued that if he couldn't have her near him, life would lose its meaning. He wanted to touch her. He wanted to push her away. Never had he been embroiled in such a conflict of emotions.

Disappointment flickered across Laura's face but Davey was too distraught to notice. "I don't need your escort. No harm will come to me in broad daylight."

Davey started to remind her that she had fallen in the river, then been caught by the storm in broad daylight, but he thought better of it. She was giving him the opportunity to bid her adieu here and now. He could sever the invisible cord that had bound him to her since that first night when he had seen her at her uncle's party, the night he had looked into her rare, expressive eyes and felt his heart constrict.

"Have you forgotten there is a band of ruffians riding around the neighborhood in broad daylight taking pot shots at innocent people?" *Oh, hell! Why couldn't he heed his better judgment?*

Laura bristled. "I haven't forgotten but since you

208

suspect my uncle is behind what happened to Susan's father, I see no reason for you to concern yourself about *my* safety."

"I never said your uncle was responsible."

"But you believe he is, don't you?" Laura glared at him defiantly, daring him to lie when she could read the truth in his hesitation.

Before he could form a reply she answered for him. "You're wrong, Davey. You're mean, and spiteful . . . and wrong."

With that she kicked her mare into motion and took off down the road leaving him to choke on her dust. If she had yelled her bitter recriminations he would have found it easier to take but the cold, calm finality of her words shook him to the core. She had chosen sides. She would stand with Fowler Dunstan and Brad Kincaid. How could she do otherwise when one man was her uncle, the other her betrothed? The war against injustice wasn't over but suddenly Davey felt weighed down by defeat.

Clouds scuttled across a narrow sliver of new moon riding high in the midnight sky. The hoot of an owl was answered by the far-off baying of a hound. The protesting creak of tired wheels could be heard long before the dilapidated buckboard rolled into sight, making its way along the rutted road that wound up the hill through the grove of orange trees.

As the rickety conveyance came to a halt, a dark-clad figure emerged from the shadows assisting a black man whose bent shoulders were covered by a blanket. The clouds parted and in the faint moon-light the whites of the negroe's eyes were clearly visible disclosing both the pain caused by the raw wounds across his back and the terror he felt at the prospect of the long journey ahead.

"You're going to be all right now," the taller man assured in an undertone assisting the injured one into the wagon bed. Quickly he spread a layer of hay over the trembling form. "There are friends to guide you every step of the way. They'll take care of you and when you are well they will help you start a new life. Trust me, Josiah. Soon you will be safe."

The escaping slave seemed to draw strength from the man's confidence and comforting words. "I trusts ya, sir."

The one in black gave a nod to the driver and with a groan and a rattle the ancient wagon moved ahead.

"God bless ya, Mistah Spectah." The muted voice was barely audible as the buckboard became one with the night.

Chapter 15

During the next week Laura managed to stay away from Pine View. She missed Susan's cheerful companionship but she didn't want to run the risk of a chance meeting with Davey Logan. It was enough that he occupied her thoughts when she was awake and haunted her dreams through the long hours of the night.

Again Laura was tempted to tell Fowler and Hester that she had decided to leave. The atmosphere at River Ridge was growing more strained with every passing day. The disappearance of another slave had brought on a rare show of temper from her uncle who seemed, for some unknown reason, to blame Brad Kincaid. This morning, closeted behind the closed doors of the library, the raised voices of the two men could be heard echoing through the first floor of the mansion. Laura could not make out their words but there was no doubting the animosity permeating from within. The humid air was fairly charged with hostility.

Unable to stand the tension a moment longer, she headed for the wide, circular staircase intending to seek refuge in her room where she hoped the walls would block out the noise below. But when she reached the second-floor landing she found her aunt pacing the carpeted hallway. The tiny birdlike woman was wringing her hands in agitation. Puffy red-rimmed eyes gave evidence to the fact that she had been crying, and as Laura drew closer she could see fresh moisture glistening on Hester's sunken cheeks.

Laura had never felt completely comfortable in her aunt's company. She had little patience with the older woman's timidity and she blamed Hester for not standing up to Bradley and Angel. Still her heart went out to the frail little lady who was so obviously distressed by the heated argument taking place between her husband and her son.

Hester scurried forward clasping Laura's arm with her thin fingers. "Oh, dear. I do wish they would stop," she moaned pathetically.

Laura managed with some difficulty to pry the clutching fingers loose, then awkwardly placed her arm about her aunt's slender shoulders. "Come, Aunt Hester. Let's go to my room for a nice chat," she urged. "I have been here for weeks and the two of us have yet to talk."

Laura moved in the direction of her bedroom keeping Hester by her side. She would have preferred solitude in which to consider plans for her future, but she could hardly leave the distraught woman out in the hall to fret and worry all alone.

Once they were inside, Laura closed the door. Thankfully the noise from the library failed to penetrate the thick wooden panel. Hester took the chair Laura indicated but immediately began to wring her hands again.

"I do so dislike loud voices. They remind me of my father," Hester explained nervously looking at the shadowed corners of the room. "His voice boomed like a cannon whenever he was angry."

Something in Hester's tone led Laura to suspect the man must have been angry quite often.

"He hated me, you know." Her words were barely audible. She continued to search the room with wild, frightened eyes as if she believed her father's ghost might materialize to chastize her for her remark.

In an effort to calm the elderly woman's fears Laura replied placatingly, "Surely you must be mistaken, Aunt Hester. After all, he was your father."

No sooner were the words out than Laura realized it was a stupid thing to say considering how she had been treated by her own sire.

Hester shook her head, causing her tight gray curls to bounce. "He hated me because I was his only child. He wanted a son. Time and again he told me I was nothing but a useless girl, a burden he would be better off without."

Laura had never considered the possibility before but now she wondered if Franklin had resented her for just such a reason. She brushed the thought aside. It no longer mattered. Whatever had caused his lack of affection toward her, she had won in the end. He may have put himself and his bevy of women ahead of her while he was alive but now she had a fortune as payment for his neglect. At least she had grown up to be self-reliant unlike the mousy little woman cowering before her.

"As soon as I came of age he arranged my marriage to Miles Kincaid," Hester continued still keeping her voice low and secretive. "I never called him Miles, of course. Not until after he died. I always called him Mr. Kincaid. It seemed more fitting since he was even older than my father. He had a plantation not far from Charleston but I wasn't allowed to go into town. He kept me locked in my bedroom most of the time."

"Locked in?" Laura's shocked gasped indicated her astonishment at her aunt's revelation. "Do you mean he kept you prisoner?"

"He was afraid I would run away. Foolish old man. I had nowhere to go," she confided.

"But surely you could have gone to your father."

"He would have thrashed me soundly, then returned me to Mr. Kincaid, and I dread to think what *he* would have done. Though, I dare say, it could not have been much worse than what I had already been forced to endure."

Laura didn't want to hear anymore. She had her own problems to worry about. But she knew of no way to end the conversation without hurting her aunt's feelings and, once started, Hester seemed anxious to share her story.

"He would come into my room at night. Mr. Kincaid was determined to beget an heir—but he was so old. Sometimes he just wasn't able to do what had to be done. Oh, he would become so angry, ranting and raving, screaming that it was my fault. Then he would make me do vile, unnatural things to his body as penance for what he called 'my wickedness.' By some miracle I finally conceived and once Bradley was born life became much more tolerable. I gave Mr. Kincaid what he wanted. After that he only came to me on rare occasions." Recalling the degradations of the past, Hester began to tremble like someone with the ague.

Though Laura had a fair idea of what took place between a husband and wife, she couldn't imagine what the "unnatural things" might entail, but her aunt's reaction was enough to convince her that Miles Kincaid had been a despicable tyrant who had taken an innocent young girl and abused her cruelly. Now she had a better understanding of what had made Hester the way she was and her feelings were wholly sympathetic. Without hesitation she went to the old lady, putting her arms around her and hugging her protectively.

"I'm so sorry."

Wrapped in Laura's embrace, the tremors that shook Hester's diminutive body gradually subsided. When Laura rocked back on her heels her own eyes were clouded but her aunt seemed cheered by her niece's tenderness. She brightened, even managing a quivering smile.

"Now, now, dear. Please forgive an old lady for carrying on so. I don't know what came over me."

"You have nothing for which to apologize," replied Laura. "It's that terrible man you were forced to marry who should be begging forgiveness."

"Ah, well that isn't possible now, is it, dear? Mr. Kincaid has been in his grave for over twenty years."

Not wishing to speak ill of the dead yet unable to think of anything kind to say about Miles Kincaid, Laura chose to make no comment. Instead she asked, "How did you meet Uncle Fowler?"

Hester became more animated when she spoke of her present husband. "Shortly before Mr. Kincaid's death he hired Fowler to oversee the plantation. Fowler was so capable. There was nothing he couldn't do. And when he came to the house, he would always smile at me and take time to give Bradley a few kind words. Despite his wanting a son, Bradley's father never paid him much mind. When Mr. Kincaid passed on I had no one to turn to. My father had died the previous year. I felt so helpless and alone. I don't know what I would have done without Fowler. He just stepped right in and took over."

So her uncle had come to the aid of a damsel in distress. The romantic notion brought a smile to Laura's lips. "Florida must have been quite uncivilized twenty years ago. Why did you leave South Carolina to come here?"

A frown deepened the wrinkles in Hester's forehead. "Such a bunch of nonsense," she complained shaking her head. "I still don't see how they could have thought Fowler had something to do with Mr. Kincaid's death."

Incredulously Laura questioned, "They? Who?"

"The authorities, my dear. Mr. Kincaid was old but he was not a sickly man. The sheriff thought it strange the way he simply went to sleep one night and never woke up. Then when Fowler and I married within a few months . . . well . . . you know how people tend to gossip?"

Yes. Of course that was all there was to it. Vicious talk by people who could not know of her aunt's mistreatment at the hands of the heartless planter, who were not aware of the way her kindly uncle had come to Hester's aid. Laura tried to put down her vague feelings of unease.

". . . So Fowler decided to sell the plantation and begin a new life here."

While Hester chattered on about their early days at River Ridge, Laura wondered how Brad Kincaid felt about the man who not only married his mother but had apparently used money from the sale of his father's property to build a plantation of his own. Resentment on Brad's part would certainly be understandable.

Laura sighed wearily as Hester continued to talk with scarcely a pause for breath. At least her aunt was in a better frame of mind. Too bad that in trying to distract the troubled woman, her own spirits had plummetted to an all-time low. She couldn't shake the premonition of disaster ahead. The oppressive weight of portending danger hovered heavy in the air.

* * *

Bradley Kincaid stormed out of the library nearly colliding with Delilah who was hurrying toward the staircase. The wide-eyed young maid stifled a scream, dropping the crisp vellum envelope she carried as her hand went to her throat.

Rather than apologize Brad clasped the girl's arm in a punishing grip and snarled, "Careless slut! Don't you know enough to stay out of my way unless I send for you?"

Trembling, the maid tried to take a step backward but Brad held her fast, increasing the pressure until his fingernails drew blood.

"I's sorry, Mistah Bradley. I'll 'member next time." Delilah's frightened eyes pleaded for mercy, but there was no softening in the pinched features of her captor.

"Why, Delilah, you know I couldn't possibly allow your impudence to go unpunished." Brad's eyes took on a feral glow. "You will come to the cabin tonight so that I may discipline you in private."

His voice was low and deadly, promising a far more severe penalty should she fail to appear as ordered.

Slowly, resignedly, Delilah nodded her head up and down, choking back the tears that threatened to fall. "Yessah, Mistah Bradley."

Her humble acquiescence served to calm Brad's ire, for now instead of fuming over the harsh recriminations his stepfather had heaped upon him, he could spend the next few hours devising a suitable chastening for the intrusive slave. He took perverse pleasure in giving Delilah time to think about what was to come. It made the lessons he taught her so much more meaningful.

Not until he thrust her aside did Brad remember the envelope which had fallen to the floor. "What have we here?" Leaning down he picked up the missive and withdrew a brief note.

"I's suppose to give it to Miss Laura," Delilah volunteered, wanting to snatch the paper from his hands but knowing to do so would probably cost her her life.

Brad scanned the penned words of Susan Ashe asking Laura to come to Pine View at her earliest convenience concerning a matter of importance. His lips thinned as he tucked the note back inside the envelope and held it out to the anxious maid.

"By all means," he sneered. "See that Miss Laura gets this right away."

As Delilah made to scoot around him, he took her arm once more. "And you will not mention my having seen it first."

"No sah."

Once free Delilah didn't look back. The letter in her hand meant nothing to her. She would deliver it to her mistress, then go to the little room off the kitchen which she shared with Sulee. There she would spend the next few hours praying for the strength to get through the night ahead.

Brad kept his eyes on the girl's well-rounded hips as she climbed the stairs. Yes indeed, he was going to enjoy reminding the bitch of her place. When Delilah reached the landing and disappeared from sight he turned and stalked toward the door to find Bart Harmon. There was someone else who needed to be taught a lesson, only in her case repentence would come too late.

He'd been a fool to ask Susan to write that note. At least she hadn't laughed at him. Laura would certainly get a hoot out of it though if she ever found out. She'd probably think it was almost as funny as the way he had stayed awake night after night worrying about her. The plain truth was he missed the aggravating woman and her uppity ways but it'd be a cold day in Hell before he admitted it to anyone. He could hardly believe it himself.

He should have waited at Pine View instead of riding out to meet her. He was going to feel like a jackass if he got all the way to River Ridge only to have to turn around and go back alone. Most likely she was busy making wedding plans and would ignore Susan's summons. On the other hand she didn't seem particularly excited about her upcoming nuptials. Truth to tell, she didn't act much like a woman in love. In fact, now that he thought about it he couldn't recall Laura ever mentioning her engagement to Brad Kincaid. It was Kincaid who'd said they were to be married. Damned strange she hadn't said a word especially after he had kissed her.

Davey's dark eyes looked inward as the memory of that kiss burned in his mind. Some unseen force locked around his heart, squeezing, then releasing, in an uncertain rhythm that sent blood rushing hot as molten lava through his veins. Her lips had been warm and willing. Yes, willing. Not the response of a woman bent on marrying someone else. Could it be a mistake? Would Kincaid have some reason to lie about his relationship with Laura? Davey wouldn't put it past the lowlife slime if it served his purpose. He should have asked Susan. If Laura and Kincaid were engaged Susan was bound to know about it.

She wasn't going to come and it shouldn't matter whether she was engaged to Kincaid or not. Laura Dunstan came from a different world where wealth and social standing took priority over everything else—especially in the mind of the Boston ice princess. From Susan he had learned about her lonely, loveless childhood. No wonder she thought money could buy her happiness.

Davey's hands tightened on the reins. He longed to shake some sense into her. If only she could see that cold cash was no substitute for the loving warmth of a family. Just because her father had been an unfeeling bastard was no reason for her to shut out the rest of mankind. Too bad she would never have an opportunity to meet the folks at Fort Brooke. His lips tilted up in a grin the way they always did when he thought about those back home. Maybe if he shared some of their adventures with Laura she would come to see how important it was to be surrounded by caring people. She might begin to look upon this land of flowers with its clear lakes and rivers, its shell-strewn beaches and glorious sunshine, as a place to plant her roots.

"Oh sure," a little voice whispered sarcastically. "You could begin by telling her about your stepmother's introduction to the territory when she barely escaped a band of renegade Indians only to be kidnapped and carted off by the infamous pirate, Jose Gaspar. I'm sure she would enjoy hearing that your father was once accused of murder, and by all means don't forget the amusing tale of your cousin's rape by the half-breed Seminole warrior she later married."

"Enough!" Davey conceded, knowing Laura would never understand that these near-tragic events had played a major role in bonding the Logans and Townsends and Hawkins together to form the close-knit clan they had become. No doubt she would look upon them as crude and countrified. Never would he subject those he loved to ridicule simply to make a point. Better to leave his family out of it.

He didn't know much about the relationship between Fowler Dunstan and his wife but from what he'd seen and heard of Brad and Angel he could not picture a happy, harmonious household at River Ridge. He wished Laura could spend more time with Susan and Henry. Now there was a fine example of how things should be between a father and daughter. He had expected the fur to fly last night when Susan and Wade told the crusty old planter they were in love and intended to marry as soon as

222

possible. But to his amazement, Henry Ashe couldn't have been more delighted, encouraging them to hurry up so he could dandle a grandchild on his knee.

Davey's wide brow furrowed. He was glad his original skepticism had proven to be unfounded but the time had come for Wade to tell Susan the truth about his past so there would be no secrets to mar their happiness.

So deep was Davey in thought, he didn't hear the horse's hooves drumming in the distance. The rider was no more than a hundred yards away when he saw her. She wore a habit of forest green blending perfectly with the lush vegetation outlining the road's narrow path. A single feather decorated the jaunty hat of matching material perched atop her auburn curls.

Bringing the stallion to a halt, Davey's heart began to hammer. Giddy and lightheaded he waited, wondering what he would say, what excuse he would give for being here. Any coherent thoughts he might have had deserted him as she closed the distance separating them. She was so beautiful moving as one with the animal. Impossible from so far away, but he could swear he smelled the delicate fragrance of jasmine. Improbable but she appeared to be smiling, her soft, sensuous lips curving upward to let him know without words how glad she was to see him.

He waved a greeting. Laura lifted her arm. A shot rang out setting the birds to flight. Then frozen in horror Davey watched as the green-clad form tilted drunkenly in the saddle, then pitched to the far side, sliding beneath the thundering hooves of the terrified mare.

Chapter 16

As he stared at her crumpled figure, Davey ceased to breathe. The sound of receding hoofbeats grew ever more faint until they disappeared completely. The killer was getting away but it didn't matter right now. Davey would find him later—search him out, then see that he fully appreciated the ancient Indian method of dealing with one's enemies. The man would die slowly, very slowly, and before he drew his last, agonizing breath he would curse his mother for bringing him into this world.

Plans for revenge came to mind instinctively, serving as a defense mechanism to block out the reality of the scene before him. But while his thoughts were focused on the future, his body was propelling him forward. Later he would wonder how he got from his horse to where Laura lay with her lifeblood forming a crimson pool which seeped slowly into the hard-packed earth. He reached out to touch her. With trembling hands he gently turned her onto her back. The unexpected moan his action evoked took him by surprise. A moment later her dark-fringed lashes lifted slowly to reveal pain-glazed topaz eyes.

"It hurts, Davey. It hurts so much."

She wasn't dead. Immediately Davey snapped out of his stupor. His first impulse was to take her in his arms and hug her until he heard her ribs crack. But long years of self-discipline and training as a doctor overrode his initial impetuousness.

"Take it easy, princess. You're going to be all right. I promise." *God, he hoped it was true. It had to be true. There were things that must be settled between them.*

Carefully he lifted her to a sitting position, cradling her with one arm as he removed the blood-soaked jacket. He pulled his hunting knife from its sheath, then slit her blouse, peeling the material from around the gaping wound high on her left shoulder. The rifleman must have been a goodly distance away when the shot was fired for the lead ball had not exited its target but remained lodged somewhere in the flesh just below the collarbone.

Damn! Davey cursed silently, refusing to let the fear gnawing at his gut show in his eyes. Removing his shirt he used the knife to slash the linen into long strips. One he folded into a pad for a compress to stem the flow of blood. With another he bound the thick square into place, winding the material across Laura's breasts and over her shoulder.

Laura had no choice but to submit to his care though the least movement sent sharp needles of pain to every nerve ending, leaving her weak and nauseous. Beads of perspiration popped out on her forehead and upper lip. She longed to give into the gray mist moving cloudlike through her line of vision but that infuriating savage wouldn't allow it. Relentlessly he kept calling her back, forcing her to endure the red-hot agony burning high in her shoulder.

So this was what the Indians did to torture their victims? It was far worse than anything she could have imagined. Why couldn't he let her die in peace? Blast his soul to Hell! She didn't even have the strength to tell him what a blackhearted knave he was.

Laura gritted her teeth against the pain but was helpless to prevent the hiss that escaped through tightly stretched lips. Though she didn't know it, Davey suffered with her, his muscles knotting each time she winced. What's more, he realized as she did not that the worst was yet to come. He was going to have to dig the ball out and soon or she would run the risk of lead poisoning. But he couldn't operate here. He needed the necessary instruments and disinfectant which he had left at the farm. Certain she would resist, he broached the subject in the no-nonsense manner of a trained professional, which wasn't easy when his emotions were threatening to tear him apart.

"The bleeding is stopped temporarily but I'm going to take you to Wade's where I have the equipment I need."

He answered her questioning look truthfully. "The slug has to come out, princess."

Laura's face which had been flushed until now

blanched white as the words penetrated her wretchedness. She shook her head from side to side making a token effort to deny that which she didn't want to accept. Rather than argue, Davey gathered her up in his arms solicitously and carried her to where the big stallion stood munching leaves from the low-hanging branch of an oak tree.

There was no way to mount without causing Laura a good deal of additional distress and by the time Davey was in the saddle holding her protectively crushed to his now-bare chest, she had lapsed into unconsciousness. For her sake he was glad. At least she would be spared the jolting ride down the rutted trail.

Laura awoke in a room not her own yet somehow familiar. A light scent of roses sparked recognition, reminding her of the day she had borrowed the clothes of Wade Callahan's dead wife. She was at the farm and Davey Logan was going to do something terrible to her—something she was helpless to prevent. She could hear him moving about in the next room. What macabre plan did he have in store for her, she wondered as panic threatened to send her into another swoon?

She tried to sit up but barely managed to lift her head before she met defeat racked by throbbing pain so excruciating she cried out her misery. Davey was by her side in an instant. No longer was he able to maintain his dispassionate air. She was hurting and with each laborious breath she took he found it more difficult to draw oxygen into his lungs. With each distortion of her delicate features he felt his facial muscles twist in concert. He wanted to rail against Fate for allowing her to suffer. Most of all he wanted to kill the one responsible for her anguish.

He hated the look of fear he saw in her shimmering amber eyes but he pushed his own feelings aside. She was like a wounded animal relying on her own weakened defenses, trusting no one.

"Easy, princess," he soothed, raising a glass to her lips as he supported her with one strong arm.

She tried to resist but he refused to be dissuaded. Finally she took a sip of the bitter draught, scowling at the acrid taste left in her mouth. At his urging she continued to drink until the tumbler was nearly empty. Almost immediately her body began to numb and her eyelids grew heavy. She welcomed the lassitude which brought relief from the heat of the bonfire burning in her shoulder. Her mind drifted amid the puffy white clouds of oblivion unaware of what was taking place in the temporal world below.

As soon as Laura's eyes closed, Davey returned to the kitchen to fetch what he would need to remove the bullet. He knew the opium would not render her fully unconscious but he had acquired a healthy respect for drugs. Better to administer too little than take a chance on proffering a lethal dose.

When he approached the bed—balancing a bowl of water, his instruments, and a supply of clean bandages—his hands trembled noticeably. But as he bent to examine the wound, Davey Logan, a man with human feelings and frailties, disappeared to be replaced by a different Davey, this one a competent doctor of medicine whose sole purpose was to save lives. He went about his task with grim efficiency, probing for the elusive piece of lead, stemming the flow of blood with a wad of gauze, speaking encouraging words that he knew went unheard.

Just when Davey reached the point where he thought he would have to back out and approach from another angle, metal touched metal. He hesitated only long enough to release a sigh of satisfaction before he eased the pincers around the ball, carefully extracting it from the soft tissue in which it was embedded.

Up until now Laura had remained relatively docile only flinching now and then as he worked. But when the lead shot came free followed by a fresh river of blood, her eyes flew open and her scream rent the air. Huge glistening teardrops streamed down her cheeks as her arms flailed wildly, seeking to punish the one who had brought her such grief. Only by thrusting his own body on top of hers was Davey able to subdue her.

"I hate you, Davey Logan!" she shrieked, finding herself pinioned beneath her tormentor.

Outside the window Brutus howled as dusk turned to night and a silvery crescent moon appeared overhead. Weakened by her ordeal, Laura's aggression was short-lived. Soon her slender form relaxed and her eyelids fluttered closed. Davey rolled to one side, then got to his feet. Turning up the lamp he applied disinfectant, then bandaged the raw, inflamed flesh. Once done he returned to the kitchen where he washed his utensils, then moved out onto the back porch to dump the pink-tinged water. Sitting down on the warped wooden step he leaned his head against the rail, giving in to exhaustion brought on by the events of the past few hours. When a dark shadow appeared around the corner of the house moving quietly toward him on padded feet, Davey held out his hand welcoming the dog's company. He felt Brutus quiver beneath his touch.

"All that shrieking and hollering make you nervous, boy? It sure did me." Davey's words were soft and soothing like the night and soon Brutus stopped trembling, reassured by the trusted voice of his master's friend.

"If we're lucky she will sleep through the night, but look out come morning. That gal's got one hell of a temper and right now she isn't too happy with me. 'Course if I hadn't gotten the slug out she might not be around to complain but I don't reckon she'll be thanking me anytime soon."

Davey didn't mind the one-sided conversation. In fact it was kind of nice to talk to someone who didn't argue with everything he said. But as the moon rose higher in the midnight sky he found his gaze drawn to the lamplit window. Ignoring the customary nocturnal noises, he strained his ears to pick up any sound that would indicate Laura was awake. The silence coming from inside the farmhouse drew his nerves as taut as a bowstring until he could stand it no longer.

Getting wearily to his feet, he tiptoed across the porch and back through the house to where Laura lay sleeping peacefully. He watched her breasts rise and fall, admiring the creamy white swells visible beneath the strip of linen girding her chest. How innocent she looked with her thick auburn hair fanning the pillow. His pulses quickened as he reached down and lifted several long, silky strands, letting them glide through his fingers. He allowed his hand to brush her flawless alabaster cheek, then smiled when he noticed the faint spray of freckles along the narrow bridge of her nose. Despite her efforts she had not totally escaped the unrelenting rays of Florida's golden sun.

There was nothing of the haughty socialite about her now. In slumber she looked young and beautiful and so very vulnerable. Davey's throat constricted until he could scarcely swallow around the lump of fear lodged just below his Adam's apple. Had the powerful lead ball hit an inch or two lower there would have been no way for him to save her. His awareness of how close he had come to losing her brought with it a dramatic realization. The wide gulf of differences between them notwithstanding, Davey could no longer deny his love for Laura Dunstan.

He pulled the covers up to her chin, then quickly removed his boots. Carefully so not to awaken her he stretched out on top of the quilt. He left the lamp burning but tried to avoid looking at the woman lying close by his side. Stretching his arms behind his head he stared up at the ceiling, searching for a way to come to grips with this startling new revelation. He had nothing to offer a woman like Laura. They had not a whit in common. He still didn't know how she felt about Brad Kincaid. As for her feelings toward *him . . . I hate you!* Her furious invective rang in his ears. Not very encouraging, he thought wryly. All in all there didn't seem to be a whole lot on which they could build a lasting relationship.

Hell! Who was he kidding? He'd be lucky if she didn't come after him with a load of buckshot once she got her strength back.

Davey moved his head to sneak a furtive glance at Laura's still form only to find he could not take his eyes from her. The quilt rippled. Her right hand came up to push the cover away. Slowly her fingers flexed, then curled back against her palm. Davey brought his arm down beside hers, so closely the dark springy hairs tickled her skin. Sensing his nearness Laura slid her hand beneath his much larger one in an instinctive, unconscious gesture. Whether she knew it or not she needed his warmth and protection. Davey's rapidly beating heart filled with happiness and hope. Against all odds he had fallen in love with this stubborn blue-blood from Boston. Against all odds he would make her his own.

"What do you mean you don't know if she's dead?" Brad Kincaid clutched the handle of the whip so tightly his knuckles turned white.

An insolent Bart Harmon answered. "I told you that half-breed bastard passing himself off as a doctor came along before I could get a close look, but I hit her all right. I saw her fall from her horse."

"You stupid son of a bitch! Your orders were to kill her and now you can't even tell me where she is! This is twice you've failed me, Harmon! That's two times too many!"

The ugly scar on the gunman's face stood out against his weathered skin. Lips, cracked and dry from long hours spent in the sun, locked tightly, holding back the countercharges Bart wanted to throw in the arrogant coward's face. He'd been hired to ride herd on a bunch of slaves, not ambush old men or pretty ladies. And even though Laura Dunstan was a snooty piece of baggage who thought she was too good for the likes of a hired hand, she sure was pretty. Too bad he couldn't sweet-talk her into his bed like he had her cousin, Angel.

Curbing his resentment Bart repeated what he had already explained. "By the time I doubled back there wasn't a sign of them. I figured *the breed* would bring her back here."

"The only thing that came back here was her horse," snarled Brad, slapping the coiled whip against his palm. "I want you to take some men. Scour the countryside," he ordered, his eyes narrowing dangerously. "And, Harmon, if she's still alive I expect you to finish the job you were sent to do."

As Bart stalked off toward the stable he wondered if it might be time to move on. He didn't really mind a little killing if the price was right, but he hadn't counted on Davey Logan getting involved. Logan was one tough hombre. Just over a year ago he and his kin had made it clear Bart wasn't welcome at Fort Brooke. He'd take some men and scout around. Then he would decided whether to return to River Ridge or keep right on going.

The first faint rays of dawn sifted through the thin curtains at the window, shadowing the room in early morning light, but Laura didn't open her eyes. Caught in the tranquil somnolence that often precedes wakefulness she lay still listening to the rooster crowing not far away. Was it just the cock who had awakened her so early? Sulee wouldn't have breakfast ready for another hour.

When she started to lift the blanket up over her head pain shot through her upper body, pain so fierce it brought her quickly out of the dreamlike state. With consciousness came awareness. With awareness came fear as she found herself firmly immobilized by a strong, masculine arm which was obviously attached to the rock-solid form molded along the curve of her back.

Pivoting her head Laura came face-to-face with a pair of familiar chocolate-brown eyes. She stared blankly at Davey, too surprised to even try and extricate herself from the band of steel holding her prisoner.

"How do you feel, princess?" His warm breath whispered along her cheek, alerting her senses to some unknown danger.

How did she feel? What a ridiculous question to ask

a lady who went to sleep alone, then awoke to find herself wrapped in a man's embrace. Good Lord! How could such a thing happen?

Laura tried to think . . . to remember . . . but her brain was still clouded by the last remnants of a sound sleep. She felt as if she had been drugged.

Blast! That was it! She remembered Davey giving her some vile concoction, then everything went blank. What had he done to her while she was unconscious? Any number of horrid possibilities flitted through her mind.

She tried to scoot toward the edge of the bed hoping to escape his treacherous grasp but immediately waves of dizziness threatened to send her back into oblivion. Breathing deeply she waited for the swells of nausea to recede. Strange how the pain seemed to stem from her shoulder. If she had been ravaged her discomfort should be located in an entirely different part of her anatomy. Laura blushed scarlet, embarrassed by her own imaginings.

Davey's black brows drew together in a worried scowl. "If you don't lie still you are going to start bleeding again."

At his warning Laura went rigid. Whatever he had done, he had practically admitted she was on the verge of bleeding to death.

"A gunshot wound is nothing to trifle with," he added, glad to see she had heeded his advice, but knowing only too well how contrary she could be when it came to taking orders.

One word exploded in Laura's mind like the

reverberating crack of a rifle. *Gunshot!* And then it all came rushing back to her.

She remembered riding toward Pine View, her thoughts in a whirl as she tried to guess what might be behind her friend's urgent summons. Had Henry Ashe fallen victim to another attack? Had that cad, Wade Callahan, finally shown his true colors and broken Susan's heart? Most importantly, would she see Davey Logan again?

She recalled looking toward the bend in the road and there he was as if she had conjured him out of her fantasies. Inside her stomach those bothersome butterflies had begun to flutter their wings and she knew the long week during which she and Davey had been apart had only heightened her desire to be near him. It was no use trying to deny her attraction to the darkly handsome half-breed. And in that moment she had felt the protective shield long ago erected around her heart start to crumble like a physical thing, its pieces scattering on the wind. Davey had won but it was Laura who experienced triumph in defeat. The future, which had once seemed so important, no longer mattered. It would take care of itself. For now she had today and Davey was waiting for her.

And then, as she raised her arm in greeting, past, present, and future had fused into one blinding moment of white-hot pain. Her memory of what happened afterward was vague. At some point she had awakened to find herself here at Wade Callahan's farmhouse suffering terrible agony. Davey had forced her to drink a vile-tasting liquid after which she had been carried off in the arms of Morpheus. She dreamed she was being attacked by a host of demons prodding and poking her with heated pitchforks. But when she opened her eyes it was Davey's face she saw. Davey, with his instruments of torture, was the one inflicting the cruel pain. She had screamed at him to stop but he had paid no attention to her pleading. Beads of sweat had glistened on his forehead. His dark eyes had been fixed in concentration on a spot above her left breast and he was hurting her dreadfully. It had seemed the worst of nightmares at the time. Only now did she understood.

"You saved my life again," she murmured through parched lips.

Davey offered her a glass of water, pillowing her head with his arm. "You aren't out of the woods yet, princess. You lost a lot of blood which is why you must rest."

Troubled amber eyes took in Davey's ruggedly handsome face. Worry and fatigue had taken their toll, deepening the hollows in his cheeks. Laura raised her right hand to stroke the dark, bristly stubble along his jaw. "It looks as if you are the one who needs rest," she commented, summoning a weak smile.

"All in good time. Right now I'm going to fix you something to eat."

Davey didn't return her smile. The gentle touch of her hand affected him deeply. Twice in less than a day he had been certain he had lost her forever; first when she was brought to death's door by a sniper's ball, again when she had shouted her hatred for him. He wanted nothing so much as to take her in his arms and hold her as he had during the long hours of the night. But other more important things took precedence over his raging desire. It was time to begin fulfilling the vow he had made to himself. He would seek out the one who had done this to her and make him pay.

Reluctantly he stood up. Laura watched as he brushed his hand over his thick black hair, wishing it were her own fingers combing the ebony thatch into order.

"Did you sleep at all last night?" she asked, knowing he had lain in bed beside her at least part of those lost hours when she had been under the influence of whatever drug he had given her.

Davey shrugged. "A little." It was a lie but how could he tell her that given the opportunity to hold her in his arms he wasn't about to waste a minute of precious time in slumber? He had thoroughly enjoyed the feel of her warm body snuggled next to his, every curve of her slender form molded perfectly to the contours of his large frame.

Laura interrupted his reverie. "You do understand that I cannot possibly remain here alone with you?"

"I understand you cannot possibly leave until you are well," countered Davey.

Recognizing the stubborn lift of her chin, he sought a compromise which would enable her to stay and at the same time protect her reputation. There was one solution to his dilemma which would also give him the excuse he needed to leave the house long enough to examine the spot where the ambush took place.

Frowning thoughtfully he broached the idea with care. "Since it will take several days for you to regain your strength, how would it be if I asked Susan to come and stay with you? I could sleep in the barn. That way I would be close at hand if you need me."

If I need you? Blast but the man was dense! Couldn't he see that she needed him right now? Would need him for the rest of her life? To have him near and not be able to touch him might prove a thousand times more painful than the gunshot wound in her shoulder, but she could hardly use that as an argument against a suggestion that made perfectly good sense.

Resignedly she nodded her agreement. "I suppose if Susan is willing to come it will satisfy the proprieties."

With that problem out of the way, Davey started for the door but was brought up short when Laura asked the question he had dreaded but knew must come. "Why, Davey? Who shot me?"

Davey had no answer. He suspected Bart Harmon and his gang of ruffians were responsible for the attack on Henry Ashe. It also stood to reason either Fowler Dunstan or Brad Kincaid had given the order. But he could think of no one who would want to harm Laura.

"I don't know," he replied candidly. "It could

have been a near-sighted hunter who mistook you for a deer."

Laura grasped the explanation hopefully. Yes, surely it had to be an accident and it was just a coincidence that it had happened so soon after Susan's father was set upon.

Continuing to the kitchen Davey put the water on to heat, then began preparing a light breakfast paying little attention to the task at hand. He was glad Laura had accepted his theory about a careless hunter. Too bad he couldn't do the same. But something told him the explanation was too simple. One way or another he would discover the truth. He only hoped the truth would not drive a deeper wedge between him and the woman who had stolen his heart.

Chapter 17

Davey raised the heavy brass knocker, then let it fall, listening to the reverberation echo beyond the double oak doors. He had promised Laura to let her uncle know what had happened though he wasn't looking forward to the encounter. He didn't like Fowler Dunstan and he knew the feeling was mutual. If the man insisted on bringing his niece home there was little Davey could do about it except argue against the wisdom of such a move.

One panel swung inward but instead of the butler he expected to see, he found himself looking down upon the smiling face of Laura's cousin, Angel.

"Why, Davey. What a pleasant surprise. Do come in," she purred, exaggerating her southern drawl.

Stepping into the foyer Davey wasted no time in idle chitchat. "I need to speak to your father. Is he in?"

Angel pouted prettily. "I'm afraid not. Won't I do?"

Finding her flirtatious manner offensive, Davey's reply was intentionally curt. "Your cousin has been injured. She asked me to inform her uncle that she is all right but it will be several days before she can be moved."

"Where is she now?" The girl seemed more curious than concerned.

"I took her to Wade Callahan's farm. After I got the lead ball out of her shoulder . . ."

"Lead ball? Do you mean Laura has been shot?" In her excitement Angel's accent became much less pronounced.

"I'm afraid so."

"But who would want to shoot Laura?"

Who indeed? "I don't know. Maybe a careless hunter." Davey decided to stick with the same conjecture he had used with Laura until he found evidence to the contrary. "She will be all right," he repeated, "but she's lost a lot of blood and needs time to recuperate which means remaining at the farm for a few days. When will your father be back?"

"I have no idea. He has been out looking for Laura all night." Her tone indicated she thought a great deal of fuss was being made unnecessarily. Batting her light lashes she sighed enviously. "So Laura spent the night alone with just you and Mr. Callahan?"

Davey resented what she seemed to be implying and spoke without thinking. "Wade has been at Pine View for the past week." As soon as the words were out he realized his mistake. Not only had he made the situation look worse for Laura, he had inadvertently jeopardized Susan's reputation in the process. What's more he had the distinct impression that Angel Dunstan was silently laughing over his blunder.

"Henry Ashe was nearly killed by a gang of gunmen," he hurriedly explained, "and since the attack Wade has been staying at Pine View to guard against any further trouble."

Angel took the opportunity to brazenly clutch Davey's arm. "It's downright scary the way people are being shot at around here. Soon every young lady in the neighborhood will need a big, strong man to look after her."

Repulsed by Angel's feigned fright and clinging fingers, Davey brushed her hand away. "I have to be going. Please give your father my message and tell him I intend to ask Susan Ashe to stay at the farm with Laura until she is well."

Angel pounced on what she saw as a chance to get closer to the fascinating and forbidden half-breed. "You needn't bother Susan. I would be happy to come with you and take care of my dear cousin."

Groaning inwardly Davey wondered how such sugary sweetness could sound so insincere. It seemed like every time he opened his mouth around the forward little hussy, he stuck his foot in it. For Laura's sake he decided a slight prevarication would be in order.

"I know Laura will appreciate your kind offer but she specifically requested I bring Susan to help her and under the circumstances to do otherwise might jeopardize her recovery. But I shall make certain she knows the full extent of your concern."

Before Angel could summon a response, Davey was out the door and headed down the walk. Without a backward glance he sprinted into the saddle and kneed his horse into action, anxious to be away from River Ridge and the strange people who lived there.

Several hours later Davey reined in the big black at the junction where the tree-lined drive leading to Pine View Plantation met the main road. There he sat for some time trying to make sense out of what he had discovered.

By estimating the distance the lead ball would have had to travel in order to penetrate but not pass through Laura's shoulder, and knowing the angle at which the projectile entered her flesh, it hadn't taken long to locate the spot where the rifleman had waited for his victim. Atop a rise about three hundred yards from where Laura had fallen, the grass had been trampled flat. The stubby remains of half a dozen thin cheroots littered the ground, a sure sign that whoever had been there the day before had lingered for more than a few minutes. The view of the road was unobstructed making it doubtful that the gunman could have mistaken his target for anything else. If Davey hadn't had his back turned he would likely have seen the attacker before the shot was fired. One thing seemed clear. The ambush had been deliberate. But the who and the why were still as much a mystery as ever.

Davey started down the path, passing between the rows of stately pines for which the plantation had been named. Soon he came within sight of the two-story structure visible beyond the screen of branches. The house was built along the same lines as River Ridge but there the similarity ended. An extension of the warm personalities of those who dwelt within permeated the bricks and mortar of Pine View, welcoming both friend and stranger alike. How different it felt from the cold, inhospitable atmosphere hanging like a dark cloud over Fowler Dunstan's estate.

Where, Davey wondered, would Wade and Susan live once they were married? It wasn't likely that his strong-willed friend would agree to abide in a household dependent on slave labor, yet neither could he picture Susan living at the ramshackle farm. The thought of Wade and Susan's wedding reminded him he hadn't had a chance to talk to Laura about Brad Kincaid. But as time passed he became more and more convinced that Kincaid had made the whole story up possibly to discourage any designs Davey might have on the young lady. Maybe Kincaid was afraid Davey was after Laura's money. The ludicrous idea brought a grin to Davey's lips.

He had nearly reached the house when the door flew open and Susan dashed out to meet him with Wade right behind her. At once Davey was bombarded with questions by the distraught blonde.

"Have you heard the news? Laura is missing! No one has seen her since yesterday! Did you run across her? Oh I'm glad you're here! Where could she be?"

Tears pooled in Susan's wide, blue eyes as words tumbled from her mouth in an incoherent rush. She appeared on the brink of hysteria by the time Wade had caught up with her. Taking her by the arms he pulled her firmly back against his chest.

"Calm down, sweetheart." There was understanding in his gentle command. "Let's get Davey inside where he is needed."

Needed? Had something else happened to Henry Ashe?

"Is your father all right?" he asked, directing his concern to Susan.

As the three moved up the walkway side by side, she replied, "Yes, yes, Papa's fine, but—"

"Susan!" Wade cut her off sharply turning his head to survey the tree-studded grounds. "Not out here!"

All this secrecy made Davey nervous. He found himself looking over his shoulder for any sign that they were being spied upon. Knowing he could ease Susan's mind on one account he leaned over and spoke close to her ear. "Laura is at the farm." In whispered tones he told her what had occurred on the road the previous afternoon, supporting her by the elbow when the color drained from her face.

Overhearing enough of the conversation to get the picture, Wade disclosed how they had come to learn of Laura's disappearance. "Fowler Dunstan stopped by this morning to see if Laura was here.

247

His no good stepson was with him and I tell you I was hard pressed to keep from laying into Kincaid on the spot. But I knew a confrontation would only make a bad situation worse."

By now they had reached the door and Davey was more confused than ever. As soon as the panel was shut he rounded on the pair. "Will one of you please tell me what the hell this is all about?"

Instead of answering his question Susan said, "Come this way. We'll show you."

They lead him up the stairs and down the hall stopping before a bedroom whose door stood partially open. Entering the room Davey noticed the curtains at the window had been drawn. Outside the sun shown brightly but here illumination was provided by the artificial light of a lamp. An elderly negro woman, her hair concealed beneath a snowy white turban, sat beside the bed rocking back and forth softly singing what sounded like a hymn. Davey's stomach rebelled at the sight that met his eyes. On the bed a dark-skinned girl lay facedown, her naked body covered to the waist with a thin sheet. Blood seeped from the lacerations crisscrossing her back. Not an inch of skin had been left unflayed.

Davey motioned the old woman aside, then knelt to examine the mutilated body of the girl. He was relieved to see that her breathing was shallow but regular. Carefully lifting the sheet he saw that her wounds extended down across her rounded buttocks.

"Who did this?" The explosive anger in his voice

sent the ancient negress shrinking into the shadows.

Henry Ashe, who had been sitting unnoticed in a wing chair near the window, spoke up. "We don't know. She was found early this morning near the irrigation ditch." He sounded tired and bewildered. By nature Henry was a gentle, decent man. That anyone could abuse another human being in such a horrific manner left him shaken.

Davey snapped out orders which Susan was quick to obey. "Bring me warm water, ointment, bandages . . ." All the while he was meticulously observing the rise and fall of the girl's chest. If her ribs were broken one might easily puncture a lung but thankfully such didn't seem to be the case.

When Susan set the water on the nightstand and Davey began the arduous task of cleansing the rent flesh, the girl moaned, managing to turn her head on the pillow. One eye was swollen shut and a deep gash sliced her dusky cheek. Dried blood crusted the corner of her mouth leading down to a smaller cut on her chin. Susan remained at Davey's side, handing him a clean washcloth when needed in exchange for the one he was using.

"Her name is Delilah," she whispered not wanting to disturb the pitiful soul lying on the bed. "She is one of the Dunstan house slaves who served as Laura's maid."

Davey gave no reply but kept on with his work. Finally he said, "That's all I can do for now." He had satisfied himself that no bones were broken but he knew the danger of infection was great.

"Come. Let's go downstairs," suggested Henry.

"I don't know about you but I could use a drink. Cassie will stay with her," he added, motioning to the old servant.

Once in the parlor, Susan paced restlessly about the room. "I simply cannot believe someone would do such a heinous thing. Do you suppose it was that awful Bart Harmon?"

Wade answered. "He's a lowlife if I ever saw one but I'm guessing it was someone else."

"Harmon may be a worthless scoundrel," agreed Davey, "but I doubt he would have the nerve to do what was done to that girl upstairs. Especially since she belongs to his employer."

After considering his logic, Susan had to agree. "But if it wasn't Harmon who could it have been?"

The three men looked at each other knowingly. It was Wade who voiced what they all were thinking. "It's pretty clear what was done to Delilah and only one man around here carries a whip."

Abruptly Susan stopped her pacing, pivoting to stare ashen-faced at Wade. "I know Bradley has an empty space where his conscience should be but I can't believe he's capable of committing such a foul deed."

Wade merely shrugged while the other two men refused to meet her eyes.

Unable to muster an argument, Susan shrieked, "If you are right, Brad must be insane! We've got to do something to stop him before he hurts someone else!"

"He may already have done just that."

Susan's mouth fell as she gaped at Davey. "Do you think he was the one who attacked Papa?"

"I believe he gave the orders. I also suspect he was behind the ambush on Laura but damned if I can figure out why."

Susan shook her head in denial. "Papa and Delilah, maybe. But Brad had no reason to kill Laura. He wanted to marry her."

Davey's heart plummeted. So it was true. For days he had argued against the possibility of a union between Laura and the cruel planter, finally convincing himself that it was nothing more than Kincaid's pipe dream, a fantasy encouraged by his overinflated ego. Now Davey had to face the fact that he had been the one wearing blinders. He had allowed himself to believe he could make Laura happy. Him. Davey Logan. A poor half-breed doctor whom she considered a savage. What a fool he'd been! What a blind, stupid fool!

"She turned him down, of course, but rejection is hardly a motive for murder."

At first Davey was too demoralized to understand what Susan was saying but the word *rejection* alerted him to the importance of what he had missed. "I beg your pardon, Susan?" He apologized, acknowledging his lack of attention and hoping she would repeat what she had said.

Susan complied without further urging. "Laura turned him down but men don't go about killing women just because they say 'no' to a proposal of marriage."

Wade put his arm around the petite blonde, hugging her to his side. "Most men don't, sweetheart, but most men don't beat their slaves half to death either."

"Thank God," Henry lamented from where he sat clutching a glass of bourbon.

The reminder sent shivers of fear through Susan's small frame. "We've still no proof that Brad committed these atrocities." Though she had to admit the finger of guilt certainly pointed in Brad's direction.

Davey was oblivious to the discussion taking place between the three. Laura wasn't going to marry Brad Kincaid. Gazing out the window he noticed that suddenly the sun had grown brighter in a cloudless, powder-blue sky. The grass appeared greener than it had a few minutes ago. Even the songs of the birds had taken on a merrier note. He was tempted to whistle a happy tune in harmony with the carefree feathered creatures as his spirits soared higher and higher, threatening to spiral out of control.

It was Henry who brought him back to earth. "I can understand why Fowler or Brad might want me out of the way. I'm the one responsible for cutting them off from their friends and neighbors. And knowing how heavy-handed Brad treats the people at River Ridge, it's possible he might be responsible for what happened to Delilah, but I have to agree with Susan. What reason could he have for wanting to harm Laura?"

"Money?" Wade tossed the idea out for consideration.

"She seems to have plenty," agreed Davey. "I figure maybe Kincaid thought I was after some of it and made up that cock-and-bull story about their engagement to keep me at bay."

"Engagement?" Susan exclaimed. "Good Lord! They were never engaged! How could Bradley tell such a lie?"

Davey grinned, still caught up in a euphoric light-heartedness despite the gravity of the situation. "Lying seems to be one of his lesser sins. But getting back to Laura's money, which incidentally I have no designs on, if something happened to her I would think her uncle stood to inherit her wealth, not Kincaid. And from what I understand Fowler Dunstan is already worth a fortune."

"For some people it's never enough," Wade commented dryly.

Staring into space Susan pondered her thoughts before she spoke, then said, "Laura once told me something that sounded peculiar at the time. I'd forgotten about it until now but I wonder if it might have some bearing. Laura's father was a successful Boston banker but in addition he inherited all of *his* father's sizable estate. It wasn't until after her father's death that Laura learned she had an uncle. And this is what struck me as odd. Fowler Dunstan was the oldest of the two brothers, yet Laura's grandfather left his entire fortune to his younger son, Laura's father."

Davey took time to digest this bit of information. Normally the eldest son received the lion's share of an inheritance when his sire died but for some reason Laura's grandfather had elected to disregard tradition. Which led to another question.

"Then where did Fowler get the money to build his plantation?"

Henry Ashe furnished yet another surprising piece to the puzzle. "Rumor has it Hester's first husband, Brad's father, left all of his money to her when he passed on."

"Making no provisions for his only son?"

"Ironic isn't it? Fowler is disinherited by his father, then Brad ends up out in the cold as well."

It was the sort of thing that could turn greedy men bitter, causing them to seek revenge. The more Davey learned, the more complex the plot became. Was it possible Fowler Dunstan was trying to harm Laura because of some feud which had taken place before she was born? And how did Brad Kincaid feel about his stepfather who had usurped what should rightfully have been his? Stretching his imagination a little further, Davey realized that if an accident should befall Laura her fortune would go to her uncle. Should Fowler then meet a similar fate, Brad Kincaid would be a very wealthy man. Where there had seemed to be no motive for the attack, now there appeared to be several.

Convinced that one or both of the men wanted her dead, Davey felt the icy fingers of fear ripple along his spine. He knew it was imperative he get back to the farm without delay. It was he who had left word at River Ridge where Laura could be found. If something happened to her he would never forgive himself.

Quickly he explained his need to return to Laura with all due haste. "I was a fool to tell Angel where she was."

"Don't berate yourself, Davey. You didn't know the danger. Besides we may be completely wrong in our assumptions."

Susan's placating words failed to ease the anxiety knotting his stomach. "I promised Laura I would bring you back with me but now it would seem you are needed here." Casting troubled eyes toward the ceiling Davey was torn between what was best for his patient upstairs and how Laura would react when he returned alone.

Understanding his dilemma, Susan started to say she would accompany him, knowing the household staff could efficiently care for the young runaway but something made her hold her tongue. Aware of the attraction Davey and Laura felt for each other she decided time alone together might be "just what the doctor ordered." Smiling secretively at her little joke, she agreed it would be best if she remained at Pine View.

Declining Wade's offer to go with him, Davey moved toward the door. "You may be needed here. Once he learns where Laura is, Dunstan will be searching for his missing slave. I'll come back tomorrow to check on the girl's progress. Meanwhile apply ointment to her wounds and keep her as quiet and comfortable as possible."

Following in his wake, Henry called out, "Bring Laura with you if she's up to it. We've got plenty of room and we must keep her safe until we get to the bottom of this mess!"

Shouting his thanks Davey sped down the drive wondering as he went just who was behind the sinister scheme to kill the woman he loved. Henry was right about one thing. They had to protect Laura at all costs. She could not return to River Ridge until the identity of the culprit was known. If Davey had anything to say in the matter, she would never go back!

Chapter 18

After Davey left, Laura drifted in and out of sleep the remainder of the morning. By the time the sun reached its zenith she'd had enough of indolence. Sitting up on the edge of the bed she found herself feeling rested and remarkably fit with the exception of the soreness in her shoulder. It was then that she noticed her riding habit hanging from a peg and heat swept over her face. Clad in nothing but her pantalettes and chemise she slowly rose to her feet allowing time to regain her equilibrium. If she had been moving at her normal pace she would have tripped over the huge black bulk sprawled directly in her path. Dark, doleful eyes looked up out of a wrinkled, homely face but Laura's smile immediately triggered a tail-thumping response.

"Some watchdog you make, you lazy cur. Why don't you go chase a rabbit?"

Brutus's tail slapped happily against the wooden floorboards. Saliva streamed from both sides of his wide mouth.

"Yuck! Has anyone ever told you what a disgusting creature you are?"

Carefully Laura stepped over the prostrate form. She pondered the idea of trying to dress herself, then decided to wait until Susan arrived to assist her. A man's shirt had been tossed over the back of the couch and with some difficulty she managed to slide her arms into the long sleeves and fasten most of the buttons. The hem of the garment stretched midway down her thighs leaving no doubt as to its owner's identity.

Dreamily she inhaled the musky, masculine scent given off by the soft cotton material. The fragrance brought to mind the moment she had awakened to find herself molded to Davey's large, muscle-corded frame. She wondered what it would be like to belong to such a man, to wake up each day cradled in his protective arms.

But as she poured herself a cup of lukewarm coffee reality came crashing down to splinter her flight of fancy. Though she was unsure as to how she would plot her future's course, none of the paths open to her included the barely defined backroads of Florida. While Davey might be content to traverse the countryside caring for Indians and settlers in the remote hinterlands, she could never be satisfied so far removed from big city life. Even her uncle's plantation, only a day's ride from Jacksonville, lacked the amenities she had grown use to in London and Boston. If they had met in another place, another time . . .

Taking a seat on the well-worn sofa, Laura

chided herself. *What ifs* and *might have beens* were for the very old who had nothing to look forward to, whereas she had her whole life ahead of her and she had the means to make of it whatever her heart desired. She was infatuated with Davey Logan because he was unlike any other man of her acquaintance. She must guard against her body's traitorous longings in order to find and maintain her place in society. Wasn't that what she had always wanted? Wealth, independence, status. These were the ingredients which had made her father and grandfather happy. It was the only recipe she knew.

Blast! What difference did it make how she felt, she ruminated dejectedly? It was a ridiculous, one-sided attraction anyway. As far as Davey was concerned she was nothing more than a self-centered thorn in his side, a walking disaster always getting into trouble. He would be better off when she was gone . . . if only she could decide where it was she wanted to go.

A green chameleon suddenly appeared on the window ledge. Laura watched the lizard move, his orange throat extending, then retracting, as he moved on fragile legs. Gradually the tint of his skin faded to a dull grayish brown color making him indistinguishable from the sun-weathered wood on which he perched. When a tiny insect flew within striking distance the reptile's sticky tongue darted out, capturing the unsuspecting bug before it was aware of the danger.

Laura shuddered despite the warmth of the afternoon sun beaming through the glass. She wanted to believe Davey's theory about the shooting, but if she had been accidentally wounded by a careless hunter why hadn't the man come forward to lend assistance? She didn't like to think it was something other than an accident but the possibility did exist. And if the attempt on her life had been deliberate it meant she had an unknown enemy. Someone much like the chameleon waiting to catch his prey off-guard. It was a frightening thought but one she would be wise to consider. The problem was that she could think of no reason why anyone would wish her harm.

Brutus heard the approaching hoofbeats first. Bounding from the bedroom he barked loudly, sending the lizard scurrying out of sight. Laura, certain it was Davey returning with Susan, remained where she sat, taking a folded quilt from the corner of the couch and tossing it over her legs. Though she hated to admit how much she had missed him since he'd ridden out that morning, the thought of his return was like a restorative tonic to her dejected spirits. He would laugh at her preposterous conjectures and most likely call her a whimsical female but she didn't care. At least his presence would rid her of her fear.

The sound of booted feet echoed across the planked porch just before a heavy knock shook the door in its frame. Laura froze knowing Davey wouldn't bother to knock.

"Laura! Are you in there?"

Her breath caught on a ragged sigh when she heard her uncle's familiar voice. "I'm here, Uncle

Fowler," she answered, tucking the edges of the quilt more tightly about her legs. "Come in. The door isn't locked."

Fowler entered with the sun at his back leaving his face shaded which spared Laura the sight of his shock at finding her there on the faded, sagging old sofa. Neither did she see the glint of anger spark his amber eyes turning them to flaming topaz. After the brief message left by the half-breed bastard he had not expected Laura to be sitting up casually sipping coffee from a chipped mug. A quick glance at the untidy room did nothing to abate his growing rage. A man's breeches lay draped over a chair; a pair of fringed moccasins were beside the cold fireplace. Only the deep-throated growl of the hairy beast who stood between him and the sofa kept Fowler from snatching Laura up by her disheveled auburn locks and hauling her out of the tumbledown farmhouse.

"Laura! Thank God you are all right. From what Angel told me, I expected to find you at death's door."

For a brief moment Laura thought she heard disappointment in his voice. *Blast! She really must get hold of herself. This was her uncle, for goodness sake. The man who loved her and welcomed her as a member of his family.*

"I'm fine, Uncle. Just very tired." Which was true. Coinciding with Fowler Dunstan's arrival had come an overpowering fatigue. Laura didn't know if she had the strength to reach the bedroom without help, but she wanted nothing so much as to curl up beneath the covers and lose herself in the downy softness of Wade Callahan's feather mattress.

Fowler started to take a step forward. "This will never do, my dear. I must get you home at once." His deprecating tone made clear his desire to quit the meager dwelling. He was brought up short when Brutus snarled, baring his fangs. Irritably Fowler ordered, "Call him off, Laura."

"I'm sorry, Uncle. Brutus won't obey anyone but Mr. Callahan and Davey." Laura wasn't sure if what she said was true or not, and she wasn't about to put it to the test. Knowing she could not possibly endure the long ride to River Ridge, the intimidating animal gave her the excuse she needed to stay right where she was.

Fowler felt his ire soar once more when he heard the familiar way Laura spoke the half-breed's name. "Just where are Callahan and Logan?"

Reluctant to confess she had spent the night alone with Davey, Laura hedged. "Both men are at Pine View. They are bringing Susan to stay with me until I am well enough to return to the plantation. Please don't worry."

She mistook Fowler's intense scrutiny for concern. The truth was, having discovered no one else was about, Fowler debated whether or not to take the opportunity to finish the job Bart Harmon had botched. Wounded as she was it would not be difficult to subdue her, then smother her with a pillow the same way he had snuffed the life out of Miles Kincaid. The only thing stopping him was that damned black demon who looked ready to eat him alive if he so much as blinked. Deciding he would have to wait until a more advantageous time presented itself, the planter changed his tactics, successfully playing the part of an anxious guardian.

"In all good conscience, my dear, I cannot allow you to remain in a place like this. After what happened, it just isn't safe."

Stubbornly Laura countered. "I am perfectly safe here, Uncle. It was an accident after all. I'm convinced the hunter who fired the shot wasn't even aware he had hit me."

That was stretching Davey's theory a bit far but it was a comforting idea.

Fowler was pleased to learn his niece had no inkling of the truth but he was not happy about the trust she seemed to place in Davey Logan. The man could be a real obstacle to his plans.

"I wasn't referring to your *accident* when I spoke of your safety. Forgive me if my candor upsets your tender sensibilities but surely you realize this man, Logan, is nothing more than a ruthless savage. As I've tried to explain to you, Indians are uncivilized creatures. Why, the heathens regard their women as . . ."

A steady thumping interrupted his lecture. Glancing down he saw that Brutus had relaxed his protective stance and was now focusing attention on the open door at Fowler's back. Damned if the slobbering beast didn't look as if he were smiling. A chill of apprehension warned him of what he would find as he slowly pivoted around.

"Go ahead, Dunstan. Tell us how *the heathen* regard their women."

Davey leaned casually against the doorjamb, arms crossed over his chest. There was nothing threatening in the pose or in his deep baritone voice. One had to read the dark forbidding color of his eyes, observe the slight flair of his nostrils to understand the depth of his fury. Unfortunately, Fowler's own anger clouded his vision, blinding him to the danger. Instead he chose to further antagonize the big man standing before him by arrogantly defending his disparaging remarks.

"Oh come now, Logan. It's common knowledge Indians think more of their horses and dogs than they do their squaws."

It was all Davey could do to restrain himself, but he knew beating the pompous ass to a bloody pulp would only support the man's ridiculous notion. Still he could not let the insult go unchallenged with Laura witnessing the exchange.

With a nonchalance he was far from feeling, Davey replied, "In other words you are saying we treat our women much the way you treat your slaves. Am I correct?"

"It's hardly the same thing," Fowler spluttered, his face taking on a crimson hue.

"You've got that right, Dunstan," agreed Davey, straightening to his full height which put him a good six inches above the older man. "It isn't the same thing at all. I don't know where you come by this wealth of knowledge you have regarding Indians but for your information when a brave marries, everything he has becomes the property of his wife—his house, his land, and his possessions. What's more Indian women are treated with respect akin to worship by their men."

Davey's brown eyes smoldered with resentment. "And there's one more thing you should know about Indians. We don't whip our women, forcing them to flee for their lives."

"Just what the hell is that supposed to mean?" roared Fowler, his cheeks reddening to an alarming brightness.

"It means you had better warn your stepson to stay out of my path if he knows what's good for him."

The veins in Fowler's forehead bulged. "Don't you dare threaten me or mine, Logan! Laura, we're leaving this filthy pigsty right now! No niece of mine is going to put herself at the mercy of a half-breed savage who doesn't know his place!"

Laura looked from Davey to Fowler, her mind reeling as she tried to make sense of the accusations they had hurled at one another. Her uncle should have been grateful for what Davey had done in coming to her rescue. Instead he had verbally attacked and insulted her benefactor. In return Davey had once again implied the slaves at River Ridge were being mistreated. In her opinion, neither of the men were acting particularly civilized at the moment. The hostile tension between the two left Laura feeling as if she was sitting on a powder keg ready to blow and she could think of no way to head off the impending explosion.

"Laura is in no condition to go anywhere, Dunstan. She sure as hell can't ride five miles on horseback!"

What he said was true but Davey knew if Laura took it into her head to leave, there wasn't much he could do to prevent it.

Having had enough of their arguing, Laura came to her feet more swiftly than was wise. The sharp pain that shot through her shoulder and left arm made her cry out. When she swayed unsteadily Davey was beside her in a flash, gently assisting her back onto the sofa.

She gasped, taking very short breaths to offset a wave of nausea. "Where is Susan?"

Davey lied without hesitation. "She and Wade will be here any minute." It was the only answer that might persuade Dunstan to leave without his charge.

His ploy worked. Fowler had seen for himself that Laura was too weak to make the trip and with Susan Ashe present to act as nurse and chaperone there was little he could say without seeming to appear callous. But conceding defeat went against the grain. In a final attempt to thwart Davey's bid for control of the situation, he said, "There is no need to trouble Susan. If you must remain here I will bring Hester to look after you."

"That won't be necessary, Uncle," Laura protested. She couldn't imagine the pampered old lady being of any use away from her fine house and servants. "Susan is already on her way."

"I don't like it! At a time like this you should be

266

at the plantation with your family, not in some squalid cabin on a run-down farm."

It was really too much. Laura was tired of arguing. She wanted to lie down until the dizziness passed. Her uncle's continued expostulations grated on her nerves causing her to speak more sharply than she normally would have. "I've really little choice in the matter. I can assure you I will return to River Ridge as soon as I am fit to travel. Until then . . ."

Taking her words for the dismissal they were intended to be, Fowler left in a huff but not before vowing he would return the next day.

Once the door closed behind the irate plantation owner, Davey turned on Laura demanding, "What, pray tell, are you doing out of bed?"

"I was bored. And don't raise your voice to me. I've had enough of shouting," she shouted, leaning her head back and closing her eyes.

"You're supposed to be bored. And . . . you're supposed to be in bed."

Her eyes flew open in alarm as she was scooped up in a pair of brawny arms. Davey's surprise equalled Laura's mortification when the quilted coverlet glided to the floor, leaving her bare feet and calves exposed. Staring in fascination at the sight of her long shapely legs and trim ankles, Davey stood rooted to the spot until his blushing burden began struggling against his hold.

"Now see what you've done! Put me down this instant!"

A man would have to be blind not to see. Davey

could also feel. Hot flames of desire heated the blood coursing through his veins. Burning fires of passion seared every nerve and sinew.

"Be still!" He wasn't sure if the command was meant for Laura or his rapidly beating heart. Neither obeyed.

Awkwardly Davey stepped over the quilt, then nearly lost his balance when Brutus refused to move out of his path. He sidestepped just in time to keep from taking a spill, then let loose a string of curses which sent the dog scrambling for cover and brought Laura's wiggling to an abrupt half. She remained rigid in his arms until he reached the bed and gently deposited her upon the mattress. Sinking into its feathery softness she wondered how he could speak so harshly while handling her with such tenderness.

Once he had her where he wanted her, Laura had expected Davey to take his leave. Instead he sat down beside her and proceeded to silently study his hands. As the minutes dragged by and still he said nothing, she felt the need to break the strained quiet.

"Shouldn't Susan be here by now?"

"She isn't coming."

Laura tried to sit up but Davey pressed her back against the pillows. "I had to lie to your uncle or he would never have left here without you." His voice held an unspoken apology. "You're safer here for now."

Safer? What an odd way of putting it. She could have understood if he had mentioned her wound, the loss of blood, the toll it would take on her if she tried to sit a horse, but his cryptic phraseology led her to suspect he meant something else. She remembered then his barely leashed fury when he had returned to find Fowler with her.

"Why isn't she coming? Has anything happened to her father?" Laura clutched Davey's arm for she knew only a matter of extreme urgency would have kept her friend from her side.

"Henry is fine, princess. But there is someone at Pine view who needs Susan's attention even more than you do at the moment."

"Mr. Callahan?"

"No."

Laura jerked her hand back. "Blast you, Davey Logan! Stop talking in riddles and tell me what this is all about!"

Davey took her hand in his, tracing the blue veins visible beneath her fair skin. "This morning one of your uncle's slaves was found near the irrigation ditch dividing River Ridge and Pine View. She had been badly beaten."

"She?"

"The woman's name is Delilah."

Laura's face registered her horror at the news. "Noooo! Not sweet, gentle Delilah!"

"I'm afraid so. Susan is with her at Pine View. I did what I could but I don't know if it will be enough."

"Oh, Davey! Do you mean she might die?"

He nodded and the fear Laura had tried so hard to dismiss returned to settle over her like an ominous black cloud. Davey sensed her trepidation even before her hand began to tremble in his. He wanted to tell her there was no reason to be frightened but there was. And unless he divulged his suspicions to her now she would return to her uncle's plantation where she would once again be in danger.

Chapter 19

"About Delilah . . ." Davey hesitantly began. "What was done to her . . . it was more than just a beating."

In response to Laura's questioning look he went on. "Her back was lacerated . . . with a whip."

He waited for his words to sink in. It didn't take long.

Ashen-faced, Laura gasped. "You think Brad did this terrible thing?"

For someone to commit such an atrocity he would have to be an unconscionable fiend. She didn't want to believe it was her uncle's stepson, yet she could see in her mind's eye the coiled black scourge the man carried wherever he went.

"But why?"

"I don't know," replied Davey, wishing with all his heart he could spare her any further distress. But he was convinced Kincaid's real target was Laura, herself, and in order to protect her he had to tell her everything. Holding her hand between his two large palms, he related what he had found atop the hill, going on to explain why he no longer thought the shooting had been an accident and that he felt Brad Kincaid was behind the ambush.

Laura listened in stunned silence, then shook her head. "Even were he capable of such perfidy, it would serve no purpose for Brad to cause me harm."

It was one thing to allege the attack had been intentional. It was quite another to accuse a member of her own family.

Davey racked his brain for some way to persuade her to at least consider the possibility. "Are you aware that Kincaid told me you and he were engaged?"

Laura thought nothing else could astound her but Davey's query proved her wrong. "That's absurd. He did ask me to marry him but I said no."

"Why?" It was an impertinent question and Davey expected her to say it was none of his business which, from her point of view, was probably right. He *hoped* she would say it was because she had fallen in love with someone else—him being that someone.

Instead she said, "I've decided marriage isn't for me. There are places I want to go, things I want to see. A husband would only tie me down."

Davey hid his hurt and disappointment behind a cloak of indifference. He had been right about her all along. She was like a colorful butterfly destined to wing her way around the world from one glittering city to the next leaving a string of broken hearts in her wake. Once she was gone he would forget her. He hoped it would be soon for as long as she remained here he would protect her, with his life if necessary; because regardless of their differences, he could not deny his love for her.

"Was Kincaid angry when you turned him down?"

Relieved that Davey wasn't going to pursue the *why* of it, Laura replied, "He didn't appear to be. Even if he was put off by my refusal, spurned suitors don't go around killing those who have rejected them."

Her argument was much the same as Susan's had been but everything pointed to Brad Kincaid as the cold-blooded villain behind the attacks on Henry Ashe, Laura, and Delilah. Davey was more determined than ever to warn Laura against playing into his treacherous hands.

"I agree that most men would not go to such extremes but just hear me out for a moment."

Laura eyed Davey warily before nodding for him to continue.

"Suppose Kincaid was after your money, and finding he could not get it through marriage, he came up with a more complicated scheme to achieve his goal."

When Laura opened her mouth to protest, he placed a finger over her lips. "With you out of the way what would become of the wealth your father left you?"

Heatedly Laura shot back. "Well it certainly

wouldn't go to Brad. As my only blood relative Uncle Fowler would be the rightful heir."

Satisfied Davey carried his theory a step further. "And what if something happened to your uncle?"

"That's ridiculous!" Laura exclaimed trying again to sit up but finding her shoulders pinned to the mattress by Davey's firm hands. "You go too far. Brad would have to be insane to think he could get away with two murders and nothing you've said explains what happened to Delilah! You are the one who is crazy, Davey Logan! Why are you doing this to me?"

Great glistening tears pooled in her eyes. Plagued with guilt for bringing her sadness, Davey relaxed his grip but continued to hold her with his steady gaze. "I'm trying to save your life, princess, so that you can visit faraway places and meet those important people who will become the center of your world."

The words stuck in his throat like a bitter pill but he knew he couldn't force her to stay. He had achieved his heart's desire fighting against all odds to become a doctor. He had no right to ask her to disregard her own dreams for the life he could offer her in this unsettled wilderness.

"Get some rest now," he advised rising to his feet. "We'll talk more later."

Leaning down he brushed the moisture from her cheeks, then moved slowly toward the door.

"Where are you going?" The note of panic in her voice brought him hurrying back.

"I'll be in the next room." The smile he gave her

was teasing. "I won't leave you again, princess. Not until you command it."

He held the whip by its handle allowing the braided length to trail along the ground. His hand tightened. His muscles flexed, infusing life into the inert leather. As Laura watched the inanimate raw-hide began to slither, slowly, purposefully toward her. Mesmerized by the viper's hypnotic twisting and turning she could not move from its path. When the serpent reached her feet it raised its ugly head and she could see two venomous fangs, one on each side of its thrusting tongue. A mocking hiss warned that the snake was preparing to strike. Still she couldn't move. The serpent drew back, then lunged forward and all Laura could do was scream and scream and scream. When she felt its insidious body wrap around her she fought against its stran-glehold, flailing out to rid herself of its deadly coil.

"Wake up, Laura! It was only a dream," Davey managed to capture her arms, then sat down beside her rocking her shivering body to and fro.

Finally his voice penetrated her fear-glazed mind. She grasped his shirt in a viselike grip pulling him down on top of her as she sobbed out her terror. Davey held her against his chest wondering if she could feel his racing heart. He'd never been as scared in his life as when he heard her screams. Murmuring words meant to soothe and comfort he cradled her head in his hands, massaging the tense muscles at the back of her neck.

"Oh, D-Davey," she stammered when she was at last able to speak. "The wh-whip turned into a snake and it str-struck me. I couldn't move, Davey. I knew it was g-going to bite me but I just couldn't move."

"It was only a dream, princess. Brutus would never let a snake in the house."

His attempt at humor was partially successful. Laura fell back against the pillow wane and spent but she gave him a weak smile.

"Is that right? And just where is our protector?" she asked in a voice more like her own.

Davey chuckled. "All that shrieking sent him under the table shaking like a leaf."

"Marvelous! He can keep the snakes at bay but cowers in the face of a little feminine caterwauling."

"Never mind Brutus. I want to see what damage you've done to your shoulder."

Deftly he unbuttoned the borrowed shirt she still wore and slid it down her arms, then removed the bandages covering her injury. Despite her thrashing about there was no new bleeding. Laura remained passive while he examined the flesh where the ball had entered, then applied a fresh dressing.

When he was finished she said calmly, "The whip in my dream . . . . Brad was holding it. Then it began to move of its own volition, coming right toward me."

Davey could tell Laura was putting on a brave front for his sake as well as her own. He knew beneath the surface her nerves were as ragged as the torn flesh around her wound. Talking about the dream might again trigger the hysteria she'd nearly succumbed to a few minutes before. Yet he recognized her need to bring her fear out into the open where she could examine it, dissect it, come to terms with it.

"It's not surprising that you had such a dream. The brain is a funny thing. It stores away what the eyes see and the ears hear. Sometimes when we are asleep bits and pieces of what we have retained creep into our subconscious minds. Memories mix together and often what we get is a distorted picture."

Laura mulled over his explanation, then said thoughtfully, "It isn't really the dream that frightens me. I know an object cannot suddenly come to life. It's the symbolism that makes me afraid. The serpent represented Brad. If he is responsible for the evil you have purported, he must be stopped and, one way or another, I have to know the truth."

Admiration showed in Davey's eyes. "You are a remarkable woman, princess." Before he could think better of it he lowered his head and kissed her lips.

Laura quivered in response. She heaved a sigh and her breasts rose, their taut nipples touching his chest through the thin material of her chemise. Davey tried to control his desire but in her innocence Laura's every breath stimulated the aching need centering in his groin.

She had no idea what she was doing to him. As her heart hammered against her ribs and every nerve ending came alive, it was her own needs she was thinking of, not his. Instinctively she reached up to lock her arms around his neck. Encouraged by her response Davey traced the outline of her mouth with his tongue. Then slanting his head to one side he deepened the kiss, forcing her lips apart.

Laura closed her eyes, savoring the taste of forbidden fruit, relishing the feel of Davey's great weight pressing upon her. She ran her fingers through his thick black hair, ignoring the warning voice that said *this cannot be.* Tomorrow she would listen. Tonight she wanted to feel and taste and smell all that she had craved and been denied.

Like Laura, Davey chose to ignore the alarms going off inside his head. The ice princess had melted beneath his touch. What remained was a woman of unbelievable passion who fired his blood as no one else ever could. As her fingers worked their magic he felt his shaft harden and begin to swell. It was the pressure of his arousal straining against his breeches that finally brought him to his senses.

Laura was an untried virgin, not some doxie from Flora's whorehouse. In addition she had been shot. Any unnecessary movement was sure to aggrevate her injury.

With the utmost regret he drew back, pausing just inches from her flushed face, his eyes riveted on her perfectly formed features. Thick red-brown lashes fanned her checks, then her lids lifted. Gone was the haughty aristocrat from Boston replaced by a lovely young maiden who had thoroughly enjoyed his kiss.

Laura sensed his withdrawal even before he released her. It was as if a special gift had suddenly been snatched away by the giver. She tried to force his head down but he placed his arms firmly on either side of the pillow. His expression was pained, indicating the effort it cost him to control his volatile emotions. He wanted her as much as she wanted him and Laura wasn't about to let him walk away until they had resolved this thing between them. He had been hers for a moment. It wasn't enough—not nearly enough. Yearning to recapture that elusive, electrifying feeling brought on by his touch, she rubbed her cheek along his forearm. The tendons rippled and through half-closed lids she saw his jaw clench.

"I want you to stay with me, Davey." Her voice was low and husky. She didn't plead; she promised. Instead of a command, it was an invitation.

Davey's breath grew labored as wave after wave of naked carnality grappled with the last vestiges of reason. Rearing back his head he cried out in a language unfamiliar to Laura but there was no mistaking the significance of his gutteral entreaty. The battle was over. She was the victor. Now he would have to show her what to do with the prize.

Cupping her face in his hands, Davey surrendered. "I was afraid it would come to this, princess, though God knows I didn't want it to happen."

"What is it you didn't want to happen?"

He whispered his confession in a voice raw with emotion. "I didn't want to love you."

Unable to say more, unable to even breathe, Davey waited. *He loved her*. Laura felt her throat constrict. She wanted to laugh and cry and shout her joy for all the world to hear. Looking up she read the fear and doubt that transformed his handsome features into a mask of uncertainty. Tenderness filled her heart as she sought to reassure him. "I love you, too, Davey," she said with a smile.

Davey could scarcely believe his good fortune. At last he had found a woman to share his life. It wouldn't be easy for someone like Laura. She would have to give up her notion of traveling the world consorting with society's elite, but together they would dream new dreams and he would see that they all came true for her.

He frowned, remembering Laura's earlier declaration concerning marriage. Was he presuming too much in thinking she would change her mind in the space of a few short minutes? There was only one way to find out. He wrapped an errant curl around his finger, taking pleasure in the silk-smooth texture of the auburn lock.

"Did you mean what you said a while ago about not wanting a husband?"

Laura pondered the question before answering. "I thought I did at the time."

"And now?"

"Every woman has a right to change her mind, so they say." Again she gifted him with a beguiling smile. "I suppose it would depend on who was doing the asking."

Davey hesitated. Laura had said she loved him but love came in varying degrees. He was not unaware of the sacrifices she would be required to make if she accepted his proposal. "What if he was a half-breed bastard with little more than the shirt on his back?" he asked tentatively.

Laura lightly delineated the contours of his beloved face, following the planes and hollows with her finger. Davey caught the roaming digit between his teeth and sucked it into his mouth. The hungry heat of his tongue sent flaming impulses shimmering through Laura's body.

Breathlessly she gave him the answer he had been waiting for. "I would say yes. Yes," she repeated loudly.

Giving out a whoop, Davey buried his face in the curve of her neck, kissing her petal-soft skin. His lips brushed a path over her ear and across her cheek, finally honing in on her mouth. His tongue against hers sent Laura spiraling beyond the heavens to a place more beautiful than any on this earth, a star-studded wonderland of rainbows and waterfalls. But her journey was shortlived. Abruptly Davey withdrew once more. The bed creaked as he rose.

"I've got to get out of here before . . . before . . ." Sweat beaded his brow as he searched for a way to make her understand that a man's control was a fragile thing easily lost in the recklessness of a moment.

He needn't have bothered. Laura knew full well where their ardor was leading and why he was determined to resist its pull. She admired him for clinging to his high principles, but right now her body's needs took precedence over an old-fashioned code of honor. Having vowed their love for one another, she saw no reason why they should each be made to suffer alone and miserable just because a minister hadn't said the proper words.

"You promised not to leave me until I commanded it. I don't want you to go."

Davey could no more ignore her appeal than he could sprout wings and fly. Conscience, be damned! Here was the woman he loved, the woman he planned to marry on the morrow as soon as he could find a man of the cloth willing to perform the ceremony. What difference would a few hours make? Laura wanted him now and, God knows, he needed her to put out the burning fires raging within him.

She watched him take off his boots, then slowly undo the buttons of his shirt. Her fingers itched to perform the task for him. His gaze held hers as he worked the fastenings at his waist alert for any indication that she had had a change of heart. What he saw in her tawny eyes was anticipation and a hunger equal to his own.

Laura had never seen a naked man before. The sight of Davey's wide shoulders and broad chest tapering to a slim waist and hips had a dizzying effect on her. His long legs were lean and well-muscled but none of these things held her interest for more than a few fleeting seconds. It was the enormous protrusion jutting out at the juncture of his thighs which gained her attention. Erect, proud, awesome evidence of pure masculinity. She was more curious than frightened by the recognizable proof of his virility.

"Do you like what you see, princess?"

Laura flushed scarlet. She had been staring openly at his engorged shaft, acting in no way like an innocent. What must he think of her?

She needn't have worried. Davey found her bold appraisal to his liking. Having had no experience with chaste young virgins, he'd anticipated a very different reaction after her first glimpse of his distended manroot. He should have known better than to expect the expected from Laura, he reminded himself. Time and again she had caught him off guard combining a rare blend of mature sophistication with a childlike knack for getting into trouble.

In answer to his question, Laura stretched out her arms beckoning him to join her. He eased down on the bed carefully, drawing her close.

"Has anyone ever told you what a beautiful, bewitching enchantress you are?" His voice was a husky whisper filled with raw hunger. He tried not to think about the feel of her breasts crushed against his chest with only her thin chemise separating flesh from flesh.

"No," she answered shakily. "And I'm not at all sure I like the description. It makes me sound like some sort of sorceress who has cast an evil spell."

Davey slid his hand along her arm, sending chills up and down her spine. "Not evil, my love, but very, very potent."

He promised himself to be gentle. He didn't want to hurt her in any way but he knew there would be a certain amount of pain which had nothing to do with her injured shoulder. The only way to lessen that pain was to make certain she was ready for him when he took her. Tenderly he stroked her back. He rubbed one foot along her bare leg. His heart leapt when her body responded to his every touch.

"I love you so much, Davey."

Laura raised her head offering him her lips. His kiss was devastating, sensual, and artfully done, causing her to wonder how many women he had known before her. But soon there was no such thing as lucid thought. Davey's tongue explored her mouth, savoring the sweetness within. Tiny sparks ignited at her core, bursting into flames; flames fanned by desire to spread like wildfire, making her fingers tingle and her toes curl.

"God, but you feel good to me, princess," he rasped hoarsely as his tongue licked at her parted lips.

He palmed her right breast, circling its pink tip until he felt the nipple harden. Laura moaned, arching her back, wanting more than the gentle kneading of his skillful hand.

"Easy, love. Let me do the work," Davey cautioned, concerned that she might further damage her wounded shoulder.

Laura tried to obey his soft command but her newly awakened body seemed to have a will of its own. The driving force of unrequited ardor surged through her veins until she felt as if she was going to burst into a million pieces. When Davey's mouth replaced his hand to nip and suckle, Laura thought she would surely die from the pleasure of it. She clasped his head to her breast and, despite his warning, drew her knees upward. Using her feet for leverage she twisted her hips trapping Davey between her long, slender limbs.

Shifting slightly, his fingers plotted a path across her flat, smooth belly moving lower at an unhurried pace until he reached the mound of chestnut curls covering her woman's heat. Laura stiffened, uttering a nervous protest as he carefully parted her thighs to caress her wet, velvety softness.

Never faltering, Davey silenced her objection with a kiss. He adored the feel of her warm, willing body molded to his. He basked in the knowledge that he was exploring the unknown where no man had ventured before. Laura's nails bit into his naked back. Her breath came quickly as her heart raced frantically toward some secret end. She felt the hot, pulsing length of him against her skin but never spared a thought for how or when the last of her undergarments had disappeared.

Poised over her writhing form, Davey braced himself on powerful arms. Then his throbbing arousal found its mark, sliding inside the sleek, tight channel leading to the springhead of her desire. He paused when he reached the thin membrane barring his passage. Looking down at her cherished face he hesitated wondering if she had any idea what was about to happen. Laura's love-hungry eyes told him she not only knew but was eager to rid herself of the obstacle nature had placed in his way. His dark, smoldering gaze never left hers as with resolute pur-

285

pose he pierced the sheer tissue, burying his shaft deep inside the snug, satiny sheath.

He felt her quiver beneath him, saw her amber eyes grow wide with wonder, heard her blissful sigh. He allowed her time to adjust to the extraordinary sensations generated by the union of their bodies. Then slowly, cautiously, he began to move.

With each stroke of his mighty sword, the building storm escalated. Laura was a raging tempest of tumultuous emotions. Pressing forward, then drawing away, Davey teased and tormented. His lips skimmed over her fevered flesh leaving a trail of liquid heat in their wake. When Laura tightened her arms about his waist, he increased the tempo of his thrusts. Crying out his name, Laura begged him to relieve the unbearable pressure threatening to tear her apart at the seams.

With one final thrust the explosion came, hurling her into space where the sky lit up in a kaleidoscope of pattern and color. She glided through time, passing beneath a rainbow's arc, then circling the pale blue moon to follow a shooting star. Gradually she drifted back to earth and to the man who had transported her into infinity.

Davey had wanted Laura to reach her climax first. He had wanted to see her expectant face when she tripped over the edge of reality and plunged into the sea of paradise. Then he had planned to resume his slow seduction and together they would climb to the highest heights. What he had failed to take into account was the effect her unleashed passion would have on him. His swollen shaft was throbbing, hot, demanding. Now there would be no holding back and he could not take her with him for there was no time.

Trembling like a mountain of lava about to erupt, he caught her to him as he found his own release. His heavy weight came down on top of her; his chest heaved while he labored to draw air into his lungs. Davey had never known such a feeling of content-ment. What had taken place between them was more than mere physical gratification. They had become one in body and soul. With his mouth close to her ear, he whispered words of love both in the tongue of the white man and that of his Indian forebears.

Laura, too, felt at peace, thrilling over her ability to inflame his senses and sate his desire.

It was many hours later before they finally fell asleep wrapped in each other's arms.

Chapter 20

Laura snuggled close to Davey nesting in the curve of his long, lean body. She luxuriated in the feel of his bare skin next to hers. When his arm tightened across her breasts, she wiggled her hips, eliciting an immediate and not entirely unexpected response from a certain part of his lower anatomy.

"Oh no you don't!" Davey rolled away from her, coming to his feet on the opposite side of the bed. "No more of your witchcraft until I make an honest woman of you."

He looked magnificent standing there in naked splendor silouetted by the first rays of early morning sunlight. His hair was tousled. A shadow of beard darkened his jaw but to Laura he was perfect in every way. And he was all hers.

"I doubt you will find a minister awake at this ungodly hour."

She hoped to entice him back into bed. She wasn't ready to give up what they had shared even for a short period of time. But Davey was determined to set things right before he touched her again. Once they were man and wife, nothing and no one would ever keep them apart.

Frowning down at her, he asked solicitiously, "How are you feeling?"

Laura wanted to say *wonderful.* Instead she replied mischievously, "Do you mean my shoulder or my . . . ?" Smiling suggestively she left Davey to finish the sentence for himself.

He cocked a black brow. "One night of lovemaking has turned you into a wanton as well as a witch. I was talking about your shoulder."

Lowering her thick lashes Laura did her best to look pathetic. "It feels quite tender when I move. Perhaps you could recommend a good physician to prescribe something for the pain."

Anxiously Davey circled the bed, his face mirroring his concern as he made a place for himself beside her.

"Dammit! I knew better than to behave like a rutting stag! Here, let me see."

Carefully he removed the bandage while Laura toyed with the lobe of his ear. Much to his surprise Davey found the swelling around the perforation greatly reduced and no new seepage evident from the hole itself. He fixed Laura with a questioning gaze. For an answer he received an unrepentant smile.

"Don't be so serious, darling," she purred, playfully running her hand over his broad chest. "There's nothing wrong with me that you can't fix with a kiss."

Davey was relieved and at the same time exasperated with her for allowing him to believe she was suffering. "Never lie to your doctor," he warned leaning down to plant a kiss on her willing lips.

Sensing his irritation, Laura quickly set about to make amends. "I'm sorry, Davey. I didn't mean to worry you. I just wanted you to stay here with me a little longer."

How could he refuse after such a contrite apology? Lifting the covers he slid in beside her, enjoying the warmth left by her body heat in the spot she vacated to give him room.

"Don't think you will always get your way, princess. Once we are married, I will be wearing the pants in this family."

"Well you certainly aren't wearing them now, so I'd best take advantage of the time I have left to rule."

Laura raised herself on one elbow and rained feather-light kisses over his upper body. "Oh, darling. We are going to have such fun. Imagine waking up in Paris or London or Rome. We'll have the world at our feet and wherever we go people will say 'Aren't the Logans a handsome pair?' "

Davey tried to laugh at her foolishness but the sound died in his throat. He wanted to believe she was joking but something told him she had never been more serious. The idea of leaving Florida and those he had vowed to help was unthinkable. Suddenly he realized the mistake they had made by allowing sexual need to take precedence over the necessity of discussing their future in more practical terms.

He had assumed Laura would be willing to give up her dreams in order to share a life with him here. Instead she apparently expected him to follow her around the world living on her largess. Davey knew he could never be any woman's paramour and it was time Laura understood it, too.

Quickly he moved to distance himself from her. He stood up and walked toward the window, staring out at the unkempt barnyard where chickens scratched in the dirt while piglets wallowed in a mud puddle left by an overnight shower. There was nothing particularly appealing in what he saw yet he felt an affinity for this rugged land where his ancestors had managed to survive for generations. Desparately Davey sought for words to make Laura understand. Turning in her direction, he saw the look of confusion on her lovely face as she waited for him to explain his abrupt withdrawal.

He decided to begin by telling her about his life before he became a doctor. "Less than ten years ago, I was a wild young buck riding dispatch for the army mainly between Fort Brooke and Fort King. I was partnered with my cousin, Beth, and the Seminoles were on the warpath. When I look back at the risks we took I wonder how either of us survived."

Aghast, Laura interrupted. "You mean the army hired a woman to carry messages while they were at war with the Indians?"

Davey chuckled. "Beth was only a slip of a girl when we began working for the military."

In answer to Laura's shocked reaction, he went on to say, "Beth isn't your ordinary female."

Laura guessed that was probably an understatement.

"She grew up like me in a fort full of soldiers and rough-and-tumble frontiersmen. Rachel, her stepmother, tried to teach her how to be a proper lady, but Beth was always more at home in buckskins than a fancy dress; more comfortable on the back of a horse than in the kitchen. It wasn't until Robin came along that she discovered the advantages of being a woman."

Though she had no idea where all of this was leading, Laura found the story fascinating. "Who is Robin?"

"Now he is Beth's husband but when they first met they were like oil and water fighting their own private battle every inch of the way. Robin was sent to Florida by his uncle, a well-known congressman in Washington, to try and settle the dispute between the Indians and the settlers. None of us knew then that Robin was not only a lawyer but also a half-breed Seminole who shared a rare friendship with Osceola, the tribe's undisputed leader."

"Good heavens! Whose side was he really on?"

"Both," replied Davey. "Robin believed the Indians and the white folk could live together in peace. He worked as a liaison between the two opposing sides and to some degree his efforts paid off. But not without great sacrifice. Many lost their lives including Osceola who died in prison."

"Where are Beth and Robin now?"

"They live in the settlement outside the walls of Fort Brooke. Robin has his law practice and Beth has her hands full riding herd on their seven-year-old twin boys and an adorable red-haired toddler who shows all the earmarks of growing up to be just like her mother."

Laura smiled wistfully. "It must be wonderful to be a part of a large family."

Davey wanted to assure her she would soon be a member of the boisterous group, but he held back. It had to be her decision and there were still things she needed to know about him before she was asked to decide.

"It was Robin who convinced me to become a doctor. Soon after he and Beth were married, I found myself floundering seeking a purpose for my life. He pointed out the lack of physicians available to meet the needs of the people who had chosen to make this territory their home. Once he opened my eyes to the unnecessary suffering going on around me, I became determined to do everything I could to help. It wasn't easy but Robin's uncle used his influence to get me into medical school and I worked hard to make up for the years I had wasted."

Laura thought she knew what he was trying to tell her. He had struggled against overwhelming odds to achieve his ambition. It was not something a man could willingly turn his back on and she admired him for his resolve.

"Darling, I understand completely. You must think me terribly selfish to suggest you give up your chosen profession. Especially since I know firsthand what a gifted doctor you are."

Davey felt a bud of hope begin to unfurl where the knot had formed in his belly. But Laura's next words withered the bloom before it had a chance to fully blossom.

"Together we will find a place where your talent is appreciated. London, perhaps, or maybe Boston. You'll have a fine office with modern equipment and a hospital nearby in which to operate."

Laura clapped her hands together enthusiastically as she planned their future, certain Davey would jump at the chance to secure a lucrative practice while gaining a foothold into society. But Davey wanted no part of her world nor would he compromise his honor and integrity for monetary gain.

Sadly he shook his head. "You don't understand at all, princess. My life is here. It's where I belong and where I want to be."

Laura challenged him with a look of disbelief. "But surely you don't expect me to live in *Florida?*"

She made no effort to hide her distaste for the newly acquired state. It hurt Davey to realize she found no beauty in this spacious, verdant land of blue skies and sunshine, warm balmy breezes and meadows blanketed with wildflowers.

"What I *expect* is of little consequence, I'm sure," he answered coldly. "But Florida is my home and I don't intend to give it up to live in some crowded, foul-smelling city where people don't know or care about their neighbors."

Rising to her knees, Laura rebutted angrily, "Blast it, Davey Logan! How would you know what it's like to live among civilized people? You're nothing but a . . . a . . ."

"Go ahead and say it, princess." His voice was as hard as forged metal. His eyes bore into her with a look that dared her to continue.

Wisely Laura backed down. "I . . . I didn't mean it." Her crestfallen visage was convincing but Davey remained unmoved.

"It seems you didn't mean a lot of things," he replied icily.

"What about us?" Laura ventured to ask when long moments passed and the silence grew unbearable.

Davey was aware of the tears brimming up in her liquid amber eyes but he refused to be swayed by a femine ploy. "Is there an 'us'?"

Blinking back her tears, Laura looked down at the rumpled covers, noticing the splotches of dried blood staining the sheet. How could he ask such a question? More importantly, what answer could she give?

Following her gaze, Davey, too, saw the telltale crimson reminder of what they had shared. He loved her. He wanted and needed her, but it had to be on his terms or not at all.

"It's up to you, princess," he said softly, answering his own question while fighting the urge to take her in his arms and kiss her into submission. Instead he gathered his things and closed the door behind him, leaving Laura to wrestle with her demons.

Once Davey was gone, Laura allowed her misery to surface as she sobbed into the pillow so he would not hear. It wasn't fair of him to expect her to abandon the plans she had made. What did he have to offer in their place?

"Nothing!" she told herself.

Love! a small voice countered.

"It isn't enough," she argued.

The voice persisted. *Well, there's that big family you have always wanted.*

"Uncle Fowler calls them a bunch of mavericks. Imagine a girl wearing buckskins and fighting Indians."

Hey! I was listening, too, and the way I heard it the only Indian Beth ever fought against was the one she married.

"Oh, shut up!"

Arguing with herself did nothing to settle the conflicting war of emotions hammering inside her head, but it did serve to end her flood of tears. She needed time to think things through in a rational manner and she couldn't do that here. Not with *him* in the next room. Not when she could still smell his musky masculine scent on the pillow, still taste the manly flavor of his lips pressed to hers.

Yet she wasn't ready to face her uncle. She would never be able to hide her fears and doubts where Brad was concerned. What she needed was a quiet haven in which to meditate alone. One place came immediately to mind. She would go to the Ashes. With Susan and her father she would feel safe from the gunman who had ambushed her. She would have an opportunity to contemplate her future and decide whether or not to reevaluate her objectives.

More than once, Davey wondered if he had made a mistake in letting Laura talk him into taking her to Pine View. She looked so pale and fragile. He could feel the sharp bones in her back poking into his chest as they ambled along the road atop his big stallion. At first she had tried to lean forward in the saddle but stubborness soon gave way to fatigue. Now she rode slumped against his body, depending on his strong arms to keep her upright.

Moving her to the Ashe Plantation would have made good sense if she had been well. God knows, he couldn't continue staying alone with her at Wade's farmhouse after the argument they'd had this morning. He would have tried to convince her with words and deeds to accept his proposal and remain here in Florida. But unless it was her decision and hers alone, there was every likelihood she would someday grow to despise him. He would have to give her the time she needed to make up her own mind.

There was also the danger of her uncle returning with Brad Kincaid and his hired gunmen. Though he had not mentioned it to Laura, Davey found it hard to believe Fowler Dunstan was totally unaware of his stepson's nefarious activities. Pine View would offer more protection from attack than the isolated farm with its one-man guard.

Inhaling a whiff of her clean-smelling hair, Davey

thought how different this day was turning out from what he had anticipated when he had awakened at dawn with Laura cradled in his arms. He'd planned to locate the minister of the little church on the hill where Nell was buried and persuade the man to say the words which would make Laura his wife. After they were legally wed he would have gone to River Ridge and informed Laura's kin, making certain her uncle and Brad Kincaid understood the lengths to which he would go in order to protect her. Instead he felt like a thief running away with the spoils. It wasn't a comfortable position to be in and he hoped soon to set things right.

Thinking Laura had fallen asleep, Davey was surprised when she turned her face up to his. He wished he had the power to erase her troubled expression. When she spoke he knew she had been pondering the suspicions he had voiced.

"If you really believe Brad is a threat to my uncle and me, and that he is responsible for what happened to Delilah, why don't you go to the authorities? Surely now that Florida has become a state of the Union, there must be laws and someone to see that they are enforced."

Davey stared at the trail ahead. Her sweet lips were only inches from his. It was all he could do not to kiss her but he resisted the temptation by focusing his attention on the winding road. He wondered if she realized what could result from their night of passion. Every instinct told him to find the nearest preacher but he knew a woman as mule-headed as Laura could not be forced into marriage against her will. Best he keep his mind on other things. She had asked him a question and though he feared his explanation would only confirm her low opinion of the place he called home, she deserved an answer.

"We've always had laws. It's just that right now there is no one to see that they are obeyed."

Laura's look of incomprehension let him know he was making a muck of things. He tried again.

"Florida has only been a state for a few short months. As a territory we were governed by territorial laws preserved by federal marshals. Now crimes like murder, attempted murder, and assault are state offenses falling under the jurisdiction of local officials. Most areas are just beginning the process of electing sheriffs who will then appoint deputies."

"In other words, people can get away with murder and there is no one to stop them." Laura's voice rose sharply as she condensed his explication into one damning statement which pretty well summed up the situation.

"Let me remind you, princess, no one has been murdered. Besides I haven't any proof that Kincaid was behind the attacks on you and on Henry. For now I am operating on pure conjecture."

"What about Delilah? Can't she tell you who beat her so horribly?"

Davey shook his head from side to side partly in answer to her question and partly because he was amazed by how little she knew about a slaveholding society. "Delilah was in no condition to tell me anything. Even if she had, it wouldn't matter as far as the law was concerned."

Laura's amber eyes grew wide with consternation. "Surely it is illegal to whip a person near to death!"

Davey made a strange gutteral noise that Laura guessed might be an oath in some foreign tongue. "Much to my regret, Florida entered the Union as a slave state. Here, as in other states where slavery is legal, Delilah isn't considered a person even by those elected to uphold the law. She is a piece of property belonging to your uncle. What he does with his property is no one's business but his own."

"Why . . . why that's the most outrageous thing I've ever heard of!" Laura spluttered. "How can a nation founded on freedom condone such injustice?"

Puzzled by her sudden heated outburst, Davey asked a question of his own. "How is it you have lived at your uncle's plantation for weeks now and you know so little about the goings on around you?"

Laura felt the color creep into her cheeks as she remembered the conversation she'd had with Delilah the night she and Davey had quarreled. At the time her heart had gone out to the pretty young maid who had been taken from her parents and forced into a life of servitude. But, preoccupied with her own problems, she had quickly forgotten the incident. Looking back now she recalled wondering why the field hands at River Ridge never sang the old spirituals that rang through the air at Pine View. Then there were the bitter arguments between her uncle and Brad concerning the mysterious disappearances of slaves and the need for hired guns like Bart Harmon. She had been blind not to see the unhappiness of those around her; blind and completely oblivious to everything outside her own selfish interests.

Lowering her eyes so Davey would not see her shame, Laura admitted, "I didn't give it any thought. I'm used to having servants . . . people who work for pay, that is. At River Ridge things seemed much the same as they were in Boston. The house was kept clean, meals were on the table when it was time to eat . . . I just didn't think," she repeated.

They rode on in silence, neither knowing what to say. Finally Laura heaved a dejected sigh. "I'm not a very nice person, Davey. I consider only myself and my own needs."

Though Davey had often criticized her inwardly for being spoiled, he now jumped to her defense. Placing a finger beneath her chin, he tilted her head until she was looking up at him. "For what it's worth, princess, I find you to be an exceedingly nice person. You are brave and loyal . . . and beautiful inside and out."

Leaning down he gave her a quick peck on the nose which earned him a winsome, if dubious, smile. Luckily it was at that moment they reached the turnoff to the Ashe Plantation. Otherwise Davey's chivalrous resolve would have been no more than a dim memory.

Chapter 21

"What do you mean she's not there?" roared Fowler Dunstan when Bart Harmon and his men returned to the clump of trees atop a rise overlooking the Callahan homestead.

Bart shrugged his shoulders, then pulled a narrow brown cheroot from his pocket, taking his time to light it. He exhaled a puff of gray smoke, then repeated, "There's no one there, Mr. Dunstan, and Logan's horse is gone from the barn."

"Did you look inside the house?"

"Hell no! They gotta dog that's near 'bouts big as a bear and none too friendly. But if anyone had been at home they'd have showed themselves with all the fuss that animal was making."

"Damn!" Fowler growled. "Where could she have gone?"

Brad sat mounted beside his stepfather. "I told you we should have come back last night," he fumed, caressing the whip coiled around his saddlehorn. "Maybe she decided to get her tail home this morning."

Infuriated by the younger man's criticism, Fowler shouted. "Idiot! If she was on her way to the plantation we would have met her on the trail."

"Then where is she?" Brad's cold, sea-green eyes challenged Fowler to come up with an answer. He resented the way his stepfather spoke to him in front of the others. He had been right last night suggesting they waste no time finishing the job Harmon had botched, and he didn't intend to stand by and be made to look like a fool because the old man had ignored his advice.

"If I could answer that, I wouldn't be sitting here wasting my time in idle conversation with a know-it-all smartass like you!" Fowler shot back.

He stretched tall in the saddle, surveying the landscape while ignoring his stepson's accusing glare. His display of temper had heightened the color in his ruddy cheeks and set a pulse throbbing in his temple. If there was one thing Fowler abhorred it was incompetence. He'd been wrong in depending on Brad and Harmon. There was only one way to make certain Laura got what was coming to her and that was to handle the matter himself.

"I think I know where she has gone," he announced after considering his niece's options. "I have a feeling we might find little Laura at Pine View with her friend, Susan Ashe."

Brad was in the mood to argue. "Why would she go there instead of returning to River Ridge? Do you suppose she suspects something?"

Fowler snarled. "Who knows what cock-and-bull stories that bastard Logan has been telling her."

Speaking around the thin cigar held firmly between his teeth, Bart asked, "Do you want me and the boys to go get her back?"

The black scowl Fowler gave him was all the answer Bart needed to shut him up.

"Well, we can't just leave her there," Brad pressed, having properly interpreted his stepfather's look.

"We can't go storming into Pine View demanding her return either. There are at least three men inside that house who know how to shoot. We'd be sitting ducks."

"Then what are we going to do?"

"For now we're going home until I can come up with a plan," stated Fowler. "And no one is to leave the plantation until I give the order."

His instructions were meant for the entire ragtag bunch of miscreants but his smoldering gaze rested commandingly on Brad Kincaid. After a long tension-filled moment, Fowler dug his boot heels into the sides of his mount and started down the slope, setting a fast pace for the others to follow.

In the parlor, Laura sat quietly weeping into her handkerchief while Susan padded back and forth in front of the window. But not one prone to tears, Laura's sorrow was soon replaced by a profound anger which quickly escalated to full-blown fury.

Wiping away the last traces of salty moisture

from her red-rimmed eyes, she declaimed heatedly, "Whoever did this monstrous deed should be drawn and quartered, then left in the sun to rot!"

Nothing Davey said had prepared her for the sight of Delilah's horribly mutilated back. Against the advice of the others, Laura had insisted on going to the young maid the moment she arrived at Pine View, but one glimpse of the damage done brought the bile rising up in her throat. Having been heavily sedated, Delilah slept peacefully unaware of her audience. She did not hear Laura's gasp of dismay and outrage nor did she see Davey reach out to steady her ashen-faced mistress.

Now the men were closeted in the library speculating on what Fowler Dunstan might do when he found his niece was no longer at the farmhouse and what they could do to ensure her safety.

"I couldn't agree with you more," Susan avowed, carefully studying her visitor whose rancor seemed to match her own. As far as Susan was concerned, there could be no question as to the identity of the one who had inflicted the brutal punishment on Delilah, yet Laura had not mentioned Brad Kincaid's name. And though Susan knew her friend was not the sort to hide from the truth, she also understood what a crushing blow it must be to discover a man you trusted was capable of such barbarous cruelty.

Having been privy to Laura's most private feelings, Susan was aware of how much Fowler Dunstan and his family had come to mean after Franklin's rejection. She wished Laura did not have to face further disillusionment because of Brad's sadistic nature.

"Davey thinks Delilah will be all right with rest and the proper care. He said you should take it easy, too. Why don't you lie down for a while?"

In no mood to be coddled, Laura ignored the suggestion, choosing instead to ask a question of her own. "What will happen to her once she is well?"

Susan's expression became guarded. "If your uncle learns of Delilah's whereabouts, he will come to take her back. She belongs to him."

Laura jumped to her feet. "Blast it, Susan Ashe! I'm thoroughly sick of hearing people refer to Delilah as little more than a stick of furniture. She's a human being!"

Susan wondered just how far Laura would be willing to go in order to help the defenseless slave she appeared to care so much about. As for herself, she had already resolved to assist Delilah in escaping her bondage despite Fowler Dunstan's legal claim. She knew she would need an ally to make the plan she had in mind work. What she didn't know was whether she dared trust the niece of the man she was determined to outmaneuver. Though she admired Laura's independent spirit, she worried that misplaced loyalty might constrain her friend to inform Fowler or, worse yet, Brad Kincaid, of the subterfuge she was plotting.

Seating herself in the spot Laura had vacated, Susan made a pretense of straightening the folds in her skirt. "Regardless of how unfair it may seem, facts are facts. According to the law, Delilah must be returned to River Ridge."

Now it was Laura's turn to pace. Long moments passed when the only sound to be heard was the ticking of the clock on the mantel. Then suddenly Laura stopped in midstride and whirled about.

"According to Davey, there is no one in authority to carry out the law." A short time ago she had despaired of finding a way to save the hapless maid. Now she felt a ray of hope. Perhaps they could use the very thing she had recently found so appalling—the lack of a bona fide peace officer—to their advantage.

Susan eyed her suspiciously. "So?"

"So it's simple. We are going to help Delilah escape," Laura replied matter-of-factly. "I haven't figured out quite how to go about it," she confessed, "but it shouldn't be too difficult since there is no one to stop us."

Susan had her answer as far as Laura's loyalties were concerned. She was tempted to remind the enthusiastic new abolitionist that Fowler Dunstan and his stepson would most definitely try to stop them should they get wind of what was going on, but she held her tongue. Laura, she reasoned, had to have some inkling of the danger involved in aiding a runaway slave. Besides Susan needed her help to save Delilah. If they formulated their plan well, they could pull it off with a minimum of risk and none would be the wiser. If the Specter could do it, so could they!

307

* * *

"Those damnable hooligans aren't going to get to either of the girls as long as they are under my roof!" An outraged Henry Ashe slammed his palm down on the wooden desktop causing Wade and Davey to exchange anxious glances.

It was Davey who voiced what both were thinking. "I brought Laura here to buy some time. Now I'm afraid it may have been a mistake. It won't take Dunstan long to figure out where she is and if he rides in with his army of mercenaries the three of us may not be able to stop them."

Henry faced the two men with stubborn determination and no little pride. "If it comes to a fight, my people will stand behind us," he declared.

Wade answered sharply. "For God's sake, Henry! You know it's illegal for a black man to bear arms! Do you want to get your entire work force hung!"

Flushing at the unnecessary reminder, Henry snapped back. "There are other ways to keep foxes out of the henhouse without shooting the varmints!"

"Just what have you got in mind?"

The old planter didn't have a ready answer to Wade's question.

"There is no law against having some of your folks posted as lookouts," Davey suggested tactfully. "That way we will have some warning if Dunstan decides to pay a call."

Henry brightened, glad to have something useful to do. "Good idea, son. I'll see to it right away."

After the door closed behind Susan's father, Davey and Wade breathed a singular sigh of relief. "He means well," Wade assured with a fond smile, "but I don't think Henry realizes how dangerous Harmon and his band of brigands can be."

Davey cocked an eyebrow. "I'd say Harmon and the rest of his bunch are pussycats compared to Kincaid. Don't forget what he did to Delilah."

"At least they don't know she is here. How soon do you think she can be moved?"

Rubbing his chin thoughtfully Davey replied, "A couple of days if fever doesn't set it. The sooner the better. I'd sure hate to see Henry and Susan get into trouble for harboring a fugitive."

"We won't let that happen." Wade gave Davey a confident grin. "I've heard tell there's some people here 'bouts willing to help runaways make good their escape."

"You don't say?" Davey arched his brow again.

Wade's face was the picture of innocence. "Yep! Heard tell this organization is headed by some reckless fool the negroes call *Specter.*"

Giving his friend a look of mock sternness, Davey chided. "Didn't your mama ever caution you about listening to rumors?"

"Sure, but that never stopped me."

Both men laughed heartily enjoying a private joke only they understood. Then sobering, Wade confided, "I hate keeping things like this from Susan."

Davey felt the same way. If and when Laura decided to give up her harebrained notions about traveling the globe in search of adventure, he wanted to enter marriage with everything out in the open. But meanwhile there were lives at stake and the risk of someone making a slip was too great.

"Be patient, Wade. Just a few more days. Once Delilah is safe, you can tell Susan all there is to know. And maybe soon the *Specter* will no longer be needed to wage war against oppression."

Wade masked his skepticism behind a hopeful grin. "I pray you are right, my friend. I pray you are right."

Having satisfied his lust, Bart rolled beyond the reach of Angel's clinging arms. He fastened his breeches, then brushed loose straw from his hair. "You'd better get back to the house before you're missed," he suggested dispassionately as he pulled a cheroot from his pocket and struck a match to its tip.

Angel's pretty pout was wasted in the dark barn where only the vague outline of her shapely body was visible. "You know they have all gone to bed. The only one to miss me will be you if I leave."

The girl's extravagant conceit grated on Bart's nerves. As far as he was concerned women were good for one thing and one thing only. Now that he'd taken what Angel had to give he preferred solitude in which to enjoy his smoke without any silly female chatter. He wished Angel would just go away and leave him alone. She was one of the best little sluts he'd ever plowed but she was getting a mite too possessive for his liking. Plus there was always the chance someone would catch them rutting in the dark. Angel couldn't seem to get the job done without a lot of unnecessary moaning and groaning and carrying on. Though Bart didn't consider himself a coward, he had a healthy respect for that damned whip her stepbrother wouldn't let out of his sight. The more he thought about Kincaid the more anxious Bart was to be rid of Angel.

Squinting through the smoke he said, "Honey, you've plumb tuckered me out. Be a good girl and run along home. I'll let you know when to come back."

Rising to her knees Angel purred, "I could make it real special for you, Bart. I know ways I'll bet you've never tried."

"I'm not a betting man, honey. Now get yourself into the house before someone finds you here." His voice was edged with impatience.

Used to having her way, Angel retorted sharply. "You think you can just snap your fingers and I will come running. Then you can shoo me away when you are finished with me! Is that how it is, Bart?"

Bart decided she had just about summed it up only she didn't seem to want to play by his rules. "Well, honey, nobody's forcing you to come when I snap," he answered coldly.

Like a spitting cat Angel flew at him. She knocked the cigar from his mouth before he could grab her arms and pin them to her sides. Furiously she hissed, "How dare you speak to me that way, you worthless two-bit gunman! You're nothing but hired help groveling at the feet of your betters! What's more you're ugly and you smell like a skunk! Everytime you touch me it makes my skin crawl! Just wait until I tell my father you've been making unwanted advances toward me!"

In a rage Bart wrapped his hands around her slender throat cutting off the hateful words. Since the day of his arrival at River Ridge Plantation, Angel Dunstan had thrown herself at him. Whenever he looked up she had been there swinging her hips as she passed, making eyes at him, gesturing provocatively until there could be no doubt as to her eagerness to get into his pants. It was she who had suggested they meet in the barn that first time and she who had taken the lead in their feverish coupling. His hands squeezed tighter. She was more debased than a common whore who sold her body in order to live. Angel was a bitch in heat who knew no season though Fowler Dunstan would never see it that way.

Bart didn't notice when her small fists ceased to beat against his chest. He didn't smell the smoke as the dry hay ignited at his feet. He didn't hear the grinding sound of splintering bone when Angel's delicately sculpted neck cracked.

The next morning amid the smoldering ruins of the barn Fowler Dunstan discovered his daughter's badly charred body. He had managed to get the horses to safety soon after smoke from the fire had alerted those at the manor house that something was amiss, but he'd had no way of knowing Angel was in the blazing inferno.

"What the hell was she doing out here in the middle of the night?" demanded Brad.

Fowler chose not to answer as he stared down at what was left of his beautiful Angel.

"Maybe she started the fire," Bart suggested. "Accidentally, of course." He went to reach in his pocket for a cheroot, then changed his mind. His first impulse, once he'd come to his senses and realized what he had done, had been to hightail it out of there. But that would have looked suspicious and he was certain the tyrannical plantation owner would follow him to the ends of the earth if he thought him responsible for his daughter's death. He wished for the hundredth time he had left a week ago when he'd had the chance. Instead he was becoming deeper and deeper embroiled in a sticky situation.

Brad snarled. "Don't be an ass, Harmon. If Angel had started the fire, accidentally or otherwise, she wouldn't have remained inside the burning building."

Trying to offer a believable explanation that would not involve him, Bart muttered, "A falling beam might have konked her on the head before she could get out."

"It would have taken time for the flames to reach the rafters," argued Brad derisively.

"Shut up, both of you!" Fowler's thundering

313

command brought the debate to a swift end. "It makes no difference now. She's dead and nothing will bring her back."

An uneasy silence followed, then Brad speculated aloud, "But this might bring Laura back."

Fowler was not so overcome with grief that he couldn't see the merit in his stepson's supposition. "You just might have something there," he nodded. Revenge against the girl who had stolen his birthright was never far from his thoughts.

He instructed Bart to ride immediately to Pine View and inform the Ashes about the tragic accident. The rangy gunman was halfway to his horse when Fowler called him back. Curling his hands into fists at his side, he issued one final order.

"If my niece is there make certain she understands that her aunt is inconsolable and needs the comfort of her loved ones in her time of sorrow."

That his wife was not as yet aware of her loss made no difference to Fowler as he watched Bart Harmon disappear around the house.

Chapter 22

"I have to go! Aunt Hester needs me!" Laura found herself caught up in a tangled web of divergent emotions. Feelings of regret over Angel's senseless death and compassion for her poor, grief-stricken aunt were twisted and intertwined with an inescapable thread of fear for her own safety. Out there beyond the security of these walls was some unknown assailant who had tried to kill her yet she hadn't the heart to turn her back on the silver-haired little lady who had already experienced so much sorrow in her life.

Davey threw up his hands. "It's a trap, Laura! Your life won't be worth a plug nickel if you leave here with Harmon!"

"You make it sound as if someone killed Angel just to get me back to my uncle's plantation!"

It was unfair of Davey to add to her fright by bringing up his groundless accusations. She needed his encouragement and, instead, he was trying to talk her out of what she had to do. If he loved her he would understand. Hester Dunstan had welcomed her into her home and treated her with kindness. Laura could do nothing less than repay that kindness by offering what solace she was able to give.

"It didn't take them long to figure out where she was," Wade commented from where he stood with his arm around Susan.

Davey's eyes remained fixed on Laura's chalk-white face. "At least they didn't come riding in with guns blazing."

"Uncle Fowler would never let that happen," insisted Laura, stubbornly defending the man who had selflessly reached out to her after her father's death.

A disgruntled noise issued from Davey's throat. Loyalty might be an admirable quality in most instances but Laura was carrying a good thing too far. The blinders she was wearing could very well cost her her life.

The tension between the pair was clearly evident to the room's other occupants. Trying to end the shouting match, Susan interjected. "I never cared much for Angel but she didn't deserve to die such a horrible death. And poor Hester . . ." She broke off, going to place her hand on Laura's shoulder. "I'm sure the shock has left her devastated."

Laura could only nod, too overcome with emotion to speak.

"I don't know that I can be of any help," her friend went on soothingly, "but I would like to go with you."

Laura felt as if the weight of the world had been lifted from her shoulders. Not only did Susan understand, she was willing to accompany her when she faced what was bound to be a strained reunion with her uncle.

"Now wait just a minute!" Wade Callahan had something to say about Susan's magnanimous offer. It was one thing for Laura to feel obliged to comfort her aunt. It was quite another to involve his fiancée.

Susan started to speak but Davey cut her off. "Wade, I'd like a word with you in private." He gestured toward the library. "If you ladies will excuse us this will only take a minute."

Without giving Wade a chance to protest he exited the room. Once the two were alone, Davey hurriedly argued his case. "I know how you feel about Susan going to the Dunstan place. I don't want Laura out of my sight either. But if they are together Kincaid won't dare try anything. There have already been three unexplainable accidents within the past two weeks."

When Wade hesitated Davey added, "Don't worry. We'll keep a close eye on them. Your engagement to Susan will give us a plausible excuse for spending time at River Ridge. Besides it will be easier to take care of that other business we have to attend to if the girls aren't here."

Wade scowled. He didn't like it but he had to admit what Davey said made sense. Finally he conceded grudgingly. "Against my better judgment I'll go along with you for a couple of days but that's all. I won't feel at ease as long as Susan is in that nest of vipers."

Davey gave his companion a grim smile. "I know it's asking a lot and I'd be a fool to say there wasn't a certain amount of risk involved. Frankly I'm hoping Laura will take a good hard look at her uncle and his degenerate stepson. Maybe she will see what's really there beneath the urbane facades they assume when it suits their purpose."

Still Wade had reservations. "Let's just hope they don't catch her looking," he replied glumly. "Especially if and when she discovers what a pair of villains they are."

The men were scarcely out of earshot before Laura whispered urgently, "I appreciate your wanting to come with me but what about Delilah? Doesn't she need you here?"

Susan clapped her hands together, her blue eyes sparkling with excitement. "Delilah is the main reason I volunteered to go," she giggled, unable to check her exuberance. "She will be in good hands while we are with your aunt, and it will give us time to make plans for setting her free without interference from Wade and Davey."

"They are going to be very angry if they find out what we are up to."

"They won't find out, although I almost wish they would. They should be ashamed of themselves for not taking an active part in securing Delilah's freedom. How can they do nothing in the face of such blatant injustice?" railed Susan whose commitment to the cause remained strong in spite of her recent inability to take part in the abolitionist movement.

Laura pondered the question, her troubled expression taking on a faraway look. "Men are basically concerned with their own affairs," she replied. Her thoughts reverted to the days when she had craved love and affection from a father too busy to show such emotions. "Perhaps they just don't see the needs of others."

"Balderdash! There are plenty of men who not only recognize the evil of slavery but play an active role in trying to abolish the practice. There is one in particular I would like to meet."

Laura smiled indulgently. "Do you mean one of these knights in shining armor has caught your eye? And here I thought your heart belonged to Mr. Callahan."

"Well of course it does," assured Susan, unable to hide a telltale blush. "But the *Specter* is such a romantic figure dressed all in black, appearing out of nowhere to come to the aid of those who cannot help themselves."

The *Specter?* Good heavens! It sounded as if Susan were describing a character out of an adventure novel rather than a flesh-and-blood being. Taking a seat on the sofa Laura began idly toying with the fringe bordering one of the throw pillows. "Please tell me more about this dark-clad paragon of virtue," she entreated. Though she suspected Susan was making the whole thing up, her curiosity

319

had been piqued. What if such a man really did exist? The possibility teased Laura's senses, leaving her slightly breathless.

Satisfied that she had her friend's undivided attention, Susan proceeded to recount everything she knew or had heard about the mysterious shadow figure called *Specter*, embellishing on his heroic exploits. Listening spellbound Laura began to form a picture in her mind. She envisioned an enormous phantom sweeping down from the night sky, his flowing ebony cape blocking out the light of the moon so no one could see his face. Like a giant raven he descended to earth, plucking one of the persecuted from under the nose of his startled master. Then soaring up into the heavens he winged his way to freedom, carrying his precious burden.

"Laura?" Davey's deep resonant voice put an end to her musings. "Are you feeling all right? You looked as if you were in another world."

Laura's amber eyes focused on her surroundings. She hadn't heard Davey enter the room nor had she heard Susan leave but for the moment they were alone. Recovering quickly she lied, "I'm fine. I was thinking about Aunt Hester and how this terrible tragedy has to be affecting her."

"Susan has gone to get some things together. Wade and I will take the two of you to River Ridge."

Laura wondered why he had decided to give in after heatedly opposing her plans but she was not about to question his change of heart. "What about Bart Harmon? Isn't he waiting outside?"

"Wade is sending him ahead to inform your uncle that we will be accompanying you and Susan to ensure your safe arrival."

There it was again. The implication that someone at River Ridge was responsible for what had happened to her. Still it was comforting to know she would not have to ride out alone with Brad's scar-faced henchman. Not that she thought Bart would dare try anything. Her uncle had sent him to bring her back and she was certain Fowler would expect her to arrive with every hair in place.

The return to River Ridge was less taxing than Laura had anticipated. Fowler welcomed her with open arms asking after her welfare while refraining from any mention of her hasty flight from the Callahan farm. He extended a cordial greeting to Susan, saying it had been much too long since her last visit. When he went so far as to politely thank Davey and Wade for providing them an escort, Laura was convinced Davey must be wrong in presuming her uncle knew something about the attack on her.

Despite his friendly manner, Fowler did not invite the men to stay and with no little trepidation they bid their charges goodbye, saying they would return the next morning to attend Angel's burial service.

On entering the house, Laura was struck by the eerie quiet. Rather like a mausoleum, she thought, unable to stem a shiver of apprehension. The curtains had been drawn against the light leaving the rooms they passed shrouded in gray shadows. Fowler paused at the bottom of the wide staircase.

"I'll wait for you in the library. I'm not very good at a time like this," he apologized. "Hester is so distraught I don't know what to say to her."

Laura felt that just being with his wife would have provided comfort but her uncle had his own share of grief to deal with and he would have to do it in his own way.

They found Hester Dunstan in her daughter's bedroom, an inordinately childlike chamber adorned with an overabundance of pink frills and ruffles. She sat in the cushioned rocker. Her tiny feet lifted off of the floor, then came lightly down again as the chair tilted to and fro. In her arms she cradled a rag doll with red yarn hair and a wide embroidered smile.

"Ssh," she whispered, hearing their approach but not looking up. "Angel is asleep. Such a good child, my Angel. Never gives me a bit of trouble."

Susan cast a worried glance at Laura as the gray head bent to place a tender kiss on the forehead of the smiling doll. At a loss as to how she should deal with her aunt's bizarre behavior Laura looked around uncertainly, then, seeing that the pink coverlet had been turned down on the bed, she quietly suggested, "Shall I tuck her in, Aunt Hester?"

She reached toward the doll but Hester clasped it to her chest recoiling from Laura's touch.

"No!" she shrieked raising blue eyes that glittered far too brightly. Her head bobbed down again and she began to croon a lullaby.

In an undertone Susan muttered, "She's as mad as a hatter."

Motioning her friend to follow, Laura tiptoed softly out the door. As they retreated the old woman continued to sing, rocking the make-believe baby in her arms.

Fowler was waiting for them in the library just as he said he would. With the heavy curtains closed, the dark-paneled room was illuminated only by the double-globed lamp burning on the corner of the huge desk. Laura had to remind herself that it was broad daylight outside for judging by the house's gloomy interior one would think it was the dead of night.

Her uncle stood up as the girls entered. "How did you find your aunt?" he asked after gesturing for them to sit down.

Laura could not contain her distress. "Oh, Uncle Fowler, she is not herself at all. I'm terribly concerned and I feel so helpless."

When her voice choked with emotion Susan spoke up. "Hester seems to have withdrawn into the past and she won't let go of Angel's doll."

Fowler shook his head sadly. "My daughter's death has been a great shock. Poor Hester. She loved Angel very much. As we all did," he hastened to add.

"We want to be of assistance," assured Susan, "but as Laura said we don't know what to do for her."

Laura turned her head to find Fowler staring at her. His eyes burned like live coals glowing red with their intensity. She wanted to believe it was some peculiar trick of the lamplight that made her feel as if he were attempting to brand her soul, but she could not quite convince herself. In that moment a trace of fear she had managed to hold at bay returned leaving her ill at ease and wishing she were back at Pine view with Davey by her side.

"For now your being here is enough." He smiled, dispelling the strange sensation which only seconds before had Laura ready to bolt from the room like a frightened rabbit. "We must be patient with Hester and hope in time she will be her sweet self again."

He was saying all the right words yet something in his manner left Laura questioning the depth of his feelings. He had never shown his wife any affection in Laura's presence, not so much as a pat on the shoulder or a warm smile across the table. Trying to place herself in her aunt's position, she knew instinctively she would want her husband with her should they suffer the heartache of losing a beloved child. However, neither her aunt nor her uncle appeared inclined to share their grief. Fowler's attitude struck her as cold and unnatural especially considering the pain and loss his wife had suffered in the past.

"I believe I will sit with Aunt Hester for a while. Perhaps I can coerce her into taking a nap before dinner." ·

As Laura had hoped, Susan volunteered to go

with her. At the door her uncle's voice brought them to a brief halt. "Brad will be happy to hear you have returned to us, my dear. He was most concerned when I told him of your accident. But then you know how much he cares about you."

Nothing in her uncle's tone could account for the sudden sense of foreboding that came over Laura at the mention of Brad Kincaid's name. Chiding herself for being a foolish ninny, Laura hurried toward the stairs. It was Davey's fault for planting doubts in her mind. Brad had always acted the gentleman whenever they were together and she had no reason to think he would do otherwise now. Surely someone else was responsible for what had happened to poor Delilah. Perhaps that someone wanted to make it appear that Brad was the culprit. Still, she decided as she mounted the steps, she preferred to avoid the inevitable encounter with her uncle's stepson for as long as possible.

It was stiflingly hot beneath the leafy branches of the big live oak tree where Angel was to be laid to rest. The brilliance of the sun overhead seemed to mock the somber gathering. Trickles of perspiration ran down the valley between Laura's breasts, the salty moisture making her feel sticky and uncomfortable. On her right Hester Dunstan stood clutching the doll she had substituted for her dead daughter. The old lady paid little heed to the droning words of the minister. While he spoke she softly hummed a tune, her frail body swaying from side to side, keeping time with the music.

Neighbors who had chosen to declare a temporary truce with their former friend in order to pay their respects, showed curiosity and in some cases embarrassment over Hester's unusual behavior. Laura, who had only pity for her bereaved aunt, glanced around the circle of people waiting for the coffin to be lowered into the ground. Across from her, Susan stood between Wade and Davey, her face solemn as befitted the occasion.

Davey looked up and their eyes met. He frowned as his gaze shifted to focus on Brad Kincaid standing to her left. There was no mistaking Davey's dislike for the man. It was plain to see in the rigid set of his jaw and the ripple of flexing muscle beneath his black coat.

Laura moved closer to Hester, hoping Davey would read the silent message she was attempting to convey. She had not encouraged Brad in any way since her return to River Ridge. She had, in fact, managed to evade him up until he appeared at her side shortly before the others arrived. Last night she and Susan had taken their meal in Angel's bedroom, not wanting to leave Hester alone. They had skipped breakfast this morning using the heat as an excuse for their lack of appetite. By the time she looked in his direction once more, Davey had visibly relaxed. A brief nod of his head let her know he understood.

The morose clergyman seemed bent on holding his audience captive as long as possible. Not until the restless stirrings of the mourners became obvious even to him did he bring the graveside service to an end. Though food and drink had been prepared for the guests, most made their excuses and took their leave without entering the cheerless manor house. Laura could not really blame them for their hasty departure in light of her aunt's comportment. As soon as the men began shoveling dirt into the deep hole containing the wooden casket, Hester loudly proclaimed it time for her baby to eat and stumbled back toward the mansion cooing to the doll as she went.

Davey caught up with Laura as she made to follow.

"Laura." He spoke her name, then lightly touched her elbow.

Spinning around she faced him, her forehead creased with anxiety. "Oh, Davey. I am so worried about Aunt Hester. You see how she is. Surely as a doctor there must be something you can do."

What Davey wanted to do was haul Laura up in his arms and kiss away the lines marring her brow. Instead he said, "I dig out bullets and set bones, princess. I don't know how to cure a sick mind."

It wasn't the answer Laura wanted to hear. "But she can't go on like this pretending that pile of rags is a real baby!"

Davey searched for something hopeful to say. His experience into the realm of mental illness was limited at best. "She hasn't had time to adjust to Angel's death."

"She can't adjust to what she refuses to accept,"

Laura replied more sharply than she intended. *Blast! It wasn't Davey's problem, yet here she was jumping down his throat.*

"I'm sorry," she murmured. Then added forlornly, "I feel so helpless."

Patting her shoulder understandingly, Davey commiserated. "I know this isn't easy for you. Maybe in a few days she will be better. I'm sure having you and Susan nearby will bring her comfort though I'd rather you were both still at Pine View."

"She doesn't even know who we are." Laura had never been more tempted to take the easy way out. All she had to do was say the word and Davey would gladly accompany her back to the Ashe's plantation away from the gloomy atmosphere pervading River Ridge. But to do so would be admitting defeat, and Laura was determined to stay and help Hester through this latest crisis.

When he saw her shoulders slump, Davey thought for a moment Laura had decided to give up the harebrained notion to remain with her batty aunt. Then she straightened her back. Her face took on that look of obstinate resolution which assured him she had not had a change of heart.

"Talk to her," he advised. "Try to get her to talk to you. Maybe something you say will draw her back to reality."

He wasn't very optimistic but it was the only advice he had to give besides telling her to leave with him while she had the chance. And he already knew what her answer would be if he tried to dissuade her from staying.

"How about taking a ride in the morning?" he suggested, hoping she might welcome the opportunity to be with him. "I could stop by for you after breakfast."

Smiling for the first time since she had awakened that morning, Laura responded with gratitude. "Thank you, Davey. A ride would be lovely."

Davey and Wade left a short time later. As much as she dreaded the hours to come, Laura's heart felt lighter. She had something to look forward to on the morrow. But first she had plans to make with Susan tonight.

Chapter 23

The girls lay facing each other in the wide bed Laura had come to think of as her own. The house was quiet for it was nearing midnight. Still they whispered, not wanting to risk being overheard.

"While you are riding with Davey, I am going home to check on Delilah. If she has recovered enough to be moved, we'll sneak out tomorrow night after everyone is asleep and take her to safety."

"So soon?" gasped Laura. "But what about Aunt Hester? If you go to Pine View who will keep an eye on her?"

Susan hesitated. "I don't think she will miss either of us and I'll only be gone an hour. You'll have to admit she doesn't seem to know we are here. Or maybe it's that we are here but she isn't. I think she's somewhere lost in the past."

Laura had to agree that their absence would probably not be noticed by the elderly woman they had come to keep company. "But how are we going to move Delilah to a place where she will be safe from pursuit?"

Susan giggled, anticipating Laura's surprise when she let her in on the secret arrangements she had been making since the attack on the Dunstan maid.

"It's all taken care of," she confided with no small degree of satisfaction. "Delilah is to be taken by ship to my cousin who lives in New York."

"But . . ."

"Ssh! Let me finish. I sent a message to an old farmer who lives a few miles north of here. I know for a fact the man is adamantly opposed to slavery and I suspect he might be working with the abolitionists. He has agreed to take Delilah to Jacksonville and put her on a ship bound for New York. I've also written to my cousin and I am certain she will be waiting at the docks. All we have to do is get Delilah to Seth Parker's place and she will be on her way to freedom."

All they had to do? The plan sounded simple enough and Laura admired Susan for coming up with a scheme that just might work. But she did not delude herself into believing the plan was foolproof. There was still the problem of getting Delilah to the Parker homestead which meant they would first have to leave River Ridge in the dead of night without being seen or heard. It was a prospect guaranteed to unnerve even the most stouthearted.

Playing the devil's advocate, Laura voiced one of several concerns. "If Mr. Parker is an abolitionist, what is to stop him from telling the man you call *Specter* about our intentions? And what if the

331

black-clad crusader doesn't approve of our involvement? Isn't he liable to try and stop us?"

"No doubt he had something to do with putting an end to the messages I used to get in the hollow tree, but he won't stop me this time!" Susan vowed, enlightening Laura about her previous association with the freedom fighters and how her ties with the group had been severed for no apparent reason. "As for Seth Parker spilling the beans, I'm not overly concerned. The likelihood of his knowing the *Specter*'s identity is too remote to constitute a real threat."

"The hell you say!" Wade Callahan's oath burst forth like a loud clap of thunder resounding off of the walls in the small one-room cabin Seth Parker called home.

Wade and Davey had come to the farm to make their own arrangements for Delilah's safe passage north. The news the old man had to share sent a usually affable Wade into a scalding fury.

"I'll wring her neck! I'll blister her bottom until she can't sit down for a week! Dammit! Why couldn't she stay the hell out of this?"

Ignoring Wade's harrangue, Seth explained to Davey. "I was on my way to find you when you two showed up at the door. I figured you'd know what to do. I just sent word that I'd help her so she wouldn't go asking someone else and get herself in trouble."

"Trouble? She'll know the meaning of the word before I'm through with her!" railed Wade.

"Actually it's not a bad plan." Davey chuckled much to his friend's dismay. "Too bad we didn't know about Susan's cousin sooner. We could have used her as a contact."

Wade wheeled around prepared to wipe the grin off Davey's face, but Seth took care of that with his next words.

"The message said she and Dunstan's niece would be bringing the injured woman here late tomorrow night. Kind of surprised me to hear the man's own kin was working against him."

Davey paled at the thought of Laura embarking on such a dangerous mission. Thank God Seth was one of the few people who knew the identity of the *Specter*. Otherwise he and Wade would have been blissfully unaware of the girls' shenanigans until it was too late to stop them. But what were they to do now? If they admitted knowing of their surreptitious activities, Susan and Laura would realize who had told and possibly even guess the reason why the old farmer had betrayed their confidence. This entire operation was turning into a fiasco.

Thinking quickly Davey said, "We owe you, Seth. Too bad we don't have a dozen more men like you working for the cause. Your place is the first stop on the road to freedom for those fortunate enough to escape their bondage and tomorrow night the cargo you are expecting will be delivered as scheduled . . . only not by those two madcap females," he added after a pause.

Seth Parker shook Davey's hand, his perceptive eyes bright with emotion. "The people don't make it this far on their own. Would that I had a son like you."

Davey cleared his throat, moved by the other's words. "Let's go, Wade," he said hastening toward the door. "We've got a couple of fillys to corral."

"I doubt a pen will hold them," muttered Wade, still fuming over his future wife's underhanded dealings. "I intend to hog-tie Susan until this whole business is finished."

"One thing's for certain," Davey declared, remembering the times he'd had to save Laura from disaster. "I won't breathe easy as long as that pair is on the loose!"

"Ah, here you are."

Laura whirled around at the sound of Brad's voice. She had known she could not continue to avoid him indefinitely but she was still startled when he came up behind her unexpectedly. After spending the afternoon talking to Hester in what turned out to be a frustrating, one-sided conversation, she had left Susan to watch over her aunt and gone out on the terrace for a breath of fresh air. The sun dipped low over the distant ridge taking with it much of the energy-sapping heat of the day.

"I . . . I just came out to watch the sunset," she replied, hating the nervous tremor that crept into her voice. She was afraid to question Brad regarding Davey's allegations; afraid to hear the answers he might give, but without those answers she could no longer feel at ease in his company. Yet he had no way of knowing why she had distanced herself from him, which didn't seem fair.

Brad looked out across the endless rows of cotton. "There's nothing quite like a Florida sunset."

The sky was ablaze with vivid horizontal bands of gold and blue and pink.

"It's beautiful," she sighed as they watched the wide ribbons blend together, creating a magnificent spectacle of modulating colors.

"But not as beautiful as you, lovely Laura," Brad astonished her by saying.

His flattering words brought a blush to Laura's cheeks. It wasn't the first time he'd used that description of her, but now she found his smooth manner, the way in which the softly spoken compliment hung in the air, extremely disconcerting.

Noting her heightened color, Brad's thin lips stretched into what Laura thought of as his almost-smile. "I'm sorry, my dear. It was not my intention to embarrass you but surely you must know how much you mean to me. I was hoping you had reconsidered my proposal. After being forced to spend the past few days with that uncouth savage, I thought you might now see me in a more favorable light."

Laura was quick to recognize the arrogance behind his pretty speech. He seemed confident that in a comparison between Davey and himself, he was bound to come out on top. But he was wrong. With an effort she bridled the urge to defend the country doctor who had dedicated his life to helping the sick and needy living in the Florida backwoods. Brad Kincaid would never understand how she could prefer a rugged frontiersman to an aristocratic planter. She didn't understand it herself. But there it was. The truth struck her like a lightning bolt, blinding in its intensity; overwhelming in its magnitude. Davey Logan was the manifestation of every dream she had ever dreamed, and in that instant she knew only one course was open to her. Suddenly, without warning or regret, she surrendered to a love she knew would be boundless and everlasting.

Brad completely misread the capitulating smile which curved her lips and set her amber eyes aglow. He had no way of knowing her thoughts were of another man, one he considered his inferior. "Your expression gives me reason to believe you have come to your senses at last. Perhaps I owe Logan a debt of gratitude. I trust he didn't frighten you with his barbaric manners while you were forced to endure his company. Your being compelled to spend the night with him was most unfortunate, of course, but under the circumstances I doubt there will be any scandal. Still it might be best if we were wed without delay. Once you are my wife no one will dare mention your name in connection with his."

Delighted with the way things seemed to be turning in his favor, Brad prattled on unaware of the effect his words were having on his listener. What began as irritation over his arrogant presumption quickly rose to white-hot fury when Brad unleashed his verbal attack on Davey.

Unable to hold back her anger, Laura hissed, "You pompous ass! You callous, self-centered peacock! You are so concerned with my reputation you haven't even asked how I am feeling. A rather extraordinary oversight for someone who claims to want to marry me, wouldn't you say? For your information, the man you call a barbarian saved my life. It wasn't the first time either. Why you aren't fit to wipe Davey's boots!"

Laura's chest was heaving; her eyes flashed liquid fire as she continued her tirade. "But you are right about one thing, Brad. I have come to my senses. Davey has asked me to marry him and that is exactly what I intend to do!"

At first Brad could not credit what he was hearing. He wanted to laugh but he didn't know how, so he simply stared at the infuriating woman who seemed determined to yank the foundation from beneath his carefully laid plans. Her face told him she was serious. In a heartbeat, disbelief turned to blind rage. His fists clenched. Too bad he had left his whip inside on the table. He wanted to feel the smooth black leather grip against his palm. He wanted to thrash the willful creature standing before him until she learned who was master. He longed to hear her beg for mercy the way Delilah had done. A few lashes across her tender flesh would change her mind about giving her body and her fortune to an ill-bred heathen. Oh, he could almost taste the satisfaction he would derive from bending her to his will.

But Brad knew her punishment would have to

wait. Susan Ashe would certainly come running if Laura began to scream. Even Fowler might frown on what Brad deemed just recompense for the insult his niece had delivered. For now there was nothing he could do but try to convince her to reconsider. Regardless of his success or failure he would eventually make her pay for foolishly choosing a bastard Indian over one of her own kind.

"My dear Laura. Forgive me if I have appeared insensitive. I simply felt it best to forget the entire debacle. What happened to you was most reprehensible; but rest assured, if I could get my hands on the man who shot you, I would flail his hide."

Laura gave Brad a look of utter loathing. He had thought she would appreciate his willingness to reap vengence on her assailant. Instead she seemed repulsed by his guarantee that the culprit, if apprehended, would be properly chastized. Silently she glowered at him as if he were something beneath her contempt.

"I understand, my dear. We all appreciate what Logan did to help you in your time of need, but you can't throw your life away just because you feel beholden to the man. Besides he's a doctor. It's his duty to care for people who are injured."

Laura's chin lifted obstinately. Rebellion was written all over her stiff features. Brad's eyes narrowed. He was growing impatient with the stubborn chit.

"All right," he compromised in a last ditch effort to make her see reason. "If you are determined to repay him for services rendered, try money! Hard, cold cash will free you from whatever debt you think you owe."

In spite of her anger, Laura couldn't help laughing but it was not a pleasant sound. She tried to imagine how Davey would react if she placed a sack of coins in his hand and told him it was payment for "services rendered." She was tempted to enlighten Brad on just how thorough the servicing had been. That would put his aristocratic nose out of joint for certain. But what had taken place between Davey and herself was no one's business but their own. To throw it in Brad's face would be cheapening something incredibly rare and beautiful.

The unexpected sound of her laughter caught Brad by surprise. He could find nothing humorous in their conversation and he suspected he was the butt of some joke he didn't understand. Catching her roughly by the arms, he gave her a shake. "This is a serious matter, Laura. I won't allow you to demean yourself by marrying that heathen," he sneered.

His ugly, pinched features and the viciousness of his grip enlightened her to another truth. Brad was not only capable of inflicting pain, he actually seemed to enjoy the opportunity to subjugate one less powerful in physical strength than himself. She could almost see Delilah quelling at the feet of the despot.

Laura tried to pull free but his hold was too tight. His fingers were bruising her skin. In panic she blurted out, "Take your hands off of me or I'll scream! I hate you, Brad Kincaid! You're mean-minded and cruel, using that hideous whip against people like Delilah who can't fight back!"

Stunned by Laura's mention of the missing maid, Brad released his hold. Before he could collect himself, Laura picked up her skirts and fled into the house, the accusation she had hurled so carelessly ringing in her ears like a death toll. Tears of remorse and fear blinded her as she ran. "Dear God," she moaned, "What have I done? More importantly, what will Brad do now?"

Long after Laura disappeared inside, Brad stood staring blankly at the door. She knew what he had done to Delilah which could only mean one thing. The black bitch was still alive, probably hiding out at Pine View. He had thought her dead after the way he had vented his rage on her following Laura's rejection of his proposal. He remembered how he had brought the whip down across her back pretending it was Laura feeling the sting of his lash. He'd tied her hands to the bedpost but left her legs free taking perverse pleasure in watching her body jerk, her hips lift each time he applied the braided leather. He had encouraged her to cry out for the sound of a woman in torment excited him. When his sex had swelled to near bursting, he had mounted her but as soon as he found his release, he had continued to discipline his captive.

Like his father, Brad knew how to keep a female in line. Too bad the old man had died before Brad was old enough to take over the plantation. Had he been of age, he would have stopped his weak, sniveling mother from marrying Fowler Dunstan. Fowler was a thief. He had stolen what belonged to the Kincaids and his mother had allowed it to happen. But they would pay for their duplicity. And so would Laura who had shunned him in favor of a worthless half-breed. They would all pay the price. Then he would have back what was rightfully his.

But first there was that damned darky to take care of. It had been stupid to untie her but he had been so sure she was dead. Before he'd had a chance to get rid of her, he had heard his stepfather shouting his name. When Fowler told him Laura's horse had returned without her, Brad had gone with him to the spot where they expected to find her body. He had thought to come back later and bury Delilah in the woods. But it hadn't worked out as planned. Both women were still alive.

Brad didn't want to think about what Fowler might do if he learned that his stepson had whipped another slave against his orders. Apparently Laura had decided not to tell, knowing her uncle would demand the return of his property. She was a meddler like all women, with a tendency to involve herself in men's affairs and that made her extremely dangerous. He would have to keep a very close eye on her. Maybe by now his ruthless stepfather had come up with a plan to hasten her demise. They needed to talk but before he sought Fowler out he would send some men to watch the Ashe Plantation. Delilah would have to show herself eventually and when she did he would be ready to grab her. Once Fowler had taken care of Laura there would be just two more obstacles in his way. The neighborhood would be shocked when his deranged mother and the man she had unwisely chosen to wed both met with a tragic accident but he doubted many tears would be shed.

Fowler Dunstan was more than a little annoyed. The attempt to rid himself of his troublesome niece and gain her fortune had failed. Instead he had lost his only daughter in a fire whose origin remained a mystery. There was still no clue as to what had become of his valuable house slave, and Hester— who had always been meek and malleable—had come completely unhinged, causing him no end of embarrassment. As if that were not enough, he was finding it increasingly difficult to keep a rein on his hot-headed stepson. And what of Bart Harmon and his men? He knew their loyalty went to the highest bidder.

Leaning back from his desk, Fowler closed his eyes. He was losing control. His position as master of River Ridge was being threatened by his stepson's vicious nature and insatiable greed. He had to act and act quickly or risk forfeiting everything he had worked so hard to acquire. If only he could come up with a way to dispose of Laura and Brad at the same time. Coming to his feet he felt the tension in his neck begin to drain away. A plan was taking shape in his mind and for the first time in more days than he could count, he smiled.

* * *

After dispatching a couple of the men to Pine View with instructions to keep an eye out for any unusual activities, Brad made his way toward the study. He was startled to see Bart coming out as he approached. Harmon touched the brim of his hat as they passed but didn't speak.

"What the hell did he want?" demanded Brad, entering to find Fowler just closing the wall safe.

Fowler took his time in answering, first replacing the painting of a marshland scene which served to conceal the secret cavity. "I sent for him. I told him I didn't tolerate inefficiency. One more blunder and he will be out on his ass."

Resenting his stepfather's high-handed ways, Brad argued, "It's my place to talk to Bart. I hired him."

Fowler's eyes took on a feral glow. "You may have invited the man here, but I pay his salary and I give the orders. Don't forget it!"

"Have you come up with a way to get rid of Laura?" Brad asked, changing the subject while he seethed inwardly.

"If you were worth your salt, the girl might reconsider your proposal and the problem of Laura and her money would be solved." Sarcasm dripped from Fowler's tongue like thick syrup.

Anticipating with delight the effect his news would have on the bigoted planter, Brad announced with equal derision, "I guess I don't have what it takes. Laura has just told me she intends to marry *Dr.* Logan."

"The hell you say!" To Brad's immense satisfac-

343

tion, Fowler's naturally ruddy cheeks changed to an ever-deepening shade of purple. "By God, she's as crazy as Hester if she thinks she can get away with this!"

When Fowler clutched one hand over his heart while he reached for his chair with the other, Brad became alarmed. It wouldn't do to have the autocratic old fool die first. That would leave Brad with no legitimate claim to Laura's money. He circled the desk and eased his stepfather into the chair.

"Calm down, for God's sake!" Brad hurriedly poured a shot of whiskey from the decanter and held it to Fowler's lips.

"I'll see her dead before I let her marry Lance Logan's illegitimate son!"

In truth the circumstances surrounding Davey's birth had little to do with Fowler's fit of temper for he, too, had been born on the wrong side of the blanket. No, his complaint stemmed from the fact that Laura, knowing his hatred for the savages, would dare defy him by seeking to marry a man whose mother was an Indian.

"We were going to kill her anyway." It irritated Brad to have to issue the reminder. What Laura wanted was of no consequence. She would not be alive long enough to see her dreams brought to fruition.

Fowler immediately regretted allowing his emotions to come into play. He had already taken steps to rid himself of his unwanted niece as well as his overly ambitious stepson. With Laura out of the way, Davey Logan would no longer constitute a threat and life could get back to normal. Only he would be a great deal richer and he would have satisfied his need for revenge against everyone who had tried to take what was his.

Bart tucked the roll of bills back into his pocket and pulled out a cheroot. Five hundred now and five hundred when the job was done. And to think he'd nearly missed out on the biggest bank roll he was ever likely to see in this life. Lucky for him he hadn't run away after he'd killed Angel. Yep, things were certainly looking up, he decided, striking a match on the heel of his boot, then squinting through a cloud of smoke.

Dunstan was one blackhearted old reprobate but he didn't hold that against him. Imagine hiring someone to do away with your niece and stepson when your daughter wasn't yet cold in her grave? Now that took guts! Too bad about the niece though. She was a real looker. Bart blew a cloud of smoke into the air. *Maybe it would work out so's he could sample her charms before he did her in. No point wasting what she had to offer.*

As he headed toward the slave quarters, Bart patted his pocket, still not quite able to believe his good fortune.

Chapter 24

They rode in silence beneath the shady canopy of moss-strewn oaks and tall towering pines. The gentle rocking motion of the slow-moving horse, the steady clip-clop of the animal's hooves, had an hypnotic effect on Laura as they traveled south along an unfamiliar path. Davey led the way with the purposeful manner of a man who knew where he was going. Their destination was of little importance to Laura. All that mattered was that they were together.

Occasionally they came within sight of the river. Once Laura paused to watch a flock of gulls overhead flying in perfect formation, winging across the narrow strip of land separating the Saint Johns from the Atlantic Ocean. A week ago she would have envied the birds their freedom, but not now, not since she had come to realize the depth of her love for the big, broad-shouldered man riding ahead of her.

Wistfully she studied the back of Davey's head

capped with thick dark hair worn several inches longer than was fashionable. She remembered its silky texture and experienced an aching need to touch him and be touched in return. But she dared not voice that need, for though he had arrived at her uncle's plantation shortly after breakfast as promised, his mood had been distant and brooding. She had looked forward to greeting him with the news that she was willing—no, anxious to marry him even though it meant giving up her dreams of adventure in far-off places. But after one look at his solemn face, she had swallowed back the words. When he had helped her to mount, then pulled in front of her making no effort at conversation, Laura began to think he had changed his mind. The possibility that he no longer loved her was almost more than she could bear. Perhaps he was taking her to some secluded spot away from curious ears in order to spare her embarrassment when he told her their brief affair had been a mistake. If so, she had no one to blame but herself.

Davey had almost lost his resolve when Laura rushed out the door, her smile more radiant than the morning sun. She had looked so young and gay. He wanted to believe it was because he was there. His dearest hope was that she had decided to accept his proposal and remain at his side forever. Then he had remembered his conversation with Seth Parker. This very night Laura and Susan were planning to deliver the injured slave to Seth after he and Wade had ordered them to stay out of trouble. How naive he had been in expecting her to obey. Laura craved adventure. She had told him so time and again just as she'd made clear her opinion of his native land. As far as she was concerned Florida was a provincial wilderness populated by rustics and savages. She probably found life here so boring she had decided to spice it up with a little excitement of her own making. If she was trying to disguise her guile behind a charming face it wasn't going to work. He was not about to be taken in by a facade of light-hearted innocence.

The more he thought about it the angrier he became until his features were set in lines as rock-solid as granite. One way or another he was going to make her admit what she and Susan had planned, then he would point out the flaws in their scheme. If necessary he was even prepared to tell her that less risky arrangements had been made to ensure Delilah's safety though he hadn't yet figured out how he would explain his involvement.

Laura wondered if Susan had reached Pine View yet. What would she say if Wade Callahan caught her sneaking into her own house. Her lips curved upward in a knowing smile. She needn't worry. Susan was clever and she had that poor sodbuster wrapped around her finger. What in the world did she see in him anyway? Surely she could do better than to saddle herself with a man who had nothing but a ramshackle farm and a boyish grin. Laura's smile faded to be replaced by a thoughtful expression. It didn't seem to matter that Wade had little to offer and no prospects in sight. Susan was head over heels in love with him and had every intention of moving into the rundown cabin once they were married. When Laura had asked in dismay how she could leave her beautiful home to live in squalor, Susan had laughed, not the least offended by her outspokenness. "It's obvious you have never been in love, my friend," she had replied sagaciously. And at the time Susan's observation had been correct. Their conversation had taken place before Laura had come to acknowledge her feelings for Davey. But now she knew exactly what Susan meant. Not once in all of her soul-searching had Laura given a thought to where they would make their home if she married the half-breed country doctor. It could be a tumbledown shack or a thatch-roofed hut. Or they might just camp out under the stars each night. Susan was right. It really didn't matter.

But what if Davey had changed his mind? How could she possibly go on without him? In what seemed no time at all he had become the center of her life, the pivotal point around which she revolved. So lost was Laura in her musings her mount edged up beside Davey's big black stallion before she realized he had come to a stop.

Following his gaze, she saw that the wooded path they had been traveling ended atop a rise. There below stood the very dwelling she had been thinking about—Wade Callahan's farmhouse where she and Davey had known their one night of rapture. He had brought her back, leading her along a circuitous route. Did he plan to dash her hopes in the very spot where they had begun? She glanced warily in his direction but his face gave nothing away.

Without a word Davey nudged his horse in the flanks. Brutus raced from the barn wagging his tail, barking in welcome. Davey's stern mien remained fixed even as the huge dog ran to greet him. Laura considered beating a hasty retreat but she would have to face the truth eventually. No point in putting it off, she sighed. Still Davey's austere mood did not bode well for what was to come.

Once they had moved into the house, he asked, "Would you like some coffee?"

"No. No, thank you."

Davey's voice didn't sound as formidable as he looked. He had even unbent enough to give Brutus a pat on the head. Having received his share of attention, the animal now lay curled up in front of the empty hearth while Laura stood nervously fiddling with her hands, wondering what to do next.

"Shall we sit down?" suggested Davey.

"Why?"

"Because it's more comfortable than standing up."

"What I mean is, why did you bring me here?"

Taking a seat on the couch Davey answered. "It seemed as good a place as any to have a private chat."

Laura felt the butterflies begin to stir. She had been right. He was going to withdraw his offer of marriage, tell her it was all a mistake. Well fine. It wouldn't be the first time she had loved someone who hadn't loved her back. She willed herself not to cry. She wished he would get it over with so she could crawl off and lick her wounds. But Davey seemed determined to prolong her agony. Indeed he waited as if he expected *her* to begin the conversation. Finally she did.

"I'm ready."

She had chosen to remain standing. Now she squared her shoulders and thrust out her chin looking for all the world like someone preparing herself to face a firing squad.

"For what?"

"To listen, of course." Why was he making this so difficult, she fumed inwardly.

Davey laughed without humor. "Funny, I thought you might have something you wanted to tell *me.*" *Damn the woman for not coming right out and admitting the truth. Hell, he was giving her the perfect opportunity to fess up and ask for his help.*

Blast the man! Could he read her mind? The possibility brought color to her cheeks for lately her imaginings had become quite sensually explicit especially when she thought of him and the night they had spent together under this very roof. *Did he expect her to admit she couldn't live without him, then wait for him to say her decision had come too late? At least she could spare herself that humiliation!*

"I don't know where you could have gotten such an absurd idea. I have nothing to say to you. Now I'd best be returning to the plantation for my aunt may need me."

Haughtily she moved toward the door but Davey was on his feet in a flash. Reaching out he caught her arms and yanked her back against his chest. He

351

was disappointed and he was angry. Neither emotion set well with him.

"Lying doesn't become you, princess," he ground out between clenched teeth as he swung her around. "And you're not very good at it," he added contemptuously.

Tears brimmed in Laura's eyes. She felt trapped and at a distinct disadvantage. How was she to maintain her pride when faced with an adversary who could discern her innermost thoughts? Her shoulders slumped in defeat. She knew he wasn't going to let her leave until he'd had his pound of flesh. With head bowed submissively she said, "You win, Davey. I'll say the words so you can have a good laugh before you send me on my way."

She took a deep breath. He felt her slender body quiver beneath his strong, unrelenting hold. "I love you," she whispered knowing none of the joy which usually accompanied such a declaration. "I want to marry you and live with you wherever you choose to live."

Davey tilted her chin, forcing her to look at him. He wasn't laughing. Shocked speechless, he watched twin streams of moisture roll down her pale cheeks. Of all the things she could have said, this was the most unanticipated. He had just about given up the hope that she might come to care for him fully and completely. Now, out of the blue, she was professing a willingness to marry him. This in spite of her less than favorable opinion of his home state and knowing he had nothing to offer her except a life of hardship. No, he amended. That wasn't entirely true. Though he would never be able to afford the material trappings she was used to, given the opportunity, he would lavish her with love and cherish her until his dying day.

Tenderly he brushed away the salty wetness. "Why in God's name would I laugh about something as important as our future?"

"B-because it's too late," she stammered, heartsick over what might have been. "B-because you are angry." She gulped as the floodgate holding back a tidal wave of misery began to give way. "B-because you don't love me anymore!" she wailed as the barrier broke, sending a rush of fresh tears flowing down in the wake of those not yet dried.

Her body convulsed as she sobbed out her wretchedness. Davey pulled her close, murmuring into her ear but she was too distraught to comprehend what he was saying to her. She struggled to breathe. With each inhalation her breasts pressed against his chest. Soon his shirt was damp where she had buried her face in the crook of his arm but still she continued to weep. Once started there seemed to be no end to the torrent of tears.

Knowing his softly spoken assurances were not getting through to her, Davey waited patiently for the outpouring to subside. He contented himself with stroking her back and running his fingers through the cascade of auburn curls which had come loose from the pins. The chestnut mass giving off the sweet-smelling scent of sunshine and wildflowers stirred his senses.

Minutes went by or was it hours? Davey didn't

know or care. Satisfied to have Laura locked safely in his embrace, he stood suspended in time. Finally her sobs began to abate and she sagged in his arms, her energy spent. Bending, he scooped her up, retracing his steps to the couch. Once seated with Laura cradled on his lap, he fumbled in his pocket for a handkerchief. Sniffing loudly, she took the handkerchief and wiped her eyes, then began nervously twisting the square of linen around her fingers.

Refusing to look at him she mumbled shakily, "You must think I'm a perfect dolt carrying on this way."

"None of us are a perfect anything, princess. You are willful and stubborn and very very beautiful—but you are not a 'perfect dolt'!"

Laura glanced up and caught him smiling. His straight white teeth contrasted sharply with his deep-tanned complexion. It was hard for her to believe this was the same man whose visage had been as dark as a thunder cloud when they had arrived here.

"You forgot loyal," she said, taking heart from his more genial countenance.

It was the wrong thing to say for Davey was immediately reminded of his purpose in bringing her here. "Ah, I have no doubt you are loyal, princess. It's only a question of to whom."

Laura was hurt by his strange response and on the heels of her pain came a swift surge of anger. After she had professed her willingness to remain with him in this humid, bug-infested territory most of which seemed to be swampland, he had the nerve to doubt her devotion! She had humbled herself before him knowing he might reject her as her father had. Accepting the fact that he might not love her was difficult enough without having to try and decipher his cryptic remarks.

Flushing from the heat of her ire she tried to pull from his grasp as she ground out. "If you can't trust me, then you don't love me so just let me go, you . . . you . . ."

"If you say *savage* I'll turn you over my knee and teach you the meaning of the word!"

"You wouldn't dare!"

"Try me!" he challenged.

Again Laura experienced the bitter taste of defeat. She thought she was all cried out until she felt her eyes filling once more. But this time the tears stemmed from frustration brought on by her own helplessness. Giving up the struggle, she implored him. "Please let me go. I don't blame you for not wanting me and I am so dreadfully tired of fighting. I want to go home."

"I think I liked you better when you were breathing fire," he quipped, loosening his hold on her arms. "And another thing . . . I wish you would stop trying to put words in my mouth."

His eyes were like smoldering embers, more black than brown and darkened by a desire he could no longer hold in check. He had longed to touch her, to kiss her, to make love with her ever since that one night of splendor they had shared. At last they were alone together and all they had done so far was

355

argue. He hadn't forgotten that she and Susan were conspiring to secretly undertake a dangerous mission which could land them both in a heap of trouble and he fully intended to take her to task for not confiding in him. But looking down at her adorable face, recognizing a tiny seed of hope in her expressive amber eyes, he decided the lecture he had brought her here to deliver could wait a little longer.

"Are you saying you still want me, Davey?" Her low-pitched voice registered her uncertainty. Inside she was trembling with fear as she awaited his reply.

Instead of answering, Davey tangled one hand in her hair, slowly pulling her toward him. His intense gaze held a potent energy which attracted her like a magnet. Laura was drawn to the power source, her heart slamming against her ribs as she anticipated what was to come. When at last his lips covered hers, her brain exploded, sending out a starburst of resplendent multicolored lights. He deepened the kiss, thrusting his tongue into her mouth and Laura thought she would die from the pleasure of his tender assault.

Too soon he withdrew. He leaned back pensively observing each subtly defined feature comprising her exquisite face. Not expecting him to end the kiss so abruptly, Laura moaned her disappointment aloud. Davey understood her need for it was no greater than his own. She had said she loved him but he needed more than mere words to convince him he wasn't imagining his good fortune.

Their clothing was an unwanted barrier but not for long. They went to work in silent unison, Laura frantically ripping at the buttons on her blouse while Davey yanked his shirt over his head. Soon they lay naked on the narrow sofa. Davey promised himself to go slowly. He wanted to touch her all over, delay that moment of ecstacy when they would come together in the only way their tortured bodies could find release. But Laura was like a caged tigress set free, wild and wanton and equally determined to waste no time with unnecessary foreplay. She needed him inside of her to make her complete and she needed him now.

The rough fabric covering the cough made her back itch but it was the prickling sensation at the juncture of her thighs which cried out for immediate relief. She could feel the length of his burning arousal searing her belly, branding her as his. She thought it must be painful to have that stiff protrusion trapped in an unnatural position between their bodies. She let one leg fall until she felt the floor beneath her bare foot. Then she bore down, grinding her heel against the smooth surface. Still she wasn't strong enough to shift him from his present position.

Davey knew what she wanted and he would see that she got it, but not yet. For the moment he was content to smother her with kisses and fondle her breasts. If only she would stop squirming. Irrepressible even in lovemaking, Laura reminded him of a stallion always straining at the bit.

"Slow down, princess," he urged, skillfully paying homage to one creamy white breast with his mouth. He experienced a thrill of satisfaction when he felt her nipple peak and grow hard as he suckled.

Laura tugged at his hair. When he reluctantly raised his head she arched her back, urging him to take the other tasty bud between his lips.

"Good, princess. Very good."

His praise held a double meaning. Not only was the piquancy of her flesh pleasing to the palate, but at some point during his ministrations she had ceased her frantic efforts to hurry him along. Now it had become a matter of keeping his own rampant desire under control. Keenly aware of his own painful throbbing, Davey couldn't help wondering which of them held the upper hand.

Working his arm between their sweat-slick bodies his fingers stroked the silky curls covering her woman's mound. "Soft, so soft." Reverently he parted her to gain entrance.

Laura whimpered, tightening her muscles to encase his warm, probing finger. She raised her hips encouraging him to further exploration. Slowly, maddeningly, he set about making her ready for him. He teased, he caressed, he experimented until he triggered the right response.

"Help me, Davey! Dear God, I need you now! I'm falling!"

Her ragged plea nearly sent *him* over the edge as she writhed in agony beneath his heavy weight.

"It's all right, princess. I have you and I won't ever let you go." He came inside of her quickly, lifting her to meet his rapid thrusts.

Laura's scream rent the air sending Brutus scurrying out the door. Her body tensed. She was afraid. She stood poised unsteadily on a pinnacle high above the earth. She had trusted Davey not to let her fall yet she was spiraling faster and faster through the air, plummeting toward the ground. She screamed again, then suddenly she was floating. No, that wasn't right. She was riding on the back of a huge bird with wings as black as midnight. Together they glided through the air, landing in the soft grass growing beside a bubbling brook. Just before she opened her eyes, Laura envisioned the transformation of the enormous feathered creature. She saw a man, large in stature, his face concealed beneath the hood of the dark cape he wore. Still dazed from her heady flight, she whispered the name which came to mind, the name of the one Susan had spoken of as if he were some sort of mythical being. *"Specter."*

Davey froze. He wanted to lift his head; ask her what it was she had said for surely he had misunderstood her. And no wonder. His heart was beating so rapidly all he could hear was its pounding in his ears. If only he had the strength to move, to open his eyes. He managed to suck in some much-needed oxygen but speaking was impossible when one was gasping for air. Besides it wasn't important. What mattered was that she loved him and was going to be his wife.

The velvety soft touch of Laura's tongue licking his lips served to push his vague uneasiness aside. He felt the now familiar ache in his loins that came from wanting to bury himself deep inside this beautiful woman who belonged to him. With no little difficulty he reversed their positions until she was on top, her knees clamped firmly along his hips. He was fascinated by her willingness to act as the agressor in their lovemaking.

Boldly Laura closed her hand around him making him forget how exhausted he had been just moments earlier. When she began firmly stroking his distended organ, he could think of nothing but the pleasure to come. As she finished working her magic and prepared to mount him, all rational thought had long since been driven from Davey's mind, replaced by a propelling force which would take them to heaven and back.

Chapter 25

Wade had known Davey for nearly a decade. They'd met when Davey was attending medical school in Charleston. One day while walking down the street from opposite directions each had seen a gang of ruffians beating an elderly black man and both had jumped to the old negro's defense. After thoroughly trouncing the bullies, Wade invited Davey into the nearest tavern to celebrate their victory and from there a close and lasting friendship had developed.

Now Wade looked at the one who had shared his triumphs and tragedies as if he were a total stranger. "You didn't bring it up? Just like that you are telling me you didn't bring it up? You took her to the farm to make her talk, for God's sake! What the hell did the two of you do all day?"

Davey didn't blame Wade for shouting. There was no excuse for what he had done or for what he had failed to do. He had set out on a mission, then allowed himself to be sidetracked by carnal desire.

The fact that he was certain no man could have resisted Laura's charms did nothing to lessen his feelings of guilt. Since the moment he had deposited his bride-to-be on her uncle's doorstep with a promise to return the next day and announce their engagement to her kin, he had berated himself for losing sight of his original purpose. How could he have been so infatuated as to have forgotten all else but the pleasures of the flesh? Easy, he told himself, remembering how wonderfully alive Laura's flesh had felt beneath his body. But there were some things which weren't meant to be shared even with a trusted friend.

Evading Wade's inquiry Davey quickly came up with what he hoped would sound like a well-thought-out alternative to the direct confrontation he was suppose to have initiated. "I think we should let Laura and Susan go through with their rattle-brained rescue." He braced himself anticipating the explosion to come. He wasn't disappointed.

After a tense moment of slack-jawed silence, Wade yelled, "Have you lost your mind? If Dunstan and Kincaid find out what they are up to there's no telling what they will do. You may be willing to risk Laura's neck but I'm not about to let Susan taken such a chance."

Davey allowed him to say his piece before he attempted to justify his reasoning. "I have no intention of putting either of our foolish females in harm's way. But don't you see, if we tell them we are aware of their plans, they'll want to know how we found out."

"So? What's wrong with telling them Seth let the cat out of the bag because he was afraid they would get themselves in trouble? Which, you mark my words, they will!"

On edge over the situation to begin with, Davey snapped back. "Do you really think anything we say will change their minds?"

Wade thought it over, then admitted, "Not unless we tell them the whole truth."

Davey wished that were an option but it wasn't. "It's too soon, Wade. In agreeing to become my wife, Laura has conceded a great deal. She's willing to give up everything she wants to stay here with me in a place she doesn't much like. Hell, she hasn't even asked where or how we will live. She has faith in me, Wade."

Sarcastically Wade interjected, "With her money she won't have to worry about having a roof over her head. Any kind of roof she wants, I might add."

Davey bristled. "Laura may not yet know me well, but I've already made it clear that I'm not interested in her money. Her faith in me is still a fragile thing. She was deeply hurt by her father's rejection. Now she has doubts about her uncle's character. And if I can prove he and his lowlife stepson were behind the ambush that nearly took her life . . ."

He let his words trail off, clamping his jaws together to hold back the suppressed anger building up inside as he thought about how close Laura had come to death. If he ever found evidence to link

Dunstan and Kincaid to the attack, he knew he would kill them both.

"What I'm trying to say is that every time Laura puts her trust in a man, she gets kicked in the teeth. If she finds out the truth about me she'll hightail it out of here so fast she'll be a blur in the distance before I have time to blink."

Though Wade understood and sympathized with his friend, he could see no way to avoid the inevitable. "She's bound to find out sooner or later."

"Then let it be later." Davey's simple statement sounded like a prayer which is exactly what it was. He hoped some supreme deity was listening whether it be the God of his father or one of those worshiped by his mother and her people. All he asked for was a little more time in which to prove to Laura that he was not like the other men she had known, men who had deceived her for their own selfish purposes.

"If . . . and it's a big if," Wade emphasized, ". . . but if I agree not to storm into Dunstan's place and drag Susan back here by her beautiful blond curls and lock her up until we have taken care of Delilah—which is exactly what I'd do if I had a lick of sense—how in the name of all that's holy are we going to make sure she and Laura don't get hurt?"

Davey gave his friend a knowing look. *"We're* not! I suggest we let the *Specter* and his dependable compatriot take care of that for us. And at the same time they're going to teach those two errant females a lesson they won't soon forget!"

* * *

"Are you certain Delilah will be able to endure the strenuous trip to Mr. Parker's by wagon?" Laura's eyes never left the narrow path along which she and Susan trod. The full moon overhead lighted their way but it was a new experience, this trekking through the woods in the middle of the night. Both women took each step cautiously, springing back whenever some unseen nocturnal creature stirred the thick underbrush lining the trail.

Nervously Susan replied. "She can make it. A few day's rest and care has done wonders to heal her wounds, but she hasn't a great deal of confidence in our ability to carry this off. You should have seen her eyes. As round as saucers they grew when I told her what we had planned. She kept staring at the ceiling. I think she was praying for Divine intervention . . . or that of the *Specter,* which to her way of thinking would probably amount to the same thing."

Mention of the phantom figure brought back memory of the strange apparition which had recently imposed itself upon her mind at the most inopportune moment. She was thankful Susan could not see her flushed face as her thoughts turned to Davey and the afternoon they had spent making love in Wade Callahan's cabin. An owl hooted not far away, startling Laura whose nerves were already as taut as a bowstring. She wished with all her heart Davey was with her now. With him by her side she would not have been afraid.

Several times during the afternoon she had been tempted to confide in him. If only she knew where he stood on the issue of slavery. True he had been upset by the atrocity committed against Delilah but his anger could have stemmed from his being a doctor. One dedicated to relieving human suffering would naturally abhor violence. It didn't necessarily signify his opposition to the established institution on which Southern planters relied.

She wondered how it was possible to love a man as completely as she loved Davey, yet not know his views on matters as vitally important as human rights. She'd wanted to tell him what she and Susan had planned but the risk was too great. What's more she'd had the oddest feeling that Davey, too, was holding something back.

At least there were no barriers when it came to the physical side of their relationship. Each openly offered that which the other needed. Likewise each accepted the offering, giving back in return. Laura supposed that was the order of things among men and women. First came attraction followed by trust and understanding. She imagined Susan, being more experienced and worldly-wise, would know if this were true. A few minutes later when they stopped to gauge the distance they had traveled, curiosity overcame any inhibitions Laura harbored about broaching the delicate subject.

Taking Susan completely by surprise, she asked bluntly, "How do two people expand their relationship beyond mere coupling?" The question seemed to reverberate through the stillness of the night. *Blast!* Even to her own ears she sounded incredibly stupid.

"Good heavens! Why would they want to?"

Relieved, Laura couldn't help laughing at her companion's frank rejoinder. Susan didn't appear to be a bit taken aback by her bold inquiry. Quite the opposite. Her reaction seemed to be generated by the ludicrous possibility that there might be some undiscovered gratification which surpassed the joys of lovemaking. Which led Laura to conclude that Susan and Wade had been engaging in the same type of intemperate behavior as she and Davey. And though there was no logical reason for it, she found the knowledge comforting.

"What I am talking about has nothing to do with the physical side of love," she assured Susan as she sought to explain. "Davey seems to have the ability to read my mind while I haven't the faintest idea what he is thinking. It's really quite annoying. Furthermore I don't know what is important to him and what is of little interest."

"Have you tried asking him?"

Laura frowned, mulling over the simple suggestion. "To tell you the truth, Susan, every time we begin a serious conversation we end up in bed—or on the couch as happened today."

"Well I hope you will have your own furnishings soon because Wade and I will be moving back into the farmhouse once we are married."

Not long ago Laura had argued Susan's decision to live in the humble cabin but now she felt a stab of envy. "I hope we will, too," she replied. "Davey hasn't mentioned where we are going to be living. He hasn't spoken much about his family either and

367

I do so want to make a good impression when I meet them. Can you tell me what they are like?"

Susan searched her memory for things she had heard Wade or her father say as she and Laura continued their journey. "I know there are a bunch of them," she began. "Davey's mother was murdered by two trappers when he was a small boy. She was an Indian princess, the daughter of a Calusa chief."

"Why was she killed?"

"I don't know. Possibly just because she was an Indian. That's all the reason some people need. Several years later Lance Logan met Davey's stepmother when she came here from England to deliver her niece and nephew to their father. That would be Andrew Townsend who was an army scout at Fort Brooke at the time. Davey's stepmother came from an old aristocratic family. Wade says she actually had a title. She was Lady Rebecca Winslow." Susan pronounced the name with an exaggerated British accent. Then she placed a finger on the tip of her nose and lifted it airily.

Both girls laughed.

"Rebecca didn't care much for Florida which was dreadfully uncivilized at the time, but somehow Davey's father convinced her to stay here and marry him."

Laura could imagine the woman's dilemma when faced with choosing between the love of her life and her homeland. As for Susan's description of Florida, she doubted it had changed much in the last twenty years.

Looking back over her shoulder, Susan's blue eyes glittered with excitement as she warmed to her narrative. "I can hardly credit some of the tales Wade has told me but he swears they are true."

"What tales?"

Bursting with eagerness to share the titillating gossip, Susan let her words tumble forth. "He said Rebecca was once captured by a band of renegade Indians. This was before she and Davey's father were married."

Laura gasped.

"And . . . no sooner had Lance rescued her from that near calamity and married her, than she was kidnapped by Jose Gaspar, the wicked pirate who roamed the Gulf of Mexico back then."

"You are making all this up," scoffed Laura, certain no single woman could have survived the merciless treatment for which the ruthless buccaneers were known.

Put off by her friend's skepticism, Susan moved ahead saying nothing more until Laura apologized.

"I'm sorry if I've offended you, but you have to admit it sounds pretty farfetched," Laura offered contritely.

"Ah, but that's only the beginning," exclaimed Susan, quickly getting over her pique. "Wait until you hear what happened to Davey's cousin, Beth!"

Beth! Laura's ears perked up. According to Susan, Davey had referred to his wild and rebellious cousin as a hellion but there had been affection in his voice at the mention of her name. She listened, enraptured by her friend's description of the tomboyish dispatch rider who had fallen in love and finally married Robin Hawkins, a half-breed warrior and blood brother of Osceola, the most powerful Seminole leader of all. As Susan related a story of love and betrayal, Laura tried to imagine how frightened Beth must have been when she arrived at the prison fortress in St. Augustine where Osceola was held following his capture. Despite her fear and the risk to her own safety, Beth had entered the fort disguised as a soldier to commiserate with the dying Indian. Deeply moved, Laura felt a lump form in her throat.

By the time she and Susan reached the edge of the woods where the shadowed outline of the Pine View manor house could be seen, Laura had heard about Lance Logan's rise from army scout to influential legislator in the newly formed state government, about Robin Hawkins's successful law practice in the little town of Tampa, and she now knew that Robin had played a major role in persuading Davey to pursue a career in medicine.

Daunted by the impression of an extraordinary family made up of brave, strong-willed men and determined, self-reliant women, Laura fretted over how she could possibly measure up. What would they think of her, a wealthy, citified girl from Boston without a single perilous adventure to her credit? Compared to the daring deeds of the Logans and Hawkins, her life had been dull and uneventful.

Then she thought of the bold emancipation she and Susan had resolved to bring about and she brightened considerably. Perhaps before this night was over she would have done something to warrant the admiration of Davey's remarkable relatives. With this in mind, she didn't know whether to be glad or disheartened by the fact that they had arrived at Susan's home without incident. It had been no problem to leave her uncle's plantation without being seen after everyone was asleep. And though it wasn't the sort of thing one looks forward to, little credit was due for having walked through the woods on a clear, moonlit night. All in all Laura had to admit her mettle had not yet been tested!

"Dammit! Wake up, Jigger!"

"Wh—what's going on? Why'd ya kick me, Nate?"

"Shut up!" hissed the man called Nate, bending over his sleepy partner. "Get up and stay down!"

Rubbing his eyes with one hand, Jigger argued. "That don't make no sense, Nate. No sense a 'tall."

"Ssh! Keep under cover, you stupid jackleg! Look there!"

Peering between the branches of a bush which hid them from view, they watched Susan and Laura creep stealthily across the yard toward the back of the house.

"What do you reckon they're up to, Nate?"

Nate ran his fingers through his heavy beard. "Don't know, but it could have something to do with the buckboard that ole nigger rigged up a little while ago and took in the woods. I'll stay here and keep an eye out while you hightail it back and get Kincaid."

Brad was awakened by a light but insistent tapping on the door leading from his bedroom out onto the balcony. Getting up, he reached for the whip he kept on the table nearby, then approached the door with caution. Through the glass he could see the silhouette of a man standing in the moonlight.

"Who is it?" he whispered, standing to one side where he would not be seen. Brad knew he had plenty of enemies and he wasn't about to place himself in jeopardy until he had identified his late-night caller.

After a moment of silence a nervous, high-pitched voice answered. "It's me. Jigger."

Brad opened the panel a crack and pulled his young hireling inside. For the second time that evening Jigger was warned to be quiet. Uncertain as to how he was supposed to convey a message without speaking, he eyed the coiled whip in Brad's hand wishing he had been left to keep watch and Nate had come to report to their quick-tempered employer. Finally in whispered tones he managed to stutter and stammer an explanation for his being there.

If Brad was startled to learn that Susan and Laura were no longer in the room down the hall, he gave no indication. He sent Jigger to saddle his horse while he got dressed. An hour later as they approached the spot where Jigger had last seen

Nate, the bearded minion rushed forward to meet them.

"They just left, Mr. Kincaid," Nate exclaimed excitedly. "All three of them. I didn't know whether to follow or not. Lucky you got here when you did." The barrel-chested lacky was puffing from exertion after his short run, making it difficult to understand his breathy discourse.

Brad stared down at Nate finding his patience sorely tried. "Three? Speak plainly, man. Who just left and where were they headed?"

"It was Miss Laura and Miss Susan. They went in the house, then they came out again. 'Cept this time they had that slave, Delilah, with them. You know, the one what's been missing. By dang, I thought we'd seen the last of her, but that's who it was all right. I'd swear to it."

Brad caressed the whip he held in his hands. His eyes gleamed with hate. "Where did they go?"

"Into the woods on the other side of the house. They was half carrying the darky between them so they couldn't have got far."

Jigger fidgeted, working up the courage to ask his cohort, "What about the buckboard?"

Brad swiveled his head around. "What buckboard?" Getting information from these two was tougher than rawhide he decided, emitting a silent curse.

"The one the old house slave took into the woods after ever'body was asleep," answered Nate scowling at his young sidekick. He wished he'd been the one to remember about the wagon.

Quickly Brad put two and two together. Obviously Delilah had been hiding out with those slave-lovers at Pine View and now they were aiding her escape from the territory. And Laura was in on the plot right up to her scrawny neck. She was stealing the property of another and stealing was illegal. It was also immoral when the property in question belonged to a man who had welcomed her into his home even if it was for selfish reasons. Well, she wouldn't get away with her treachery. He would see to that! Three unarmed women would be no match against the pistol he carried in his pocket. He preferred his whip when it came to meting out punishment but he couldn't afford to leave evidence that would cast suspicion his way. A few well-placed bullets would have a more lasting effect. And with Laura out of the way once and for all, he could turn his attention toward getting rid of his mother and step-father.

Satisfied that the culmination of all his careful planning was in sight, he gave instructions to the two men awaiting orders. "I'll handle it from here on out. Go back to the plantation and act like nothing has happened. There will be a bonus for each of you at the end of the month."

"If you live that long," he added softly as they rode away.

Brad was much too thorough to risk leaving anyone alive who might connect him with what was about to take place.

* * *

Moonlight illuminated the wide sweeping lawn as Fowler made his way toward the cabin shared by Bart Harmon and his men. He didn't know what had roused him from a sound sleep but once awake he couldn't ignore the niggling sensation that something was amiss. On reaching the small frame building he heard a dull thud followed by a groan, then a crash. He wrenched open the door without announcing his arrival and nearly fell over the prostrate body of Nate Fuller. Sparing only a glimpse at the battered face of the unconscious man, Fowler looked at Bart, his penetrating amber eyes demanding an explanation. Rubbing his knuckles, Bart returned his employer's stare dispassionately.

"I assume you have a good reason for what you are doing to this man." Fowler nodded toward Nate who hadn't stirred since his weighty body hit the floor.

Cool as a cucumber, Bart replied, "Sure do. I caught these two trying to sneak back to their quarters and they didn't want to tell me where they'd been. It being so late, I reckoned there was mischief afoot. And I'll just bet junior here is ready to tell us all about it."

Until then Fowler hadn't noticed the trembling youth standing in the corner, his arms penned behind him by one of Bart's men.

"Well, Jigger, what have you and Nate been up to?"

In a high squeaky voice Jigger pleaded. "Please, Mr. Dunstan, tell 'em to let me go. I . . . I have to take a leak real bad."

Bart's cynical laugh lacked any trace of compassion. "We're gonna do more than scare the piss out of you if you don't start talking."

Fowler had to agree with Bart that the pair had been up to something. Otherwise they would have admitted straight off what had kept them out so late. That being the case, he decided not to interfere with the interrogation.

Bart took a step in Jigger's direction. Seeing that his boss was not going to intervene on his behalf, Jigger began to cry and would have crumpled to his knees had the man behind him not held him clasped in a firm grip. Broken phrases tumbled out between sobs and soon Fowler was able to piece the story together. He was furious when he learned that his missing house slave had been given asylum by Henry Ashe. He was livid when he heard that Laura was at this very moment endeavoring to move the girl farther from his reach. But, for Fowler, the ultimate betrayal, the most infamous act of disloyalty, the deed which swept him into a murderous rage was that committed by his own stepson. Brad must have known or at least suspected where Delilah was hiding and what Susan and Laura were planning to do. Why else would he have secretly posted guards to keep an eye on the Ashe plantation? No doubt Brad was responsible for the maid's flight from River Ridge in the first place. And now the double-dealing ingrate had set out on his own to take care of the matter. Like as not he would screw up again, Fowler fumed, wondering why it was his fate to be saddled with a bunch of incompetents.

"Let him go," he instructed the man holding Jigger. "But see that he and Nate stay put until we get back. Harmon, you come with me. It's time for you to earn the money I've paid you."

He lead the way to the makeshift stable which had been hurriedly erected to shelter the horses until a new barn could be built.

"We're going to get my property back," he said when they were mounted. "Except for Delilah, I don't want anyone else left alive. I'll leave it up to you to take care of my niece and her interfering little friend, but Brad Kincaid is all mine. Understood?"

The orders were issued in a brittle voice as chill as a bath in winter. Bart nodded his understanding, thinking as he did so that Fowler Dunstan was one cold-blooded son of a bitch.

Chapter 26

Laura cradled Delilah's head in her lap, tucking the blanket under her shoulder. She found it to be much more frightening traveling the main rode in the back of the buckboard than walking along the forest path. For one thing it was considerably darker here with the thick-leafed branches overhead blocking out the moonlight. And cast in shadow the bushes on either side of the track took on eerie shapes like ghostly dancers swaying in the breeze.

She and Susan had agreed it would be best not to talk. No point in taking a chance on attracting the attention of some roving band of thieves who might have made camp nearby. But Laura missed her friend's lively chatter. She doubted their voices would invite any more notice than the jangling harness on the mule-drawn conveyance. Still she hesitated to add to the noise. She had no idea how much farther they had to go in order to reach Seth Parker's farm. They'd been traveling less than an hour according to her estimation and already the journey seemed endless.

They heard the horseman coming up on them from behind long before they saw the figure of the rider and his mount. This was the moment they had hoped would never come, for the dense forest of trees and tangled underbrush made it impossible to maneuver the wagon off of the narrow lane. After warning the injured slave not to make a sound, Laura quickly tossed a light layer of loose hay over her, then scrambled up on the plank seat beside Susan. Reaching beneath the board she pulled out two bonnets made of dark material with wide half brims. The rider caught up with them as they finished tying the streamers beneath their chins.

"Whoa!" yelled the unwanted traveler, grabbing hold of one harness and bringing the team to a halt.

"Leggo, Mistah. Wez already powerful late gettin' back to the farm and our five big brothers are most likely out beatin' the bushes lookin' fer us right now."

Susan's attempt at imitating a local farmer's daughter was creditable and might have fooled an unsuspecting stranger. But Brad wasn't taken in for a minute. Both girls were so intent on keeping their heads lowered Brad managed to draw his horse back beside them before they realized who had accosted them.

"Five big brothers, you say? I do declare, ladies, I'm quaking in my boots."

Recognizing Brad Kincaid's sardonic voice, Laura and Susan raised their heads at the same time, each giving the man a defiant glare. Despite her semiconscious state, Delilah also identified the malevolent tyrant who had so cruelly used her. She began to wail from under the hay. When Brad's attention was diverted momentarily by the maid's piteous cries, Susan took the opportunity to snap the reins against the mules' rumps.

"Giddyup!" she shouted.

The animals obeyed, but they were no match for a horse and soon Brad was once more in control.

"Try that again and I'll shoot those two jackasses. Now get down. Both of you." The pistol he held in his hand convinced them that he meant business.

When Laura started to climb out on her side of the buckboard, Brad yelled, "Hold it! This way!" He motioned with the gun, indicating that she was to follow Susan. So much for her quickly devised plan to duck into the woods using the wagon for cover.

"What are you going to do with us?" Laura knew how a cornered rabbit felt as she stood on the ground next to Susan while Brad remained mounted with the weapon pointed in her direction.

Susan answered before Brad could open his mouth. "If he's smart he'll let us continue on our way."

Brad sneered, "And why would that be so smart, you meddlesome bitch?"

Ignoring his vulgarity she answered boldly. "Because if you take Delilah back to River Ridge your stepfather is going to want to know what happened to her. I doubt he will be pleased with the way you've treated his *property*. I rather imagine he will be quite furious. He might even decide to give you a taste of your own medicine." She glanced pointedly at the whip coiled around the horn of his saddle. "On the other hand, if you let us go Fowler need never know what a loathesome creature you really are."

Brad's narrow features drew together, contorting his face as he scowled contemptuously. "Who said anything about taking the slut back to River Ridge. I'm more of a mind to finish what I started."

Susan and Laura exchanged helpless looks. Up until now neither had fully understood the depth of Brad's depravity. With understanding came fear which left them with knees trembling and stomachs churning.

Horrified Laura exclaimed, "Surely you don't mean you intend to kill her?"

The wails from inside the wagon bed grew louder.

"Ah, but that is exactly what I intend to do, lovely Laura," countered Brad with the cocky assurance of a man who knows he holds the upper hand.

"You'll never get away with it," Laura promised heatedly. "Susan and I will see to that!"

Susan groaned while Brad feigned an expression of regret. Too late Laura realized that her careless vow had left their adversary with no choice but to rid himself of them as well. That bit of insight made her more angry than frightened. She and Susan had no weapons. They would be no match against a gun and a whip. But she wasn't about to just lie down and die.

"If you kill us all, how will you explain our disappearance to Uncle Fowler?"

"I won't have to explain anything," he replied mildly, "because you aren't going to disappear. Your bodies will be discovered right here come morning. No doubt Fowler will puzzle over where you were going in the middle of the night dressed in that getup." His mustache twitched his disapproval. "But he won't expect me to know anything about it since he will have no reason to think I was any place but home in bed when you were set upon by a band of thieves. Naturally I'll have to bury Delilah in the woods so he won't guess what you were really up to, but once that is done there will be nothing to link me with your unfortunate demise."

His total lack of emotion as he spoke about cold-bloodedly murdering three women caused Laura to wonder if Brad was entirely sane. Susan put the thought into words.

"Are you crazy, Bradley? Laura's right! You'll never get away with it! There are others who are privy to our plans. If something happens to us they will know it was no accident."

What Susan said was true. The faithful old servant who had hidden the wagon in the woods knew what they were about and Seth Parker was waiting for them at the end of the trail, but Laura felt it was unlikely either man would come forward with information. To do so would mean implicating themselves as accomplices in the illegal venture. It might force Brad to reconsider if he thought Davey or Wade or Susan's father was aware of their activities, but Laura knew he was too smart to consider such a possibility. He would guess, and rightly, that none of the three would have allowed them to take on such a dangerous mission alone.

Her supposition proved correct. "If someone else is aware of the foolish games you play, that person poses no threat to me. He or she is obviously too cowardly to take an active role in your little drama and will turn a blind eye to what takes place here tonight."

Laura wasn't surprised to find that Susan's ploy hadn't worked. Their only chance now was to keep Brad talking and hope someone would happen along before he tired of the conversation. Considering the lateness of the hour it was a very slender hope.

Taking a step forward, she willed herself to remain calm. "I have a proposition to make. Before you pull that trigger you had best hear me out."

To her amazement Brad laughed. "A proposition, my dear? By all means continue."

Humor was so foreign to Brad's nature, it took Laura a moment to collect her thoughts.

"I have money. A lot of money. But you already know that. If I'm not mistaken you were willing to marry me in order to get your hands on my wealth. Let us go and I will give you one hundred thousand dollars. We will disappear, the three of us. I promise you will never hear from any of us again. Let everyone think we have simply vanished from the face of the earth. You'll be a rich man, Brad. Rich enough to buy your own plantation."

Again Brad's laughter rang out. It was a grating, discordant cackle which left Laura fighting the urge to retreat. Eventually the sound drifted away and Brad's thin face reflected all of the pent-up hatred he had harbored for the past twenty years. "Why should I settle for such a paltry sum when I can have it all?" His vindictive words struck her with such force Laura lost her resolve and jumped backward.

He leaned down, enjoying her discomfort. "Yes, lovely Laura. I intend to have it all. Once you are dead, your fortune will belong to your next of kin, the *kind* and *generous* Fowler Dunstan who happens to despise you for taking what should have been his. He's a good actor. Much better than I had expected. It was highly entertaining watching him pander to you, pretending to feel pity for the poor little rich girl whose father preferred his whores to his own daughter."

Badly shaken by Brad's malicious aspersions, Laura clutched her throat. "I don't believe you." Her voice wavered uncertainly. She didn't want to believe she had been so easily duped, but it didn't take long for the seed of doubt to take root. Questions she had tried to push aside suddenly demanded answers. Why had her father never mentioned a brother? Why had her grandfather left everything to his youngest son? What had prompted Fowler to seek her out after Franklin's death?

Brad was quick to take advantage of her vacillating emotions, using the opportunity to repay her for rejecting his suit. "Surely you don't think he invited you here out of concern for your welfare. Nothing could be farther from the truth. To put it bluntly, my dear, you are the sum total of everything my stepfather abhors in a female. Your cool disdain and your independent spirit make him want to puke each time he is forced to endure your company."

In a crude and hurtful manner, Brad made what most would consider attributes sound like character flaws of which to be ashamed.

"Shut up, you foulmouthed blackguard!"

Caught up in her own misery, Laura had almost forgotten Susan until she heard her friend upbraiding their captor.

"It's all right. I want to hear what he has to say." Speaking with dispassionate self-control which was belied by the churning inside her, Laura faced her tormentor. "If Uncle Fowler despises me, why did he invite me here? Why has he begged me to stay?"

"Money!" Brad smirked, answering her question in a word.

"That makes no sense. Uncle Fowler is already a wealthy man."

Brad shook his head, denying what most people, including Laura, thought to be true. "Fowler has made some bad investments lately and those shiftless field hands of his seem to be deliberately working against him doing everything they can to slow down production. I can assure you all that will change once I take over. Indolence will not be tolerated." He stroked the wicked scourge meaningfully.

385

No longer was Laura merely stalling for time. A need to learn the truth had now become uppermost in her mind. "Why does he believe my father's money should be his?"

"Your grandfather cut Fowler off without a cent; refused to acknowledge him as his son because he was born on the wrong side of the blanket. Years ago Fowler's mother was a common housemaid working for the Dunstan family. Apparently her services extended beyond the 'normal duties' of a domestic and she ended up in your grandfather's bed. When he discovered she was pregnant, he kicked her out. It must have been rough on a lad growing up with no father and a drunken whore for a mother." His voice lacked any trace of sympathy.

"After she died Fowler went to see his negligent sire. All he wanted was a stake so he could start fresh someplace away from the hellhole where he had lived his entire life. But the pious old bastard denounced him; said he had only one son, that being your father."

Laura had never met her grandfather for he had succumbed to some mysterious malady years before her birth. But she remembered the portrait hanging above the fireplace at the Dunstan's country estate. The stern visage on the face of the man in the painting attested to the elder patriarch's implacable disposition. Despite the amber eyes so like her own and the neatly trimmed beard which had a softening effect, the artist had captured the image of a stubborn, uncompromising individual. Laura had always avoided the room where her grandfather's spirit seemed to dominate from beyond the grave. It was easy to imagine the senior Dunstan turning his back on his mistress and her son. Still Fowler had no right to blame her for his father's indifference.

"If what you say is true Fowler himself should be holding that gun," she mused aloud, gesturing toward the pistol. Fresh shivers of fear tripped along Laura's spine. The strange glow which she now attributed to madness was back in Brad's eyes.

"Fowler had every intention of killing you once he learned you had refused to marry me. The morning after he found you at that wretched farmer's shack with the Indian bastard he went back with enough men to finish the job Bart Harmon had botched."

Brad snickered when he heard Laura suck in her breath. "That's right, Laura. Harmon fired the shot that was supposed to put an end to you, only he missed his mark and Logan showed up before he could try again. Fowler also gave the order to have your father killed," he informed Susan with an utter lack of feeling. "My stepfather doesn't appreciate being shunned by his neighbors. If not for Logan and his friend, Callahan . . ." He let his words trail off ignoring Susan's look of outrage as he turned his attention back to Laura. "The reason Fowler isn't here tonight is because I chose not to tell him that his niece is an ungrateful thief. To do so would have placed me in the position of having to justify my means of disciplining that rebellious slut you are trying to hide beneath the hay. Besides my plans are much more far reaching than just getting rid of you three. Soon I will be the master of River Ridge Plantation and with your wealth in my control, I will be the most powerful man in all of Florida. You really should have married me when you had the chance. Now it's too late."

Susan found it impossible to keep quiet any longer. "I've heard enough of this moronic drivel! Regardless of how he feels about Laura, Fowler isn't going to sit idly by while you commandeer his holdings."

Her voice fairly dripped with sarcasm. Laura wished she would stop making maligning references to Brad's mental state. Sooner or later the man was bound to take exception to her deprecating remarks.

"Ah, but I haven't explained the next step in my plan," Brad sneered, relishing the opportunity to impress his listeners with the meticulous details of his evil scheme. "Fowler and my dotty mother are scheduled to have the next unfortunate accident."

He paused to ponder an idea beginning to take shape in his sick brain. "I do believe they are going to happen upon the same band of brigands who will be blamed for your own deaths!"

The reminder that they were soon to die brought a strangled outcry from Laura. "You fiend! How can you speak of murdering your own mother and the man who has been a father to you?"

Brad's lip curled over small, sharp teeth giving him the appearance of a wild beast preparing to attack. "A father? Fowler? He's never treated me like a son. He murdered my real father in order to get what should by rights belong to me. I saw him coming out of the master bedroom the night before Pa's body was discovered. My stupid mother was already so besotted by the man I knew she would never believe he had killed her husband so I kept quiet. For years I've bided my time waiting for a chance to avenge my father's death."

Laura's head was spinning. She had wanted answers but now they were coming too fast and furiously for her to take in all at once. One thing, however, seemed clear. If what Brad said was true, he and Fowler were both seeking revenge for similar reasons. Each man felt he had been wrongfully denied his birthright, and each was willing to kill in order to get even.

Brad glanced around nervously, his hand tightening on the pistol. There were still some questions remaining to be answered but Laura knew her time was running out.

"Why did Uncle Fowler encourage me to accept your proposal knowing marriage would give you control of my money?"

It was an attempt to keep him talking. She was also curious as to why her uncle would risk losing that which he wanted so badly.

Brad fidgeted in his saddle, scanning the line of trees on either side of the road. "It was the only way he could make sure you stayed here. He was afraid to kill you outright. The neighbors were already suspicious about some of the goings-on at River Ridge. Too many slaves disappearing and that sort of thing. I agreed to put your money into the plantation once we were wed. In return he would leave everything to me. The old fool thought I would be satisfied to lick his boots until he died a natural death. I played along with him knowing revenge would be that much sweeter when I told him he'd been duped. I was going to make sure he knew just before I killed him. But you refused to cooperate, didn't you, my dear? Who could have guessed you would prefer a filthy savage to a man of quality? Your stubbornness proved most inconvenient. It left us no choice but to get rid of you."

Laura straightened her shoulders, taking some small amount of comfort in knowing she had not fallen in with their evil schemes.

"I'm really sorry it has to be this way, Laura."

The sincerity in his voice took her by surprise. For a moment she thought he might actually care about her just a little. But his next words quickly banished any such notion.

"I was looking forward to bringing you to heel. One sound thrashing would have done wonders."

Shuddering uncontrollably Laura found her gaze drawn to the devil's whip. Seeing the fear and revulsion in her face, Brad felt his shaft begin to swell. Unlike most men, he derived little satisfaction from bedding a woman and none at all if his partner proved willing. He achieved a perverted form of sexual gratification by generating terror in others. Shifting in the saddle he pressed his erection against the hard leather, enjoying his discomfort almost as much as he enjoyed the discomfort of the woman standing in front of him.

"Too bad I haven't time to demonstrate my prowess with the lash. I'm sure Delilah can vouch for the fact that it's a stimulating experience."

The mere mention of her name was enough to frighten the petrified slave. Her wails increased with ear-piercing intensity. The woman's caterwauling resounded in Laura's head, pounding against her skull. She put her hands over her ears in a vain attempt to block out the noise, then closed her eyes unable to bear the sight of her iniquitous persecutor. Brad was going to kill them and they were powerless to stop him. She'd been a fool not to confide in Davey. He would have helped Delilah. In her heart Laura had known Davey would never turn his back on someone in need. But now there would be no opportunity to tell him of her faith and trust. Tears welled up behind her closed lids as she heard the pistol cock and realized too late that the only dream which held any meaning for her was about to slip away.

Chapter 27

A shot rang out. Laura heard a scream. Susan or Delilah? She couldn't be sure. It was of no consequence since the gun had been trained on her. She waited for the searing pain which would signal the beginning of the end. Long seconds ticked by. Still she felt nothing. This was not like the other time when she'd been ambushed by Bart Harmon. Then the bullet had struck with such force she'd fallen from her horse. Her shoulder had felt as if it were on fire almost immediately.

Dreading what she would see yet unable to stand the suspense any longer, Laura slowly opened her eyes. From atop his mount Brad Kincaid looked blankly down at her, the pistol still clutched in his hand. He swayed to one side, then toppled to the ground. Only a small amount of blood seeped from the neat round hole in the middle of his forehead.

"He didn't give you any choice, Mr. Dunstan. You heard him say you were going to be next."

Bart Harmon need not have bothered making

392

excuses for the man who stood over Brad's unmoving body with a smoking gun in his hand. Fowler Dunstan showed no sign of remorse.

"Double-crossing cowardly bastard! Death came too easy to the son of a bitch." Fowler drew back his leg and gave Brad's inert form a vicious kick.

Before Laura had time to get used to the startling realization that she was still alive, her uncle turned to his henchman and growled, "I'll get the darky. You know what you have to do."

His words held an ominous finality. Though she had escaped certain death once this night, Laura knew her luck was about to end. Strangely enough she was no longer afraid.

"So everything Brad said is true. You murdered his father, didn't you?"

Fowler paused in midstride, keeping his back to her. "His father deserved to die. Brad got what he deserved as well."

"And what about me, Uncle? Do I deserve to die?"

Continuing toward the buckboard, Fowler made no reply.

Half a mile away, just beyond a sharp bend in the road, two men heard the loud report of Fowler's pistol echoing through the copse of trees.

"What the hell! Who fired that shot?"

"I don't know but we're damn sure going to find out!" answered the giant shadow figure whose menacing voice held a ready challenge.

Without another word they kneed their horses in the flanks and took off at a dangerously fast pace. The dark cape worn by the larger of the pair billowed out like the wings of a huge bird of prey as they closed the distance separating them from the source of the gunfire. The sound of thundering hooves left the four people who stood in the middle of the trail frozen in their places.

Fowler was the first to recover. "Shoot them, damn you!" he yelled at Bart who stood gaping at the dark-cloaked figure swooping down on them like one of the web-winged creatures of Slavic folklore.

"Specter." Susan breathed the name in awe.

Laura stared at the larger of the two riders. Her heart began to race. Though she could see nothing of the man's face beneath his flowing mantle she knew this was the one worshiped by the slaves, feared by their owners. His bearing was proud, his course straight and true. She pictured a grim face with nostrils flaring and a firm set to his lips.

"I gave you an order, Harmon! Shoot those interfering jackels!" There was a note of panic in Fowler's shrill command.

Suddenly Bart snapped out of his stupor. He raised his gun but not quickly enough. Before he could squeeze the trigger a burst of flame erupted in a deafening roar as the oncoming horseman fired first. The scene blurred for Laura. As in a dream she watched Bart slowly slide to the ground.

The two men reined in their horses, kicking up a cloud of dust. Wearing a wide-brimmed hat pulled low over his face, the smaller of the pair dismounted and made his way toward the fallen gunman. There was something familiar about the way the man moved. He stripped off the glove covering his right hand and bent to feel Bart's pulse. Just then a shaft of moonlight pierced the tree branches overhead illuminating the kneeling figure. Susan cried out once, then proceeded to faint dead away leaving Laura to gape in horror at the man's badly scarred palm. His flesh appeared to have been burned. Rough red ridges puckered up like twin serpents side by side.

"He's alive but just barely." Wade Callahan's face was clearly visible as he raised his head to speak to the dark apparition still seated atop his big black stallion.

With a grunt of disgust, the man pushed back his cowl. Laura felt the hairs lift on the back of her neck. The butterflies in her stomach began turning somersaults as she forced her eyes to meet those of the one called *Specter*. She already knew his would be soft velvety-brown. What startled her was the way in which they seemed to plead for understanding.

Fowler's voice tore through the night, interrupting their silent communion. Taking a step toward Wade he railed, "You're not a farmer! You're a no-good slave stealer! Branding obviously didn't teach you a lesson but this time I'll see you hanged!"

Slave stealer? Laura looked again at Wade's up-turned palm. Those weren't snakes; they were letters. *SS* had been deliberately burned into his hand.

She shuddered, wondering how anyone could inflict that sort of pain on another human being. Then she remembered Delilah and what Brad had done to her. It seemed there was no limit to man's inhumanity to man.

Her features softened as she gave her attention to the caped figure she now knew to be Davey Logan. Her Davey. The healer whose curative powers went far beyond what he had been taught in medical school. There was no hiding what she felt at that moment: respect, admiration, and most importantly, love.

"Don't move, Dunstan, unless you want to wind up like your hired assassin." The first words Davey had spoken since his dramatic appearance were both bold and menacing. The gun he held pointed directly at the enraged planter served to support his ability to make good on the threat.

"Who the hell are you to be giving me orders?" Fowler looked quite literally ready to explode. His golden eyes glittered dangerously. His ruddy cheeks puffed out to an alarming degree.

Not the least intimidated, Davey replied, "I'm the man who's going to see that you burn in hell for trying to kill the woman I love."

In a remarkably short space in time, all color drained from Fowler's face, leaving his florid skin a sickly white. "So, Logan! You're the bastard responsible for stirring up trouble around here?"

Her courage renewed now that Davey was with her, Laura retorted sharply, "If I were you, Uncle, I'd be careful who I called a bastard."

Just at that moment, Susan moaned and began to stir. The movement diverted Davey's attention for no more than a split-second but it gave Fowler just enough time to grab Laura from behind. Quickly he pulled the pistol out of his pocket and pressed the barrel into her side.

"Stay back," he warned, "or I'll shoot the bitch! Throw your guns into the bushes, both of you. And, Logan, get down from that horse nice and easy."

They did as they were told, neither willing to risk lives by trying any heroics.

"I'll be leaving now and I'm taking my niece with me. If we are followed, I won't hesitate to kill her."

Fowler backed toward his horse, dragging Laura with him. After she was mounted he heaved himself up behind her, then kicked the animal into motion. Soon they were swallowed up by the darkness.

Wade hurried to Susan's side.

"I don't understand any of this," she wailed, "but we have to stop Fowler. He needs Laura right now to make his getaway, but he will have to kill her eventually in order to get her inheritance."

Davey scrambled to find his weapon in the tall grass. "Wade, toss Harmon in the wagon with Delilah and take them on to Seth's. I'm going after Laura."

Wade wrapped his arms around Susan. "But you don't know where he's taking her."

"I have a pretty good idea." Davey hoped he was right.

"I'd better come with you," volunteered Wade reluctantly.

Casting a knowing glance from Wade to Susan, whose expression was growing more thunderous by the minute, Davey chuckled despite the seriousness of the situation. "You'd better stay with your woman, my friend. I believe you have some explaining to do."

"Won't this be nice? An uncle and his dear niece traveling together. Our first stop will be Boston where I shall lay claim to my fortune. Oh, but you will no longer be with me by that time. Such a pity. I can see the headlines now. 'Young woman falls overboard.' Happens quite often, I understand," Fowler clucked, rifling through the contents of his safe. He removed a stack of papers and a wad of bills which he stuffed into a small black satchel. "I believe I will head West after that. I understand the land beyond the Mississippi holds a number of opportunities for a resourceful man. Or should I say a man with resources?"

Laughing over his clever play on words, he smiled at Laura. "I really hate to leave all of this but with my newfound wealth it won't be difficult to begin again.

The good humor in his gloating voice grated on Laura's already ragged nerves. By the dim light of the lamp on the desk she could see satisfaction written on his beefy face. She wondered where Davey was. She knew he would be searching for her but would he guess that her uncle had brought her back to River Ridge or would he expect them to be halfway to the coast where Fowler could make good his escape?

Thus far no mention had been made of Hester Dunstan. The house was deathly silent. Did he intend to leave his wife behind? Laura hoped so for she doubted Hester was aware of the duplicity her husband and son had been plotting. It would be wrong to include the old lady in his fugitive flight.

Laura shifted in the chair where Fowler had thrust her. She wished she could tell him exactly what she thought of his perfidy but the gag in her mouth made it impossible for her to do more than seethe inwardly. Exhausted from the long night's ordeal and frustrated by her helplessness, she blinked back tears which threatened to spill. She would not give her uncle the pleasure of seeing her cry. Heavy drapes were drawn across the windows, blocking out the early dawn. She contemplated the idea that this might be her last day on earth. As is so often the case among young people, Laura had never given much thought to what lay beyond death. There was too much living to be done. Now, however, the future looked bleak and the idea of passing through Heaven's gates without Davey by her side was a frightening and lonely prospect.

Blast it, Laura Dunstan! Stop acting like a maudlin dolt and start thinking of a way to get yourself out of this pickle.

Laura wanted to remind the niggling little voice that with her hands tied her options were decidedly limited, but this was no time to argue even with herself. Besides she could not sit around and wait for help to come. The odds of someone reaching her before it was too late did not appear to be in her favor. So when Fowler returned his concentration to the safe, she rose slowly and began inching toward the door. If she could get out of the room without being seen, she might be able to find a place to hide until Davey figured out where she was. Scarcely daring to breathe, she prayed no board would creak beneath her feet. Her heart was racing by the time she reached the open threshold. She was going to make it.

"Why, Laura, what are you doing downstairs at this hour?"

Only the gag covering her mouth prevented Laura from screaming when she saw Hester Dunstan standing in the exit. With the woman's arrival, any chance of slipping away unnoticed vanished like a fleeting thought. Dressed in a flowing, high-necked nightgown and beruffled cap set slightly askew atop her silver ringlets, Hester wore the dazed expression of a small child awakened from a dream. In her arms she carried the smiling rag doll.

Her wrinkled face puckered in a frown. "Fowler, whatever are you doing?"

Fowler was already across the room before she spoke. Grabbing Laura roughly he yanked her away from the door and dragged her back to the chair.

"Stay put, dammit!" he barked, shoving her down upon the seat.

Hester's frown deepened. "There's no need to shout for goodness sake. You'll wake the baby."

Laura felt as befuddled as her aunt was acting. Hester seemed oblivious to her niece's predicament, making no comment on the fact that she was bound and gagged.

"Why are you both awake at such an early hour? And where is Bradley? His bed hasn't been slept in. I don't understand. It's all so very confusing."

Her wrinkled face brightened as she began to search the room, peering into each shadowed corner. "Bradley loves to play tricks," she confided, bestowing a vague smile on Laura. "He thinks it's great fun to pop out from some nook or cranny and startle me."

Laura couldn't find the humor in scaring a timid soul like Hester, but such a prank seemed in keeping with Brad's warped personality.

Fowler growled impatiently. "Hush up, Hester. Go back upstairs and feed the . . . baby."

"She isn't hungry yet. Now where is that naughty boy?" she whined, stooping to look under the desk.

Fowler slammed his fist against the wood top. The force of the blow jarred the oil lamp, moving it closer to the edge. So surprised was Hester by the sudden loud noise, she straightened abruptly, dropping the doll she had been holding.

"Your son is dead, you demented old hag! I shot him before he could shoot me! Now get out of my way!"

Hester had fallen to her knees to retrieve the doll, and her position made it impossible for Fowler to reach the bag containing his money and documents. On hearing her husband's appalling declaration, she sprang to her feet with amazing agility for a woman of her years.

Curling her fingers into claws, she lunged forward, emitting an unearthly shriek. "NOOO, not Bradley!"

Her nails raked one cheek, leaving four trailing ribbons of blood running from Fowler's eye to his jawbone. Grabbing her hands he proceeded to give her a vigorous shake.

"He was a mad dog, Hester! He was going to kill us both!" His amber eyes glittered with hate as he spoke of his stepson. His words offered nothing in the way of comfort. "Now I've got to get out of here. Logan's right behind me!"

"Closer than you think, Dunstan," came a deep voice from the doorway.

Fowler drew the pistol from his pocket as he whirled around to face his adversary. At the same time Hester snatched up an ornate silver letter opener lying on top of the desk. Before the planter could fire a shot, his wife plunged the dagger into his back.

"Monster!" she cried as Fowler slumped forward, knocking the lamp to the floor.

The oil which had splashed on the rug and the drapes ignited, spreading quickly. Spurred into action by the sight of the flames, Laura leaped to her feet. Davey was there beside her before she had taken a step. Scooping her up in his arms, he started for the door, scanning the room for Hester Dunstan, but she was nowhere in sight.

Laura buried her face against Davey's chest in an

effort to keep from choking on the thick smoke. Panic seized her when she tried to breathe. With the gag still covering her mouth, her nasal passages burned from the fumes she was forced to inhale. She had seen her aunt dart out ahead of them and was relieved to know Hester had remained rational enough to escape the blistering inferno.

Soon they were a safe distance from the house. For Laura the gray dawn had never looked brighter. Davey placed her on the dew-damp grass, then removed the handkerchief from her mouth. Thankfully she sucked in great gulps of the fresh morning air. Her chest heaved. Her eyes watered as she coughed out the pollution in her lungs.

Davey knelt beside her, resting his hand upon her shoulder while he watched the flames work their way up to the second floor of the mansion. He knew it was too late to help Fowler Dunstan. Hester was still nowhere in sight and he wondered if she had run to the slave quarters to sound the alarm. Then she appeared like a tiny wraith standing on the balcony above the terrace.

"Oh, my God!" he whispered, unable to believe she had not fled the house when she'd had the chance.

Tongues of fire reached out to lick at the hem of her gown.

Clutching at Davey's arm, Laura croaked, "Do something! You've got to help her!"

Davey sprinted across the lawn as fast as his legs would move but he was still some distance from the flame-engulfed structure when Hester climbed upon the narrow railing clutching the smiling rag doll to her breast. His heart pounded with the rise and fall of each booted foot. Desperately he ran, praying he would not be too late. He saw Hester teeter unsteadily upon the ledge. He watched as she swayed toward the burning timber. Then, letting go of the doll, she began to flail her arms in windmill fashion as she tried to right herself.

Screams from Laura and her aunt sounded in unison just before Hester toppled forward, landing with a sickening thud on the bricks below.

Chapter 28

Laura and Davey stood looking at the smoldering remains of the River Ridge plantation house. Little was left save the towering brick chimneys and even they were now blackened from smoke and soot.

Hester and her son had been laid to rest beside Angel on the shady knoll overlooking the river. No trace of Fowler Dunstan's body was found after the hellish flames burned themselves out. Precisely speaking his flesh had been consumed by fire, but to those who knew the truth, his fate was the result of the all-consuming greed which had pervaded his soul.

Laura spoke reflectively. "It's hard to believe a house can be so beautiful on the outside, so evil on the inside. I'm glad it's gone."

"The house was never evil, princess. Only the people dwelling within it. I wish I had been able to save your aunt. Hers was a senseless death."

Laura touched Davey's arm, finding comfort in

the strength and vitality emanating from his warm, solid presence.

"There was nothing you could do. We both assumed Hester had escaped ahead of us."

"Even so I wish her life could have been spared. It was suicide to go back upstairs once the house was ablaze. I wonder why she did it."

"Perhaps she was searching for happier times," mused Laura.

"At least we know now what happened to Angel."

"I didn't think a man like Bart Harmon would feel the need to cleanse his conscience before he died."

Davey shrugged. "I doubt he had time to confess all of his sins, but according to Wade, Bart admitted he'd strangled Angel in a fit of rage."

Cocking her head to one side, Laura wrinkled her brow. "Don't you think it's about time you told me the truth about your friend Wade?"

Davey chuckled her beneath the chin but made no immediate attempt to satisfy her curiosity.

"Well?" she prompted.

"You win, my persistent bride-to-be," he finally replied, taking her hand in his. "Let's walk down by the river and I'll tell you everything you want to know."

Davey waited until they had reached the familiar path running parallel to the fast-flowing waterway before he spoke again. Then he began by explaining how he had met Wade in Charleston.

"We remained close friends during my internship," he went on. "I stood up with him when he married Nell. It was a big wedding. Wade's family is among the most prominent in the Southeast. His father is part owner of an import firm and about the time I finished medical school, Wade and Nell moved to Savannah where Wade was put in charge of one of the branch offices. After that I returned to Fort Brooke and we lost track of each other for a while until they turned up here."

"This is a long way from Savannah," Laura commented when Davey seemed disinclined to continue.

Davey nodded. "You could have knocked me over with a feather when I discovered Wade and Nell had bought the old Hawthorne place."

Laura wondered what could possibly have induced the young couple to leave a thriving town like Savannah to live on a run-down farm in the backwoods of Florida. Anticipating her question, Davey answered before she could ask.

"Wade was always a champion of the underdog. Not long after they moved to Savannah he was caught trying to smuggle some runaway slaves onto a ship headed north. The fugitives were returned to their master, and Wade . . ."

". . . was branded as a slave stealer," Laura finished for him, closing her eyes against the reality of such a gross injustice. "That's the most barbaric thing I've ever heard of! Surely someone could have stopped it! Where were the authorities while this atrocity was taking place?"

"Probably holding Wade's arm steady while the

iron was being applied." Davey's answer was brutally honest. "Helping a slave escape is a crime, princess. Wade was tried as a thief and found guilty. He would have been hanged if not for his father's influence. All things considered, his sentence was relatively light."

Light? Having one's hand disfigured, not to mention the pain Wade had been forced to endure, seemed an enormous price to pay for an act of mercy. However, when Laura considered what might have resulted she could see Davey's point.

"So they came to Florida?"

Davey gazed out over the water, watching the reeds along the far shore bend with the breeze. "They were no longer welcome in Savannah and Wade felt returning to Charleston would only cause his family added embarrassment."

"Tell me about Wade's wife. What happened to her?"

A faraway look appeared on Davey's handsome face. "Nell died the way she had lived—unselfishly. She was the kindest, most gentle person I've ever met. She shared Wade's views about slavery. Come to think of it, I never heard her disagree with him about anything. She thought the sun rose and set according to his wishes."

"Then she didn't mind living here?"

Davey smiled when he heard the skepticism in Laura's voice. "As astounding as it may seem to you, some people actually like this *savage* land."

Giving him a playful poke in the ribs, Laura retorted saucily, "And others like the *savages* that call this land home."

Then sobering she asked again, "How did she die?"

"Wade and Nell were fishing downstream from the public landing. When they heard a steamer sound its horn, Wade went around the bend to the dock. He was expecting some supplies and wanted to see if they were on board the arriving boat. While he was gone Nell spotted a young negro girl clinging to a log in the water not far from shore. She recognized her as one of the slaves from your uncle's plantation. She could see that the girl had been beaten and was barely able to hold on to the piece of driftwood. Instead of calling for help, Nell swam out by herself. She got caught in the current and was dragged under. The girl managed to scream loud enough to alert the men on the dock but when they arrived Nell was nowhere in sight. Wade dove in and finally found her body tangled among the weeds."

Laura shivered, remembering her own brush with death when the river had tried to claim her. "Wade must have been devastated."

"Losing Nell nearly destroyed him. He blamed himself for bringing her here to begin with and then for leaving her alone on that fateful day. He also blamed your uncle after learning from the young slave of the abuses carried out against the people at River Ridge. It was then he decided to become a part of the abolitionist movement."

Davey stooped to pick up a flat stone. With a

practiced swing of his arm, he sent it skipping out across the water. "I never thought he would find another woman he could love. But now that he has Susan, I foresee a bright future ahead for the two of them. They both deserve happiness and together I believe they will have it."

Laura thought about what lay ahead for the unlikely pair. "I know that they love each other but will love be enough? Wade certainly has no knack for farming and I can't picture him living a life of ease at Pine View. How will he support a wife?"

"He's planning to run for sheriff," replied Davey, as if it were the most natural thing in the world for a convicted felon to seek a job as peacemaker.

"You're joking."

His dark eyes sparkled with suppressed humor as he shook his head from side to side.

Laura opened her mouth to speak but all that came out was bubbling laughter. What poetic justice, she thought as Davey's uninhibited guffaws were added to hers. The sound of their merriment sent a long-legged blue heron who had been fishing along the bank soaring into flight. The disgruntled angler winged his way across the water, squawking raucously, but Davey and Laura paid him no mind.

Wiping tears of mirth from her cheeks, Laura leaned into Davey, circling his waist with her arms. Caught up in the hilarity of the moment, she giggled lightheartedly, "With Susan campaigning for him, the other candidates don't stand a chance!"

Epilogue

Davey stood outside the post office idly toying with the letter he held in his hand. After three months of marriage he still could not believe his good fortune in having found a woman like Laura. He had been pleasantly surprised at the way in which she had adjusted to her new life here in the small but growing community of Tampa. His large and boisterous family had not intimidated her in the least. In fact, she seemed to enjoy being related by marriage to a goodly portion of the town's inhabitants.

From their first meeting Laura and Rebecca had felt a kinship toward each other. They laughed as they compared their experiences in England. Both had attended Miss Haversham's Academy for Young Ladies and though Laura had been under the supervision of the original Miss Haversham's niece, apparently the two old maids had run the establishment in much the same manner. Likewise their charges had used similar ploys to circumvent the rigid rules set down by their headmistresses.

Davey had known Laura would get on well with his cousin Beth for they were as alike in spirit as two peas in a pod. Sure enough the two women had immediately combined forces which often placed him and Beth's husband, Robin Hawkins, at a disadvantage especially since the families lived next door to one another. But it was a nice location and the townspeople took pride in having a doctor and a lawyer living and working right there on the main street.

The sight of the stagecoach clammering around the corner trailed by a cloud of dust put an end to Davey's daydreaming. He saw Laura coming out of Mr. Dodd's mercantile as the rocking conveyance pulled to a stop in front of the store. As she started toward him the door of the coach opened and a heavily gowned matron descended the steps. Beads of moisture glistened on the obese woman's forehead as she shook out her skirt while giving her surroundings a mutinous look.

Laura paused to speak to the newcomer. After a brief exchange, she continued to weave her way between horses and buckboards, hastening in his direction. Davey expelled his breath. His wife's flushed cheeks were a sure indication that her meeting with the disgruntled visitor had not gone well.

"Blast that damn Yankee!" Laura spluttered, thrusting her basket into Davey's stomach. "Do you know what she said? Well I'll tell you! She had the nerve to call Florida an uncivilized hellhole! And that's not all! She went on to inform me that the roads were bad, the accommodations worse, and the food was unfit for human consumption! Can you believe it?"

"She must be a fast talker to have said all of that in so short a time." Davey choked back laughter inspired by Laura's rapid-paced, clipped way of speaking. "I don't suppose you had a chance to get a word in."

"I certainly did!" she snapped. "I told her the stage ran in both directions and she could just get right back on it if she didn't like it here!"

"Well that's what I call putting her in her place, princess. By the way, you have a letter from Susan."

Instantly Laura forgot all about her confrontation with the woman on the stage. She snatched the envelope from Davey and ripped off the seal. After scanning the missive she clapped her hands in excitement and announced gleefully, "Wade won the election!"

"Was there ever any doubt?"

"One can never be certain when it comes to politics," came her sage reply.

"What else does she have to say?"

Laura read aloud: *We've added a room to the farmhouse in anticipation of a new arrival due in about seven months.*

"Oh, Davey! They're going to have a baby! Isn't that wonderful?"

Grinning, Davey agreed. "Now that's the kind of new arrival one can look forward to."

"She goes on to say her father is well and the people seem content. She and Wade hope we will visit them soon," she finished happily.

Laura tucked the letter away and took Davey's arm as they started to walk the short distance home. After a while she said, "It was kind of Henry Ashe to take my uncle's people in and accept the responsibility of providing for them."

"Henry's a good man, princess. They'll be happy at Pine View."

What had occurred following Fowler Dunstan's death was still a mystery to Laura. She had offered the slaves at River Ridge their freedom, believing they would welcome the opportunity to escape their bondage. Instead her pronouncement had been met with bewilderment and, in a few cases, stark terror. It had taken an explanation from Davey for her to understand.

"They are like orphaned children," he had said, "not knowing how to survive on their own."

Though he was adamantly opposed to slavery, Davey understood why Laura's magnanimous gesture had caused fear among the people. They had not become slaves overnight and it would take time to prepare them to live as free men and women. Living at Pine View they would be encouraged to grow their own crops; the children would be educated.

At the time, what Davey said made sense, but now Laura wasn't so sure. "If you really believe they are unable to take care of themselves, why did you help so many escape?"

Up until now she had avoided questioning Davey about his role as the *Specter*. With the death of her uncle and his stepson, the work of the night rider

414

had come to an end and she didn't want to think about the danger her beloved had faced during his reign as savior to the oppressed. But after careful consideration, Laura recognized a certain ambiguity in his original explanation.

Davey understood her confusion, though at the moment his mind was centered on other things. Still thinking about the baby Wade and Susan would soon welcome into the world, he put his arm around his wife. Her waist was so slender he could circle it with his hands. He hoped that would change soon for he would like nothing better than to see her belly swell big with *their* child. He was seized with the urge to scoop her up and carry her straight to bed where they could lose themselves in the present and leave the past far behind.

But knowing he would have to satisfy her curiosity first, he replied, "The *Specter* provided a way for those who chose to leave. The men and women he helped knew that to remain at the plantation would mean certain death. There are people in the North who are willing to assist former slaves and teach them how to become independent. But as you have seen, not all are ready. The move to Pine View may seem like a small step, but it's a step in the right direction."

Steering her up the walk leading to their front door, Davey was anxious to put the matter to rest. He knew the day might come when the *Specter* would again be called upon to rise up and do battle against the forces of evil, but right now he was more concerned about his own urgent needs.

Laura regarded him thoughtfully. "It's nice to know we aren't the only ones who believe slavery is wrong. In fact it wouldn't surprise me if someday those who feel as we do band together to put an end to the abominable practice."

They entered the house and Davey paused to kiss the tip of her nose. He smiled in anticipation of the hours of loving that lay ahead. "It wouldn't surprise me either, princess," he responded, squeezing her tenderly as they continued toward the bedroom. "It wouldn't surprise me at all!"